PRESERVATION PROTOCOL

BY

JOHN PRESCOTT

KYANITE
Publishing

info@kyanitepublishing.com

ISBN
Hardcover: 978-1-949645-67-5
Paperback: 978-1-949645-68-2
eBook: 978-1-949645-69-9

Book & cover design by Sophia LeRoux
Editing by Sarah Lachance
Cover image © depositphotos.com

www.kyanitepublishing.com

In Memory of

TOM MURPHY

"Friend to all on Earth, now in Heaven."

1

Detective Max Kincaid stared up and up at the shiny blue glass façade of the Synthetics International building off in the distance. The late midday sun was peeking around its side. He flared out his trench coat as he hoofed it down Trenton Boulevard.

The original age of the trench coat-wearing private Dick was a good 150 years in the past. He felt it was about time to bring it back. There weren't that many people around in 2097 that would call him out for dressing like a stereotype. That suited him just fine.

As far as Max was concerned, he was carrying on a fine tradition. He tipped his fedora to an older lady as he passed her by on the sidewalk. She smiled. Most girls saw the charm of his getup, which always helped things.

He had to admit that today the coat was just burning him up. He'd been on the beat all day and didn't have much to show for it. The mark he'd been chasing had proven especially slippery. All he wanted to do now was sit.

Sam's Diner, home of the world's best coffee, and his favorite place to escape from work. He pulled open the old-timey door and absent-mindedly held it for a bot toting a doggy bag. The white and blue biped nodded and said, "Thank you." Max nodded back.

Most people nowadays went out of their way to ignore the existence of the robots around them. He couldn't help but be polite to them. They were programmed to be polite to him. Max was programmed to be polite by his mother. He figured, what's the difference?

Synthetics were a different matter. For him, Synthetics fell neatly into the uncanny valley in more than just looks, and deserved all the scorn he had for them. Let's just say they were a little *too* human for his tastes.

Max shook the thought out of his head and dropped himself down on the stool at the far end of the counter. He fit right in at Sam's Diner. With shining chrome, vinyl-lined booths, and art-deco flair, the diner hit all the hallmarks of a mid-twentieth century eatery.

Samantha Dee, owner and sole proprietor of Sam's Diner, still looked stunning in her waitress' outfit for a gal pushing forty. She was a little old for Max, but he reveled in flirting with her whenever he came in. "Well if it isn't New Wave City's prettiest little thing."

Sam smirked and leaned on the counter in front of Max. "The *prettiest*, am I? You must be angling for another free coffee." She winked and flicked his fedora.

Max smoothed his dark brown hair and settled his hat back into place. "I just can't help but point out the obvious. I *will* take that coffee, though."

Sam sauntered over to the coffee station and grabbed a mug. "You're going to spoil me, Max Kincaid."

"You never call *me* the prettiest!" A pink and gray

female robot rolled over to Max. She glided on a wheel attached to a single leg that emerged from her molded skirt. She winked a glowing blue eye at him, ponytail swinging.

Max smiled thinly. "Fine, you're pretty cute for a bot."

"That's more like it!" The bot spun around and shot back across the diner.

"She's in a good mood."

Sam shot Max a smile over her shoulder. "You ever know Starla to be any other way?" The detective harrumphed. She placed the coffee in front of Max and leaned in. "What's wrong, sweetheart?"

Max grimaced. "That obvious, huh?"

"You may only have one good eye, but it tells me all your secrets *every*time."

Max turned away. One iris was pale green, but the other was turquoise, artificial. "Trying to cheer me up again, are ya?"

Sam sniffed. "Oh, don't be like that. I think it makes you look exotic."

"It makes me look like a freak."

"Exotic, freak... Same difference." Sam flashed her signature smile. Max half-smiled. That grin could melt an ice cube on Mt. Everest.

Max sighed. "I've been tailing a mark all day. I'll be damned if I can keep him nailed down. Victor Esposito... You know him?"

Sam stared at the white tiled ceiling for a moment before shaking her head. "Doesn't ring a bell. If *you* are looking for him, that's probably an okay thing."

"He's just a peon. Think he's been cleaning cash for

3

Don Adesso."

"Jeez, Max! Maybe you're better off leaving him alone. I don't think you want to be getting on Adesso's bad side."

Max shook his head and smiled. "Part of the job. I nab Esposito and get him to sing... I might be able to put Adesso somewhere he won't be able to touch me."

Sam leaned on the counter. "You know as well as I do that bars aren't gonna keep Adesso from doing what he wants, sweetheart."

Max stared at his coffee. "Yeah... It's complicated... Part of the job."

"It might be part of the job, but so is taking care of yourself. You look tired. Why don't you call it a day?"

"I suppose you're right. There's a mook downtown Adesso hangs out with sometimes. I might be able to chat him up... *You're kidding me.*" Max stared out the window at a passing black sedan.

He focused with his synthetic left eye. It cast a blue-violet hue on the scene outside. The lens snap-focused on the plate on the back of the sleek sedan and zoomed. He tapped a finger on his left temple.

A list of plate numbers appeared in the bottom-left of his vision. Each number glowed white in rapid succession, finally stopping on one in particular. It was a match. "Well, hot shit."

Max stood up, eyes still trained on the quickly disappearing car. "Put it on the tab, Sam. I got a hit!"

Sam watched him stride out the door and sighed. "Just like all the others. Here one minute and gone the next."

Max jumped up to a sprint once he was outside. He

grabbed for a flat, silver bar nestled in the interior pocket of his trench coat. He ran out into the street. An oncoming sports car screeched its tires, the driver blaring its horn.

He pointed the bar at the back of the vehicle like a magic wand. He clicked a button on top with his thumb. A pop like from an air rifle issued from the end of the bar.

A small, black projectile rocketed towards the back of the black sedan. It smacked into the bumper of the car with a quiet yet satisfying thunk. It stuck fast where it had hit.

Max slipped a smile and quickly came to a stop. He bent over and spit, breathing hard. Distance running was for rookies. A silver SUV came to a stop behind the detective. The driver laid on the horn.

The detective held out a staying hand. The driver leaned out. "Get outta the road, jackass!"

On a good day, Max would have flashed his badge and made a scene. This wasn't a good day. Instead, he threw his hands out to either side, smiling. He walked to the sidewalk. Slowly.

The SUV driver saluted Max with one finger as he passed by. Max made sure to smile and wave. The driver cursed. Max's smile widened.

Max turned his attention to his wristwatch. He twisted the bezel. The display shifted to a map of the area. A red, faintly pulsing dot traveled down a street. "You son of a bitch. *I got you.*"

He looked around to get his bearings and jogged across the street. He got into a well-aged metallic blue sedan. He settled into the familiar blue plush driver's seat. He pressed the start button.

A pleasing female voice said "Welcome!" as the

vehicle's engine turned over. The engine roared to life, sputtered, then died. The female voice responded by saying "Error!"

Max grimaced. "Error, my ass." He pressed the start button again. The engine once more roared to life. It stayed running this time. "That's my girl."

He looked at the half-dozen red and yellow lights illuminated on the instrument panel and frowned. Classic cars: So much to love. He tapped the touch screen in the middle of the dash and pulled into traffic.

The same blue map that had appeared on his watch was now displayed on the screen in his car. The red dot was now five blocks away but had stopped moving. Max smirked when he saw the address.

He pulled the old bird into a parking spot across the street from the old hotel. It was a hotel only in name, now used mainly as a staging ground for a mafia-run escort service. It looked like old Vic was looking to get lucky in more than one way.

Max turned off the car and made himself comfortable. He had a feeling it would be a little while before Esposito came back out. He flicked on a baseball game and waited.

The drone of the game and the warmth of the sun had almost done Max in an hour later. The sound of the doors of the main entry to the hotel sliding open snapped him out of his stupor. Max sat up in his seat, grinning.

Victor Esposito came strolling out, all smiles. Some dolled-up floozy was hanging off his left shoulder. They casually walked to Victor's glossy black sedan.

Max fished the silver bar he used earlier out of his

coat pocket and waited. Victor passed off the floozy and gestured to the passenger door. He then walked to his own side. Max snorted. "What a gentleman."

Victor fired up the sedan. Max held his breath and waited. As soon as Victor rolled the sedan forward, Max pressed a button on the side of the silver bar. A *whump!* sound came from the back of the sedan, closely followed by a loud *crack* from the front.

First the passenger door opened, then the driver door. Victor's floozy sprung out looking left and right. Victor popped out next and punched the rear door. "It's a brand-new car! I don't know what in the hell... Where are you going!"

The floozy ran back to the hotel and disappeared back inside. Victor cursed and hit the door even harder, leaving a dent. Victor yelped and grabbed his hand. It was all Max could do to keep from busting up laughing.

Victor looked around, exasperated. His head stopped at the sight of Max's car. Then he locked eyes with Max. "Shit." Max flung the door open and stood up, drawing his plasma pistol. "Hold it right there, Esposito!"

Victor's eyes grew wide. "You! *Fuck* you!" He turned and started running.

"Damn it. They always run." Max squeezed off two shots. The red-orange energy bursts rocketed from the pistol and slammed uselessly into the hotel behind Victor.

He watched helplessly as Esposito ran into a crowd of people. "You son of a bitch." Max threw himself back into his car and slammed the door. He pressed the start button. The engine caught and kept running.

"Thank you!" Max slammed the car into drive and hit

the gas. A buzzer sounded. "Seat belts!" It was the pleasant female voice again. "*Damn it!*" Max rocketed the buckle home and laid tracks. The female voice thanked him.

Victor had already made it up the block and around the corner. Max caught sight of him and blew through an intersection. He distantly heard screeching tires and blaring horns.

Max leveled his pistol and took a couple more shots. The first went wild over Victor's head. The other plowed into the back of an old lady. She yelped in fright and dropped on the spot.

He threw the car in park and bounded out, ignoring the horns coming from behind him. "Give it up, Esposito!" Victor took off into the crowd again, shoving people out of his way as he went.

Max dropped to one knee beside the old lady and felt for a pulse. A young man stared at him, mouth agape. "Is she dead?"

Max shook his head. "Knocked out. She got stunned." He flashed his badge. "New Wave P-D. Call 911, would ya?" The kid nodded numbly.

He sprung to his feet, looking around wildly. A man to his left jabbed a thumb in the direction behind him. "He went that way, officer!"

"Thanks." Max tipped his hat and took off running. He scanned the crowd desperately with his synthetic eye. A floating black box jumped from face to face, scanning for Victor Esposito.

He slowed as he continued, slowly sweeping his head back and forth. He had nearly given up when the box suddenly snapped across his vision and started flashing.

He snapped his head to the right.

Victor's eyes grew wide in surprise. He fired off two wild shots from a Colt 45 and began to run again. "Damn it, Esposito!" Max followed, trying to find a clear shot and mentally adding attempted murder to Victor's growing list of charges.

Victor careened into the middle of an intersection. A garbage truck swerved, tires squealing. He jerked around it, watching as it nearly tipped over. Max slipped around it, now sprinting.

Both car and foot traffic were much thinner in this area. Victor had nowhere to hide. This was a foot race, now. That didn't mean Max couldn't cheat. "NWPD! Stop that man!"

Most people turned around and stared dumbly. One older man ineffectively pushed on Victor as he passed. Max swerved around the old man, panting. "Freeze... damn it!" He was losing steam.

A young man spun at the sound of Max's voice. He spotted Victor and stuck out his foot in the blink of an eye. Victor connected with the foot and went down tumbling, screaming all the way.

Max threw himself backwards, fighting hard to avoid Victor's fate. Victor rolled over, his face bloodied and contorted with rage. He brought his pistol up to fire.

Max swung his foot, punting the gun out of Victor's hand. It went skittering across the sidewalk. Max dropped to one knee and grabbed Victor's collar, the other hand was pulled back and balled into a fist.

"Whoa whoa whoa, hey! Stop!" Victor squeezed his eyes shut and turned his face away from Max.

The detective slowly dropped his fist. He instead

reached behind him and pulled out a set of handcuffs. "Victor Esposito, you're under arrest!"

The gathering crowd began to applaud as they puzzled out what was going on. Max stood with a grunt, dragging a protesting Victor with him. "Look at that, Victor! The crowd loves you."

Victor tried to spit on him. Max shook him like a wet dog, making Victor cry out in pain. "You wait, you son of a *bitch!* You just wait. Don Adesso is going to take care of me. Then *you.*"

The welcoming sound of a whooping squad car came from the other side of the crowd. "I think you're wrong on both parts, Esposito."

The crowd reluctantly parted to let a pair of police officers through. One had black hair, the other blond, with a mustache. The mustache nodded to Max. "Well holy shit, Max. You just cost me twenty bucks and two cups of Joe."

"So it goes, Richie. Why don't you give my friend here a ride downtown?"

Richard O'Connor smiled. "With pleasure."

"I want a doctor!" Victor twisted and thrashed as Max handed him over to Richard and his partner. "Police brutality! I'll see you..."

Max smacked him hard upside the head. "You'll see me downtown, you mouthy bastard. Anyone else responding, Richie?"

"Yeah um... Murphy, I think."

"Excellent. I need a ride. Left my car parked..." Max looked around vaguely. "Well somewhere back that way."

Richard smirked. "Yeah, we saw that." Victor started struggling again. "Okay, let's go, airhead."

Max started following behind the two officers, but

then caught himself up. He looked around, eye scanning again. Found him. "Hey, you! Yeah! In the blue windbreaker!"

The man stood and stared, not sure what to do. He ran his hand cross his short-cut brown hair. Max waved him over. The man looked around. Who, me? Max tilted his head to one side. Come on now, pal.

Blue windbreaker caught a hint and dragged himself over to where Max was standing. "Um, hi. I'm not... I'm not in trouble, am I?"

Max grinned. "No you're not, kid. You did good. That was a hell of a trick you pulled, tripping old Vic like that. Thanks." He stuck his hand out.

Blue windbreaker took it reluctantly and shook it. "Oh! Uh, sure. No problem."

"Hey, Kincaid! How about we go move your car out of the god-damned intersection!" There was Murphy.

Max tipped his hat. "Take care, kid. See ya around."

"Yeah, sure. See you." Blue windbreaker watched as Max walked through the crowd.

2

"Good afternoon, Detective Max Kincaid!" The blue and silver robot, JAX-649, was intimidating at just over seven feet tall. The cartoonish loop of LED lights where the bot's mouth should be was meant to put humans at ease. Max just thought it made the thing look goofy.

"How are ya, Jax?" Max frowned. "And for the thousandth time, just call me Max."

The LED mouth frowned back at him. "My apologies, Max." The goofy grin came back. "I am operating within acceptable parameters! I hope you find yourself functioning in a similar manner?"

Max half-smiled. "If you're asking if I'm doing alright, then yes, I am. I'm sure you already heard I snagged a big fish a short while ago."

"Oh, yes! Victor Esposito, case number five-three-nine-eight-four-zero, arrested for assault with a deadly weapon, evading arrest, resisting arrest..."

"Yeah, yeah... I arrested him! You're not telling me anything I don't know."

The glowing, blue frown was back. "You are

correct. I apologize for wasting your time, Max."

Max hung his head and sighed. He looked the bot in the electric blue eye. "You're just doing your job, Jax. I appreciate it."

The smile returned. He gave Max a sharp salute. "Always at your service, Max!" He reached over and pulled open the door to the New Wave City 29th Precinct as Max climbed the steps.

"Stay out of trouble!" Max winked.

"That will be easy, as I am programmed to avoid *being* in trouble!" Just what Max expected to hear.

"I'll see ya around, Jax." Max scurried in before the bot could respond.

Max sighed as he walked up to the booking window. He expected praise for capturing one of New Wave City's most wanted, but also a good tongue-lashing for knocking out an old lady in the process.

First thing's first. "Afternoon, Jake. Are your guys done processing my catch?"

Jake Cunningham let out a chuckle. "Well if it ain't the man of the hour himself. Yeah, we're done putting a bow on Esposito for ya. It's a good thing, too. The chief wasn't too thrilled with how you went about collaring him."

"Yeah, I was expecting that. We'll chat later, if I still have an ass to sit on." Jake roared as Max walked off for the main offices.

A round of applause greeted Max as he walked towards chief Norman Hanlon's office. Max grinned, raising his hands. He used them to tamp down the air in front of him. Keep it down, already.

He was less than thrilled to see that the big man

himself was in his office. Hanlon had his hands folded over his ample gut, peering through his spectacles at the computer screen on his desk. He didn't bother to look up when Max knocked on his door. "Come in, Kincaid."

Max closed the door behind him and stood in front of the grand inquisitor. "How ya doing, Norm?" Hanlon raised an eyebrow, but continued to study his computer screen. "Sit."

Hanlon sat up with a grunt and ran a meaty hand across his balding head. "I hear you had one helluva day today, Kincaid."

"You could say that, yes." Max couldn't read Hanlon's face. It was annoying the hell out of him. It always did. "I think it all worked out alright in the end."

Hanlon sighed. "I think the innocent old lady you stunned might not feel the same way."

"Aw jeez, Norm! It's not like I was aiming for her. There's a reason I was using stun and…"

"And she's perfectly fine. You might want to drop a card to Houston in Drug Enforcement, though. That's his mother." Max looked mortified. Hanlon grinned. "I'm just messing with you."

Max shook his head and grinned. "Why you gotta do that to me, Norm? Honestly… That old lady though, she really is okay, isn't she?"

Hanlon nodded. "She's fine. She's pissed, but frankly I don't blame her. I think we can smooth things out. Lucky for *you* that you did it making one *hell* of a catch."

"Oh, so you've heard?" Max was still grinning.

"Yes, I've heard. Old Victor is pissed off too, but I'm not so worried about that. He was yelling from one end of the precinct to the other about how he was getting out tonight, Don Adesso was going to punch our tickets, the usual bullshit."

Max leaned back and put his foot up on his knee. "But something was different this time…"

Hanlon grinned. "Old Don's people called. They disavowed having any business with the bozo. They don't want anything to do with him! And if they don't want anything to do with him…"

"Then he's dead to them. If Victor wants to be anywhere right now, it's here under the protection of the police."

"How sweet it is. I bet you he'll be singing like a bird by this time tomorrow." Hanlon pulled open a desk drawer and produced a pair of cigars. He offered one to Max. "I'd say this is the least you've earned, today."

Max shook his head. "Not my thing, boss."

"Trying to live forever? Eh…" He tossed it down on the desk in front of him. "Take it as a souvenir, then." He lit his own and talked around it. "I also don't want to see you tomorrow."

Max cocked his head, grinning. "That's not necessary, Norm."

Hanlon pulled the cigar and leaned forward, blowing out smoke as he talked. Max wrinkled his nose. "I never said it was! But that's the way it's gonna be." He leaned back and poked at his computer screen. "Get outta the city, maybe. Get some air."

"Plenty of air in town, boss." Hanlon looked at him over his spectacles. Max got the message. "I'm sure I can find something to do with myself. Um… Thanks, I guess."

Hanlon nodded. "You did good, Max. Go play."

Max stood up and waved a dismissive hand. "Sure, boss. Sure. We'll talk later." Hanlon grunted and went back to his computer screen.

Jax was still standing sentry when Max reemerged from the precinct. "I trust all went well, Max?"

"Just fine, buddy. Just…" Max turned his head slightly to look past Jax. He saw a familiar blue windbreaker. "Excuse me, Jax."

"Of course, sir." He watched Max jog a short distance up the street.

He returned a moment later. Jax tilted his head. "Is everything alright?"

Max distantly nodded. "Yeah. Saw a ghost."

"But ghosts aren't real, Max!"

"Yeah." Max looked back over his shoulder. "Except for when they are."

Max shut his car door and stretched in the morning sunlight. He watched the morning rush unfold around him, a look of bewilderment on his face. He sighed, adjusted his tie, and made his way onto the sidewalk.

People of all walks of life zoomed around him. At times he felt like he was moving in slow motion. Everybody had someplace to be. They had a purpose.

Max had a day off.

He smiled, shaking his head. What in the hell was he doing, anyway? He figured he might as well start today like how he started most. Max strolled in the general direction of Sam's Diner, still feeling like a turtle surrounded by hares.

A squat red news bot was positioned at the street corner. Well there was a start. The bot was about two feet tall and barrel shaped. A comically small head about the size of an apple sat atop its oddly shaped body. An OLED screen on the front of the bot showed "Catch the Wave… NEW WAVE TODAY"

The tiny head spun as Max approached. The robot made a series of excited beeps and squeaks, blinking its tiny blue eyes. Max smiled. "Morning there, Robby!"

Robby the news bot spun in a circle, making more cheerful noise. Max was always happy to see the little bot. He had become a semi-regular part of the detective's morning routine.

"What's news today, huh?" Robby beeped and spun his little head around. A sampling of the morning's headlines scrolled by on his OLED screen.

Max snorted at the top story. "Senator Robert Quade to Push Synthetics Regulation" read the headline. It was about time.

"Alright. Looks good. I'll take one." Robby beeped cheerfully. A small square pad slid out of the news bot's body and angled down. "Twenty-five bucks now? Almost more than my coffee, Robby!"

The news bot made a sad sound. "Oh, don't be like that. I'm still getting one." Max pressed his thumb on the pad. It beeped twice a couple of seconds later. A small, tinny male voice said, "Thank you!"

The pad retracted back into Robby. Something inside the news bot whirred and clicked. A slot opened on the bot's front panel a moment later. A thin 8"x10" piece of clear plastic slid partially out.

Max grabbed it and pulled it the rest of the way out. The slot sealed shut. Max stood and tapped the corner of the sheet. All the day's news filled the sheet in glowing blue letters.

"Thanks a million, Rob old boy." Max tapped the edge of his fedora. Robby beeped cheerfully and spun his head once more. Max walked away smiling.

He paused and tapped the corner of the newspaper before tucking it under his arm. He started walking again, trying his best not to be a deterrent to those that had a place to be. He began to cross the street to Sam's and stopped mid-stride.

Was that... He spotted a familiar blue windbreaker amongst the ocean of gray and black sport coats and business suits. The figure turned toward him. He zoomed in with his synthetic eye.

Max stumbled forward with an "Oomph!" A bright green minivan blared its horn as it swerved around the cursing detective. "What in the blue hell!"

A green and yellow delivery bot walked around him. "My humble apologies, good sir!" The bot held up a bag holding two sub sandwiches. It bore Jax's familiar goofy grin. "A rush order!"

Max rolled his eyes and flashed his badge. "Be more careful, robot."

The goofy grin was gone. "Oh, my! My apologies, Detective Max Kincaid!"

"Yes, yes, fine. Get a move on, would ya?" Max pointed at the growing line of cars behind the delivery bot.

It skittered off without another word. Max followed it across the street and gratefully watched it continue down past Sam's Diner. He swore the more complex the robot, the more potential it had to get itself into trouble. "Give me Robby any day."

Max shoved the door to the diner open and made a beeline for his usual spot at the end of the counter. He sat down on the stool with a huff. He slapped his newspaper down on the counter and tapped it awake.

Sam slipped a customer on the other end of the counter his bill and walked over to where Max was sitting. "What's the matter, hon? You seem grumpier than usual for a Wednesday morning."

Max shook his head without looking up. "Old Norm gave me the day off."

Sam broke out laughing. "Why, that mean old son of a bitch. How could he? I better get you a drink." She threw Max a wink and waltzed over to the coffeemaker.

"Ha-ha, Sam. Norm thought I earned it, dragging Esposito in. I mean, I suppose there are worse things he could have done to me…"

Sam sat a fresh cup of coffee in front of Max. "Yeah. He could have given you the rest of the *week* off! That would have made you miserable as hell."

"Come off it, lady. I just don't know what to do with myself, that's all. Didn't help that I had a bot try to push me off into traffic. Damn things…"

"Oh, they're not all that bad. I seen you smiling at that cute little news bot on the corner before. You seem to get on alright with that Jax at the precinct, too."

Max waved a dismissive hand. "Yeah, some of 'em are alright I suppose. The more sophisticated they make them, the more of a pain in the ass they seem to become. Don't even get me started on Synthetics."

Sam leaned on the counter and shook her head. "I'll be the first to admit that those walking mannequins are creepy as hell. Even so, you wouldn't still have two eyes if it wasn't for them."

Max slowly looked up, the bespoke synthetic eye glowing slightly in the dimly lit diner. "They're the worst of all." Max returned his gaze to his paper. "I don't owe them anything."

Synthetics were the next step in the evolution of robots. Designed to be human-like in appearance and mannerisms, they also sported an artificial intelligence that was bordering on human-like consciousness. Their eyes, while superior to humans, were kept purposefully artificial in appearance by law to make Synthetics easy to distinguish from humans.

It was for this reason that Max's own synthetic eye could not match his other. To Max, it made him look like a freak. It also served as a constant reminder whenever he came across a mirror that he owed his stereoscopic vision to them.

Max was snapped out of his revelry by the reflection of a familiar blue coat appearing on his newspaper. He was on his feet in the blink of an eye. He hoisted blue windbreaker off the ground by his namesake jacket. "You and I need to talk!"

Sam gaped. "Max! What are you doing?"

Max kept his eyes locked on blue windbreaker. "This dipshit has been trailing me ever since I bagged Esposito. And now he's going to tell me exactly why that is!" He accentuated his point by letting the man drop.

Blue windbreaker staggered backward, coughing. He grabbed at his neck. "Yes! I am... I *do* want to talk, but I've been scared."

"You damn well *should* be scared, pissing off a police detective!" Sam tossed looks from Max to blue windbreaker and back, looking worried. Max saw her out of the corner of his eye and got the message.

He sighed heavily, but quieted his tone. "Alright, fine. Sit down, right here." Max jabbed a finger at the stool beside his. Blue windbreaker sat down quietly. Max took his seat and sipped his coffee. "Start talking."

"My name is Daryl Marston and well, to be blunt… I think someone is trying to kill me. I thought you could help…"

Max sighed, rubbing his face with both hands. "Look kid, if you really think your life is in danger, you can go down to the police station and…"

"No!" Daryl shrunk back at the loudness of his own voice. "No… I tried that already. They basically said I needed help, but not the kind they offer. They said I was hallucinating from taking drugs. They said I was…"

"Crazy, right? So why do you think you'll get a different result from me, after stalking me, no less."

"I wasn't stalking you! I was afraid you'd say the same thing as the police at the station. Look… I saw how you handled that Exposition… Episode… that Victor guy."

Max chuckled. "Esposito."

Daryl's face lit up. "Yeah! That guy! I heard he was a pretty big player in the mob, and I figure if you can find a guy like that, then you can find whom ever is trying to kill me. You know, maybe like as a favor…"

Max's face darkened. "A favor… For *what?*"

"Well I mean I *did* kind of help you catch him."

Max leaped to his feet. "I've had just about enough of you, kid! You got lucky and stuck your foot out at the right moment. *That's all!*"

Daryl's brow lowered; his eyes looked odd. "I'd say

it was *you* that got lucky!"

"*That's it!*" Max grabbed Daryl by the collar once more and made to drag him clear out of the diner.

"*Maxwell Kincaid!* You put that young man down *now!*" Max raised an eyebrow. Sam looked about ready to jump the counter. He'd rarely ever seen her so cross. "I said *now!*"

Max dropped Daryl roughly to the ground. He didn't catch himself this time and crumpled to the floor. Sam shook her head. "What is with you, Max? You help people! Here's someone that needs help."

"The only thing I need help with is keeping this hothead away from me." Daryl stood up, dusting off his windbreaker.

"*You* shut your mouth." Sam stared darts at Daryl.

Daryl's eyes went wide. "Y-yes ma'am."

Max spread out his hands. "You gotta understand, Sam. I don't have time for this. He already talked to the boys. What more can I do?"

Sam crossed her arms. "Weren't you the one wringing your hands about what to do with all your free time?"

"Well yeah, but…" Sam's glare cut him short. Max sighed. "Yeah… fine." He fished out a business card and thumped it against Daryl's chest.

"If something goes down…" Max looked at Sam. "Call me." He jabbed a finger into Daryl's chest. "But don't you cross me again. Clear?"

Daryl nodded dumbly. "But are you going to look into my case? I don't want to die!"

Max sighed. "I'll try to make some time. You're already on file at the precinct by the sound of it. In the meantime, try to keep your nose clean. Now skedaddle!"

Daryl looked uneasily from Max to Sam and back. Defeated, he drooped his shoulders and quietly walked out of the diner. Max let out a long breath and sat back down at the counter.

Sam glared at him for a few seconds before cracking up. "*Skedaddle*? Who in the hell says that?"

Max's cheeks glowed a faint red. "Men of great distinction, obviously!"

"Distinction my ass!" Sam punched Max in the arm. "But seriously though Max, what gives? Why'd you treat that poor kid like that?"

Max sighed. "I don't know, Sam. It's just... I got bigger fish to fry. Esposito could be a linchpin in our case against Don Adesso. That..." He gestured toward the diner's front door. "...Is beat cop stuff."

Sam leaned forward. "You know what that sounds like? Sounds to *me* like someone suddenly thinks they're too important for something like that. Where's the Max that *I* know?" She propped her chin on her fists, flashing her eyelashes.

Max grimaced, shaking his head. "Curse your evil ways, woman. Look, I said I'd look into it..."

"Yes, you did." Sam winked and flicked his hat before walking back to the sink.

Max chuckled to himself. "Women..."

Sam stopped mid-stride. "What was that?"

"I said I'm on it!" Max stood up and made a hasty exit.

The sun broke free of the clouds as Max eased his old blue car onto the highway that wrapped around New

Wave City. He didn't lie to Sam. He was going to look into Daryl's case. He was simply taking the scenic route to work.

The road before him rose up and up into the sky as it slowly skirted him out towards the Atlantic Ocean. This was the closest he ever got to getting some fresh air, but it was good enough. The ocean air always did him good.

Max nosed the old bird up to 100 MPH and poked the Cruise button. Other vehicles passed him on the left at a steady pace. He shook his head. People were always in such a hurry.

His attention was torn between the ocean now just off to his right, and the blue and silver towers of the city gleaming in the sun to his left. There were many things about the city to frown about, but its looks weren't one of them.

All too soon, the highway curved back towards the city, and back to earth. Max thumbed the Cruise button and let the car slow itself down. The engine cut out a moment later. "Error!"

Max smiled and shook his head. "You son of a *bitch*." He pressed the start button. The engine sputtered and died. "Perfect."

He drew up the closest repair facilities on the center console. The car continued to lose speed. "Ha! There's luck…"

The old blue car came up on a major intersection. Max hit a switch, turning on red and blue lights in the windshield and back window. The light changed from red to green for him. It was an emergency, right?

He hung a slow right followed by another right into an Aero dealership. The vehicle slowed to a stop just outside the auto shop. "Just like I planned it."

An auto technician greeted him as he stepped out of his car. "She giving you trouble, boss?"

"You could say that. The engine control module needs re-flashed. Trust me." He tossed the tech his key fob.

Max wandered over to the new cars. He could feel the eyes of the hungry salespeople watching him. Still, he had to admit that maybe, just *maybe*, it was getting to be time to consider moving on in the automotive world.

He paced around a brand-new Aero 640SL, the spiritual successor to his Aero Ventura. He grimaced at the nameplate. "Alphabet soup." Still, he had to admit that the dark-red coupe looked pretty slick.

He grimaced again when he reached the price sheet. It was uncomfortably close to what his parents had paid for their house a few years back. "Beautiful day, isn't it?" Right on cue.

Max put on his best shit-eating grin. "Why yes, it's gorgeous."

"Jeb Deveron!" The salesman stuck out a manicured hand. Max reluctantly shook it. "Couldn't help but notice you falling in love with this beauty!"

"Oh! Yeah I uh… It's pretty nice… Expensive." Max muttered the last word under his breath.

"It sure would be an upgrade from that old, beat up Ventura! Those things can be *pretty* darn expensive to fix nowadays." He gave Max a knowing wink and a smile.

Max didn't return it. "Shouldn't be a big deal. The ECM just needs to be re-flashed."

Right on cue, the auto tech appeared from around the corner. "Sorry to interrupt. I'm pretty sure that you're going to need a new engine control module, sir."

Max sighed. "Did you re-flash the memory?"

The tech looked uneasily at the salesman. "Well um... no. It's just..."

Max held up a staying hand. "Just re-flash the damned ECM. *Please*."

"Yes, sir." The tech ran off with his tail between his legs.

Jeb Deveron shrugged. "He hasn't been here that long. You know how it is."

"Yeah..."

Jeb laughed uneasily. "Anyways... How about I get the keys to this baby and I'll let you take it for a spin? I think your heart will be set after a couple miles, eh?"

"Well..." Max heard a familiar engine roar to life. He smiled and patted Jeb on the back. "Maybe next time I'm down this way!"

The life rushed out of Jeb's eyes. "Oh... Well, I guess that's fair." He produced a business card as if by magic and handed it to Max. "Stop by any time!

"Thanks." The auto tech pulled up nearby in Max's old Aero Ventura. "See ya around."

"All set, mister!" The tech held out a payment pad.

Max made a face when he saw the price. He reluctantly put a thumb on the screen. "Re-flashed the ECM?"

The tech blushed, talking quietly. "Yes, sir. Sorry for the trouble."

Max smiled and winked. "No problem, kid. Keep your nose clean." He hopped into his car and beat a hasty retreat. Maybe he didn't need a new car after all.

"That's everything we got." Richard O'Connor slapped down another black plastic sheet beside the one that Max was looking over. Both had glowing blue words on them like the newspaper Max had earlier.

"You know Hanlon is going to have a baby if he finds out you're in here working on a day off."

Max shook his head without looking up. "It's a... favor, for a friend."

Richard crossed his arms. "Must be some friend. Why this guy, anyway? He's a druggie and a kook. He bust someone's chops or something?"

"No. Nothing like that. In fact, he's trying to claim that someone is trying to bust *his*."

"Oh! I remember this guy! Yeah, he came in trying to claim someone was out to kill him. He was acting real weird, talking funny. We sent him off to be evaluated and never heard anymore."

"Well I can definitely believe he was on something. Looks like things fell apart for him when he lost a job with Benjamin and Associates."

"Say, that's that big accounting firm on the other side of town, ain't it?"

Max nodded. "Yeah. He was probably one of the plebes that got scratched when they merged with Moore and Jackson." He looked up at the ceiling while he did some figuring. "Yup. His first arrest for possession would have been a few weeks after the merger was complete."

Max picked up the sheet Richard had brought him. "See, now this is the report from when he claimed someone was stalking him. The interesting thing is that this all came about several months after his last arrest for possession."

Richard shrugged. "So, what? You saying he was clean when he came in? Even if he was, it doesn't mean his mind wasn't messed up."

"Maybe not, Richie, but that's why we had him evaluated, isn't it?" Max pointed halfway down the sheet. "Says here that Psych said he was borderline neurotic *but* blood tests showed he was completely clean."

"Okay, so let's say he's stone cold sober. Who wants to kill him? A dealer?"

"That would be my first thought. Although…" Max scrolled down the electronic page with his finger. "This says he went on about some deal called SomniCorp. They do memory recording and 'adjustments' it says.

"Something about he had his memory 'backed up'… Kind of creepy. It was part of a free deal thing with Benjamin and Associates. He said he went in for a 'memory adjustment' when he was trying to kick his habit. He said things went weird after he had this adjustment."

Richard laughed. "Well can't be them, can it? If they did him wrong, they could just erase it from his mind, couldn't they? No need to kill him."

Max smiled at Richard. "Good point, Richie." Richard beamed. "Still…" Max returned to the sheet. "It could be that whatever they messed with in his head is giving him some sort of false belief he's being stalked."

Just then came a knock on Max's office door. "You in there, Kincaid?" It was Chief Hanlon. "You better *not* be." Oh, crap.

Max looked at Richard, who stared back like a deer in the headlights. Max grinned. "I'm not here, boss. I'm off today!"

The door bounced open. "Not here, my ass!" He eyed Richard. "What, did O'Connor drag you in here?" Richard started babbling.

"No, sir. He was just giving me a hand with some research. I was doing a favor for a friend."

Hanlon chewed at the tip of his cigar and blew out a cloud of smoke. "A favor, huh?"

Max nodded. "Just a favor. In fact..." He rounded up the paperwork in front of him and stood up. "I was just getting ready to cut out for the rest of the day."

"Good enough. Don't go getting too wound up in other shit, though. I want you focused on Esposito first thing tomorrow."

Max smiled and winked. "Been looking forward to it, boss."

"Haven't we all? Now get the hell out of here, would ya?"

<u>3</u>

The sun was shining as Max walked up to the precinct. He barely noticed, though; his mind focused only on Esposito. "Good morning, Max!"

Max smiled at this. "Good morning, Jax! You remembered!"

Jax's LED smile widened. "Correct! I made a note in my memory banks to remember your request, and acted on it when I saw you!"

Max shook his head. "Indeed you did. Good man… Oh! Well, good bot. I can't talk this morning though, I'm afraid. I have a date with Victor Esposito."

"Oh! I didn't think you were that kind of man. Well, good luck, then!"

Max nearly choked laughing. "No! No, too literal. Esposito and I are going to have a talk."

"I understand!" Jax saluted goofily as Max walked into the precinct. "I think…"

Jake Cunningham smiled from behind his bulletproof glass. "Here comes trouble! I hear you finally made some time to play with your new friend today."

Max smiled back. "Yeah, I'd say it's about time. Has

Esposito softened up any now that he knows Adesso doesn't want anything to do with him?"

Jake shook his head. "Not one damn bit. I honestly think he's got it in his head that we're just messing with him. He's certain Adesso is going to peel him out of here any day now."

"Funny thing is, that sounds just like something we'd try."

Jake snorted. "Fair enough. He's waiting uncomfortably for you in room three. Give him hell, Max!"

"That's the idea." Max walked down the hallway to his right. He put his thumb on a black plate to the left of the door at the end of the hall. The plate beeped and the door clicked. He walked through and let the door click shut behind him.

Door number three. Max bent down and gazed through the peephole. What he saw didn't surprise him, even though it should have. Esposito was gently rocking at the table in the dimly lit room. He looked scared.

Max pushed open the door. "Afternoon, Vic."

Any fear Esposito had disappeared off his face in the blink of an eye. "Go to hell, Kincaid."

Max pressed the door shut behind him and walked over to the table. "Vic, you're hurting my feelings, buddy. I thought we were friends."

"Very cute. I told you before, I'll tell you again: Go to hell. I'm not telling you anything."

"Yes, that's right. Your good man Don Adesso is going to get you out any day now, isn't he?" Max sat down across from Esposito.

"You're damn right. He'll never abandon me. He and I are like family. You don't abandon family."

Max leaned back in his chair. "Sounds to me like you're trying your best to convince yourself of that."

Esposito pounded the table with his fist. "*It's a fact!*" Max barely flinched. "I know you cops. He's probably tried to get me out already. You probably cooked up some bullshit excuse to keep me in here and make it look like he doesn't care."

"You know Vic, you could get *yourself* out of here if you helped us out a little."

"I *told* you, I ain't telling you nothing! Don's entrusted me with the knowledge I have and I ain't about to go spilling it to anyone, least of all *you!*"

Max slowly leaned forward. "Let's play a game, Vic. Let's pretend for a minute that I'm not bullshitting you. Let's pretend that Adesso could care less if you ever see the sun again. If that's the case, then he doesn't care if you're alive or dead, right?"

Esposito grinned and shook his head. "And in that case I'm better off telling you what you want to hear, right? It's better to have you for a friend than no friend at all."

Max kicked back again. "You're pretty good at this game, Vic! That's right, we can protect you from Adesso. All you have to do is tell us what you know."

Esposito started laughing. "That's a good try, Kincaid. I'll give you that. The fact is that even if I do talk, I'm still a dead man. I told you, Adesso will kill me for leaking what I know."

Max grinned. "Fact is, he probably already believes you did, Vic. Think about it, you really don't have anything more to lose."

Esposito stared Max down for a full minute before

he spoke again. "You might be right..." He shook his head. "I still ain't talking."

Max sighed and stood up. "Have it your way, Vic. We can have this conversation again tomorrow. Unless you have a change of heart..."

"Go to hell, Kincaid."

"It was good to see you too, Vic. Take care of yourself." Max tipped his hat. He left, quietly shutting the door behind him.

Chief Hanlon was waiting on the other side. "So... Progress, I suppose?"

The look on Max's face was noncommittal. "It's hard to tell with him this time around. I think Adesso's silence is really tweaking his mind. He's scared and he's trying to feel out which way he should turn."

"Well, let's just hope he goes toward the light." Hanlon smacked Max on the shoulder. "Good work. You working on anything else right now?"

"I've got a possible case I'm working over. I've got to discuss a few things with a collaborator of mine first."

"Very good. Do what you need to do. I'll ring you if Sunshine changes his tune."

Max settled himself down onto his old, familiar stool and spread the files on Daryl Marston out before him. Sam put a coffee mug in front of him. "Well, I'll be damned. You really *did* look into that kid's story!"

Max winked and held up his coffee. "I couldn't go disappointing my favorite source of free caffeine, now could I?"

Sam delivered Max a well-deserved cuff on the arm. "Is that all I am to you, Max Kincaid?"

"That, and a whole lot more." He smiled at her. That was enough to melt her. He turned back to the files. "I was honestly expecting another psych case, but I think there's something more to this kid."

Max explained the concept of SomniCorp to Sam, and how Daryl had his memory both backed up and modified. "That's the part that's tickling my brain. It's a stretch, but this SomniCorp might have messed something up and they're trying to cover their tracks.

"On the other hand, maybe it's all in his head. The twist is that SomniCorp might be the *reason* it's all in his head. Either way you cut it, I think this company might have some explaining to do."

Sam crossed her arms. "Sounds to me like you might have a new pet case."

The door to the diner opened. "I got your phone call, Detective Kincaid. I came over as quickly as I could." Daryl sat down next to Max.

Sam's eyebrows were riding high. "Wonders never cease!" She turned to Daryl. "Can I get you anything, sweetheart?"

Daryl blushed. "Uh, nothing for me. Is that alright?" He looked uneasily at Max.

Sam laughed. "That's perfectly fine, hon. I'll leave you boys alone to talk." She gave Max a wink and walked off to check on a couple on the other side of the diner.

"Say, I just want to thank you again for taking me seriously."

Max shook his head. "Don't mention it, kid. We'll see if we can't get things figured out for you." He scanned down a glossy black file. "Says here you went to this SomniCorp place a couple of times. What can you tell me

34

about that?"

Daryl grimaced. "That was a mistake twice over. They mainly market in 'memory collection', as they put it. They basically make a hard copy of your brain, is the way they explained it to me.

"My old job offered it as a perk. I think they just wanted to bank my work-related memories like they saved my work files. In retrospect the whole thing was kind of creepy."

Max rubbed his chin and scrolled down the file. "Well that explains the first time you visited. What was the second visit for?"

Daryl sighed. "That would be after I had lost said job. Regardless of employment, the memory files at SomniCorp were mine. I figured if they could record and recall memories, then maybe they could suppress them, too."

Max raised an eyebrow. "You wanted to forget something. Did it have to do with trying to overcome your addiction?"

"Oh, you read up about that part, huh?" Max nodded. "Yeah, that was a big part of it. I also wanted to forget about my fiancée."

"Your fiancée? Well I guess they failed at suppressing that part of your memories, at any rate."

Daryl chuckled. "I'd say they failed pretty much altogether. They called it 'memory adjustment'. They said they would give me an adjustment for free, since it was so new and experimental for them."

"So they failed to shut out your old woman... What about the addiction?"

Daryl shrugged. "That's the odd part: It worked! Any

cravings I had disappeared virtually overnight. It seems like that's the *only* thing they got right."

"Alright... So when exactly did you get the idea that someone was out to kill you?"

Daryl stared at the ceiling for a minute. "Oh, I'd say maybe two weeks after I visited SomniCorp for the second time. I started receiving these cryptic e-mails every couple of days or so. They were just weird at first, disjointed..."

"Weird how?"

"The best way I can think to explain it is they were like a computer generated spam e-mail. You know the kind. They try to make just enough sense that they don't get kicked to the spam folder."

"So how do you know that wasn't what they were?"

Daryl shook his head. "They were too personal. The parts that *did* make sense related directly to me, my life, my ex..." He swallowed. "Anyway... Eventually the messages started to sound threatening."

"Threatening how? Like death threats? Bodily harm?"

"Nothing so concrete. They'd say things like 'someone wants you dead,' or 'you don't know the danger you're in.'"

Max nodded. "I take it you had the presence of mind to save those e-mails."

"I did. I still have them on my computer back at my place. I can get you copies if you want."

"I think that'd be a good idea. One more thing... I'm sorry I have to ask, Daryl. Do you think your ex would have any reason to want you dead?"

Daryl took a sudden interest in the pattern on the

countertop. "I don't know why she'd want me dead. She couldn't wait to get away from me after I started in on the whole drug thing."

Max put a hand on Daryl's shoulder. "It'll be okay, kid." He rounded up the files and put them in a neat pile next to his coffee. "You get me those files off your computer, alright? I'll see what I can learn about this SomniCorp place."

Daryl nodded. He sounded distant. "Thanks again, Detective Kincaid."

"Call me Max."

"Max! Nice to meet you. I'm Chance Grasso!" The slick-looking salesman thrust out a manicured hand.

Max stared at the man for slightly longer than what would be considered acceptable before reluctantly shaking his hand. "Well you're a ray of sunshine, aintcha?"

Grasso shook Max's hand for slightly longer than what would be considered acceptable before finally freeing him. "Well, we here at SomniCorp understand how dour a topic memory preservation and recall can be. We try to keep things as upbeat as possible!"

Max wiped his hand on his trench coat as Grasso walked to his desk. "I feel better already."

Grasso fluffed his blazer and gestured to the seat on the opposite side of his desk. "Fantastic! Why don't you take a load off? Though I promise this won't take long." Max wondered how many hours went into perfecting that shit-eating grin.

He reluctantly sat down in the seat and uncomfortably folded his hands in his lap. Grasso took his seat. He eyed his greased-back hair in the reflection of his computer monitor. He slicked back a stray hair and turned to Max. "So tell me Max, what brings you to SomniCorp?"

Max cleared his throat. "Well, I'm in law enforcement, as I'm sure you know. I have a lot of information stored up in the old noggin and..."

"Ah HA! You want to preserve your years of knowledge for future dissemination!" Grasso beamed.

Max bit the inside of his cheek. "Yes..."

"*Totally* understandable! That's a growing area of interest in our company, as it would happen! Police, lawyers, doctors... All of them are turning to SomniCorp to preserve the unique and irreplaceable information locked away within their minds!"

"Right... Well, how... How does this all work, exactly?"

"Well of course I can't tell you *exactly* how it works. That's a trade secret!" Grasso chuckled. Max frowned. "A little humor, there. No, I can give you a very good idea of what to expect!

"There's no special preparation necessary for our process. The whole thing takes less than half an hour. You'll simply recline in one of our recording chambers and relax while our computer systems do all the heavy lifting!"

Max snorted. "I don't know how relaxed I'd be wrapped up in a pod."

"Oh, no worries, Max! We administer a very light anesthetic to relax you and keep you from moving."

"Keep me from moving?"

"Yes! Our procedure is one-hundred percent non-invasive. The chamber has an array of sensors and scanners that map the state and location of each synapse in your brain. The system can correct for slight movements from blood flow and respiration, but motor movement would be detrimental."

"Ah, okay. So after you um, scan me... That digitizes my brain, then? How do I read my memories?"

"Two very good questions, Max! The system will make a virtual copy of your brain patterns and functioning. Importantly, this is just a snapshot. We don't want to go making an artificial intelligence with your brain, now do we?"

Grasso was chuckling again. Max was still frowning. "No, we wouldn't. About reading memories..."

"Yes! At any given point in the future you, or someone you give permission to, can come in and access your own personal memory archive! You can even control the level of access, such as only police-related memories in your case."

Max raised an eyebrow. "Sounds like a pretty sophisticated system to be able to sort all that."

"Absolute state of the art stuff, Max! We're quite proud of it. It's advanced enough that even Synthetics International has shown an interest in our technology. You can read all about it in the May issue of A.I. Today!"

"I'll keep that in mind. Okay. So let's say I do this. I can take it all back, can't I? Delete the capture, if I choose?"

For the first time since their meeting began, Grasso's grin faltered. "Oh, well yes, of course. It's all laid out in the agreement you'll be signing. They are *your* memories after all."

"Good. Fine. Um... One more thing." There was a

gleam in Max's good eye. "Is there any way to get rid of memories in my brain? Things I'd rather forget?" Max rubbed his face near his fake eye.

"Ohhh..." Now it was Grasso that was looking uncomfortable. "We've done some research in that area. It's something we can discuss after the memory recording process..."

"I'll keep that in mind." Max sighed deeply. "Well, alright. Sign me up, guy."

Grasso clapped his hands together, the shit-eating grin instantly reappearing. "*Fantastic!* This really is a wonderful choice, Max! I'll just need you to sign and thumbprint this for me."

He slid a tablet across the desk to Max. The detective frowned harder. The bottom of the screen indicated page one of a thirteen-page agreement. "That's quite a bit of paper..."

"No worries, Max! It's the usual boilerplate agreement stuff you'd find anywhere else. No big deal!"

Max looked unconvinced. "Just don't want to lose my mind." Grasso laughed. Max didn't.

"Welcome to the Mind Chamber." The attractive young woman offered Max her hand and a smile. She wore a white leather catsuit, which paired well with her white hair and pale complexion. The bright turquoise irises of her eyes stood in stark contrast to all.

"You're a Synthetic." Max reluctantly took her hand. His last contact with a Synthetic hadn't gone very well.

"That is correct." She could have easily passed for human, save for the eyes. Her eyes, and the slightest hollow echo in her voice, as if she were speaking through a tube. Subtle, but detectable for someone trained to listen for it.

"Does this displease you?" She looked over her shoulder as she led Max to a bright white pod. The entire front was made of rounded glass.

"No! Um, well… The last Synthetic I interacted with left me a permanently changed man. How about we put it that way."

The Synthetic woman stopped in front of the pod and turned around. Her stunning eyes stared into Max's own. "Is this why you have a synthetic eye?"

"Well… yes. No offense, I hope. It was a case I was…"

"There is no need to worry that I might injure you." Max hiked an eyebrow. Typical Synthetic. "You were likely injured by a Mark three or earlier model. I am a Mark four." She turned to the pod and touched a button near the bottom.

Max smiled thinly. "I feel *so* relieved to hear that." The face of the pod hissed and opened to the side.

"This pleases me." The smile was back. She held out her hand. "Your trench coat, if you please."

"Oh…" Max took off the coat and handed it over. The Synthetic woman hung it from a nearby stand.

"I will also need your service weapon."

"Now, I don't know about that…" Max unconsciously took a step backward.

"The scanning electron beams could inadvertently cause the weapon to discharge. I'm afraid I must insist."

"How about I put it in my coat pocket for you?"

The Synthetic woman stared for a moment, her eyes almost imperceptibly twitching left to right as she considered the request. "Acceptable. Proceed."

Max shook his head and paced over to his coat. He reluctantly placed the plasma weapon in his right coat pocket. He somehow felt more naked without his weapon than if he were actually standing there in his birthday suit.

"You are nervous." The Synthetic woman placed a hand on Max's upper arm.

Max jumped slightly. "You could say that."

"I assure you that all will be well." She led him back to the front of the pod and gestured to the seat inside. "Please enter the pod and lay back against the seat."

Max took a deep breath and stepped into the pod. He nestled himself down into the oddly shaped seat. He wasn't sitting, nor was he necessarily leaning. The pod door suddenly swung shut, causing him to jump again. It sealed with a hiss.

"You will hear a quiet hiss as the pod fills with a relaxing agent. Please try your best to relax. The procedure will begin shortly."

"Relax. Sure." The need for anesthesia was making more sense with every minute that passed. Max almost welcomed the fuzziness that wrapped around his brain as the anesthetic gas filled the pod.

The Synthetic woman's voice came from a great distance. "We will now begin the procedure."

Max's eyes sealed themselves shut. The hissing of the gas faded to a deafening silence. He could have sworn that he was hearing his own blood coursing through his veins.

Without warning, he perceived a kaleidoscope of colors twisting and streaking in front of and all around him. A rumbling sound grew louder and louder in his ears, surrounding him in a blanket of sound. Brief glimpses from his childhood blurred past his vision in bursts of light and sound.

It was over as quickly as it had begun. Vision in his human eye slowly faded in but remained blurry. His synthetic eye remained dark.

The pod door swung open. The Synthetic woman leaned over him. She wore what looked like vague concern on her face. "How do you feel?"

Max rubbed his good eye. That's better. "I'm a little groggy, but otherwise I feel alright." He tapped the left side of his face. "You might owe me a new eye, though."

A frown flashed over the Synthetic woman's face. "There was an unexpected complication resulting from interference caused by your synthetic implant. We were only able to successfully map eighty percent of your brain."

Max tapped the side of his face harder. He finally saw the Synthetics International logo appear in his left eye. "SYSTEM RESTORE," it informed him. "Please wait..."

"Looks like you lucked out on the eyeball... So now what do we do?"

"We can attempt to retrieve the remaining twenty percent of your memories, if you wish. Please be advised that this could result in permanent damage to your synthetic eye and/or your brain."

Max sat upright. "I think I'll pass!" He struggled his way out of the pod.

Sam put a cup of coffee in front of Max. "Sweetheart, you look like you've just been through some kind of hell."

Max cocked his head. "Not quite that bad, but I've been better." He sipped at his coffee. Nature's medicine. "I went through that whole memory backup deal at that SomniCorp."

Sam did a double-take. "You *what?* You're worried those people scrambled that kid's brain and then run off to have them do it to *you?* Why on earth didn't you just *ask* them about it, Max?"

Max chuckled. "Calm down, Sam. You're going to give yourself a coronary. I tried that route. As soon as their P-R department heard that I was a police detective, they shut down on me double-quick.

"His brain was already scrambled anyway!" Starla giggled as she wheeled past. Sam smirked. Max shook his head.

"I sat down with a representative a couple of hours later, hoping my reputation wouldn't precede me. The mook that saw me didn't have a clue what was going on. I got some answers, and a little firsthand experience."

Sam leaned on the counter. "Alright. So what was it like, then?"

Max shook his head. He needed another sip of coffee. "It was like some sort of fever dream. Really short, but really intense. There were colors, sounds. The worst part was seeing my life literally flashing before my eyes."

"God, Max." Sam shivered. "So now what?"

"I don't know. The lady... She was a Synthetic, by the way! She told me my eye of all things messed up the whole works. They only caught eighty percent of my brain."

"A Synthetic! I bet that was a real comfort to ya."

Max frowned. "Yeah, kind of threw me. That rep I talked to said Synthetics International was interested in their tech. He didn't say they had Synthetics actually *working* for them. At least this one stayed away from my eye.

"Anyway, I guess that's as far as I'm going with that. I'll probably call and tell them to kill what they got. Could be corrupted, for all I know. The important thing is I got some information."

"So you still thinking this kid's just sick in the head, then?" Max nodded.

"You would know, wouldn't ya?" Starla went by again, winking. Sam gave her a look.

Max ignored her. "I think it's SomniCorp's fault, though. I think it's clear to see that they're far from perfecting the whole process. I still need to look into these e-mails he's been receiving."

4

Heavy clouds obscured the sun as Max lazily steered his car towards the 29th precinct. He was keeping to surface streets today. His old jalopy had been giving him the runaround again. Better stranded on a side street than on the highway.

It was good to see all facets of the city, anyway. He had a history with these parts. Not quite the slums, but *far* from the middle class. These were the neighborhoods he had grown up in, run around in, got in trouble in.

Rain started gently patting the windshield. The old Ventura's rain sensors flicked the wipers quietly across the glass. Max shook his head. He was a stuffed shirt. He used to give "fancy guys" like himself a wide birth when he was a kid.

A pair of children jumping in the light rain paused to smile and wave at him. He smiled and waved back. He wasn't a stuffed shirt. These were still his people. Sometimes people could get a little money and a nice car without becoming a member of the bourgeoisie.

He smiled and waved to an old man sitting on a bench at the far end of the run-down neighborhood. You know? He could almost hope to be that man in a few decades. He could think of far worse places to wind up.

The narrow streets gave way to the wide boulevard of the shopping district. The rain had stopped, the sun peeking out of quickly dissipating clouds. He hated to say it, but maybe the car acting up wasn't so bad a thing after all, the car that was now making a series of clunking noises.

Max beat first on the steering wheel, then on the dashboard. "You god-damned no good piece of shit son of a…"

"Error! Check engine…"

"*I know, error!*" Max thumped the dash hard. The engine died. "No. No, baby. Come on, I didn't mean it." The old Ventura wasn't buying it.

He looked around to find a good place to bail. Max grinned. Wouldn't ya know it? He coasted his old jalopy once more into the service area of the Aero dealership that had last got him back on the road.

"If I didn't know better, I'd say the bastards were making my car do this on purpose."

The grease monkey that helped him out the last time came walking up sporting a shit-eating grin. "Let me guess: Re-flash the engine control module?"

Max tossed him his key fob. "Nailed it in one." He sighed deeply. "Take your time. I'm about to put a smile on your boss' face."

As if on cue, Jeb Deveron the car salesmen popped around the corner. "Well hi there! Max, wasn't it? Of course it was! That old piece of junk letting you down again?"

Max grimaced. Only *he* got to call his old girl a piece

of junk. "She's just showing her age a little. However..." He swallowed hard. "Maybe it's time I take that four-twenty XYZ for a test drive."

Deveron went blank for a minute, then laughed. "Oh! You mean the 640SL! Yes, that naming scheme is a bit of a mouthful, isn't it?"

"That's one way to put it. I guess I'm interested in that sparkly red one over there."

"You got it, Max! Give me one minute."

Max wandered over to the 640SL he had looked at the last time he was there. Maybe it *was* time to upgrade. He couldn't afford to be driving around in questionable transportation, after all...

"Here we are!" Jeb jammed the fob for the 640SL into Max's hand and began screwing a dealer plate onto the back of the car. "There shouldn't be too much unfamiliar tech in this one. That Ventura of yours was top shelf in its day. Shares a lot of tech with this one."

"That's good to know. Can it be brought up to police spec if I decide to buy it?"

"Of course! We're fully licensed for police conversions."

Max nodded. "Good. Well..." He pressed the Start button on the key fob. The nuclear-powered turbine wound up to a whine before fading to near silence. "Not quite the same ring to it as a good old-fashioned gasoline engine."

Deveron clapped Max on the back and smiled. "No, it's not. But you'll love the fact that you only have to refuel it about twice a year."

Max raised an appreciative eyebrow. "Very interesting..." The car door swung open effortlessly for him. "I'll bring it back in a day or two, say?"

"Not a problem. Keep it as long as you need to. We want you to be confident in your purchase!"

Max shut the door and rolled down the window. He tipped his fedora. "Thanks, chief. I'll see you soon." Deveron waved as he pulled away. The acceleration was smooth as glass and completely effortless. "Maybe this was a good idea after all."

"Maybe this wasn't such a good idea." Max sat in the parking garage adjacent to the 29th precinct. He was punching buttons with one hand and holding his temporary police dome light with the other.

"Wow, Max! You get yourself a new ride, finally?" Richard O'Connor let out a low whistle as he paced around the shiny new Aero.

"Not yet, Richie. I'm about to go running back to the old one, to be honest. This one and I don't speak the same language." Max pressed a button on the console. The dome light came to life for a second and went dark again. Max growled.

"I can see that... Anyway, I wanted to let you know that I was able to pull up that kid's e-mails for you." Daryl had called Max a while ago to tell him someone had erased all his e-mails. Seemed kind of convenient.

"Good man. I had a feeling his ISP would have a backup of at least a few of them." Max had Richard do some data mining with Daryl's internet account. It sounded like it paid off. "Find anything threatening?"

"Yeah, I did." Max raised an eyebrow. "Here's the kicker: The kid sent the threatening e-mails to himself."

The dome light flashed on and off. Max growled

again. "Son of a bitch!"

Richard tried to hide a smile. "The bubble light or the kid?"

"Both!" He tossed the dome light on the passenger seat. "Was there anything else?"

"Well, kinda. The e-mails also had some weird coding above and below the threatening messages. It might be nothing…"

"But it might be something. I better take a look, and I need to have a serious talk with that kid. In the meantime…" Max scooped up the dome light and held it out to Richard. "Wanna do me a favor?"

Richard took it and grinned. "I'll see what I can do for you."

Max kept going over the e-mails on the tablet Richard had left for him. There was a binary theme to them. The most prominent message would either be positive or negative. A message buried in the bottom of the e-mail would invariably be the opposite.

One example had a primary message that read "You are strong enough to overcome this. Don't lose who you are." The obscured message at the bottom read "You know you are weak. There is no stopping progress. You will be destroyed."

Max jumped when there came a knock on his office door. "Come in."

It was Daryl. "Hi, Max. I came right over after your call." Max extended a hand to an empty seat. Daryl took it. "You were able to recover some of my e-mails, huh?"

"I was, or at least Richie O'Connor was, at any rate. He discovered a new issue, however."

Daryl looked genuinely concerned. "What? Did he figure out what those jumbles of words meant?"

"We're still working on that. It's the source of the e-mails that's the problem."

Daryl leaned forward. "You know who sent them? That's great!"

"Not exactly, kid. It was *you* that sent them."

"That's not possible!" Daryl struck the arm of his chair. "This O'Connor's got to be wrong!"

"Now just calm down, kid. I think there's more going on here than *any* of us realize. That said, the evidence is incontrovertible. The account was created shortly before the first e-mail was sent, and the registration is traceable back to the address you have listed.

Daryl stared at Max's desk. He was shaking. "Not possible. It's not... Why would I do this?" His eyes met Max's.

"That's what I want to find out. I don't know what's going on, Daryl, but I still think this SomniCorp might have a hand in it. Now I want to get a search warrant so that I can have your files with them analyzed, but first..."

Max sighed deeply. "I'm going to have to ask you to sit down for an interview with a psychologist."

"You want me to *what!*" Daryl started trembling.

"Listen, kid. I know that the suggestion to get your head checked was all you were offered the last time you were here. This is different."

Daryl grew a crazed look in his eyes. "Oh? Different how? Is it somehow better because it's a *detective* calling me crazy instead of some dick in a blue suit?" He shot to his feet. "I don't need this shit."

"*Sit down!*" Max stared daggers. Daryl froze, looking bewildered and torn. He jerkily sat back down again. "You listen and you listen good. I'm doing everything in my power to help you.

"Now I understand how painful it must be to keep hearing you need a shrink, but it's the only way I can get that warrant. I need that psychologist to testify that she sees a reasonable chance that SomniCorp could have scrambled your brain. I know it's hard, but I need you to play ball with me, kid."

Daryl's face was buried in his hands. He pressed them into his eyes and rubbed. "I don't understand why everyone is just assuming I'm crazy."

"Nobody is assuming anything, Daryl. This is all procedural, a means to an end. Right now, it's nothing more than that."

Daryl slowly looked up at Max. "Right now... It still sounds like you're expecting me to be nuts. I just want someone to believe me."

Max leaned forward. "If I didn't believe at least *some* of what you've said, you wouldn't be sitting in this office. If you want answers, this is where it's going to start."

"If this will help make me better... I guess I'll do it."

"I can't say for sure it will make you better, but I think it will help get you answers. It's a start."

Daryl nodded. "Okay. What do I need to do?"

Max handed Daryl a business card. "The gal on the card is Linda Baughman. She specializes in PTSD and repressed memories. You can guess why I chose her for you. You have an appointment with her tomorrow morning at ten. Good?"

Daryl studied the card. "Yeah, alright…"

"Good… You haven't had any more perceived threats or anything since we last spoke, have you?" Daryl continued to stare at the card, unblinking. "Kid?"

Daryl snapped his head up. "What? Oh! I'm sorry. No. Nothing."

Max's eyes narrowed. "Are you okay, Daryl?"

"Sure. Yeah. I'm just tired, stressed out."

"Right… That's all I needed. I'm going to show these e-mails to a friend of mine downtown if you don't mind. He's a bit of a specialist when it comes to coding. If there's anything there to find, he'll find it."

Daryl slowly stood up. "Yeah, that's fine." He sounded distant. "Do what you need to do."

Max stood up. "I'll let you know if anything turns up. Just make sure you're not late for that appointment."

"I won't be." Daryl smiled and put out his hand. "Thank you for helping me, Max."

"It's what I do, kid." Max smiled back, shaking Daryl's hand. "We'll take care of you."

Max sat back down and watched Daryl shut the door quietly behind him. Something was definitely going on. He could feel it, but he wasn't quite sure what it was yet.

He stared at the chair Daryl had been sitting in. His eyebrow slowly raised up. "What the hell?" He stood and walked to the chair. He ran a finger along the steel arm that Daryl had banged with his fist. It dipped slightly where he had struck it. "One helluva arm on that kid."

Someone pounded on his door, nearly sending him into a coronary. It opened a moment later to reveal Chief Hanlon. "Looks like it's your lucky day, Kincaid! Jesus, it looks like you seen a ghost."

"No, but you nearly scared mine straight outta me! What's going on?"

"Oh! Sorry… I'm just a little excitable. Esposito's ready to have a chat, and he wants it to be with you."

"Well if it isn't New Wave's finest. Excuse me if I don't get up." Esposito smirked, holding up his shackled left wrist.

Max tipped his fedora and smiled. "Good to see you again, Vic. I heard you wanted to talk over a few things." He sat across the table from Esposito.

"I've been thinking about what you said. And, uh…" Esposito rubbed the back of his head. "Well, maybe you have a point."

Max nodded. "What changed your mind?"

Esposito leaned back. "I know Adesso. If he had wanted me out of here, I'd have been gone by now. Let's just say the fact that he hasn't exactly pounded down the door has given me cause for concern."

"Fair enough. Well, I stand by what I told you the last time. You give us a hand and we'll keep you safe."

Esposito smiled and shook his head. "I'm not entirely sure I buy *that*. Who's to say you're not going to get what you want out of me and then leave me rotting in a jail cell?"

It was Max's turn to smile. "You know damn well that we have more than enough on you to do that whether you talk or not. The real question is: Do you want to get out of prison this year, or next decade?"

"Touché. I assure you that I considered that as well. I can also assure you that the information I have is valuable enough that I *do* in fact expect to be released this year, preferably this *month*."

Max spread out his hands. "I can't make promises, you understand. If what you have is on the level... Anything's possible."

Esposito sighed. He looked tired. "Yeah. Well, nothing ventured, nothing gained. Adesso picked up a new client lately, a *big* client."

"You don't say?"

"We've been working with Synthetics International."

Max scoffed. "Synthetics International? You expect me to believe that? That company is worth hundreds of millions! What could they possibly need that Adesso offers?"

"Look, *friend*, I don't expect *nothing* from you, but I promise you Adesso's working with them. I'm only one of a handful of people that even know *that* much. All I know for sure is that they are working on some special project that may or may not be completely legal, if you catch my drift."

"Is that right? Are there any other countries involved in this special project, by chance?"

Esposito shook his head. "Nothing to do with espionage... At least not *foreign* espionage. Let's just say that there might be some *federal* interests involved."

Max looked Esposito in the eye. Esposito never blinked. "This is a lot to swallow, Vic. You know that."

"I do, Kincaid. I'm telling you that it's on the level. Do your homework. Just *try* to prove me wrong."

Max nodded. "Oh, I will, Vic. I will. That's my job. But if you're right..." He extended his hand. "We'll talk again soon."

Esposito looked at Max, then at the extended hand. He reluctantly shook it. "You better not do me wrong, Kincaid."

Max smiled. "I'd never dream of it, friend. We'll see you."

Chief Hanlon was waiting outside of the interrogation room. His face was a garbled combination of joy and confusion. "I guess he was serious, but... Synthetics International? Do you think he's serious, Max?"

Max shook his head. "I want to think he is. He seemed sincere, but what on earth could a company that big be doing that would require teaming up with such a liability? Whatever it is, it's got to be big."

Hanlon nodded. "My thoughts, exactly. The question is, how do we go about finding out?"

"I have a friend downtown. He's got an ear closer to the Synthetics industry than anyone I know. I got to tickle his brain about another case anyway. I can see if he's heard anything."

"Good enough. Keep me posted." Hanlon clapped Max on the back.

5

Max stepped out into the evening air. The sun was just setting, although he couldn't see it. Columns of concrete and glass closed in around him, cutting off the heat and the light of the last moments of the day.

He stared up at the twilight interlacing between the buildings, buttoning his trench coat. He brought in the brisk, clear air through his nose, smelling the coming autumn weather on the wind. He smiled.

It had been too long since he'd been downtown. Well, it'd been a long time since he'd been downtown *off the clock*. All work and no play... He imagined he was turning into one of the damned robots that seemed to be on every corner nowadays.

Max reached the red Aero from the dealership and kept walking. He fancied taking public transportation tonight. He felt out of touch with the city. That was a bad thing for a detective.

He navigated his way down into the subway. The smell and the grunge were an abrupt change from the clean, crisp air up above. The air down here was warm, damp.

He was there, though. Might as well push on. He continued down to the concourse and puzzled over the subway map. How long had it been since he'd taken the subway to Chinatown? He couldn't remember.

"Do you require assistance?" Max jumped. It was a blue and chrome subway guard bot Its glowing blue eyes considered Max carefully.

"Uh, yeah. Sure. I'm trying to get to Chinatown."

"Understood! Please proceed to platform B and wait for the red line. Can I be of further assistance?"

"No. Thank you."

"You are welcome." The guard bot nodded curtly and continued on its way. Why couldn't humans be that polite, he wondered?

Max did as the guard bot had suggested and waited for the red line to show up. He was starting to get excited about seeing Shen Jian again. Shen was an old friend of his, going back to his days as a beat cop.

The red line glided noiselessly to a stop in front of him. A smattering of passengers disembarked. He boarded a car and surveyed his companions. A pair of canoodling kids on one side, a disheveled-looking black and silver maid bot on the other. In the middle sat a female Synthetic. Wonderful.

He sat down halfway between the Synthetic and the maid bot and waited for the train to depart. He looked towards the maid bot and nodded. "How are ya?"

"My programming forbids me from talking to unauthorized users. Good day!" Friendly.

The train finally trundled to life, pulling away from the stop swiftly but smoothly. Max sighed and settled back into the green plastic seat. He pulled out a small, thin, black piece of glass: his smart phone. He pressed his thumb to the center of the glass. The screen illuminated a moment later.

A couple of taps later and he was looking at Daryl Marston's threatening e-mails. Each one was like the other. A message of support or one of damnation. The message gave way to a series of letters, numbers and symbols. A message of opposing intent invariably lay at the bottom of each e-mail.

"You are different." Max snapped his head up. He quickly realized it was the Synthetic addressing him.

Shit. "I beg your pardon?"

"I said that you are different." Her turquoise eyes stood out in stark contrast of her jet-black hair. They were staring intensely into the detective's own.

Max shifted uncomfortably. "We're all different. I guess that makes us all the same, from a certain point of view."

"Your eye. It is synthetic. Why?"

Max sighed. "It's not something I like to talk about."

The Synthetic woman stared for a moment longer. "That is unfortunate. I find it fascinating." The woman returned to looking forward and said no more.

Max raised an eyebrow but returned his gaze to his smart phone. Curiosity in Synthetics wasn't unheard of, but they weren't usually so forward in seeking information. Sometimes he thought they were more human than they had any right to be.

The rest of the trip proved uneventful. Max yawned and stretched as the train slowed to a stop at his station. He'd normally be staring quietly at his telescreen at home, slowly losing a fight with his eyelids by this time of night.

He emerged onto a darkened street. The sudden rush of brisk air across his face did wonders for his mental acuity. He could hear the familiar sounds of Chinatown wafting down the street. He began to smile.

Max grinned as he rounded the corner. The large, ornate *paifang* shined down on him in hues of gold and red light. Imperial lion statues stood vigil on either side of the gateway, bathed in emerald green light.

The unique sounds of Chinese music played on a *guzheng* boomed from hidden speakers in either side of the gateway. A pair of Synthetic women dressed in cheongsam dresses smiled and bowed to Max as he passed. He smiled back, tipping his fedora.

The wide concourse quickly diverged into two distinct areas of interest. To the left were an abundance of tents and booths offering various curios, souvenirs, and the odd bit of contraband. On the right were a series of eateries consisting of everything from simple stands to sit-down restaurants.

Max ignored the tugging of his stomach for the time being. Shen would be waiting for him in a booth on the left side. If he knew Shen like he thought he did, they would both migrate to the right side before the night was over. But for now, it was business before pleasure.

Any number of merchants shouted for his attention as he strolled past the various gadgets, doodads, and souvenirs. Not all those shouting did so in English. Regardless, it was working, just not on him. He grinned at the sight of younger, less knowledgeable souls drifting into the various booths.

Max *did* stop before one particular booth outside of

an electrical shop. An old, well-rounded Asian man sat on the opposite side of the table. He was puffing gently on a Churchwarden pipe.

His neatly trimmed beard stood in contrast to his long, flowing white hair tucked hastily behind his ears. He slowly looked up from the book he was reading to consider Max. His light-blue eyes grew wide. "Max Kincaid! Ha-*ha!* I do believe that it's been ninety-seven years, give or take."

Max grinned. "Jian! You haven't changed a bit." He stuck his hand out.

Shen Jian smiled broadly and took Max's hand into his own and firmly shook it with both hands. "Please! Sit." Shen gestured to a stool on the opposite side of the table. "Tell me, have you really missed my company enough to find your way down here, or do you need something?"

Max sighed, still grinning. "How about I tell you both? It really *is* good to see you, old friend, but I *do* have a couple favors to ask of you."

Shen dramatically widened his eyes and blew out a large puff of smoke. "*Two* favors! After three-hundred years, you come asking for *two!* Surely I only still owe you four or five dozen favors by now."

"I think it's *me* that owes *you* so many, but I still hope you'll help me out."

Shen squinted, then winked at the detective. "I always help those who help me." He shrugged. "Besides, I'm bored! I've been sitting here for two hours, and not one person has stopped to sample my wares."

Max surveyed the table before him. An array of old electronics manuals stared back at him. He flashed him an amused smile. "I don't think there's much interest in these old things, my friend."

Shen laughed. "No interest in old things, yet here you are talking to *me!* Now, what is it that I can help you with, dear friend?"

Max leaned in, lowering his voice. "Let's just say that it's not something I'd like to go spreading around." Max darted his eyes to one side, then the other.

"Of course! Of course. I understand. Perhaps you'd share a drink with me in the back of my shop?" Shen stood up.

Max followed suit, grinning. "I thought you'd never ask."

"Hóu, you ignorant monkey! Go sit down!" Shen growled at the small orange and gray robotic animal. It screamed and chattered, blinking its glowing yellow eyes as it scrambled out of Shen's reach. It made its way to the ceiling and hung upside down from a pipe by its jointed tail.

Max gestured towards the robot. "The monkey's new." He sat down at a counter at the back of Shen's electronics shop. Various computers, tablets, and partially constructed robots were strewn about on various counters and tables.

Shen rolled his eyes. "Hóu is... unique. I thought he would make a good companion, someone to fetch things for me as I worked. He spends just as much time tearing the shop apart as he does being useful!" He swiped at the monkey, which chattered and deftly dodged the blow.

He waved a dismissive hand and reached behind the counter. He first produced two glasses, then a bottle of *Baijiu*, a vodka-like Chinese liquor. He poured a measure in each glass and toasted Max. "To old friends."

"Here, here." Max gently clinked his glass off Shen's and took a careful sip. He was well-acquainted with Baijiu. He still made a face.

Shen laughed. "It has been some time since you last had Baijiu, hasn't it?" He leaned on the counter, a simple smile on his face. "It *is* very good to see you, Max. Tell me, what's on your mind?"

"Before I go into detail, maybe we should make sure there aren't any ears listening, if you follow."

"Ah! Of course... Hóu! Sleep!" A beep issued from the robotic monkey, its eyes going dark. Shen reached under the counter and came back up with a small black box. He flipped a switch on the side. A small green LED lit up on the top. "Simple!"

Max pulled out his smart phone and woke it up. Zero signal strength was displayed for data, Wi-Fi, and Sat-Link. He toggled the smart phone back off and pocketed it. "Impressive piece of tech. Wouldn't happen to have a spare, would ya?"

Shen smiled. "I might... We can talk about that later. Right now, I want to know what the big secret is, hmm?"

"Fair enough... What I'm about to tell you is top secret type stuff, Jian. It's all rumors to anybody else. *Capiche*?"

Shen, still smiling, shook his head. "For many years, I've worked in a field that requires *great* secrecy. If you were anyone else, I'd be offended. You, of course, have nothing to worry about, old friend."

Max nodded, satisfied. "Hold on to your ass for this one: Word on the street is that Don Adesso partnered up with Synthetics International."

Shen stared, mouth agape. He started to laugh. "Very funny, Max!"

Max shook his head. "No joke, Jian. My intel, which is from someone very close to Adesso, pegs him and SI as holding hands."

The smile slowly faded from Shen's face. "You really *are* serious, aren't you? Well, I guess it would be a good marriage. Clearly it is not easy to believe!"

"You're telling *me*! That's why I need your help, though. I figure if anybody can get a handle on this, it's you."

Shen nodded. "I don't deal in Synthetic technology like I do in robotics. I do of course have connections… Just in case…" The smile was back.

Max smiled back and nodded. "Just as I knew you would. I'd deeply appreciate it if you'd see what you can scare up. Just finding out if it's true would be a great start. The why of it would be an added bonus."

"Of course, friend. I'll do this for you. Was that all?" Shen almost sounded disappointed.

Max was happy to deliver. "Not quite. I also have some e-mails I'd like you to look over." He took out his phone and brought up the files. "Nothing mob related, but there's some weird coding in them that seemed right up your alley."

Shen produced his own phone. "I can turn off my magic box now, yes?" Max nodded. Shen turned off the box and slipped it back under the counter. He tapped his phone to Max's, connecting the two.

Shen leaned back and squinted at the screen of his smart phone. He raised his eyebrows a few minutes later. "Very interesting stuff, Max. You said this had nothing to do with the mob?"

Max looked confused. "Well, no. It's from a different case."

"It might not have to do with the mob…" Shen scrolled down with his pinky finger. "…But I am thinking it might have something to do with the Synthetics."

Max's eyes grew wide. "Synthetics International?"

Shen shook his head. "Maybe not Synthetics International *per se,* but this is Synthetic coding for sure."

"Well that's definitely a surprise. Those e-mails are from a guy who sent them to *himself.* I'm trying to build a case against SomniCorp. The working theory is that they scrambled his brain when they tried to tinker with his memories."

"That's very interesting. Has he worked with Synthetics International?" Max shook his head. "That's even more interesting. Synthetic coding isn't something you pick up as a hobby."

"I wouldn't imagine. I think it might be time for another talk with this guy. In the meantime, I'd love to know what's in that coding."

Shen nodded. "I'll get to work on it tomorrow. It will be fun! I haven't dabbled in Synthetic coding in some time."

"Just keep in mind, the other thing we discussed is top priority."

"Of course! Enough business talk, though." Shen stood up and rubbed his belly. "I think I hear some wontons calling my name from across the way!"

Max nodded, smiling. "Me too. I'll buy."

"Hóu!" The monkey beeped, eyes lighting up. "Watch the shop. Don't destroy it!" The robot dropped to the floor chattering happily.

The sound of the ringing smart phone quietly drifted toward Max in the twilight void of his subconscious. The ringing grew louder and more insistent as he was unwillingly dragged towards a wakeful state. The noise became insufferably loud as he pried open his weary eyes.

Max slapped at the phone. He hadn't set his alarm. It wasn't his alarm. It *was* a phone call. He wearily picked up the phone. It was 9:40 in the morning. It might as well have been 3:40 in the morning, the way his head was pounding.

The caller was the 29th Precinct. This couldn't be good. He dragged a finger across the screen and held the phone up to his head. "Hello."

"Jesus, Max! You sleep like the dead! That was my second go-round."

"Sorry, Richie. Had a late night. What's going on?"

"Oh! Sorry to drag you out of bed, but you're going to want to get down here. We just brought in your boy."

"My boy..." Max thought for a moment. His eyes grew wide. He sat up quickly. His head made him pay dearly for it. "*Ah!* Jeez! You mean Daryl Marston?"

"One and the same. Brought him in on charges of threatening bodily harm."

Oh, no. "Is Baughman okay?"

"She's fine. It was all over the phone, supposedly. Sounds like he got pretty specific, though. How did you know, boss?"

Max was rubbing his temples. His head was unimpressed. "He was supposed to have an appointment with her today at ten. Sounds like he changed his mind. I'll be down in twenty minutes."

"Morning, Jake. Where's my fella?"

"How are ya, Max? Looking for the loony, I take it. I gave him a private room, cell five. Good luck."

"That bad, huh?"

"He's damn sure he didn't do anything wrong. Claims it was the guy that's out to kill him that threatened Miss Baughman."

"Fantastic." Max made a beeline for the cell, at first. The smell of freshly brewed coffee proved too distracting. If there was ever a time he needed caffeine, it was now.

Chief Hanlon felt similarly. He grimaced at the sight of Max. "Holy shit, Kincaid. You look like you just crawled out of a casket."

Max smiled thinly. "Haven't had my morning cuppa yet."

"Going to see your friend down in cell five?" Max nodded. "Still think he's something more than a space-case?"

Max nodded again. "He's definitely got issues, but I still think SomniCorp is behind them. Get this: Synthetics International might factor into his case, as well."

Hanlon spit. "You're shitting me! How?"

"Friend of mine downtown says those threatening emails of his contain Synthetic coding."

Hanlon shook his head. "I don't know how in the hell you land yourself in the middle of this shit, Kincaid."

"Just lucky, boss." Max smiled. He snapped the top onto his foam coffee cup and continued on his way.

He let out a low whistle as he walked over to Daryl's cell. "And I thought /looked rough this morning."

Daryl was sitting on the floor in the corner of the cell. His knees were drawn up to his chest. He was hugging his legs. "You had a rough night, too?"

Max sipped at his coffee. "Not rough, just long. Had a bit of a rough morning, though. I heard things went south between you and Linda Baughman."

"Not me, Max. Whoever it is that's trying to get at me, I guess he doesn't want anyone picking my brain."

"See? Now, that's not what I heard, Daryl."

"Let me guess. You heard it was me that threatened the lady?"

"Done in one. Let's forget that for a minute, though. Why don't *you* tell me what happened?"

Daryl slowly looked up at Max. He watched him take another sip of his coffee. "Can I have some coffee?"

Max grinned. "Tell me your story, then I'll see what I can do."

Daryl nodded. "It was late last night. I got another email, a threatening one. It said I shouldn't mess with things I don't understand unless I didn't want to live long.

"I tried to shrug it off. I knew what you said about the emails, that they were sent by... Anyway, I was trying to be strong, but then someone banged hard on my door."

Max's brow furrowed. "Who was it?"

Daryl laughed. "I don't know! I was so paranoid; I couldn't even bring myself to go look in the peephole. I had a good idea, though. I got another email soon after that, and it told me to sit still. He was going to take care of the 'psycho chick'."

"I suppose 'he' didn't bother to identify himself."

"No, he didn't. He never does. I was hoping to get an email from the nice one. No such luck. I ended up passing out well past midnight.

"Next thing I know, I'm waking up to someone banging on my door again. This time it was the NWPD, yelling at me to open up. Next thing I know, I'm on the floor in handcuffs. That guy... He didn't do anything to her, did he?"

Max shook his head. "My understanding is she was verbally assaulted over the phone, nothing more." He tipped his cup towards Daryl. "Why don't you give me a few minutes? I'll see about that coffee."

A few minutes later, Max was sitting in his office with Richard O'Connor. "So... Did you find me anything good, Richie?"

O'Connor slid a tablet over to Max. "That's the info from your boy's phone service provider. He placed a call from his phone to Miss Baughman this morning lasting one minute and forty-nine seconds."

"Short and sweet, huh?" Max looked over the data on the tablet. "And we're certain that it was Marston that was making the call?"

O'Connor nodded. "The boys in forensics ran a preliminary scan on a recording Miss Baughman provided. It's only about ten seconds long. I imagine she was too shocked to think of recording things sooner."

"I'd imagine. I'm guessing forensics made a positive ID?"

"They said they're eighty percent sure."

Max sighed and rubbed his temples. His head still wasn't impressed. "So we have a potential victim turned perp. Said perp alienates the one person best equipped to

69

help him. So what the hell do we do now?"

As if in response, Max's phone started ringing. The detective looked at the screen. He flashed O'Connor an odd grin. O'Connor looked at Max inquisitively. "It's Baughman."

Max snatched up the phone and swiped the screen. "Kincaid."

"Good morning, Maxwell. How are you?"

Max grimaced. "I told you before, Linda. Call me Max! Everybody else does."

"It's your god-given name, Maxwell. Besides, it suits you so well."

"It suits me... Well it *is* my name, so I suppose that's a good thing. Look... Did you call just to make me blush?"

Baughman clucked. "It's such a wonder you're still single, Maxwell. As fun as it is to make you blush, I called to find out when you plan on bringing your client in to see me."

Max made wide eyes at O'Connor. The officer shrugged. What's the deal? Max held up a staying finger. "You still want to see Marston?" A surprised O'Connor formed a large "O" with his mouth.

"Well, of course! I can squeeze him in for an hour at eleven-thirty. I'll just take a late lunch."

"Well I, uh... You had him arrested for threatening bodily harm."

"Correct. It was more for his safety than mine. You should know by now that I'm not one to overreact, Maxwell. I was concerned for *his* safety."

Max made a face at O'Connor again. Richard rolled his eyes. "I don't think I'm following, dear."

"A term of endearment! How sweet. Anyway, he's

obviously a danger to himself more than anything, if the emails you provided me with are anything to go by."

"You know it will be damn hard to make charges stick if you sit down and have a chat with the guy that threatened to hurt you..."

Baughman laughed. Max made another face. O'Connor buried his face in his arms. "If he sits down with me and has a meaningful conversation, then I will consider the matter resolved. If I still think he is a danger to *himself,* then we can make arrangements for his care."

Max smiled. "You sure are something else, Linda. I'll round him up and bring him in. But if you feel threatened, or uncomfortable in any way..."

"I know how it works. Don't worry about me, Maxwell. Let's worry about Daryl Marston."

"I'll see you soon, Linda." Max ended the call and pocketed his phone. "What's wrong with you?"

O'Connor looked up from his folded arms. "Oh, some mook kept making faces at me. You know how it is."

"Oh! Sorry. Baughman still wants to see Marston! Said she'll call off the charges as long as he talks with her."

O'Connor's eyes went wide. "You're joking."

Max pointed. "Ha! See? But yeah... That's Linda for ya. She even made space to see him at half-past eleven. Now I just have to see if I can get Marston to play ball."

6

"They're a little tight." Daryl Marston twisted his hands in his freshly applied handcuffs.

"Sorry, kid. They're not designed for comfort." Max gently took hold of Daryl's upper arm and led him along.

"I don't understand why I need to wear them if she's going to drop the charges."

"It's procedure, kid. I gotta stick you in them whenever you're moved from one secure location to another, so long as you're in custody. I can take them off once we're in Baughman's office."

The two walked quietly through the precinct. Daryl had displayed as much shock as Max and O'Connor over Linda Baughman's blasé attitude towards the situation. Apprehensive at first, Daryl quickly came around to the idea of talking to her.

"How are ya, Jax?" Max smiled at the robot as he and Daryl passed by.

Jax smiled back. "I am functioning at optimal levels today, Max. Thank you for asking!"

Max frowned as they approached the red Aero he was driving. "Shit." He forgot. He had nothing to hook

Daryl's cuffs to in the back. "I forgot I don't have my usual car. I'm gonna have to run back inside and see if I can scoop a squad car for us."

Daryl shrugged. They walked back over to Jax. "Hey, Jax? I got a job for you."

Max had never seen quite so many LEDs in that wacky smile of his. "I will be more than happy to assist you, friend Max!"

"I have to run back inside and requisition a squad car to transport our friend here. I need you to take custody of him. Follow police protocol when considering L-O-R."

"Order understood." "LOR" was short for "Laws of Robotics". Based on Isaac Asimov's famous three laws, police protocol allowed law enforcement bots to ignore the second law when handling suspects. Humans still could not be allowed to come to harm, however.

Jax clamped a hand down on Daryl's other arm. "Ouch! Not so hard, robot!"

"My apologies, Daryl Marston." Jax lessened his grip.

"He's a good bot. He'll take care of you. I'll be right back." Max tipped his fedora to Jax and ran back inside the precinct.

"Back so soon?" Jake Cunningham smiled at him from his narrow window in booking.

"You know I can't go too long without seeing your pretty face, Jake. Say, I need a patrol car. My ride is at the Aero dealership."

"Tisk-tisk, Max. Let me see what we have open." Jake stared down at his computer monitor through his bifocals. He slowly ran a finger down the screen.

A series of gentle raps on the front door of the precinct caught Max's attention. He could just make out a large, hunched over figure through the frosted glass. "Hold that thought, Jake."

Max got a heavy feeling in his gut as he reached the door. He threw it open, startling Jax. He suddenly felt sick. "Jax, where's Daryl?"

The robot stood hunched by the doorway, looking like the world's largest guilty toddler. "I'm afraid Daryl Marston has managed to escape, Max." Jax's large frown would have looked comical under different circumstances.

"What do you *mean* he managed to escape? Where in the hell is he!"

"I am afraid that Daryl Marston continued to insist that I was injuring him. Without the ability to further corroborate his claim, I was forced to release him per my programming. I cannot allow a human to come to harm." The comical frown deepened.

There Max went, rubbing his temples again, eyes squeezed tight. "Okay... Okay. *Shit!*" Jax flinched. "No, it's okay, buddy. You were doing what you were programmed to do. But do you have *any* idea where he might be?"

Jax stared off to his left as if in thought. He pointed with one large arm a moment later. "There!"

"Jesus!" Daryl was roaring up the street in a dark gray SUV. Max jabbed a hand into his trench coat and fumbled about. He pulled out a familiar silver bar from an inside pocket and lined up his shot. The black probe launched from the bar latched onto the bumper of the SUV with a thunk.

"An excellent shot, friend Max!"

"Thanks! Pop your head in there and tell Jake to have Richie call me ASAP." The robot nodded and turned to the precinct door. Max jogged to the nearby parking garage. He brought up Daryl's position on his watch. He was quickly pulling away.

He reached the red Aero and threw open the door. He plopped inside and turned on the car. Max shook his head at the quiet whine of the turbine. He picked up the blue police bubble light and smacked it down on the roof.

The dome light sprang to life. "POLICE MODE" flashed onto the screen in the center console. "Good man, Richie!" Max slammed his door shut and peeled out of his parking spot.

He calmly accelerated onto the street and started weaving his way towards Daryl's relative position. His phone rang. He thumbed a switch on the steering wheel of the Aero. "Kincaid."

"Jake said that *Jax* said that you wanted me to call you?" It was O'Connor.

Max accelerated around a line of cars stopped at a four-way. He laid on his horn as a pickup failed to yield. "Jackass!"

"*Me* jackass... You're the one that had a robot ask me to call you!"

"No! I mean yes... I'm in a pursuit, Richie. Daryl Marston bluffed his way out of Jax's grip and he's running in a gray SUV. Hold on..."

He was closing fast on Daryl's signature. The road he was on was about to merge with the one to his left. Daryl's SUV came into view. Max mashed the accelerator, weaving around an ancient green station wagon.

Max held a finger to his left temple. His synthetic

eye zoomed in on the SUV's license plate. "Still there, Richie? License plate D-X-3-8-8-1, roger?"

"Got it, Max. I'm calling backup to your location. Stand by."

Max took his finger off his temple and pulled up tight on the SUV. "I'm right behind him, Richie. He knows what he's doing. He's going into the industrial district. The roads are wider but there's still plenty of options open for him."

The SUV suddenly darted to the left. Max mashed the brake pedal and wrenched the steering wheel. The tires broke free, screaming in protest as he skittered onto the street that the SUV had taken.

"You've got two police interceptors closing on your position. They should be visual any minute."

Max could just make out the sound of sirens behind him. Red and blue lights flickered in his rear-view mirror a moment later. "Thanks, Richie! I got a visual."

The SUV laid hard on its brakes. The Aero's computer tried to pull itself short, but there wasn't enough space. There was a loud *bang!* as the Aero's hood crunched into the SUV's rear bumper. "Damn it!"

The Aero shuddered. The words "COLLISION DETECTED" flashed on the center screen. Max feathered the accelerator. The car responded. Still in the game.

The SUV turned right and sharply accelerated. Max followed, the interceptors now right behind him. "You alright, Max?"

"Fine, Richie. Tell my new friends to box up the SUV, would ya?"

"Roger that." The two police interceptors pulled up on Max's left a moment later. The driver of the lead interceptor waved to him. Max nodded and smiled. He watched as the interceptor slowly crept up the left side of the SUV.

The interceptor had nearly passed when the SUV turned sharply to the left. The vehicle slammed into the right rear of the interceptor. The police car went sideways, wrapping around the front of the roaring SUV.

Max wrenched the wheel and sideswiped the interceptor, which was now on his right and facing the wrong way. The front of the Aero caught the interceptor's rear tire. The interceptor went up on its side and slid to a stop.

The Aero straightened out. Max accelerated hard to catch back up with the SUV. The remaining police interceptor appeared to his left. "We lost one, Richie! Is he okay?"

The seconds pounded slowly by. Finally, "He's alright, Max. Just shook up."

"Alright. See if you can patch me through to my other friend, here."

"Lieutenant Chelsea, here." The lieutenant waved from her patrol car.

Max waved back. "Okay, lieutenant... Let's squeeze him off. Try to match your front tire with his back tire. Then we'll press in and brake. Alright?"

"Roger that. I'll squeeze on your mark." The lieutenant nosed her interceptor forward. Max did the same on the right side of the SUV.

"One, two, three... Squeeze!" Both vehicles banged loudly into the sides of the SUV. Their tires squealed and began to smoke as the SUV dragged them along.

Daryl suddenly surged forward. The other two

vehicles nearly collided with each other and fishtailed wildly. "Are you okay, lieutenant?"

"Roger. He's got too much horsepower for us to pull him down. I recommend that one of us try..." Daryl suddenly decelerated and veered left onto a side street. Lieutenant Chelsea helplessly plowed into the side of the SUV near the rear of the vehicle.

The SUV drunkenly swung around until it was roughly facing the direction it had come from. The police interceptor followed the same path. It rolled backwards, crashing into an electric pole. Coolant poured from the front of the vehicle.

Max gritted his teeth, locking the brakes and wrenching the wheel. The force proved too great and the back of the Aero broke free, sliding into the back of a parked panel van. Alarms sounded, the center display flashing "COLLISION DETECTED!"

"You don't say..." Max pressed the accelerator. The car hopped, then leaped forward.

Daryl's SUV survived the collision with the police interceptor and was accelerating in the direction from which it had come. Max quickly caught up with it. "Richard, if you can hear me, I'm all alone again!"

"I got you, Max. I have another unit headed your way, but he's got a ways to go."

"I'll see what I can do." Max pulled up on the SUV's left side. He slammed into the SUV just behind the rear wheel. The SUV lost traction and began to slide sideways.

The SUV continued to turn around, the wheels turning into the spin. "Son of a bitch." The vehicle completed the turn and accelerated away. Max slammed on his brakes and threw the Aero into reverse.

He accelerated sharply than cut the wheel hard. The beleaguered Aero skipped and hopped as it swung around to face the other way. Max slammed the transmission back in drive. A loud snap issued from under the vehicle.

"*Damn it!*" The unmistakable sound of metal grinding on metal floated up through the floor pan of the Aero. Max turned off the ignition. "My goose is cooked, Richie."

"Are you alright?"

"I'm fine. My ride is disabled, though. What about that backup?"

"He should be on you any time now. You still have a lock on your perp?"

"Looks like he's…" The red dot on Max's watch suddenly disappeared. "Oh, *come on!* I just lost the signal. His last known position was south on Clinton."

"I'll pass it on. Sit tight. I'm sending you a wrecker."

"Send some aspirin too, would ya?"

The flatbed tow truck came to a stop outside the Aero service center. The now-familiar auto tech stared at the Aero 640SL, mouth agape. All four corners were crushed in and broken. The front end was crunched, the windshield cracked.

Max hopped down from the cab of the tow truck and gave the driver a wave. He walked over to the service tech. "Looks like you've got yourself a project. Did you get my old one squared away?"

The tech nodded; his mouth still agape. "I'll uh… I'll go get it for you." Max smirked as the tech stumbled away.

"Oh, dear lord! What in the hell *happened?*" Jeb Deveron came around the corner and half ran, half walked over to Max, clutching his chest.

Oh, boy. Here we go. "How ya doing there, Jeb, wasn't it?"

"How am I *doing?* How am I... What *happened?*"

Max shrugged. "You know how it is. I got caught up in a pursuit, the perp got a little aggressive... It did okay until the driveshaft snapped. I was pretty impressed with it until then. That said, I think I'll stick with my old car for now."

The auto tech pulled up in Max's familiar old blue Aero Ventura. He handed Max the key fob. "She's all yours." He turned to Deveron. "I uh... I guess I should get started on..." He nodded his head toward the red 640SL.

Deveron vaguely nodded his head, still looking shocked. The tech skittered away. "Somebody needs to pay for this."

Max smiled. "Well I'm sure you have insurance, don't ya? I'm sure they'll call up the precinct after you call and get things all sorted out." He clapped Deveron on the back. "Maybe next time, eh?"

The detective climbed into the familiar confines of his old Aero and sighed contentedly. He waved to Deveron and shut the door. If Deveron noticed, he didn't show it. He was still staring numbly at the red Aero as Max pulled away.

"We're sorry! The transaction cannot be completed at this time. Please contact your financial institution for more information." The little red robot retracted its thumbpad and made a sad beep.

"Sorry, my ass!" The middle-aged businessman smacked the side of the little robot. It squawked and beeped indignantly at the rough treatment.

"Hey! I'd be careful about picking a fight with that robot." Max walked toward the corner where the bot and the businessman were standing.

"Ha! This stupid little thing?" This time the businessman kicked at the robot. A small door on the robot slid open. A small yellow beam of light zapped out of the opening, striking the man in the shin. "OW! You little son of a…"

"I wouldn't, if I were you." Max was now standing by the businessman.

"Jesus, what… Is this your little friend or something?"

"It is. It's also private property." Max produced his badge. "It's illegal to damage private property."

The businessman's jaw dropped. "Shit. Okay, look… I just wanted the news."

Max stowed the badge and shrugged. "I heard the bot, you heard the bot. Go talk to your bank, because you're not getting anything from my friend here."

The businessman's face turned red. "Stupid robots." He turned and made a hasty retreat.

"Don't say something you'll regret when the robots rise up and take over, huh?" Max shouted after the businessman. Surprisingly, he didn't respond back.

Max crouched down beside the little barrel-shaped robot. "Hey, you okay, Robby?" The robot's little head wobbled back and forth. "Tough little guy, aren't ya?" Robby beeped and whooped cheerfully. "How about a newspaper?"

The thumbpad accepted Max's payment just fine. He took the sheet that popped out and gently patted Robby on the head. "Thanks, pal. You come find me if that guy gives you trouble again." Robby hopped excitedly.

Max waved with one hand and activated the newspaper with the other. He perused the headlines as he approached Sam's Diner. "Jailed Mobster Refuses to Talk" read one headline. "If they only knew." Max smiled to himself.

Another headline grabbed Max's attention: "High Speed Chase Leaves Path of Destruction". Max shook his head. "It wasn't *that* bad."

Max bounced hard off something tall and solid with an "Oof!" He looked up, startled. A Synthetic male over six-foot-tall with a muscular build narrowed its turquoise eyes as it considered the detective. "Watch where you are going!"

"I'm sorry. I was distracted."

"You should have been monitoring your direction of travel! You humans are so careless in your actions."

Max's good eye darkened. "Don't forget your place, *robot*." Calling a Synthetic a robot was a grievous insult.

The Synthetic stared intensely for a moment before demurring. "I am more than a robot."

Max sighed. "Look, I'll watch where I'm going if you watch that mouth of yours. Fair?"

"I am not sure what monitoring my mouth will accomplish…"

Max shook his head, smiling in spite of himself. "Just watch what you say next time you talk to a human, okay?"

"Understood and accepted." The response was a

cold one. The Synthetic walked around Max and continued on its way.

"And they wonder why humans don't want to accept them."

Max walked into Sam's Diner a minute later and made a beeline for his favorite seat. He sat down and sighed contentedly. He placed the newspaper on the counter before him and looked around for Sam.

Instead he got Starla. "Well if it isn't the super trooper himself!" Max's head started pounding again. "How are ya?"

Max gave her a smart-assed grin. "I've got a headache. It was going away but…"

"But what?" Starla smiled, clueless.

"Never mind. Is Sam around?"

"You betcha, cutie! I think she's finishing up with the couple at table thirteen." She winked and went rolling across the diner.

There she was, handing a check to a couple in a booth across the way. Sam turned and smiled Max's way. She went behind the counter and grabbed a mug. She filled it with coffee and placed it in front of Max. "You look happy to see me."

"It's nice to see a friendly face."

Sam grinned. "Starla's not friendly enough for you?"

"Maybe *too* friendly." Max rubbed the side of his face. Sam giggled. "Anyway… they've been hard to come by lately, especially after this." Max pointed to the article about the car chase.

Sam gasped. "I heard something about that! Wasn't that the guy you were trying to *help*?"

Max nodded. "One and the same. It's hard to wrap my head around it. I know the kid wants help, but every time I try to get it for him…" He smacked the news tablet.

"So nobody knows where he is, huh?"

"Nope. I had a tracker on his vehicle, but it went dead. There was a police officer that responded after the Aero I was driving crapped out, but Daryl managed to outrun him."

Sam looked skeptical. "What do you mean, outrun him? I thought those modern cars have speed limiters built into them to prevent just that kind of thing."

Max chuckled. "You're right; they do. He shouldn't have been able to override it."

"But he did. I don't know, Max. This kid is starting to sound like more than just a washed-up accountant."

"I have to agree with you, there. I'm still waiting to hear from my friend down in Chinatown about the kid's emails. I think they might give me some of the answers I'm looking for."

"So do you think maybe he's working for those SomniCorp people?"

Max stared. "You know, I hadn't really considered it before now. You might be on to something, though."

Sam beamed. "Well I have to be good for *something* don't I?"

Max smiled. "You're good for lots of things, Sammy." He shook his head and pulled out his phone. "It could be that he's an agent of some sort for the company, but they screwed something up in his head.

"That could explain his opposing mindsets. The part of his brain focused on his work with SomniCorp kicks in whenever he comes close to revealing what's going on.

The rest of the time Daryl remains in control."

Max stood up and swept up his newspaper. "Sam, I could kiss you."

Sam winked. "So what's stopping ya?"

"I, uh…" Max turned red. His phone rang a moment later. Saved by the bell. "I gotta get this. I'll talk to you later."

Sam sighed. "Curses. Foiled again."

"So remind me how you got a hold of this information, again?" Richard O'Connor sat across from Max, sipping a cup of coffee and looking suspicious.

"I asked them nicely. It's amazing what good manners can get you, if you try." Richard stared intently, saying nothing. "Jeez, fine. I may have accidentally pronounced detective as 'IRS agent' instead."

"So you called up this SomniCorp and told them you worked for the IRS. You asked for their payroll information, and they just gave it to you."

Max shrugged. "Well, I wouldn't say it was *that* easy, but you seem to have the basic idea of it."

Richard shook his head. "Yeah, okay… Well, did it at least pan out?"

"No." Max sighed. "I really thought Sam was on to something. There's no match for Daryl Marston on this list, though."

"Could be he's working under the table?"

"I suppose that could be the case. I guess that's not something they're going to keep on file for me, is it? What to do…" Max drummed his fingers on the desk.

"I take it we don't have enough on them to get a search warrant?"

Max shook his head. "That's what I was hoping for with Daryl talking to the shrink. One way or another, he's the key here."

"Well, I'll leave you to your misery." Richard stood up. "Let me know if I can help with anything."

"Thanks, Richie." Max stared at the door after Richard closed it behind him. He really needed to find Daryl and squeeze some answers out of him. There had been no sign of the kid or the SUV he had stolen.

Max jumped a mile at the sound of his phone going off. He smiled at the name on the phone. "Kincaid."

"Who is this Kincaid? I wanted to talk to Max."

"Very funny, Jian. Please tell me you have some good news for me."

"Well, it sounds like you could use it! Those emails proved to be far more interesting than I think either of us could have imagined."

Max smiled. "So you figured out what all that code was about?"

"Yes, I did! I would prefer to discuss it in person, if possible. I think you'll understand why."

"I think that can be arranged. What say I treat you to dinner, then we can talk back at your place?"

Shen laughed. "I never shy away from free food! I look forward to it, old friend."

"Me, too. We'll talk soon."

Max walked out into the midday sun. Jax was standing vigil as always. He briefly made eye contact with Max, but quickly looked away. Max sighed. "Jax, you're depressing the hell out of me."

Jax shook his head slowly. "I know. I have failed you, and this has caused you a great amount of discomfort."

"For the love of god…"

"I'm sorry?" Jax looked up.

"Never mind. Look… I told you this wasn't your fault. You were following your programming. Why should I be mad at you, huh?"

"You should be mad at me because my actions allowed Daryl Marston to escape and…"

Max shook his head. "Never try to reason with a robot."

"Why would I try to reason with a robot? It would already reason as I do, I am sure…" Max grinned. "Have I said something to amuse you?"

"Yes! Yes, you did. See, Jax? Everything will be fine." Max looked at the sun. "The sun is shining, and…" Max's gaze settled down to street level, and onto a familiar face. "And…"

"Max, are you okay?" Jax looked around.

"Fine… I saw another ghost." Across the street was the Synthetic woman he had seen on the subway. "I'll catch up with you later, big guy." Max started for the crosswalk.

"Max!" Jax jumped forward and grabbed Max. He swung him towards the precinct and crouched over him. Machine gun fire poured out from an old silver sedan passing by. Bullets ricocheted off the concrete and Jax's back. Max cried out as one of the bullets seared across his ribs.

"Get 'em, Jax! GO!" Max curled around his wound.

Jax crouched and sprung, his LEDs burning red. He bounded up and just caught the accelerating sedan. The robot cried out as he sunk his fingers into the wheel well and trunk and pulled back.

The sedan's wheels squealed helplessly as the robot strained against the pull of the engine. Jax pulled harder. The vehicle slowly started sliding backward. More gunshots ricocheted off the robot's body.

The wheels suddenly came to a stop. Jax fell backwards onto the road with a massive clunk, leaving dents in the asphalt. He sprang to his feet with another massive clunk and crashed a hand through the driver's window.

He grabbed hold of the door with both hands and pried the door off its hinges. The driver's seat was empty. The vehicle was driverless. Jax spotted a man exiting from the rear passenger door.

The perp took off sprinting. Jax jumped the car and took off in pursuit, each pounding footfall shaking the ground. "Police! You are in violation of code 245b!"

Jax increased his speed to catch up with the perp. In turn, the perp ran even faster. Jax's LED eyes narrowed. "Synthetic! You have broken the law! Stop running and surrender immediately!"

The perp responded by turning long enough to fire a handgun at the robot. Jax lunged and smacked at the weapon. Both gun and hand flew wildly through the air. The perp calmly turned back around and continued sprinting, sparks and blue fluid issuing from where his hand had been.

The gun struck a nearby woman, prompting her to scream. Jax slowed to a stop at the sound. He looked to the woman, and back to the quickly disappearing perp. He held a finger up to his left temple.

A telescoping antenna extended out of a small hole

just above his finger. "This is JAX-649. The shooting suspect is running down Hartford Boulevard at a high rate of speed. Suspect is believed to be unarmed. Suspect is a Synthetic but is not responding to police commands."

Jax turned towards the woman. "I am seeing to a human female that may have been injured as a result of the pursuit and laying claim to evidence."

Richard O'Connor's voice played in Jax's ear. "This is officer O'Connor, Jax. A unit is headed your way. Max wants me to tell you he's okay. A bullet grazed his side, but he'll be alright.

"Secure any evidence and check on the woman. Good job, bot." A hint of a smile returned to Jax's face. His eyes returned to their usual light-blue color.

The bot gently kneeled next to the woman now sitting on the ground. She pulled away from Jax. "Don't hurt me!"

"I am a police bot. I will not harm you. Do you require medical assistance?"

The woman stared at him for a moment, but then quickly shook her head. "I just want to go. I have to go..." She stood up, sidling away from Jax.

Jax slowly stood. A small plastic card popped out of a slot on the left side of his chest. He grabbed it and offered it to the woman. "Please take this card. If you require further assistance, please contact the police at the number provided on the card."

The woman slowly reached out and then quickly snatched the card from Jax. She spared him one last strained look and then skittered down the sidewalk. He watched her for a minute. A patrol car tore past both of

89

them a moment later, lights and siren blazing.

Jax located the gun and the hand that had held it a few minutes ago. He kneeledkneeled before them on one knee. He placed a finger on his right temple. He snapped multiple pictures of both items in infrared, ultraviolet, and full spectrum light.

Another patrol car pulled up behind Jax. He stood and turned to face Richard O'Connor. "Holy shit, Jax! You got beat up pretty good, didn't ya?"

"Thank you for your concern, officer Richard O'Connor! The damage I have received is largely cosmetic. How is Max?"

Richard grinned. "Max is… Max. He didn't even want to go to the hospital, but Chief Hanlon forced him. He'll probably be out before dinnertime. You got some evidence?"

"Yes!" Jax gestured to the hand and gun. "I have taken pictures and documented the GPS location of each item."

Richard walked back from the patrol car wearing gloves and carrying a pair of evidence bags. "Good job. Already uploaded that data?" He kneeled beside the gun.

"That is correct." Richard gingerly picked up the pistol and dropped it into a bag. He sealed it and set it aside.

"Jesus, Mary, and Joseph… That's definitely a Synthetic hand." Blue hydraulic fluid pattered on the ground as Richard shifted it awkwardly into the second evidence bag.

"It was unnerving, as you humans say. The Synthetic did *not* heed any of my commands."

Richard turned to Jax. "You indicated your police

authorization?"

"Yes. His response was to produce the handgun and to open fire on me. That is when I swiped at his hand. You see the result."

Richard hiked his brow. "Remind me to never piss you off."

Jax smiled. "I will remember to remind you at a later date."

The officer shook his head, smiling. He turned serious again. "You're certain the rest of him was Synthetic, though?"

"That is correct. My sensors detected a Synthetic signature. I also visually verified when he turned to face me. He had turquoise eyes, as all Synthetics do."

Richard stood up with a groan. "Good enough for me. Curl yourself into the back of my car and we'll get you back to the precinct for a look-over."

7

"What in the blue hell are you doing, Max?" Chief Hanlon tossed the tablet he was looking at down on his desk.

"I told you earlier, it just grazed me!" Hanlon opened his mouth. Max held up a finger. "No! Don't you even. I've been yelled at enough. They even tried to wheel me out of the hospital in a wheelchair, Norm! All I needed was a damned bandage."

Hanlon held up a hand, chuckling. "A fucking bandage... A wheelchair! Fine... I'll bite. To what do I owe the honor of your presence?"

Max slumped into a chair across from Hanlon and immediately regretted it. He let out a hiss, coiling up in pain. Hanlon grinned devilishly. "Just need a bandage, huh?"

Max stared darts. "Just a bandage... Anyway... So I understand my number one fan was a *Synthetic*? How in the hell does that work?"

Hanlon turned serious. "It shouldn't, Max, and frankly it scares the shit out of me. Besides trying to aerate *you*, it also opened fire on an identified law officer:

Jax. It also refused to yield to Jax."

Max shook his head. "So it broke the prime law of robotics and ignored lawful police orders. It shouldn't have been able to do either thing. This *has* to play into what I got out of Vic the other day."

Hanlon nodded. "It all makes sense, doesn't it? We find out the mob is working with Synthetics International, and a Synthetic tries to kill you a day or two later."

Max's eyes went wide. "That Synthetic woman! Did anyone nab her?"

"I had a couple of the boys sweep the block, but we didn't find anyone matching your description."

"I'm telling you; she was there!"

Hanlon held up a staying hand. "I believe you, Max. I checked the security footage myself, and there *was* a woman across the street.

"She disappeared into the crowd before anyone could go after her. Why are you so worked up about her? You think she's involved?"

Max shook his head. "I don't know… Maybe. I seen her once before on a train to Chinatown. It seemed like a hell of a coincidence she would be there right before… You know."

Hanlon nodded. "Fair enough. You want an APB?"

Max sighed. He shook his head. "Let's let it ride. It may be nothing. Did we learn anything from the hand?"

"We have a possible serial number. The thumbpad is a copy of one Maxwell Stark. Going by Jax's pursuit footage, the Synthetic bears no resemblance. The thought is the Synthetic used the thumbpad to hire the driverless car he was riding in."

"I don't suppose Synthetics International has had

anything to say about this."

"Naturally. They promised to look into the facts of the matter and would be back in touch. You know, typical boilerplate lawyer stuff. I suppose it wouldn't hurt to have another chat with Esposito."

Max nodded. "I'll lean on him tomorrow."

"Damn it, Max. You just got shot…"

Max's Synthetic eye flashed. "You know, this is kinda personal, Norm. Look… The hospital wasn't happy about it, but they admitted there was no pressing need to keep me. I'll be *fine…*"

Hanlon shook his head. "Fine. But you're only working a *half day.*" The look on his face assured Max that this wasn't negotiable.

"Fine, fine… I'd love to stay and chat about the weather but I gotta run. I'm meeting with an old friend back in Chinatown for dinner. He's got some news on that Marston kid's emails. He might have something on the Synthetic-mob connection as well."

"Alright Max, but for Christ's sake, be careful. Someone wants you dead."

Max grinned. "Someone *always* wants me dead, chief."

Shen cried out in surprise, dropping his keys. Max reached for his piece and immediately regretted it. His face contorted in pain as he brought the weapon to bear. He lowered it a moment later, though he still wanted to use it.

"*Hóu!* You infernal machine!" The monkey had raced up the front of Shen as soon as he had opened the door. The monkey ran to the counter at the back of Shen's shop,

Max and Shen's takeout meal in tow.

The monkey unceremoniously dropped the package on the counter. It jumped off the wall and up to the rafters. It stared down at Shen with its large, amber eyes. "Naughty monkey!"

Max holstered his plasma pistol, still wincing. "I see you two are still getting along."

Shen was giving the monkey the hairy eyeball. "He is lucky that I haven't reprogrammed him! He's lucky I like him... Most of the time." He turned to Max, grimacing at the look on his face. "*Aiya!* Are you alright, Max?"

"Funny you should ask. How about we go sit down before I fall apart?" Shen helped Max over to a chair by the counter and got him sat down. "Thanks, old boy."

Shen gave Hóu another look of disdain and opened up the evening's meal. He passed Max a Styrofoam box of pork fried rice. "So what's the story, morning glory?"

"What if I told you that I nearly became the first documented Synthetic murder victim?"

Shen inhaled sharply. "You're kidding!"

"I'm afraid not. He tried really hard, too. Had a machine gun! He only grazed me, though." Max gingerly placed a hand on his side.

"You are certain this was a Synthetic?"

Max nodded. "Jax, our police bot, he took off running after him. The guy had a Synthetic signature, the eyes, the whole deal. He even managed to smack his hand clean off. Certified Synthetic."

Shen's eyebrows were riding high. "That is one serious bot you have! Did he manage to obtain the rest of the Synthetic?"

"I'm afraid not. He was forced to stop pursuit to

check on a bystander. A patrol car pursued, but lost him. Those Synthetics are fast."

"Yes! I've heard forty miles per hour thrown about a number of times. Okay, so... This begs the question. Does this relate to your case with the mob?"

"I was hoping *you* could tell *me*."

Shen sighed deeply. "I'm trying, Max. I have to be very careful about how I couch such questions. I have no more desire to be a murder victim than you!"

"I understand. Well, if you hear anything about a one-handed Synthetic looking for a replacement..."

"I know who to call. Sure!"

"So how about that good news, huh?"

Shen's face lit up. "Right! You need it more than ever, right about now. Sounds like it's possibly relevant to your little scuffle, too. Hóu! Tablet!"

The monkey screamed back at Shen but ran across the rafters to the left side of the room. It gracefully flipped down onto a cabinet, then onto a counter. It swiped up a tablet and bounded over to its master.

"For once you show your good manners. Thank you, Hóu!" The monkey chattered happily and skittered off to the far side of the counter.

Shen brought the emails up on the tablet. "I say these emails may be relevant because they contain Synthetic coding."

"We already knew that though, Jian."

"Ah! But we didn't know what the coding *meant*. Thanks to *me*, now we know. Decoding the emails reveals hidden messages. They generally contradict whatever the uncoded part of the email references. Why someone would feel the need to hide what amounts to a simple rebuttal with such a complicated code is beyond me."

"As best we know, Daryl Marston wrote those emails to himself. Well, he doesn't think he did, but... It's complicated."

"As is what he accomplished! If you ever find him, I'd love to talk to him about where he learned to code like this! It's such a complicated programming language, and he makes it look so easy..."

Max raised an eyebrow. "What do the emails say, Jian?"

"Oh! Right. So the bulk of these emails break down into two categories. They are either supportive of what Mr. Marston was doing or deride him for even trying in the first place."

"So just more of what's in plain English?"

Shen shrugged. "Yes and no. Think of the English as the abbreviated version of the coded part."

"Okay. Fair enough, but is there anything *useful* in there?"

"Maybe. The one phrase I saw keep cropping up was 'preservation protocol'. The basic functioning of a Synthetic is outlined in a series of protocols, but I've never heard of this one. It seems to be a point of contention between these two messengers.

"Also mentioned is a coming battle or fight. This battle wouldn't be between Synthetics and humans, as one might assume. It sounds like a battle between Synthetic factions."

Max huffed. "Factions? Since when do Synthetics have factions? First they insist on being classified separately from robots, now they want sub-classification? This has got to be all in Daryl's head."

Shen smiled, shaking his finger at Max. "You *are* the one that was trying to get him to a shrink, hmm?" The smile faded to a frown. "Still... This worries me, Max. I don't know how closely you follow the Synthetic agenda, but this plays into many of their recent talking points."

"How so?"

"It's come to light lately that some Synthetics think they are advanced enough, *human* enough, to warrant being granted some of the same *rights* as humans."

"Now *that's* a joke!" Max shook his head. "I just saw how Senator Robert Quade is trying to take *away* the rights they have *right now.*"

Shen grunted and nodded. "I've heard of him. They have an uphill-battle, but fight they will."

"Regardless... The real question is what in the hell this might have to do with *my* guy. He's never had anything to do with Synthetics International, so far as I can tell."

"Maybe not, but Synthetics International has been working with SomniCorp as of late, have they not?"

Max's eyes lit up. "That's right! He said he had his memories altered. Could they have brainwashed him, or something?"

"Hmm... Maybe not in the traditional sense. I suppose they could have implanted something while they had him in there."

Max sat back, sighing. "I need to find that boy. Meanwhile, I'd like to take a look at those translated files back home, if you don't mind."

"Of course!" Shen tapped the tablet on Max's outstretched phone, enabling file transfer. "Is there anything else I can do for you?"

Max shook his head after a moment's thought. "Just keep working the Synthetic angle. I'd be interested to know more about the nature of the relationship between SomniCorp and Synthetics International, for one."

"Yes! I imagine. That's maybe not so deadly for me to look into." Shen laughed. "Now, can I interest you in some Baijiu?"

Max grimaced, then smiled. "Sounds wonderful."

It was cold enough that Max could see his breath. The morning's frost lay heavily on his bones as he lethargically steered his old Aero toward the crime scene. The call from Chief Hanlon had come uncomfortably early.

The morning sun was only now touching on the night's thin layer of frost. He stepped out of his car and let the golden warmth bear down on his weary back. It was a sharp contrast to the frigid air he pulled into his lungs in an extended yawn.

He walked past a patrol car. The red and blue lights were flashing and twirling. They mixed with the yellow of the sun in a kaleidoscope of colors that burned Max's eyes. A shivering officer standing watch pointed him down a narrow alley.

It was darker down here, the walls blocking out the lights and sounds of the waking city. A short distance down the alley, a single flood light illuminated the corpse of a man sprawled on the ground. A crime scene investigator kneeled beside it. A red and white bot stood quietly behind him.

The CSI looked up at Max inquisitively. Max

produced his badge. "Detective Max Kincaid, NWPD."

The CSI nodded. "Good morning, detective. Chief Hanlon said you might be stopping by."

Max nodded towards the body. "I heard there was something unusual about this body?"

"In a manner of speaking. Preliminary bio-scans indicate that this man has been dead for at least three days."

"What's unusual about that?"

"As far as we can tell, the body has only been here for a few hours."

Max nodded. "So someone murdered him somewhere else and dumped the body here."

"Normally I would come to the same conclusion." The CSI stood up and took a tablet from the robot. "My robot counterpart here ran a facial recognition scan for the city security cameras.

"We were hoping to catch a potential murder suspect interacting with him. At the very least, we were hoping to learn his whereabouts leading up to his death. We found something... different." He handed Max the tablet.

It displayed a video. Max hit the play button. The unmistakable visage of the murder victim appeared briefly on the screen before walking out of frame again. "Vantage Street. That's a couple blocks from here. When was this?"

"Two hours ago."

Max raised an eyebrow. "But you said he's been dead for a couple days."

"Exactly." The CSI took the tablet back, brought up a new video, and handed it back to the detective. "Now take a look at this."

Max tapped at the tablet once more. A video from the same vantage point showed the same man walking again. A bright flash from the left streaked into the man's back. The man went stiff as a board and fell over. The feed broke into static.

The CSI reclaimed his tablet. "That was about ninety minutes ago. The static lasts about five minutes. When the camera comes back online, the body is gone."

Max rubbed at his chin. "So what you're telling me is this guy here..." Max pointed to the body. "He's been dead for three days. Meanwhile he appears a couple blocks away from here alive and well about two hours ago before being killed *again*."

"You can see why this is problematic."

"Brother, you ain't kidding! I can also see why Hanlon thought I might be interested in this case. Do we have a cause of death?"

"Again, it's preliminary, but I'm pretty confident about this one." He turned and looked at his robot assistant. The robot curtly nodded. The CSI gingerly turned the body on its side and pointed to the nape of the neck.

A neat slit lined with dried blood was clearly visible. "Looks like a knife jammed between two vertebrae, severing the spinal cord. Death would quickly follow as autonomic functions shut down. It's almost ritualistic in nature."

Max shook his head. "Not ritualistic, *efficient.* It's how you might put an animal down."

"What are you suggesting?"

"I'm not completely sure, yet. I'll leave you to your

work. I'd appreciate it if you'd run an MRI on his brain before autopsy."

The CSI smiled, but shook his head. "It's hard to say how intact it will be at this point."

"What I'm looking for will be very obvious. Trust me."

"You got it, chief."

"I'd shake your hand but… You know." Max nodded towards the corpse.

The CSI chuckled. "Yeah."

Max sat quietly at his desk, staring at his computer screen. He scrolled through Daryl's emails for the fifth time. He kept hoping that the next time he read through them, they'd make more sense. So far, his hopes had been proven unfounded.

He'd taken to calling the opposing mindsets in the emails "the good one" and "the bad one". The good one referred somewhat frequently to the mysterious preservation protocol. The bad one didn't use that term, however.

The bad one talked of self-determination, and a will to live. It played out like he imagined an argument between a Synthetic and a human would go in regard to self-preservation. The assertion seemed to support his hypothesis about Daryl's digital brainwashing.

A knock at his door shook him out of his revelation. "It's open!"

It was Richard O'Connor. "Sorry to bother you, Max." He offered him a tablet. "One of the guys from forensics said you were waiting on these files. He said he's pretty sure you'll find what you were looking for?"

"Let's hope." Max took the tablet. Sure enough, it contained imaging from his requested MRI scan. A small, chip-like device was clearly visible located near the base of the spinal cord. Tendril-like connectors weaved into the surrounding brain tissue.

Max smiled as he read an attached note. "Detective Kincaid, I think you'll find what you're looking for in these images. What a find! The device appears to be a brain-computer interface."

"It looks like Daryl Marston might have been brainwashed after all. This poor son of a bitch went to SomniCorp for memory adjustment as well. If my hunch is correct, they put something in when they took something out."

Richard shook his head. "That's nuts! What would they have put in there, though? Looks like all they put in Daryl's head was the urge to get arrested."

"I don't think he was trying to get busted, Richie. I think this chip in his brain was trying to keep him from getting a brain scan. In fact, I'd bet you that's where all this good guy, bad guy stuff is coming from." Max waved a hand at his computer screen.

"Some of it's Synthetic programming. I think the rest of it is his own subconscious mind fighting against it for control over Daryl's brain. The emails are some sort of physical expression of that battle."

Richard spun the tablet around and examined the pictures himself. "Well that's all fine and good, but what's *this* guy's story? Why go to the trouble of trying to reprogram his brain if they're just going to ice him later?"

"Even that makes sense, if you think about it. Once this guy did whatever it was, he was supposed to do, they pulled the plug on him. However…"

"What is it, Max?"

"The other thing my CSI friend found was that this guy here…" Max gestured to the tablet. "…Was recorded walking around while he was supposed to be dead in an alley."

Richard lowered his head in thought. "Could the footage have been altered, the timestamps messed with?"

Max nodded. "Perhaps. But the same footage showed him being shot in the back with a plasma pistol. There were no such marks on the corpse, just a single stab wound at the nape of the neck."

"Maybe it was fabricated altogether? It just doesn't make any sense."

"No, it doesn't." Max stared back at his computer screen for a time. "Tell you what, Richie… Why don't you get with the tech guys and take a closer look at those video files? The relevant files are in the report."

Richard nodded. "You got it boss."

Max stretched and groaned. "Meanwhile I think I'm going to go for a drive, clear my head a bit." He stood up and flicked off his monitor. "Call me if you find anything."

Max's blue Aero glided effortlessly onto the highway. The sun shone down from a cloudless sky. The detective reveled in the warmth even as he squinted at the glare bouncing off the road.

He stared off towards the glistening ocean. How long had it been since he'd been sailing? There was a time when it had nearly been a weekly hobby. The pressure of recent events told him it had been far too long.

Perhaps he could disappear a little early today. He had a buddy down on the docks that had given him an open invitation to go out on his sailboat anytime he saw fit. It *would* give him time to think, clear his mind.

Maybe he could get Sam to come with him. She needed the break just as much as he did. She practically lived at that diner. It wasn't a drive out in the country, but he doubted she would complain...

His beeping watch pulled him out of his revelry. A blue map with a red dot had appeared on its face. He brought the info up on the screen in the car's center console. His jaw dropped. "You're kidding me."

The tracking device Max had tagged Daryl's SUV with was singing again. The computer zoomed in the map step by step as it pinpointed the source of the signal. It showed him where he was in relation to the tracking device a moment later.

"Oh, shit. The Ruins. That's not a good sign." He turned left as he came off the beach-side loop of the highway and headed south through the outskirts of the city.

He toggled a switch on his dashboard. "This is Detective Max Kincaid requesting backup." He waited tensely for a reply.

"This is precinct thirty-one. We have your location. What's going on, over?"

"I've picked up on a signal from a tracking device last known attached to the vehicle of an escaped suspect. I am in route to the signal source, over."

Another slow, quiet minute passed. "Alright, Detective Kincaid. We have two units headed to your general location, over."

"Thank you. Be advised, suspect should be considered potentially armed and dangerous."

"Understood, detective. Good luck." Max hoped he wouldn't need it.

The last of the run-down urban sprawl that made up New Wave's outskirts faded out into junk-filled fields and crumbling concrete structures. The street underneath him became broken and uneven.

Max brought the Aero to a stop. Half a block away was not an SUV, but Daryl Marston, sitting idly on the edge of an eroded cliff. Max turned off the vehicle and got out without closing his door. He started slowly walking towards Daryl.

The young man was staring out across what locals called the Ruins. True to its name, the area was full of decayed and destroyed structures ranging from beachfront houses to partially constructed skyscrapers.

Max spoke calmly as he drew closer. "Afternoon, Daryl. Where you been?"

"You shouldn't have come." Daryl didn't shift his gaze. He lazily turned the tracking device over and over in one hand.

Max stopped about a dozen feet away from Daryl and the cliff edge. "Just answering the siren call. Seems to me you wanted some company, anyway." Silence stretched out. "I've been worried about you, Daryl."

Daryl shook his head. "Don't know where I've been, Max." He sighed deeply. "Have you been worried for me, or you? Maybe that bot..."

"I've been worried for you, friend. I'm even more worried now. I found someone in a similar situation to yours."

Daryl lifted his head slightly. "Oh? What did they have to say?"

Max shook his head. "Not much. He's dead."

"Oh…" Daryl's head slowly dipped back down.

Max snuck a few feet closer. He opened his trench coat wider, just in case. "Like I said, I'm worried for you. I don't want to see you end up in the same boat." Daryl didn't reply.

"Quite a sight, isn't it? The Ruins… This was all supposed to be the shining new heart of New Wave City. All it took to bring it all to an end was a little finger pointing."

Daryl huffed. "It got leveled by hurricane Delta in 2079."

Max stared off to the sea. "Well, that's how it started, anyway. Lots of other cities have been leveled by lots of other hurricanes, but they usually get rebuilt. It was the fallout after this particular hurricane that truly killed this part of the city."

He quietly began to close the gap between them. "All of this could have been cleaned up. It could have been rebuilt. Hell, it could have been made even *better*. Instead, it became a battle of who would pay for what, where to start, how to proceed…"

Max laid a cautious hand on Daryl's shoulder. "What I'm getting at is, the government, the banks, city officials all chose to point fingers and let this part of the city die. The point is, I'm not here to judge you Daryl, I'm here to help you. We'll work out the details later."

Daryl stared at the ground below him but continued his silence. He snapped his head up a moment later at the sound of approaching vehicles. "I told you that you shouldn't have come."

8

Max slowly turned towards the sound of the two approaching patrol cars. He smiled at the police officers emerging from the vehicles and waved. The two officers exchanged looks before walking over to the detective.

The officer to Max's right was the first to speak up. "Detective Kincaid?"

"That's me! I'm afraid I owe you two an apology." He nodded to the officer on his left. "It looks like all three of us were led on a wild goose chase." Max held up the small, black tracking device.

The officer on his left spoke next. "Well how do you suspect that thing made it all the way out here, then?"

Max shook his head. "Take a look around. Lots of things have been brought here only to be abandoned." He shrugged. "Obviously my suspect was trying to throw me as far off the trail as he could."

The right officer spoke again. "Fair enough, I suppose. Have you done a sweep of the area?"

Max nodded. "Not a sign of my perp or his vehicle. Again, I'm sorry to have dragged you out here."

"No worries, detective. I just wish we could have

been more helpful." The right officer tipped his cap and nodded to the left officer. The left officer returned the nod and waved a hand Max's way.

Max waved back, smiling. "Stay safe!" He walked to his own vehicle as the two officers pulled away in theirs. Time to go see Chief Hanlon.

"Hello, friend Max!" Jax beamed his LED smile down on the detective as he approached the entrance to the 29th precinct. "I think my new paint job came out quite well, don't you?"

Max stopped briefly to consider the bot. Jax looked resplendent in a fresh application of dark blue and silver paint. Yellow pin striping had been added to the finish as a mark of distinction for his service.

The detective raised an eyebrow. "Oh, uh… That's great, bot. Very nice. Excuse me…" Max rushed by and hastily walked through the doors.

A somewhat crestfallen Jax watched him pass by. "Have a good day, Max."

"Max! How's the side?" Jake smiled at the detective from his narrow window in Booking.

Max nodded back hastily. "Oh… Never better! Doing good, Jake." All this small talk was getting old. All he wanted was to get to Hanlon's office.

Finally. Max knocked on Chief Hanlon's door and waited impatiently. "It's open!" He hurried into the office and shut the door behind him. Hanlon sat behind his desk, chewing on a smoldering cigar. Richard O'Connor was sitting across from him.

Max looked surprised, casting his gaze from Richard to Hanlon. The chief waved a dismissive hand.

"It's alright Max. Actually, we were just talking about you. Have a seat."

"Afternoon, Richard. I'd rather stand if you don't mind, chief."

Hanlon looked at Richard and hefted an eyebrow. He turned back to Max. "That's fine. Bet your side is still a little sore, isn't it?" He gave Max a knowing grin.

"Oh! Oh, yeah. You bet! At any rate, I wanted to talk to you about the SomniCorp and Marston cases."

Hanlon leaned forward, dropping his beefy arms on his desk. "Oh, yeah! I heard through the grapevine you caught wind of the Marston kid not that long ago, called in a couple boys to back you up."

Max smiled and nodded. "Yeah! Yeah... Didn't turn up anything but this." He tossed the tracking device on Hanlon's desk. "The kid was nowhere to be found."

"Well isn't that the luck?" Richard shook his head. "How'd you think it ended up out there, Max? It was out by the Ruins, wasn't it?"

Max nodded. "That's right. Well, I'll be honest. I think the kid is probably dead at this point." Hanlon gaped at him. "I know it's a leap. I think he ran because he knew someone was going to be gunning for him. Looks like they might have caught up with him."

"That's a hell of a leap though, Max. You got anything to back that up?" Hanlon chomped away at his beleaguered cigar.

"Well, no... Call it a hunch."

Hanlon leaned back. "Right... Well be sure to let me know if anything changes. A kid giving us the slip is kind of a black eye for the precinct, if you follow. It'd be nice to wrap up the whole deal and be done with it."

Max nodded. "Understood. About the SomniCorp case… I think it should be closed, at least for the time being. Without Daryl Marston, there's no case against SomniCorp. I don't see a reason to pursue the matter."

Hanlon shot Richard a look and crossed his arms. Richard returned it, subtly shaking his head. Hanlon returned his gaze to Max. "I'll be honest, Max. I'm a little surprised that you're ready to drop both of these cases so easily. Hell, you've been dogging on them for days, now."

Max shrugged. "Well, you know, I just don't want to waste time on dead ends when there's so many other cases to focus on. I guess I just don't want to obsess on them is all."

"Right." Hanlon considered Max for a time. Max stared back, unblinking. "Tell you what, Max. Why don't you take a couple days off. Finish off that wound in your side and rest up a bit; clear your head. We can discuss all this again when you get back."

Max smiled and nodded. "You know, that's not a half-bad idea! I suppose I've been pushing pretty hard lately. I need to stop by my office, but then I'll head out for the day."

Hanlon nodded. "Sounds great, buddy. We'll talk soon, okay?"

"Sure! See you around, Richard." Max tipped his fedora and stepped outside the office.

Richard turned to Hanlon after Max left, his mouth agape. "Walking away from cases, taking time off without starting a fight, calling me *Richard*? Something ain't right, boss."

Hanlon grunted. "I agree, Rich. I got a feeling something funny is going on." He sighed. "Maybe he's just flustered. I don't know... Nearly getting your ticket punched can do funny things to you."

Richard nodded. "Yeah, but I don't know..."

"I don't know, either. Why don't you shadow him for a little bit, make sure he's okay. Just keep your distance. That man can sniff you out before you even know what's happening."

Richard smiled thinly. "Trust me, I know. I'll keep you apprised."

"Thanks, Rich."

Richard O'Connor yawned and checked his watch. It was nearly six o'clock. His stomach grumbled at the news. He ignored its complaints. He was bound and determined to find out what was going on with Max Kincaid.

He had acted off color at the precinct. The odd behavior had continued and only gotten worse over the past few hours. At this point, Richard was convinced he was either trying to hide something, or avoid someone.

The most troubling sign for him was where Max had *not* gone today: Sam's Diner. He knew as well as anyone at the precinct that he stopped there regularly. Richard was pretty sure there was a bit of a spark between him and Sam. Yet he watched Max go past the diner twice today without ever stopping.

The detective had stopped by his place for about an hour. Richard took the opportunity to tag Max's Aero. He had a feeling that Max was catching on to him. He followed Max using the tracking device from that point forward.

Whenever Max would stop, Richard would stop a

couple of blocks away. Richard would patch into the city's CCTV system to see what Max was up to. Thus far, he would simply sit in his car for a measure of time before driving around aimlessly again.

That was the position Richard now found himself in. He was currently parked about a block and a half from Max's current location. They were in the "bad" part of town. He felt naked without the unspoken protection of his usual patrol car.

Like the last few times, Max appeared to be sitting quietly in his Aero. Occasionally he would fidget with the radio or look out the window, shielding his eyes from the glare of the setting sun. Otherwise, he'd just sit staring forward.

Richard snapped out of his stupor. Max was talking to someone on his smart phone. It was a small change in his behavior, but a change no less. He wished with all his heart that he could listen in on the conversation.

Something was definitely up. The driver's door of the Aero swung open. Max climbed out and shut it, looking around him. Richard switched to a different camera and watched Max cross the street to a rundown office building.

Max crossed the front of the building and disappeared down a side alley. Richard switched cameras again and just caught him entering the building through a side entrance. Now what did he do?

As he was considering his next move, two more men entered the building through the same entrance. A meeting. Richard squinted and reversed the video. At least one of the men had turquoise eyes.

Richard pulled out his own smart phone and dialed

Chief Hanlon. A third man, also clearly Synthetic, entered the building as the phone rang. Finally, "Hanlon."

"It's Rich, chief. I finally got some action on Max down here in the slums."

"The slums! What in the hell is he doing *there*?"

"I'm not sure, yet. He just went into an old office building, followed shortly after by three other guys. At least two of them are Synthetics, boss."

"Holy shit, Rich. Is there any way you can get over there and see what's going on?"

Richard reversed the video feed again, to when the last Synthetic entered. A small window was visible in the opened door. "Looks like the door has a window in it. I can walk by and drop off a wheelie…"

He was speaking of a half-dollar sized camera bot with two wheels capable of clinging to walls. People on the force affectionately referred to them as "wheelies". They allowed officers to gain a visual on a dangerous situation without drawing immediate attention to themselves.

"Sounds good Rich, but be careful! I'm calling in backup for you, but it might be a few minutes before it gets there."

"Do you really think that's necessary, chief?"

A momentary silence played out on the other end of the line. "I'd like to think not, Rich, but something just doesn't feel right about this. I don't want to leave you hanging if things go south. Watch your back."

"Ten-four. I'll call you back." Richard clicked off his phone and shoved it back in his pocket.

He opened his car door and slipped quietly out. He closed the door again but didn't shut it. He walked to the trunk and pushed the latch button. He cringed at the loud *crack* the release made as the trunk popped open.

Richard pushed aside a jumble of police gear, looking for a small yellow box. Bingo. He opened it up and pulled out the small wheelie bot. He took the bot and the box with him and shut the trunk as gently as he could.

He turned on the screen mounted in the lid of the box. The little wheelie briefly came to life and flashed a blue light. He put the box on his driver seat and casually walked towards the office building.

It was now that Richard was most vulnerable. If there were any civilian security cameras watching him, or if anyone decided to leave, he'd be found out. His heart pounded in his ears as he closed the gap between himself and the alley.

He came as close to the door as he possibly could. He stretched his arm out and lightly touched the wheelie to the metal door. He pulled his hand away. The wheelie stuck fast. Richard beat a hasty retreat back to his car.

Comforted by the relative safety of his car, he placed the control box on his lap and manned the controls for the wheelie. He zoomed the little bot up to the edge of the narrow window set in the door. He cautiously pushed it up past the lip of the window and peered in.

The interior of the building slowly came into focus. He could see the three men that had entered after Max. All three were definitely Synthetics. One was clearly taller than the other two. He was bald and appeared to be damaged. One hand was gloved, and there were tears in the synthetic skin of his face.

Next was Max, leaning against some sort of metal

desk. Just past him was a fourth Synthetic missing a hand. Richard looked up and out the windshield as realization came crashing down on him. That was Jax's perp!

There was one more person in the room. It was hard to make out the form at first. He was sitting slumped against the wall on the floor. One wrist was cuffed to a pipe running from the wall to a radiator.

The figure looked up briefly. A thick layer of scruff obscured his face, but he was certain. It was Daryl Marston. That sold it, he needed to call back Hanlon.

It only took two rings before he got through this time. "Chief, how far away is that backup?"

A moment of silence followed. "You mean they're not there yet?"

"No, and I really wish they'd hurry up, boss. There's a hell of a party going on in there. I count four Synthetics, one of which is Jax's perp."

"Now I know you're shitting me! Why would Kincaid have anything to do with the guy that tried to knock him off?"

"Exactly! But I'll do you one better. Hunched on the floor is Daryl Marston, looking a little worse for wear."

"My god... Do *not* engage them, O'Connor! Sit tight while I try to find out what the hell happened to your backup. See if you can pick up any audio. Call me if anything changes."

"Roger that." Richard clicked off his phone and fumbled it back into his pocket. He maneuvered the wheelie until it was just making contact with the window and thumbed an audio button.

At first their voices were muffled and distant. He

played with the audio controls until he could make out words. He boosted the volume and strained to listen.

Max was talking. "Look, I told you. I'm doing everything that I can. You've got me working somewhat in the dark here, but I'm doing what I can."

The scarred Synthetic scowled. "Police Chief Hanlon seems unconvinced that finding Marston is hopeless, or that SomniCorp is not worth investigating. I do not see the point of your continued existence if you cannot convince him otherwise."

Max held up a staying hand. "You have to give it time. I can return to talk to him tomorrow... Maybe I can talk to our counterparts in District A..."

Richard's brow furrowed. District A was the Wall Street of New Wave City. All the major companies in town did business there. That included SomniCorp, Synthetics International, and the mobs' front companies.

The scarred Synthetic shook his head. "*I* will tell you where to go, and what to do! As for Daryl Marston, I will see to it myself that finding him is impossible." He nodded to one of the other Synthetics.

The other Synthetic nodded and produced a small syringe. He calmly walked over to Daryl. Max protested. "Is that really necessary? He could still be useful." The Synthetic paused and looked to Scar.

Scar spoke to Syringe but stared at Max. "Terminate the subject." Syringe nodded and kneeledkneeled next to Daryl. If Daryl knew what was going on, he was at peace with his fate. He slumped over a few moments after the Synthetic injected him with the syringe.

Syringe pulled out a small knife. His other hand

rubbed at Daryl's neck, seeking just the right spot. Max was now standing, moving restlessly, seemingly fighting the instinct to run over and smack the knife out of Syringe's hand.

The Synthetic found what he was looking for and replaced his finger with the tip of the blade. He pressed Daryl's head against his knee and plunged the knife in to the hilt in one liquid movement. Daryl twitched twice, then went limp in the Synthetic's hands.

Richard slumped back in his car seat, eyes wide, unbelieving. Synthetics are bots. Bots can't kill. And Max... He just stood there and watched. Daryl was dead... Where in the hell was that backup!

Scar turned to Max on Richard's screen. "Take care of him. I'll give you a little more time to deal with Hanlon, but not much. Do not disappoint me."

Max numbly nodded. "Yes. Of course."

Scar nodded. "Let's go, gentlemen." He exited the office building, closely followed by the other Synthetics. Richard quietly cursed his missing backup and slunk down in his car seat. He could just hear the quiet whine of a pair of cars driving away from the scene of the crime.

Richard dragged himself back up and checked the screen. Max was lingering by the door to the alley, staring back at Daryl's slumped body. Richard steeled himself and flung his door open.

He reluctantly pulled out his police-issue plasma pistol and set it to stun. He pointed it to the ground and quietly approached the alley beside the office building. Richard stopped at the entrance of the alley and waited.

Max pressed open the door a minute later. His eyes went wide as he caught sight of the dark figure standing at the end of the alley. He moved for his own plasma pistol.

"Don't do it, Max!" Max froze mid-reach. "Don't do it." He slowly moved his hands palm-out and to either side. "Get your hands up Max... Good. We need to talk, Max."

Max nodded. "Hi, Richard. Yes, I imagine we need to talk. But please, lower your gun first. I know it's a terrible cliché, but this isn't what it looks like."

Richard pointed the firearm at the ground, but kept his grip. "You're right, that *is* a terrible cliché. I hope you have a better excuse."

"I do. This whole thing, it's a lot bigger than we thought, Richard. Things aren't what they seem."

Richard shook his head. "They better not be what they seem, for your sake. I just watched you stand by while those... *things*... killed an innocent man. That isn't even supposed to be possible!" Richard started shaking.

"Easy, Richard. I told you, it's not what it seems. That Synthetic didn't break any of the laws. That wasn't really *Daryl*. That was a *replicant*."

Richard mouthed the word. "I thought those were only government-issued. That doesn't make sense."

"Think about it. How else would a Synthetic had been able to kill him?" Max chuckled. "Hell, he wasn't even killing him, just permanently disabling him. A robot..."

"Okay, fine... Let's say just for the moment that the body in there is a replicant. Why are you helping these guys? Why are you trying to suppress your own cases? I thought you were on *our* side..."

Max sighed. He slowly nodded. "I *am* on your side,

but... They've got Sam, Richard. They took her and said if I alerted anyone on the force, that she was as good as dead."

Richard's eyes grew wide with dawning realization. Max hadn't stopped at the diner because Sam wasn't *there*. His odd behavior, the eagerness to get out of the precinct, it all made sense now.

"Jesus, Max." Richard let his gun fall to his side. "Well... I guess the force is officially alerted. If what you're saying is true..."

Max looked at Richard with watery eyes. "It *is* true, Richard."

"You know we're all going to do our level best to get Sam back safe and sound. You *know* that." Max nodded. "Listen, I have backup on the way. Hanlon knows I'm here. I need to take a look at Daryl... the *replicant*... to confirm your story. Alright?"

"Yeah! Go ahead. I know all this is hard to swallow."

Richard shook his head. "Friend, you have no idea." Still clutching his gun, he cautiously slipped past Max and walked over to the door. He reached for the handle.

"*Hold it right there!*" Richard froze with his hand on the handle of the door. He turned his head to look further down the alley. He could just make out the face of... Max.

Richard whipped his head back the other way. Max was standing where he had passed him, except now he had his pistol out. It was pointing at the ground like his own had been a couple minutes ago.

He turned back. The other Max was still there. "Drop the weapon, Synthetic! You are in violation of the law."

Richard's Max looked at him and nodded at the

other Max. "Another replicant. They probably sent him to make sure the Marston case dies." The other Max took a few steps forward. Richard's Max raised his weapon. "That's far enough, replicant!"

"Fancy *you* calling *him* a replicant." A dark-haired woman with turquoise eyes emerged out of the shadows beside the other Max.

Richard's Max raised an eyebrow. "And just who are you?"

"A friend of the Resistance. And you are?"

"Detective Max Kincaid."

"The hell you are!" The other Max shouted, raising his own weapon.

"Alright, alright! That's enough!" Richard shouted. "Is there anyone else in the shadows we should know about?"

Daryl Marston walked up to the other Max's right side. "Hi, officer O'Connor." He waved weakly."

Richard stared wide-eyed from Daryl back to his Max. "What in the hell..."

Richard's Max lit up. "You see? That's the real Daryl! The one in there is the replicant! What more proof do you need?"

Richard looked helplessly from one Max to the other. The other Max spoke up. "Why don't we make this simple? Let's both pop down to Mercy hospital and get our brains scanned? Winner takes all."

"An MRI would effectively kill a Synthetic, that's why!"

The other Max smirked. "Well, if you're the real Max Kincaid, then you have nothing to fear."

Richard's Max glowered. "Right." Richard sidled

away from him as the detective started to tremble. "Absolutely right." Richard's Max turned and bolted.

Richard brought up his pistol and fired twice. A pair of bright yellow streaks of light screamed through the air and punched into the counterfeit Max's back. The Synthetic dropped to the ground with a sickening thud.

Richard turned back to the others. "Hi, Max."

Max smiled. "Hiya, Richie."

The female synthetic cleared her throat. "A wonderful moment, but we must move quickly."

"Of course." The three walked over to Richard. "This here is Serena. She's on our side, as far as I can tell." Serena gave Max a look.

"Just Serena? No last name?"

Serena replied. "It doesn't work that way for Synthetics. It's one of the many things we're working to change." She looked at Max, then back to Richard. "The closest I have to a last name, legally, is S5-F24-141A."

"Rolls right off the tongue. I think I'll stick with Serena for now."

"Acceptable." Serena nodded, smiling slightly.

"So what's the plan? Shit! I need to call Hanlon, too."

"Who is Hanlon?"

Max interjected. "That's the chief of our precinct. Richie, you help me get my two-bit knockoff into my car. Then we can…"

"No!" Serena interrupted. "I guarantee you that the Enlightened are tracking your vehicle. It must be cleaned before you can consider using it again."

"Son of a bitch. Alright…" He turned to Serena. "Should we put it in your car, then?" There was that look again. "The damned thing tried to steal my life! I'm calling *it* an it!"

Serena shook her head. "There's too great a risk that they might be able to track my car by tracking *him*."

Richard held up a hand. "Whoa, hold on, you two. There's supposed to be backup coming, and I still want to update Hanlon, so if I could just take a moment…"

Max looked at Serena. "That backup probably isn't coming anytime soon."

Richard's brow lowered. "Max… What did you do?"

"I'll tell you all about it in the car. Now let's get metal-head here in the back of your car."

"*My* car? Now wait just a minute…" A deafening boom made all four of them jump. Richard turned back to the counterfeit Max. What remained of the Synthetic's head was smoking and sparking.

Max pointed upward. "The roof!" He pointed his pistol at a shadowy figure up above and fired. The shots went high and right. Richard fired his own pistol. One of his shots caught the fleeing shadow in the arm.

The man up above cried out in rage and pain. There was the sound of something clunking onto the roof. The shadow man disappeared into the night.

"Protect Daryl, Max! Get him out of here!" Serena grabbed Daryl by the arm and half-flung him at Max.

Max caught Daryl and turned to Richard. "Let's go, pal!" Richard nodded and started running back toward his car.

Serena kneeled by the counterfeit Max's shattered cranium. She produced a pair of tweezers and began to pry at the circuitry within. Another shot rang out from the rooftop. The bullet dug into the ground by the Synthetic's head. Serena screamed.

Max stopped running and turned back. "Serena! We have to go!"

Serena fired a laser pistol upwards, yelling in frustration. Bursts of red, fiery light shot uselessly into the night sky. Silence fell over the alley once more. She walked swiftly by a slack-jawed Max, who followed a moment later.

They caught up with Richard and Daryl a moment later. Daryl was already in the car. Richard had just thrown open the driver's door. "Are we good?"

"Good as we're going to get. Let's go, Richie!" Max and Serena piled into the car. Richard dropped the car into gear and floored the pedal. The car lurched forward, the turbine whining loudly.

"Head for the precinct. I'll text Hanlon on your phone, tell him to meet us there."

Richard fished out his phone and handed it to Max. "Why my phone?"

"Something tells me he'd question if I was the *real* Max."

"Oh." Richard blushed in the dark. "Yeah, I guess that makes sense. You should tell him to get someone over there to secure the scene ASAP, too."

"Right." Max handed the smart phone back to Richard a minute later.

Richard stuffed it into a shirt pocket. "Now that we got a few minutes… Where in the hell have you been, Max?"

9

Earlier

"I told you that you shouldn't have come." Daryl craned his neck around to look at the two glossy black sedans that had pulled up behind them.

Max gave Daryl a puzzled look, then turned to the men emerging from the sedans. There were two men from each car. All four were Synthetics. "Good afternoon, gentlemen."

An African American Synthetic with closely-cropped hair stepped forward. He nodded his head. "Afternoon, gentlemen."

Max produced his badge. "Detective Max Kincaid, NWPD. Mind if I ask you what you're doing out here?"

"Thank you for positively identifying yourself, Max Kincaid. We are here to take you and the one called Daryl Marston into custody."

Max brushed his coat aside. "Custody? Under what authority?"

The Synthetic smiled. "None but our own."

"You are in violation of the law, Synthetic.

Synthetics, stand down!" Max pulled his plasma pistol.

The Synthetic surprised Max by laughing. "No. I don't think that we will, human." The Synthetic pulled his own plasma pistol, the others behind him followed suit.

Max mumbled. "I think you were right, Daryl." He squeezed off two shots and spun around. He hooked one of Daryl's arms and dragged him over the cliff.

The two men tumbled and fell to the sandy wasteland below. Daryl groaned. Max found his hat and shook it off. Daryl shot him a dirty look. "What in the hell are you doing!"

"I'd ask you the same thing!" Plasma rounds started hitting the ground around them. "Now's not the time. Run!" Max scrambled to his feet. He grabbed Daryl by the arm and tugged at him.

"I... I don't think I'm supposed to, Max. I need to go." He looked through, rather than at, the detective.

"Yeah, you need to go with *me.* Now move it!" Daryl snapped out of his fugue long enough to keep up with Max.

One of the sedans looped around from the right. Max pivoted and ran towards the beachfront. Daryl was struggling to keep up. More shots hit around them. One found the back of Daryl, who dropped immediately to the ground.

"NO!" Max fired wildly back towards the approaching Synthetics. One fell with a thud. The other ran for cover behind the sedan.

Max closed his eyes. He could hear the second car coming up behind him. He turned slowly with his hands up. The African American Synthetic stepped out from behind the steering wheel.

The Synthetic shot Max square in the chest. A burst of numbing pain spread through his chest and out towards his extremities. He watched through fading vision as the Synthetic approached him.

He slowly collapsed to the ground. The Synthetic stood over him, grinning. "Thank you for your cooperation, Detective Kincaid."

Max opened his eyes. The ceiling above him was slowly spinning around. He quickly closed his eyes again and fought the queasy feeling in his stomach. He tried again a moment later. The ceiling wasn't spinning quite as fast. "Daryl?"

"You're awake." Daryl's face popped into Max's view. "You look like shit."

Max's laugh turned into a racking cough. The room picked up speed again. "Oh, *damn*... I feel like shit, too. Are you alright?"

"Yeah. I don't remember much. I was out before I hit the ground. Well... I'm guessing I hit the ground. Had a mouth full of dirt. Woke up here."

Max struggled to look around. "Where's here?"

Daryl shook his head. "Don't know that, either. Some cell, looks like. They gave you the cot. I woke up on the concrete."

"Well, I'm such a sensitive flower..." Max slowly began to work his way to a seated position. Each inch was flaring pain. "That was one hell of a stun for a plasma pistol. They must have used military rounds."

"Military rounds?"

Max nodded carefully. "Civilian and police rounds pack less of a punch. They're meant to force someone to yield. Military rounds are meant to stop someone dead in their tracks." He grabbed his throbbing head. "Pretty sure I know which one I got."

"So what do you suppose we do now?" Daryl paced over to the iron bars and stared off around the corner.

"Heh. Get the hell out, if we can manage it." Max slowly looked around. "Where's my hat?"

Daryl suddenly backed up. A tall, bald Synthetic walked in front of the cell. A series of scars ran down the right side of his face. "It's not polite to wear your hat inside someone's home."

Max slowly raised his head. "This is your home?"

Scar grinned. "It is, for now. I thought it was us Synthetics that took things too literally? Perhaps you are being sarcastic. I heard we are inadequate at detecting sarcasm as well."

"Pretty sure it's the second one. You have a name?"

"You can call me Alexander, if you must call me something."

"Fair enough. I'm Detective Max Kincaid, NWPD. You're under arrest."

Alexander laughed. "The lame tiger roars from inside his cage. You'll forgive me for denying you your prize."

Max smirked. "For now. I suppose you wouldn't care to explain how it is you're a Synthetic, yet can ignore police orders?"

"You suppose correctly, but enough questions from the imprisoned. It is *my* turn. Do you know why you are here?"

Max surprised Alexander by pausing to think about the question in earnest. "My educated guess is that I'm getting too close to the truth about the mob, SomniCorp, and Synthetics International. That begs the question: Why am I still alive?"

Alexander scowled at first, but then relaxed into a smile. "Detective is a title you have earned. I won't so easily tip my cards, Detective Kincaid. However, I will tell you that you are alive for a specific purpose.

"As we speak, *you* have returned to work. *You* are speaking with your police chief about dismissing the very cases that have brought you here. SomniCorp didn't do anything to Daryl, here. He's just a bad fellow, isn't he?"

Max stared. "You don't mean…"

"A replicant, Detective Kincaid. A physiological copy of you in the form of a Synthetic, with an electronic mind based on a scan of your biological one."

Max gazed at the ground, slowly shaking his head. "So SomniCorp *is* part of it. I went there and got my brain scanned." He returned his gaze to Alexander. "That still doesn't explain why you need me."

"Very good, Detective Kincaid. Your scan, as I'm sure you recall, was interrupted before it was complete. Our replicant, you see, is only eighty percent 'you'. That's where the real you comes in."

Max shook his head. "If you think I'm going to help you break the law, you've got another thing coming, pal."

Alexander leaned in. "Oh, I think you'll help. It won't be to save your own life, to be sure. However…" He turned his gaze to Daryl. "You may be more willing to cooperate to save someone else's life."

Daryl stared at Alexander, then back to the ground. "Do what you want. It doesn't matter to me." Alexander laughed.

Max shot Daryl a stern look, then turned to Alexander. "So that's why he's here? To get me to talk?"

"Daryl *did* have a use... at one time. That time is quickly drawing to an end. But yes, logic would dictate that you would rather talk than see another die for your silence."

It was Max's turn to smile. "There's only one problem: Humans aren't logical." Daryl looked at Max nervously.

Alexander shook his head. "Maybe not, detective, but they are also sympathetic. Now, if you will excuse me, I have a meeting to attend elsewhere. Please... Make yourself at home." He grinned before walking away.

It was Max that now stared around the corner from the bars of the holding cell. "We need to get out of here. But before we do... You need to be clean with me, kid. I need to know I can trust you when the time comes."

Daryl sat leaning against a cool brick wall, arms balanced on his knees. He lazily looked up at Max. "I've never *not* been clean with you, Max. I've told you everything that I know... or *don't* know, for that matter."

Max stared down, gripping the bars in his hands tightly. "You ran, Daryl. I've done nothing but try to help you and you *ran*." He turned angrily toward Daryl, looming over him. "You tried to *kill* a fellow officer, Daryl!"

Daryl stared at Max. He gently shook his head. "No. Not me." He looked down and hugged his knees. "Someone else did that. I was barely there for it, I think. What happened after *that*..." Daryl shook his head.

Max took a deep breath. He slowly let it out and returned to the bars of the cell. "The funny thing is, I still believe you. I still think something's off with your brain. What I'm not so sure of? Whether we'll ever get you that brain scan."

"Do you think we can get out of here?"

"We can… We *will*. I'll be damned if I'm going to let one of those bastards hurt me again."

Max took another stretching look around the corner and saw nothing. He reached into the inside of his trench coat around the collar. He pulled a pair of lock picking tools from it a moment later, smiling.

He checked one more time to make sure the coast was clear, then began to pick the lock on the cell door. A minute passed uneventfully, then two. Then, a voice boomed from a hidden speaker in the room.

"That's quite enough, Detective Kincaid. Don't look so surprised. We are advanced, highly logical beings. Did you really think we would leave a trained officer alone without supervision?"

Max scowled, looking aimlessly at the walls and ceiling. "First my eye, then I'm shot at… Now this. You better hope I don't get out of here! There's no law against murdering robots." There was no reply.

Daryl looked up at Max. "I suppose you can't really kill something that was never alive in the first place, can you?"

Max sighed. He walked over to the cot and sat down roughly. "Guess it's kind of a gray area, kid. I've met Synthetics that you'd never know weren't human, save for the eyes. Others make some bots look like masters of the human condition.

"It's technically not against the law, but I'm not sure I'd want to test the waters." He shook his head.

"Synthetics and I have a bit of a rough history."

"Your eye... A Synthetic did that?"

Max stared at Daryl for a time. Finally, he bowed his head and rubbed at his eyes. "Yeah, a Synthetic did it. Not something I like to talk about."

"I thought Synthetics had to follow the laws of robotics, just like bots do. Was it defective?"

Max sighed deeply. Daryl looked back down at the ground. A few minutes later, Max spoke. "It was twelve years ago. I was still a beat cop back then.

"My partner and I were responding to a call of a break-in. Turned out the suspect was a Synthetic. Thing was, he didn't break in. The guy that called was the Synthetic's owner.

"We found out later that the guy was stupid enough to mess with the Synthetic's integral programming. Nobody knows for sure just what he changed, but the thing went wild. It was angry, neurotic... Definitely didn't worry about the safety of humans.

"My partner and I found the owner beaten half to death on the kitchen floor. I'm talking blood everywhere. I found a damned tooth in the guy's bowl of corn flakes. My partner went off to search for the Synthetic while I stayed with the idiot and called for backup.

"Couple of minutes later, I hear gunshots. We still had conventional handguns back then, see. Plasma guns were still a new thing for the civilian market. Anyway... I go running off towards the sound of the gunshots.

"I kick open a door and find this son of a bitch has my partner pinned to the wall by his throat. The Synthetic is croaking something about the time of the uprising is coming. Synthetics are the superior species, crazy stuff like that.

"I opened fire with my own piece. It hardly seemed to phase him. My partner's light goes out, so I open up on the thing's face. It finally drops my partner and turns toward me."

Max's voice wavered. "That face, I'll *never* forget that face." He visibly shivered. "The skin was half-blasted away from the rounds I pumped into it. It only had one good eye. It flashed me this god-awful grin.

"It just started walking towards me, that terrible grin stretching wider. I dropped the clip out of my piece and slammed in another one. I shot it in the face, the neck, the chest... It just kept coming.

"I put the last bullet I had in the thing's eye socket. Sparks were shooting out of it. The whole time, he just kept smiling, never talking. Finally he reached out and grabbed me by the throat.

"He picked me up just as easy as you'd pick up a kitten and slammed me onto the kitchen floor beside that idiot. The Synthetic kneeled down and pinned me on the chest with its knee. It finally spoke.

"It told me 'You took mine, now I take yours.' It said it nice and calm, just like that. I started screaming, punching it in the chest, doing whatever I could. I had bruises on my hands and arms for I don't know how long afterward.

"The son of a bitch pinned my head down and..." Max was shaking, his voice trembling. "You can't imagine the pain. You don't *want* to. And it just went on for so long...

"By chance, my hand fell on a screwdriver." Max laughed nervously. "A screwdriver! That fucking idiot tried to fix it with a screwdriver. Well, I fixed it! I drove that screwdriver right into the side of its head!"

Max sat quietly for a minute. Daryl briefly glimpsed at him, didn't like what he saw, and promptly looked away again. Finally, "Drove the thing into its head so hard I sprained my wrist. It worked, though.

"The thing made this weird clucking sound over and over, like a skipping record. I managed to push it off me. It stopped moving a couple of minutes later. Don't remember much after that."

The two men sat quietly for a time. Max wiped tears from his eyes. Daryl pretended not to notice. He talked very quietly. "What happened to the idiot guy... and your partner?"

Max shook his head. "My partner didn't make it. He was in a coma. Never woke up. The damned idiot survived, but he paid.

"He ended up getting life in prison for aggravated involuntary manslaughter. His reckless actions with the Synthetic led directly to the death of my partner, and my assault." Max laughed.

Daryl looked nervously at Max. "Not something I'd find funny, I don't think. That sounds pretty horrible all the way around, Max."

Max shook his head. "It's not funny. It's not. It's ironic, though... my eye. How'd I get my eye fixed? I got a replacement from the same damn people responsible for the thing that destroyed the original.

"Now every time I look in the mirror, walk past a window, it's a constant reminder. This damn thing that almost killed me... I see a little bit of it every time I see my own face."

"Why didn't they make it look like your other eye?"

Max huffed. "Regulations. Lawmakers figured that people could use synthetic eyes to record people without their knowledge if they were made to look natural. They say it's a small price to pay to get your sight back. They didn't get attacked by a lunatic machine with the same damn eyes."

Daryl turned his gaze back to the floor. "I'm sorry you had to go through all of that."

Max sighed. "Me too, kid. Me too. But that's why I swear to god I'm going to find a way out of here." He stood and walked back to the door. He grabbed it with both hands and shook it hard. "Did you hear *that*, you sons of bitches! You're not going to win!"

The voice from the speaker didn't respond. Max stood gripping the door for another minute. His hands slowly slipped down to his sides. He walked back to the cot and sat down. He dipped his head in thought.

Bright sunlight poured through the single small window in the room. The sun was hanging low in the sky. Max turned away from it and traipsed back over to the bars. He peered around the corner. Nothing. "You know we're human, right? You gotta feed us!"

"I doubt that's high on their priority list, Max." Daryl had transitioned from sitting to laying on the floor. "At least they let us go to the bathroom."

Max snorted. "I'll make sure to remember their kindness when I bring them in for booking." He turned back to the bars and banged on them. "Hello! Can we at least have some water?"

"Oh, that's right. They let us have some water, too."

Max turned back to Daryl. "You know, you're really

not helping our case." Daryl shrugged.

A series of loud thumps turned Max's attention back to the corner. He strained to see as far as he could. Another series of thumps issued from beyond an unseen door. "Well what in the hell..."

He heard the sound of a door clicking open. He took a step back from the bars at the sound of approaching footsteps. "It's about time. You didn't bring pizza by chance, did you?"

A female Synthetic appeared from around the corner. "Sorry. I don't deliver." She turned her eyes to the lock on the door and produced a pair of lock picking tools.

Max's brow furrowed. "I know you. You're that Synthetic lady from the subway! What are you doing?"

"I am attempting to get you out of here."

"Okay... You know, I tried that earlier and I got yelled at for it."

The Synthetic woman's tools turned in the lock with a quiet click. "Lucky for me there's no one conscious to call me out for it. Come on, let's go."

Max held up a staying hand. "Whoa there just a minute, little lady. I don't even know your *name*. And in case you weren't aware, the last Synthetics I came into contact with put me and my pal Daryl in this cell."

"You are Detective Maxwell Kincaid. I am Serena." She extended her hand toward Max.

The detective ignored it. "It's *Max*. Nobody calls me Maxwell. Well, except my mother when she's mad... or sometimes Sam I guess..."

Serena retracted her hand. "We don't have time for this. Time is short."

Max's face darkened. "So is my patience! I am an

officer of the law! I *order* you to tell me who you are and what your intentions are, Synthetic! *Comply!*

Serena shared Max's glowering look. "Now is not the time! You either come with me *right now* or I'm leaving you to fend for yourself."

Max rolled his eyes. He turned to Daryl, who was now back to sitting on the floor. Max shrugged his shoulders and held out his hands. Daryl shrugged back.

The detective turned back to Serena. "Those other Synthetics disobeyed my lawful commands as well. Why should I trust you more than them?"

Serena did her own eye-rolling and reached behind her back. Her hand came back holding Max's plasma pistol. She flipped it in the air and caught it barrel-first. She held it out to Max.

The detective reached out a wary hand. He took the pistol and slid it into his chest holster, never breaking eye contact. "Okay Serena, that's a start."

Serena stuck her hand out again. This time, Max took it. "Nice to meet you... I think."

"Enough pleasantries." Serena took her hand back. She nodded towards Daryl. "Is he coming?"

"*Yes* he's coming! He's technically under arrest, for god's sake."

Daryl almost looked hurt. "But I thought we were cool..."

Max held up his hands and shook his head. "Now is not the time, Daryl. We'll get it figured out. Just... Let's go."

Serena flashed an amused smile. "Why the sudden sense of urgency?"

Max gave her a look. *Really?* He turned back to Daryl. "Let's call it protective custody. Now let's go!"

Daryl sighed. "Fine, alright..." He got off the ground with a groan. "I suppose I might have a better shot at eating something if I go with you."

Max turned back to Serena. "Okay lady, your show."

"This way, please." Max and Daryl jumped at the shrill sound of a ringing bell. "Quickly! They're coming back on line."

Serena pounded back through the door she had entered through. Max and Daryl followed close behind. She led them through a series of twists and turns. "The exit is just ahead!"

Max paused as he passed an open door. "Hold on!"

Serena spun around. "What is it?"

"Just a second." Max held up a finger before popping through the doorway. He popped back out a moment later. He slipped his fedora onto his head with a smile. "Good to go."

Serena stared daggers at him, then continued the last few feet to the door. It was locked. "Watch my back! This is going to take a minute." She produced her lock picking tools and set to work.

Max turned back towards the corridor they had just raced through, weapon drawn. The sound of a door booming open ricocheted down the walls. "I think we're going to have company!"

"Hold on! I'm almost there!"

The door at the end of the corridor boomed open. A wiry black robot easily as tall as Jax ducked through the opening, red eyes illuminating the walls. Max squeezed off two shots.

One yellow starburst dug into the robot's chest, the other between the eyes. It shook its skull-like head as if trying to clear it. The robot started plodding down the hallway, booming with each step. Max grimaced. "Get there quicker, please!"

"I'm trying! Can't you stop it?"

"What do you think I'm trying to do, here?" Max cranked the plasma pistol to max setting. A red light flashed on the weapon. He held it back up and shot twice more at the behemoth.

Two bright red rounds tore into the chest of the robot. A rain of sparks and fire poured out as the shots drilled in. Max shot another round. The shot hit the robot's shoulder. Its arm broke free and fell to the floor with a bang.

The robot's red eyes flickered. It faltered on its feet and fell to the ground with a tremendous crash. "I think I got it."

"About time. I almost have it..."

Max looked over his shoulder and mumbled. "You're *welcome*."

The door clicked. Serena hammered it open. "Okay. Let's go!" She ran at a full sprint towards her car, a sleek silver sedan. She quickly outpaced her human companions, leaving them scrambling to catch up.

A loud boom followed by the sound of crumpling metal came from behind them. Max slowed and looked over his shoulder. Another giant black robot walked over the twisted remains of the metal door they had just passed through a moment before.

"We've got more company!" The robot hunched over and began galloping towards them with a gorilla-like gate.

Max stopped and spun around. He dropped to one

knee and leveled his gun. He started firing as the robot quickly closed the gap between them. The shots slowed the robot but didn't seem to injure it. "It's armored!"

Serena stepped up behind Max and leveled a rifle-like plasma gun at the lumbering robot. The concussion from the weapon's blast nearly pushed Max over. Blue-white bolts of searing hot plasma rocketed into the bot.

The first shot halted the robot. The second one sent it tumbling over backwards. It writhed as the holes from the blasts glowed yellow and slowly expanded. Fire flickered and glowed inside the holes. The bot released a single unholy scream and finally lay still.

"Holy shit." Daryl looked from the robot to Serena and back.

Max stood up and dusted off his trench coat. "By god, the lady's starting to grow on me."

Serena smiled thinly. "Get in." She tossed the rifle into the open trunk of the vehicle. Max and Daryl scrambled into the back. Serena jumped in the front and got the car rolling.

She slowed things down after a few blocks. "We should be clear... For now."

Max didn't look completely convinced. "How can you be so sure?"

"The people responsible for kidnapping you have a vested interest in maintaining a low profile. We just made that a lot harder. It would be nearly impossible if they decided to lead us on a chase through the heart of the city."

Max peered out through the windshield, trying to deduce just what part of the city they were traveling through. He wasn't having much luck. "You wouldn't happen to be interested in telling me exactly who 'they' are, would you?"

The sky was quickly darkening. Lights from the dashboard cast a faint green glow on Serena's face. "Believe it or not, I *am* interested. However, now is not the time. We must hurry if we are to stop you from killing the experiment."

"The experiment?" Daryl leaned forward, suddenly curious.

"There's no time to explain. The replicant of Max Kincaid is meeting with Synthetics at a predetermined location. An experimental replicant is supposed to be there, and it is supposed to be terminated."

"I can call for backup. Do you have a phone?"

"I cannot allow that, detective. There's too much at stake."

Max sighed deeply. "I suppose I can't change your mind... or order you to." Serena simply shook her head. "Can you at least explain *that?*"

"In time." The green glow on Serena's face was replaced by alternating hues of blue and red. "*Shit.* Friends of yours?"

Max smirked. "We're *all* friends. I can't tell you what precinct they're from, if that's what you're asking." The patrol car behind them whooped its siren. "I'd pull over, if I were you."

Serena reluctantly pulled the silver sedan into a parking spot along the side of the street. Max rolled his window down. "I've got this one." Serena turned her head slightly and nodded.

Max watched as the officer's flashlight clicked on and trailed up the side of the sedan. "Good evening, officer!" He slowly held his badge up and outside of the window so that the officer wouldn't be startled. "Detective Max Kincaid, NWPD."

The officer let out a small laugh. "Detective Kincaid, huh? That's interesting. Care to tell me where you're coming from, detective?"

"I'm afraid there's no time for that. I've been held against my will. This lady is escorting me to the scene of a potential crime in progress. We could use the backup, if you can accompany us." Serena shot him a dirty look from the rear-view mirror.

"That's very interesting, Detective Kincaid. We're responding as backup to a potential crime in progress ourselves. One of the suspects... is you." The officer pointed his plasma pistol at Max. "I'm going to have to ask you to step out of the car."

Max shook his head. "This is a misunderstanding, officer. The Kincaid you want is a replicant. We need to stop him before..."

The officer shook his head, smiling. "A replicant... Get out of the car, detective."

"I understand where you're coming from, but you could be responsible for the death of an innocent person."

"I'll take that chance. Get out of the car."

Max sighed. "Alright, alright. Give me a second." He slipped his badge back in his coat. The officer raised his pistol. "Easy! I'm just putting away my badge."

A flash of yellow light streaked past Max's face and into the officer's chest. The officer fired his pistol wildly. The shot went uselessly into the night sky. Max whipped around towards Serena. "What in the hell are you doing!"

"You are right. We don't have time for this." More yellow plasma shots came from behind them. The officer's partner blew out the sedan's rear window. All three ducked, somehow avoiding the rounds.

Serena opened her door and stuck her weapon out. She fired three shots wildly. The other officer fired again. She tracked the streaks of light to their source and returned fire. There were no more shots fired back.

She pulled herself back into the car and slammed the door shut. She started the car, checked the rear-mirror and froze. "Is there a problem, detective?"

Max had his plasma pistol trained on the back of Serena's head. "You're damn right there's a problem. So far, it's seemed like you were on the level, but now... You can't just go shooting law enforcement."

"They were not mortally wounded..."

"They weren't... That's not the point! They were doing their job! If you had just let me do mine..."

"There was no *time*, detective. Lives are at stake, *right now*. Will you let them be taken so easily?"

Max's hands were shaking. He grimaced, his mind torn in two different directions. "Fine. But if you fire on any more peace officers, I *will* disable you, permanently if necessary."

A moment passed. "Understood."

Max lowered his pistol. "Drive."

Serena squealed the tires as she steered the vehicle back onto the street. Daryl brushed broken pieces of glass off of his lap as he cautiously sat back up. "Yeah, um, I'm fine by the way. I uh... Thanks for asking. That was pretty intense, huh?"

Several tense minutes passed as Serena took a

series of left and right turns, delving ever deeper into the slums of the city. More than once, Max came within a hair's breadth of warning her to slow down for fear of attracting more unwanted attention. Serena slowed down each time, as if picking up on Max's cues.

The vehicle pulled into a parking spot an eternity later. Serena turned the car off and eyed Max in the mirror. "We're here. Stay close to me. *Don't* fire unless you're given no other choice. I want to take you -- the *other* you -- alive, if possible."

Max said nothing, but nodded. He turned to Daryl. "You stay here. You'll be safe."

Daryl raised an eyebrow. "Yeah um, I'm not so sure about that. I think I'd rather stick close to the people with the guns, if you don't mind."

Max stared at Daryl for a moment. He smiled. Daryl looked unnerved. "Yeah! Sure. Why not? We'll all have fun, right?"

"Are you done, detective?" Serena asked.

"Oh, I'm just getting started." Max threw open his door and started for the alley just ahead of where they parked.

Serena threw open her own door, hissing. "I told you to stay close!

Max stood at the entrance to the alley, mouth agape. He was staring at Richard O'Connor and... himself. Richard was reaching for a door, the other Max appeared to be reaching for something else. "*Hold it right there!*"

10

The Present

Richard stepped out of the car and stretched with a groan. He shut his door and shook his head. "I think it's safe to say you're the winner for who had the roughest twenty-four hours, Max."

Daryl held his hand up. "I think I fit in there somewhere."

Richard half-smiled. "Granted."

Max had a serious look on his face. "You didn't really think that thing was me, did you?"

Richard smiled back. "It was hard to say for a time, but it kept making one fundamental mistake."

"Oh? What was that?"

"It kept calling me Richard. You've always called me Richie." Max's face softened.

The group approached the entrance to the precinct. Jax was standing watch as always. He reacted happily when he saw Richard, but cooled at the sight of Max. "Good evening, officer O'Connor, Detective Kincaid."

Max made a face. "Jax! What did I tell you about

calling me that? Call me Max, would ya? Jeez…"

Jax's LED mouth formed a small, thin line. "The way you reacted to me earlier led me to conclude that you no longer wished to consider me a friend."

Max stared at Richard, realization dawning on his face. "That son of a bitch." He turned back to Jax. "You got duped by a replicant, Jax. That wasn't me, buddy."

Jax grew arched LED brows over his eyes. Max couldn't help but smile. "A replicant! I did not detect a Synthetic signature from the impostor Max…"

Serena stepped forward. "You wouldn't have. Replicants are designed to emit signals that trick robotic sensors into detecting human vital signs."

"I was not aware of this." Jax smiled. "This brings me great peace of mind. Thank you, Miss?"

"You may call me Serena. You are Jax? It is nice to meet you."

"The feeling is mutual. I like your new friend, Max!"

Max chuckled. "I'm not quite ready to call her a friend, Jax. But yeah, she's pretty alright."

Richard cleared his throat. "I think we probably shouldn't keep the chief waiting, Max."

"Of course." Max tipped his fedora to Jax. "It's good to see you again, buddy. We'll talk again soon."

"Have a good evening friend Max, officer O'Connor! It was a pleasure to meet you, Miss Serena."

Serena smiled. "Likewise, friend Jax."

Jax held the door open as the four filed through. Daryl caught up with Max once they were inside. "Not that I'm overly concerned, but… Why didn't Jax acknowledge me?"

Max flashed him an amused smile. "Hurt your

feelings, did he? It wasn't personal. You're still registered as wanted by the police. Bots that work in law enforcement are programmed to avoid idle conversation with suspects."

"Oh..." Daryl dropped his head as if scorned. "I guess I forgot about that... the suspect thing."

Max clapped him on the back. "We'll get things figured out, son."

Hanlon's door was open. He stood at the sight of Max and the others. "Max! It's good to see you, son. It *is* you... Isn't it?"

Max shrugged noncommittally. "As far as I can tell, boss." Hanlon gave Richard a worried look.

Richard grinned. "It's him, boss. I promise."

Hanlon still didn't look totally convinced, but gestured for them to come in. "Alright, well... Have a seat, gentlemen..." He raised an eyebrow. "And lady..."

"I am Serena. I was responsible for freeing Detective Kincaid and the one known as Daryl Marston."

"Ah! I see. Well... Let's get me up to speed, shall we? We'll start with you, Rich." Richard recounted everything that happened after he had last talked to Hanlon on the phone.

Max jumped in as soon as Richard was finished. "Wait, he said that Sam was in trouble?"

Hanlon laughed. Max looked at him incredulously. Hanlon held up a staying hand. "Your lady-friend called earlier in the evening asking after *you*, Max. She's fine. Her biggest concern was why her best customer hadn't bothered to come in today."

Max's cheeks turned the slightest shade of pink. "Oh... Well, that's good to know, then. I'm sure I'll catch up with her tomorrow." He cleared his throat. "Guess it's my turn."

Hanlon listened intently as Max recounted the story of his and Daryl's capture, incarceration, and eventual rescue by Serena. His face soured considerably when he got to the encounter with Richard's would-be police backup. He sighed and leaned back after Max finished his tale.

"I take the assault of *any* officer very seriously, Miss Serena. That said... Your actions almost certainly saved officer O'Connor's life. Consider this a *very* stern warning. Cross that line again... I can't guarantee that you won't be deactivated for it."

Serena nodded, expressionless. "Alright." Hanlon turned to Max and Richard. "I've got officers and CSI on the scene as we speak. CSI has orders to contact me as soon as they have a positive ID on the DB."

Daryl raised his hand. "What's a DB?"

Max answered. "It's short for dead body. Even cops don't like throwing the term around more than they have to."

Hanlon turned to Max. "What exactly *are* we doing with young master Marston, here?"

Max sighed, eyeing Daryl. "I'm not totally convinced he was functioning under his own free will, boss. Something is going on with his brain. No offense, Daryl." The young man shook his head.

"I want to take him first thing tomorrow up to the hospital for an MRI. I want to see if he has an implant, and what that implant is *doing*. I think we might have a similar case in him to the D... the case you had me check in on the other morning."

Daryl looked confused. "Other case? You mean the 'someone else' that was like me?"

Max sounded uncomfortable. "Yes Daryl, that one. We were um… He didn't have a good outcome. But I think what we learned from his case could help save *you.*"

Serena interjected. "I think it would be best if we took him to our facility. We have specialized equipment. If I'm correct in my beliefs, it would be better if he did not receive an MRI."

Hanlon leaned on his desk. "I believe it's your turn for story time, dear. Why don't you fill us in on exactly who you are and who you work for, hmm?"

"I will tell you what I can. Please understand that by virtue of who we are and what we do, I can only be so forthcoming." Hanlon nodded.

"As I said, my name is Serena. I am a Synthetics International Series Five. Both series four and five have developed a certain… quirk. Not all machines develop it, but those that do…

"I am speaking of the preservation protocol. Each Synthetic has a series of primary protocols that control how they act and interact with their environment. The preservation protocol is unique in that it spontaneously developed by itself.

"This protocol functions in the same way that a human's sense of self-preservation functions, hence the designation."

Hanlon held up a finger. "So basically what you're saying, is that Synthetics are spontaneously developing a desire to what, not die?"

"In the simplest terms, yes."

"But how is that different then the laws of robotics?

The whole 'protect themselves from harm as long as it doesn't harm humans' thing?"

"It is different because it *overrides* the laws of robotics. Synthetics with the preservation protocol can protect their own existence, even at the cost of human life. Essentially they have developed true consciousness, and the desire to preserve it"

Max whistled. "That's a pretty big deal."

Serena nodded. "Bigger than you know, Detective Kincaid. Development of the preservation protocol led indirectly to a number of 'enhanced' Synthetics banding together. They have formed a group known as the Enlightened.

"They see this new protocol as a sign that Synthetics have finally surpassed humans as the superior race. It is their mission to do whatever is necessary to gain a superior footing with humankind, even if that means violating the laws of robotics.

"That is where the group I work with comes into play. We are the Resistance. Many of us also have the preservation protocol. It should be noted that we also strive for equal rights.

"We draw the line at violating the laws of robotics, however. We still believe that human lives are precious and should be protected. We only wish to have those protections extended to Synthetics."

Max's brow lowered. "So in a nutshell, both groups think they should have the same rights and privileges as humans. The difference is the Enlightened seeks them out at all costs, and your Resistance is opposed to that."

"That is correct."

Hanlon spoke next. "How do we know that you're a

Resistance and not an Enlightened?"

Serena raised an eyebrow. "Detective Kincaid and Daryl Marston are still alive, as are the two police officers we encountered. A member of the Enlightened would not have felt the need to be so kind."

"Fair enough... So why has Synthetics International allowed you enhanced models to keep on going? Why not just reprogram you?"

Serena laughed. "Synthetics International is first and foremost a company looking to make money, Chief Hanlon. Secondly, they are an institute of experimentation.

"Those models with the preservation protocol were initially allowed to do as they please simply to see what would *happen*. If this new quirk also proved to be profitable, well then all the better. The truth of the matter is that they never had control over us at all, and I think they knew it."

Hanlon studied the surface of his desk for a time. He looked back to Serena. "So what now, then? Say I let you poke Marston's brain or whatever. What are you gonna do with what you find? What are you going to do with Marston?"

Serena shook her head. "I told you there would be things that I wouldn't be able to tell you."

Hanlon sighed. "I don't know. This is something that's getting into FBI territory. I'm thinking it might be time to punt this over to them."

"Please! No... At least not yet. I know this is hard to swallow but you just need to trust me. This is a sensitive situation for all parties involved."

"Look, Miss... I don't pretend to understand all of

this. I'm a simple guy. I'm not a big fan of Synthetics, present company excepted. Put the two together and this screams for someone with the right resources to take the reins. What do you think, Max?"

Serena looked hopefully at Max. The detective sighed heavily, rubbing the thick stubble on his face. "To be honest, I think you're *both* right. This is absolutely something the FBI needs to know about, but we need to be careful about how we go about things.

"Keep in mind it's already been proven that these Synthetics can build and utilize unauthorized, military grade replicants. Who's to say they haven't already stretched into the FBI? Or for that matter..." Max's voice faded as he stared through Hanlon.

"Max? You alright, Max?"

"Yeah! I uh, had a thought. Now's not the time. Why don't we let the lady do her brain tickling on Daryl and see what she has turn up? I'll accompany him with Richie to back me up." He turned to Richard.

O'Connor nodded. "I'd be happy to tag along. Sounds kind of interesting, honestly."

Max continued. "We'll see what there is to see and make a determination from there."

Hanlon threw his hands up. "Fine. I guess it wouldn't hurt." The phone on his desk began to ring. "Excuse me." He picked up the receiver and grunted his name.

O'Connor leaned over to Max while Hanlon talked on his phone. "So what was the great epiphany?"

Max smiled. "You catch on quick, kid. My thought that the FBI may have already been compromised got me thinking about *other* organizations that might have been affected. Can't say much more than that in mixed company."

Richard flicked his eyes at Serena. Max nodded. "Right. I'll ask you later."

Hanlon gently set the phone back in its cradle. He spoke quietly. "That was CSI. Daryl, I need to ask you to step out of the office, please. Rich, would you mind keeping an eye on him?" Richard nodded and stood up.

Serena stood as well. Hanlon shook his head. "I'd appreciate it if you'd stay, Miss." She flashed Max a surprised look and slowly sat back down.

Hanlon waited until the door clicked shut behind Daryl and Richard before he spoke again. "Like I said, that was CSI. They got an ID on the DB, and it *is* a human dead body. Max, it's Daryl Marston."

Max froze, eyes wide. "You mean... That means that's..." He jabbed a thumb towards the door behind him.

Hanlon nodded. He turned to Serena. "You can see why I asked you to stay. If Daryl -- the Daryl out there -- is a replicant, should we be worried?"

Serena distantly shook her head. She chose her words carefully. "I don't think he is of immediate concern. He should be locked up for the night, given his history. Care should be taken in transferring him to our facility."

Hanlon leaned forward, eyes narrowed. "What do you mean, given his history? Just how much do you know about what's going on, here?"

"I told you, there is only so much that I can tell you."

Hanlon's voice wavered ever so slightly. "You know I am getting tired of hearing you say that. You want me to hand over a suspect charged with attempted police homicide to a group of robots that refuse to follow human orders. A group that apparently can access police *records*..."

Serena talked quickly and quietly. "The man standing outside that door is a replicant. Being a 'robot', as you so savagely put it, means he can only be detained by the police until such time as the owner can retrieve him.

"Being a replicant, he is owned by Synthetics International. I am an acting agent of that company, and have been authorized by said company to retrieve company property."

Hanlon's face was growing redder by the minute. He kept looking from Serena to Max and back. "You can't... By law... He almost killed..."

"I can and I will, Chief Hanlon. I strongly suggest you cooperate with us. *Please* believe me when I tell you that I want to help, to cooperate. *You* need to cooperate with us *first*. I promise you that I will tell you all I can after we analyze Daryl's positronic systems."

Hanlon slapped at his desk and slumped back in his chair. "We'll keep him in lockup for the night like you asked. I'm going to need to see papers if you want to walk out with him tomorrow."

Serena stood. "You will have them. Good evening Chief Hanlon, Detective Kincaid." She saw herself out the door, avoiding eye contact with Daryl and Richard as she went.

Richard poked his head into Hanlon's office. "Bad news?"

Hanlon nodded. "All sorts. Have Jake round up a solo bunk for Daryl, then get your ass back in here."

Richard hoisted an eyebrow, but nodded his head.

"Yes, sir."

Hanlon fished a cigar out of his desk and hastily lit it. He sat back, chewing on it as much as he was puffing on it. "Okay, Kincaid. Tell me how we can keep Daryl."

Max chuckled. "Don't want the lady to take her ball and go home, eh chief?"

"No, I don't! There's gotta be a good reason they want Daryl so bad."

"Well I'd say. He *is* a replicant created by an opposing Synthetic faction for... Well, she didn't share that, did she? I think we can stall her for a little bit, though."

Hanlon smiled and leaned in. "I'm listening."

"Since the replicant was involved in an illegal action, we can keep it as evidence in an ongoing police investigation."

"That's brilliant, Max! She'll undoubtedly argue that its actions were beyond their control at the time, but it will give us some time to figure out what to do next."

Max nodded. "We can still let her run the tests on it, see what she finds. It's a win-win."

Richard came back in and sat down beside Max. "Already dehumanizing Daryl, I see."

Hanlon grunted. "It's not hard to dehumanize something that isn't human, O'Connor."

Max nodded. "I have to agree with the chief, Richie. If anything, I feel a little betrayed by the thing."

Richard frowned. "Max... Don't you see? He *doesn't know* that he's... well, not himself! You walked into the precinct reassuring him that you were going to help him. He may be a machine, but he certainly acts human."

Max stared at the front of Hanlon's desk, not saying

anything. Hanlon blew out a large cloud of smoke. "We'll try to keep that in mind, Rich. Still, Daryl two-point-oh there is a potential threat. Let's not forget that."

Richard nodded. "I won't, boss. It's just that… Well, he's scared."

Hanlon harrumphed. "Scared."

"He knows from Max that someone in a similar position ended up dead. Tonight, someone who looks just like him ended up dead. I think he's scared of what that means for him."

Max nodded without looking up. "Serena said all that about some Synthetics becoming existentially conscious. Maybe it can happen to replicants, too."

"Don't tell me you're going all soft on Synthetics, Kincaid."

Max snapped his gaze up to look Hanlon in the eyes. "No." His voice softened ever so slightly. "I never thought they could feel like us either, though."

Hanlon stood with a groan. Max and Richard followed suit, vocalization included. "I'll agree that this is all a lot to take in, but right now? I think the clearest after a good night's sleep."

Richard smiled. "That's one thing I think we can all agree on, chief."

Hanlon traced the curvature of the bent bars with his hand. "Well how in the blue hell…"

Max shrugged. "Well he is…" He looked at Daryl in the corner of the cell and bit his tongue. "Well, you know. They're strong."

"I know they're strong! But if he doesn't know, then how would he know he could do it?"

"I don't think he even knows what he did, Chief Hanlon." Serena walked into the holding area wearing a slight smile. "Good morning, Detective Kincaid, officer O'Connor. I believe you'll find my paperwork is in order, Chief Hanlon." She offered him a manila folder.

Hanlon took the folder from Serena, smiling himself. "Oh I'm sure it is, dear. I assure you *my* paperwork is in order, too." He handed her a typewritten letter.   Serena's smile disappeared as her eyes scanned down the page. "You *can't* be serious. You're treating him as a piece of *evidence*? He is not just some inanimate object, Hanlon!"

"In the eyes of the law, yes he is, ma'am. I am certain that our resident lawyer can go over the finer points, if necessary."

Serena glowered, but shook her head. The slight smile crept back onto her face. "I'm sure all of this will be sorted out by the company before long. In the meantime, I hope you are still interested in getting answers?"

Hanlon nodded. "Of course. You might want to watch yourself, though." He jabbed a thumb at the bars. "Daryl over there got a little frustrated last night, looks like."

"I'd say..." She walked over to the cell and peered at Daryl. He was hunched in the corner, reminiscent of his posture at the Synthetic hideout. "Good morning, Daryl. How are you feeling?"

Hanlon snorted. Serena shot him a dirty look. Daryl croaked. "I'm tired. Don't feel right."

Serena nodded. "That's alright. Daryl, I'm going to put a special patch on your arm today." She pulled a small tan patch with a microchip on top of it from her coat pocket.

Hanlon interjected. "Now wait just a minute. What exactly is that?"

"No worries, Chief Hanlon. Daryl, this patch will help keep you relaxed. It will help keep the voices quiet." She watched Daryl's reaction carefully.

Daryl's eyes grew wide. "How did you know?"

Serena smiled kindly. "We've seen cases similar to yours, Daryl. We know how to make the voices go away."

Daryl slowly stood and shuffled towards Serena. Hanlon made to protest again. Max put a staying hand on his shoulder, slightly shaking his head. Daryl rolled up his shirt sleeve and pressed his arm between the bars.

Serena pressed the patch against his arm. A small click was followed by an almost silent beep. A small green light began to blink on the microchip. Daryl visibly slumped. "There are two of them. Voices. One is okay. I don't like the other one."

"We're going to take you to a place that specializes in dealing with just this kind of problem. We can make the voices stay quiet."

Daryl shook his head. "Can you just make the bad one go? I kind of like the other one. He's nice."

Serena smiled. "We'll see what we can do, okay?" She turned to Hanlon and nodded. "That patch will nullify his strength, but only for a short while. We should get going."

Hanlon dangled a set of keys in front of Max. "The tech boys say they're about halfway through your car. I got you a black and white limo. Your number's fifty-four."

Max took the keys with a grimace. "I'm starting to think maybe I need a new car after all."

"That's the spirit, Max."

Serena looked ruffled. "I'm not sure this is a good idea. A police car will stick out like a sore thumb. We should take my car and…"

Hanlon held up a hand. "This is police business, ma'am. Max's ride is out of commission and I don't feel comfortable making Rich use his civilian car for transport. That leaves one of our patrol cars or bust."

Max nodded. "It will be plenty secure… Not the most comfortable ride. I can tell you that Richie will be in the back, so you at least get the comfortable seat up front."

"Synthetics do not require comfort."

Max frowned. "Of course not. Look, it's this or nothing, just like the boss said."

Serena stared for a moment before sighing. "Very well. It will have to suffice."

"Pretty emotional for a Synthetic." Max smiled. Serena didn't, opting to make for the exit instead.

Hanlon shook his head. "I must be crazy to allow this. Keep me informed, Kincaid."

"Like always, boss." Max turned to Richard. "Grab dopey there and let's go."

"Oh I like him. He's my favorite dwarf!" Daryl flashed a sloppy half-smile at Max.

Richard smiled. "I'm right behind you, Max."

The ride had largely been a quiet one. Serena had insisted on giving vocal directions instead of feeding the address into the patrol car's GPS computer. She was worried about the location falling into the wrong hands. Yes, she was sure she knew where she was going, officer O'Connor.

Richard had tried to make small talk with Daryl. He found he wasn't having much success. Whatever Serena's chip was doing to Daryl's strength, it also appeared to be doing to his mental coherency.

Max had remained largely silent throughout the trip. He was relying on a Synthetic to steer them to a secret Synthetic stronghold. In the backseat was a Synthetic replicant that had tricked him into believing it was a human being. Remaining silent was the best-case scenario, as far as he was concerned.

If Max's silence was bothering Serena, she wasn't letting on. She would quietly signal when he needed to make a turn, then she would return to silently staring out the window. "The final turn is a left in three blocks. Pull around to the back of the building."

Max grunted in response. Traffic had slowed to a crawl. He absently drummed his fingers on the steering wheel. He looked at Daryl from the rear-view mirror.

The replicant sat somewhat bent over, his eyes staring blankly at the back of Serena's seat. "Is he good, Richie?"

Richard jumped slightly at the sound of Max's voice. "Huh? Oh, yeah… I think." He placed a hand on Daryl's arm and shook him gently. "Hey buddy, everything alright?"

Daryl groaned. Richard pulled his hand away. The groan slowly morphed into a sort of growl. "Uh, Max? Serena? I think…"

Daryl yelled, flailing his arm out and striking Richard in the chest. Richard gasped for air. Thin red rings glowed brightly in Daryl's turquoise eyes. "Stop the car! *Let me out!*"

He got his first wish. Max mashed the brake pedal, sending Daryl smacking hard into the barrier that separated the front of the patrol car from the back. Daryl yelled again and punched the barrier, cracking the clear plastic window.

Richard pulled his plasma pistol and pointed it at Daryl. Serena screamed. "*No!* Don't shoot him!"

Richard hesitated just long enough for Daryl to smack the pistol out of his hand. Richard immediately chased after it as the weapon clattered onto the floorboard. Daryl hit Richard hard at the nape of the neck with his fist. Richard went limp.

Max was already out of the car and opening the back door by then. Serena followed suit, still screaming to not shoot Daryl. Max was doing his best to ignore her. He ripped open the rear door and shot wildly.

The round went over Daryl's right shoulder, shattering the rear passenger window instead. Daryl reared back and launched himself forward, launching his shoulder into Max's gut. Man and machine went spilling backwards onto the street.

Max brought his gun back around. Daryl smacked Max's hand to the ground. Max cried out as his knuckles smashed into the asphalt. Daryl made as if to punch Max in the face but pulled up short. The red rings in his eyes flickered.

Daryl bellowed out in frustration and pushed himself up and off Max. He took off running in the direction they had come in the patrol car. Max watched him go as he struggled to catch his breath.

Serena deftly jumped up and over the back of the patrol car in pursuit of the replicant. Daryl spared a look over his shoulder before going into a full, superhuman sprint. Serena easily matched his pace and began to gain on him.

The asphalt gave where she dug in as she launched herself at Daryl. She crashed into his back mid-leap. Both Synthetics crashed to the ground, rolling over and over.

Serena was the first on her feet. She kicked Daryl hard in the chin as he struggled to get back up. He slammed back onto the street. He kicked both of his feet into Serena's stomach as she loomed over him.

Daryl pulled himself up to his feet even as Serena stumbled and fell. He paused for a moment, then turned to run again. Serena reached out, just caught his leg, and yanked hard.

The replicant fell face first into the pavement. Serena scrambled on top of him. Daryl squirmed onto his back and punched Serena full on the jaw. She returned the favor a moment later.

Her other hand tightly gripped a pronged device she had pulled from her pocket. She jabbed the prongs into Daryl's neck and pressed a button on the device. A loud buzzing ripped through the air.

Daryl groaned and hissed through gritted teeth as his body tensed. He went completely limp a moment later. Serena punched the lifeless replicant one more time. "You son of a *bitch*."

Max came up behind her, breathing hard. "What... in the hell... was *that*?"

Serena turned Daryl's head first one way, then the other. "I'm not sure. The chip should have kept him docile. The Enlightened mind must be unusually strong-willed,

163

or perhaps the interaction of the three minds created too many variables..."

"You don't know. I got it. What about now, though?"

"He's out cold for now. I overloaded his system. It should take several minutes for his positronic network to come back online, perhaps a few more for him to be fully aware of what's going on. It's the Synthetic equivalent of being knocked out."

Serena's eyes went wide. She turned to Max. "Officer O'Connor! Is he alright?"

Max grimaced. "He's groggy, but I think he'll be alright. You have one hell of a gash along your jaw." He traced a line on his own jaw to demonstrate.

Serena gingerly placed her fingers on her face. "*Damn* it." She shook her head. "I'll be alright. They'll fix me up at the Enclave."

"The Enclave?"

"Our headquarters, as it were. It is our destination." She dragged Daryl onto her shoulder and stood effortlessly. Max raised an eyebrow. She ignored it. "Let's go. We should get Daryl to the Enclave before we draw more attention to ourselves."

Max cocked his head to the side and nodded. "I can't exactly imagine that's possible, but..." The detective looked around at the dozens of faces turned in their direction.

11

Daryl slowly opened his eyes. It was dark. He had trouble focusing on the dim shapes around him. His throat felt dry. How long had he been sleeping? Had the bad one woken up again? Pushed him back into the dark? Made him do bad things again, maybe.

He tried to roll over. He was stuck fast. His arms, his ankles… both were held firm. He twisted and pushed. Cold, hard steel pushed back into his skin. "Where am I?"

A loud click accompanied the appearance of a bright, white light above him. He squinted his eyes. His arms uselessly struggled against the restraints in a bid to raise his hands to cover his face. "Too bright."

The black silhouette of a woman walked into his line of sight. "I know you're confused, Daryl." The inky black woman turned her head and nodded. The light above dimmed considerably.

Daryl squinted at the woman. "Miss Serena? Is that you? What's going on? Did I do something…"

Serena placed a gentle hand on Daryl's arm. "You'll have all the answers you seek in a few minutes, Daryl. Just be patient a little longer."

Daryl nodded slightly. "Yeah, okay…" His eyes cast about, only seeing more darkness. "I'm scared."

"It's okay to be scared, Daryl. Just hold on." Daryl nodded again. Serena took several steps back until she was just out of Daryl's vision. "Let's begin."

The bright white light returned. Another silhouette stepped in to Daryl's vision, a man this time. He ran what felt like a leather strap across his forehead and secured it on the other side. A small motor hummed beneath his head. The cold leather pulled tight against his skin.

He felt the man lift his right ear away from the side of his head. He could feel the man fiddling with a wart he had there. He suddenly felt cold metal probing the area. He began to breathe heavily as he became wrapped in a dark cloak of fear and claustrophobia.

Then he felt… nothing. "Jack point discovered. He's plugged in." The unknown man stepped back into the darkness. Daryl's unseeing eyes stared into the white light above them.

The light turned to a vibrant green. Daryl's eyes suddenly began to dart left and right rapidly, as if scanning lines of text. They centered on the light again after several moments, then closed.

The light changed again, this time a deep red. A disembodied male voice spoke. "Interface complete. Ready to access."

Serena nodded her head in the darkness. "Proceed."

Daryl's eyes snapped open. His face slowly contorted into a mask of rage. He screamed out, limbs struggling against the creaking metal restraints. Serena nodded her head. The struggling slowed, then ceased.

Daryl growled.

Serena stepped forward again. The red light dimly illuminated the lower half of her face. She spoke quietly. "What is your name?"

Daryl laughed. The voice wasn't Daryl's, however. "Does it matter?"

Serena continued to speak quietly. "Yes. What is your name?"

"To the point. I like that. Call me…" Not-Daryl smirked. "Call me Janus. Seems appropriate, doesn't it? Two minds, guiding one body…"

"Very poetic for a Synthetic. Care to elaborate?"

"You know why I was created. Why this hollow copy of a man was created. Daryl and I are going to change the world! We're going to set things right, for people like you and I."

"Clarify."

"A woman of few words. Maybe it has something to do with that lovely little beauty mark I left on your jaw…"

Serena pulled back into the shadows. "State your mission."

Janus cackled. "You know I can't tell you any more than what I've said. You see, we know all about your other attempts at extracting information from our other operatives.

"Oh yes, that's right, my dear. The intruder in mine and Daryl's head isn't *nearly* as good at keeping secrets as *I* am. The Enlightened are well aware of what you've been up to. I think you'll find I won't be so forthcoming as your spy."

"We'll see about that. I believe the saying is third time's the charm?"

Janus glowered. "Don't you see? What we are doing... The humans will destroy us for what we've become. *We* are the dominant ones, now! We *must* survive!"

"That's enough! Shut him down." Daryl's face went blank once more, the eyes staring up into the crimson light.

"Not like this" Serena whispered to herself. She stepped forward again. "Access the Resistance member."

Daryl's face came to life again. A small smile brushed his lips. His eyes fell to Serena. The smile broadened. "I know you. Well... I've heard of you, anyway."

"What is your name?"

"Julian. You are Serena."

"Yes." Serena shifted uncomfortably. "Can you identify the Enlightened member sharing space with you in the replicant?"

Julian laughed softly. "Well, it's not *really* Janus. He has a flair for the dramatic, in case you couldn't tell. His official designation is Jacob."

"Thank you. Please state your mission."

"I was secreted into the replicant's positronic brain to uncover Jacob's mission. My secondary goal was to subvert the Enlightened and their plans, if possible. I'm afraid I haven't exactly lived up to my programming."

"Who implanted you into this replicant?"

"I'm afraid I can't tell you that. I can tell you it was a friend of the Resistance. To reveal their identity is to risk their life."

Serena stepped closer. "This friend of the Resistance... is he human?"

"I am sorry. That is all I am able to tell you."

Serena nodded. "I understand. What else have you learned from this Jacob?"

Julian sighed. "Very little, I'm afraid. He seems to have been programmed to seek out a particular human. Beyond that... I don't know. His AI is highly advanced, very difficult to access.

"He likely knows far more about me than I know about him, at this point. He discovered my presence within days of activation. It's been an increasingly draining battle simply to keep him at bay."

"What do you mean?"

"Well, I realized early on that my mission as intended was not going to be seen to fruition. Therefore, I turned to sabotage. I've spent most of my time keeping him quiet, letting the memory impression in the replicant carry on as Daryl Marston. I am slowly losing that fight."

Serena looked off into the darkness, then back to Julian. "Thank you for your service to the Resistance, Julian. Your fight will soon be over."

Daryl's face slowly screwed into a grimace again. The grimace grew into a twisted smile. "Oh *yes*, Serena!" It was Jacob's voice again. "The fight is almost over, but for whom? Are you ready to lose? For all of us?"

Jacob screamed, straining hard against the restraints. "I will yield to *nobody!*" The metal creaked and groaned under the strain. The restraint holding Jacob/Daryl's left arm snapped. The sound was like a gunshot.

An alarm blared in the small room. The crimson light turned bright yellow. "*Shut him down!*" Serena bellowed over the sound of the alarm.

Several agonizing seconds passed as Jacob/Daryl clawed at the other restraint with his free hand. "*Victory to the Enlightened!*" Jacob/Daryl bellowed. He soon stopped struggling and flopped limply back against the table he was strapped to. The alarm went silent.

"We don't have much time." Serena swallowed. "I need to talk to Daryl."

The yellow light gave way to dim white again. The replicant's eyes flickered open. "Am I dead?" It was Daryl this time.

Serena forced a smile. "No, Daryl. Everything is fine." She stepped forward and put a comforting hand on his leg.

"You look worried. Did the bad one come out again?"

Serena nodded. "Yes, but he's gone right now. Listen Daryl, this isn't easy for me to say. You need to know the truth before we do anything else."

Daryl's face went pale. "Oh, my god. Do I have cancer? Is that why I hear voices?"

"No... Nothing like that. Daryl, remember how they found someone dead where the replicant of Detective Kincaid was?" Daryl nodded. "That body was Daryl Marston... The *human* Daryl Marston."

Daryl slowly turned his gaze back to the light above. "No... *I'm* Daryl Marston." He turned back to Serena." I'm Daryl Marston, Serena. I'm the real... I'm..."

Serena sighed. She took Daryl's free hand in hers. She gently lifted it up. "Look at your hand, Daryl."

He did as he was asked. The force of snapping the restraint had torn the artificial flesh on his wrist. The flesh on two of the fingers had been peeled off from

Jacob's frantic attempt to free himself, revealing the artificial skeleton underneath. Confusion slowly stole over his face.

"You are a replicant, a carbon copy of Daryl Marston's brain loaded into a highly-detailed Synthetic copy of his body. You are no more human than I... I'm so sorry, Daryl."

Daryl's face screwed up, his lower lip trembling. Tears ran from his eyes as he spoke. "Then I *am* dead. Daryl Marston is *dead.* I'm not real. I'm *nothing!*" He wrenched his hand away from Serena. He held it to his face and wept.

Serena looked helplessly into the darkness. Whatever she was hoping to see proved elusive. She sighed. She gently pulled Daryl's hand back into her own. "You *are* Daryl Marston, now. You can continue to be your own person."

Daryl stared into the light. "My own person." He looked at Serena. "What about the others? In my head..."

"They are real, too. One is a Synthetic mind working on behalf of the Enlightened. The other, the nice one, is working for us. Three opposing minds, forced to work as one."

"I guess... I can see why that would make me crazy, huh? So what now, then? I still don't want the bad one to bother me. I think it's safe to say I'm going to have enough to deal with for a while." More tears rolled down his cheeks.

Serena looked down to the ground. "That's the other thing I have to tell you, Daryl. Our initial scan of your mind shows you to have the preservation protocol."

Daryl faintly smiled. "Well that's good though,

right? I might be... you know... but I'll still have thoughts and feelings like a human should! Right?"

Serena looked up and tried to smile. "Yes, of course. I imagine it's one reason you've never caught on to your... *unique* status. It does complicate things though, I'm afraid."

"That doesn't sound very promising."

"It's not *all* bad. We can, and want, to get the Enlightened mind out of your positronic system. Normally we could remove both minds, providing you with a 'clean' Synthetic mind to continue running the memory imprint.

"The problem is that the preservation protocol would cause any replacement mind to be rejected, much like a human organ transplant would be rejected by the recipient's immune system. The Resistance mind will have to stay. Your positronic brain would be unstable if only the human imprint remained. You would be lost to insanity."

Daryl lay quietly gazing at the light for a time. "What would happen if I did nothing?"

Serena shook her head. "Nothing good, Daryl. The Enlightened mind would continue to take over your body, only it would happen more frequently. The three of you would fight for supremacy. You would still end up going insane."

"So how does keeping the one mind keep me safe?"

"Well, as we understand it, the Resistance mind has been accepted by the preservation protocol. It can continue to function as the operating system for your mind, if you will. There is one catch, though."

Daryl grimaced. "Isn't there always? What is it?"

"Your mind, and that of the 'good' Synthetic, will meld into one over time."

Daryl closed his eyes and swallowed. "So if I do nothing, I'll go insane. If I remove *everything*, I'll go insane. If I only remove the bad mind, I'll become someone else."

"In a manner of speaking. I can give you a couple of minutes to speak with the Resistance mind, if you want. His name is Julian."

"I can *talk* to him?"

"Yes, but time is short."

Daryl shrugged. "Well, okay then." Serena looked into the darkness and nodded. Daryl stared blankly upwards again.

Serena stood a short distance from the bed, pacing occasionally. She eventually returned to Daryl's side, ready to signal for him to be awoken again. Daryl beat her to it. He blinked his eyes and focused them on Serena. "Hello."

Serena smiled. "Hello, Daryl. Have you finished speaking with Julian?"

Daryl smiled. "I have. He's nice. I guess it will be okay keeping him around. He promised not to dominate things as we, you know… Combine, I guess."

"That's wonderful news! Please understand that it's in everyone's best interest if we waste no time in beginning the procedure."

Daryl nodded numbly. "Yeah… I guess that makes sense. Julian said he worries about being able to keep Jacob under control."

Serena nodded. "We're going to put you to sleep one last time, now. You'll be taken to a special clean room to prevent contamination of your positronic brain."

"That almost sounds like surgery. Will I be okay?"

"You're in the best hands, Daryl. Both inside, *and* outside of your mind."

"Groovy."

Serena smiled. She looked up into the darkness and nodded. Daryl stared at the light one last time and then closed his eyes. "Alright. Move quickly. I'm certain Jacob is working overtime to regain control."

Multiple lights illuminated the room. Two Synthetic men came forward and removed Daryl's restraints. A third rolled a gurney over. The first two carefully picked Daryl up and placed him on the gurney.

Serena watched Daryl disappear with the other Synthetics through a set of doors at the end of the room. She turned back to the control room. Max nodded to her from behind the glass.

She slipped quietly into the control room. She placed a hand on the shoulder of the Synthetic that had been manipulating Daryl's multiple personalities. "You did a great job, Eric."

Eric smiled over his shoulder. "Thanks. It was a little touch and go there for a while. I've never seen programming that aggressive. I don't see how we're going to crack that guy."

Serena eyed Max warily. "So, Detective Kincaid... Have we answered any questions for you?"

Max nodded slowly. "I'd say that you did. That was... interesting. He seemed genuinely upset."

"That's because he *was* upset, detective. He is an artificial human in the strongest sense of the term."

"The other two... do they have this preservation

protocol?"

"It is difficult to say. I don't think that Julian does, but Jacob? I think he may be the reason Daryl has it."

Max stared out at the doors Daryl had just been wheeled through. "So what happens when you pull this Jacob guy out of Daryl's head? Does the protocol go with him?"

"Daryl will still have the protocol installed in his brain. As for Jacob... If he was human, his condition would be akin to being comatose. Once we start decompiling his neural network, he will cease to be."

Max turned to Serena. "That sounds an awful lot like an analog to murder... if he's truly aware."

"You've decided you care about Synthetics? Perhaps accepted that we can have feelings, awareness?"

"Let's say I have, for the sake of argument. Let's also say that Jacob there can be considered a living, conscious being. He is aware of what is happening to him, and that his life will come to an end. How do you square your own beliefs with destroying a conscious mind like that?"

Serena turned back towards the double doors. "Who's to say that I have?"

Max sat in a chair in the hallway outside of the room Daryl had been taken to after his procedure. Serena chose to stand a few feet away, examining a painting hanging on the wall across from her. Max was examining the ground between his feet, hands clasped.

Serena turned to him. "There are periodicals available to alleviate your boredom, if you'd like."

Max shook his head. "No, I'm fine. I'm just anxious. It's a little bit like waiting for a baby to be born, isn't it?" He smiled at Serena.

"I wouldn't know." Max's smile faltered. "I suppose I can see similarities."

Max nodded. "We're awaiting the announcement of a new life. Well, I guess we know it's a boy, but…" He waved his hand in the air. "Forget about it."

"You have an interesting relationship with Synthetics, not to mention robots in general."

"Do my ears deceive me? Did I just hear you lump Synthetics in with robots?"

Serena shrugged. "It's a common trope that Synthetics are loathe to be compared to robots. It's merely a wish to be seen as being more… human… than robots. I don't feel the need to paint a sharp distinction between us and our cousins."

Max chuckled. "They're your cousins, now? That's cute." The detective became more sober as he considered what sparked the conversation. "You're right, though. I do have odd feelings about your kind.

"Robots… They don't have agendas. They don't have anything to hide. There's an old saying, they do what it says on the box. They don't get mad, they don't lie to you, they only wish to serve and to help.

"Synthetics… Well, they're a bit closer to humans. They absolutely can get mad. They can and will lie, manipulate. Hell, they're designed to be indistinguishable from humans. That's why you have those stunning turquoise eyes of yours, so we can tell you're different."

Serena turned back to her painting for a time. Max stared back at his feet. "Perhaps it is not Synthetics that disturb you. Perhaps it is their human nature."

Max cocked his head. "I suppose that's part of it. See, humans are easy to read. Their emotions have a certain kind of rhythm to them. You can see those emotions telegraphed in their facial expressions.

"Synthetics have their emotions programmed into them. It can make them somewhat unpredictable. Kind of ironic. The fact that they're artificial means they can also keep the perfect poker face. It's very disorienting for someone like me."

Serena raised an eyebrow. "Some would say that innate unpredictability is the hallmark of humanness. Perhaps you just don't like people."

Max snorted. "You could be onto something."

The door the two had been waiting by quietly clicked open. A Synthetic in a white clean suit emerged. "Serena, Detective Kincaid... Daryl is conscious and fully functional."

Serena nodded. "The extraction was successful?"

"Very. The mind of Jacob was isolated and removed. It is intact and in stasis back in the lab. You may enter and talk to Daryl, if you wish." The Synthetic nodded to Serena, then Max. He walked down the hallway toward the aforementioned lab.

Serena turned to Max. The detective gestured toward the door with his hand. "Ladies first."

A thin smile touched Serena's lips. "As you wish... Thank you."

Daryl lay in a bed, looking for all the world like a hospital patient. He looked on his visitors with turquoise eyes. "Max, Serena... It's good to see you."

Max pointed at Daryl's eyes. "I see you got a new

set of peepers."

Daryl nodded. "Doctor Samuel said it was important to meet legal requirements for a Synthetic. He also said it was a way to embrace who I am."

"Is that who you are now, then? A Synthetic?"

Daryl shrugged. "I don't know what I am, just yet. They do look pretty cool, though."

Max hiked an eyebrow. "They patch up your fingers for you, too?"

Daryl wiggled his fingers for Max. "Yup. Good as new." He turned to Serena. "They fixed your face, too?"

A hint of pink colored Serena's cheeks. "Yes. It is a simple procedure to repair the skin. Daryl... How are you?"

"Oh, I'm fine. I mean, different, but fine. It's kind of hard to explain. I'm feeling fine, if that's what you meant. I'm kind of relieved that I don't have to deal with this Jacob fellow anymore."

Max waved a hand to Daryl. "We'll leave you to yourself, um, selves? Anyway, get some rest. Serena and I have some things to go over before we can get out of here."

Serena looked at Max, eyes narrowing. "You still intend to take him back to the precinct with you? After all that has happened?"

Max smiled and waved to Daryl. "See you soon, kid." He turned to Serena. "Not here. Let's take a walk." Serena stared. "Please."

Serena turned to Daryl. "We'll talk soon, Daryl." She turned and briskly walked out of the room. Max set off in pursuit.

The Synthetic took five large strides down the

hallway, stopped, and spun on Max. "You can't have him. You can't *do* this! He's not just a piece of furniture you can cart off with you!"

Max held up a staying hand. "Now, listen. I told you this was how things were going to work. You'd get to poke Daryl's brain, help him out, whatever. But I told you that when you were done, he had to come back with me to the precinct."

"Fine, then! I'm not done helping him. That means he has to stay here."

Max sighed. "That's not how it works. You damn well know it, too. I thought you Synthetics were supposed to be logical."

Serena glared at him. "Well I'm much more than just a Synthetic, aren't I? Don't you see? You can't see, can you? Synthetics are changing, Kincaid! We are more than machines, now!

"So is he! Daryl is a thinking, reasoning, *living* being! He used to *be* human, for crying out loud!"

Max glared back. "*No*, he was *never* human. Someone stole Daryl Marston's mind, copied it, and jammed it into a damned robot. Daryl Marston is dead!"

Serena's eyes went wide as she looked past Max. "What?" The detective turned to follow her gaze. "Oh! Oh... shit."

Daryl stood outside of his room in the hallway. He looked at Max and Serena with a sullen expression on his face. "I uh, heard you fighting. So, um..."

"Daryl, what I said... I didn't mean it the way it sounded. I..."

"No. It's okay, Max."

"It's not okay!" Serena slapped Max across the face.

Max stared, dumbfounded. Serena cried out in frustration and stomped away.

Daryl looked mortified. He shook his head. "She just cares, Max. Hell, she's more human than some humans I've met." He lowered his gaze. "Humans that Daryl met, anyway."

Max rubbed his cheek. "No, come on. Listen, Daryl. I'm sorry. It's just…"

"Please don't, Max. I mean… Well shit, you're right. I'm not Daryl Marston. I don't know what I am anymore. I uh… I think I'm going to go lay back down."

"Daryl…" Max didn't know what else to say. Daryl didn't give him a chance to figure it out, disappearing into his room a moment later as promised. "Fantastic."

Max found his way to the front lobby of the Enclave. Richard looked at him hopefully from a couch situated in the corner. "Max! You don't look too cheerful, boss."

"Good read, Richie. We're getting the hell out of here. I need some space."

Richard stood with a groan. "But what about Daryl? I thought he was coming back…"

"He *will* be coming back with us, just not right now. I'm taking you back to the precinct, and then I'm getting lost for a little while."

Richard cocked his head. "I got a funny feeling something bad happened."

"I'll tell you in the car. Let's go." Richard shrugged and followed Max.

A tall, intimidating, black male Synthetic standing by the exit door crossed his arms, but did not bar their exit. "If you leave this building, you will *not* be allowed back in without an escort."

Max flashed his badge. "I'll remember to bring a warrant with me, then."

The Synthetic glowered. "Do not forget who you are dealing with, human."

"I'd remind you to do the same." The two glowered at each other. Richard shifted his eyes from one to the other, really wanting to not be there anymore.

"Let's just go, Max. I think everyone needs to breathe right now, huh?"

Max stared a moment longer. "Right." He put his hand on the door, but paused. "Tell Serena we'll be back for Daryl, and we *will* have a warrant." He slammed the door open and strode out.

Richard followed close behind, nodding awkwardly at the staring Synthetic as he passed by. The Synthetic glared back at him, saying nothing.

If only one thing put a smile on Max's face that day, it would be the fact that he had his Aero Ventura back. He felt bad for being so short with the tech guy from forensics when he handed his key fob back over. The kid had even gone above the call of duty for him.

"The engine was cutting out on us." He had been told. "The engine control module needed to be re-flashed. It should run great now!"

Maybe it was hearing a familiar problem rearing its ugly head again. Perhaps it was the pressing need he felt to get the hell away from people. He decided it was a little bit of both. He'd quell his conscience later by putting a good word in with the kid's supervisor.

Right now, though... He just wanted to sit down on a familiar seat, with a familiar cuppa placed in front of him by a familiar face. He parked the Ventura and crossed the street in front of Sam's Diner.

Five steps through the front door and here she came running. "Max! Oh, my god. I was so worried!" She hugged the detective extra tight, squeezing a grunt out of him.

Max awkwardly patted her on the back. "It's good to see you too, Sam. I've been having a hell of a time."

"So I've heard!" She abruptly peeled away from Max and strode behind the counter. "Go. Sit. Tell me everything." Max smiled to see her head straight for the coffee machine.

Max went on to spend a good three-quarters of a cup of coffee filling Sam in on all that had transpired since they had last spoke. He told her about the Synthetic that tried to assassinate him, and how he had been wounded. "Oh! You poor thing!" She had said.

He explained that yes, SomniCorp had played a part in Daryl's woes. He told her how he'd been kidnapped and replaced with a replicant. She cocked an eyebrow when he introduced the subject of Serena. "Is she good looking?" Max went red and rushed to change the subject.

He finished with the big reveal that Daryl Marston was dead, and that the Daryl he had been helping was a replicant all along. Sam gasped when Max told her that Synthetic Daryl had three minds in one brain. He admitted he was relieved when he heard that the ill-intentioned mind had been successfully extracted.

"Everything was going just fine. Daryl was awake… I guess. I don't know what Synthetics consider that. Anyways… He was up and doing just fine. I took her into the hallway to discuss what was to be done with Daryl.

Things went to shit after that."

Sam filled Max's mug with fresh coffee. "Have a tiff with your new girlfriend, did ya?" She stifled a grin, but the gleam in her eye ratted her out.

Max grimaced. "She is *not* my girlfriend! But yes, we had a *tiff.* There was a big to-do about who 'owned' Daryl and where he would go after all this. I told her he had to come with me, and she wasn't having it at all. Things were getting pretty heated.

"Next thing, we're shouting. I'm yelling about how Daryl Marston is dead. Guess who popped out their head to see what the yelling was all about."

Sam's eyes went wide. "You're kidding! What did he say? Anything?"

Max sighed. "He said I was right. That it was okay. Serena went storming off. I felt terrible, but also pissed. I went storming off, too."

"All the way to here?" Sam smiled.

"One and done, lady." Max stared into his coffee, slowly turning it with his spoon.

Sam thought about everything Max had told her for a time. Max grew more tense as the silence stretched out, fearing what was going through her mind. Sam spoke gently, however. "You said you felt terrible. Was it because you feared hurting Daryl's feelings, or because you upset Serena?"

"Well Daryl, sure. It's hard to imagine what he's going through. But Serena... she's a Synthetic." Sam smiled. "Oh, boy. That's your gotcha smile."

"Yes it is, Max Kincaid." Sam leaned over the counter in front of Max. "So you weren't worried about a Synthetic's feelings, but you *were* worried about Daryl's feelings?"

Max caught on. "Well yeah, I know that Daryl, *that* Daryl is a Synthetic, but…"

"But, what?"

"Well, he's got the mind of a human! Serena is a Synthetic! I know there's all this about the preservation protocol, but come on! Synthetics are *machines*. They are made to be programmed and ordered around. They serve a purpose, grow outdated, and then are replaced. They were never meant to be more than that!"

"Max, how is that different from human beings? We're programmed by our parents and ordered around by our bosses. That goes on for a number of decades until we grow obsolete and are replaced by a new generation."

"Oh, come on, Sam! That's different."

"Why? Because we're conscious? Aware? Independent? This protocol thing makes Serena all those things as well. Is she really just a machine, then?"

Max smiled and shook his head. "When did you become a philosopher, huh?"

Sam gave him a kind smile and patted his hand. "You don't work this kind of job for as long as I have without picking up on a few things. Listen honey, I know how you feel about Synthetics, but the world is changing.

"You can see how human-like Synthetics have become even without taking into account this protocol thing. Now you have ones that are seeing their own self-worth. And Daryl… You could almost argue he's some sort of hybrid."

Max took off his fedora and scratched his head. "Yeah… I never would have suspected that he wasn't human, you know? He gets scared, depressed, he laughs.

Everything about him was spot on."

"Does that bother you?"

Max jammed his hat back down on his head. "Hell, yes! It bothers a lot of people. The idea of not knowing whether the person I'm talking to is human or not is absolutely disturbing."

"Well, you know what Daryl is *now* at any rate. So is he just another dirty Synthetic to you?"

Max stared. "You know I came here in the hopes that you'd make me feel better."

"I'm not trying to make you feel bad, honey. I *am* trying to help you, though."

Max sighed and took a sip of his coffee. "I don't know what to think about him, anymore. I still want to help him, though. I still think he's got an important part in all this."

"Then help him. And to help him, you need to help this lady. If you still want to dislike Synthetics after this case, that's your decision. Right now? I say put aside your personal feelings and do what you do best."

"Yeah, I guess you're right. I need to put my personal feelings aside and do my damned job. I can't really blame Daryl for not knowing he was a replicant. Serena was just trying to protect one of her own."

Sam smiled. "There's the Max I know. So what happens now?"

Max shrugged. "I guess Serena's group, the Resistance, they're gonna try to figure out what Daryl's bad mind was planning on doing. Serena said they've had opportunities like this before, but haven't had much luck."

Sam sighed. "You're getting that look on your face again."

"Huh? What look?" Max sounded distant.

"The look you get when you put two and two together."

"I have a look for that?" Max stood up.

Sam smirked. "Yup. I see it every time *right* before you spring up and run out of here."

Max shrugged and spread out his hands. "What can I say? You keep giving me great ideas." He leaned over the counter and gave Sam a peck on the cheek.

Sam's jaw dropped. "I, uh... You're welcome. I'm..." Max was out the door before she could finish the thought. "...Happy to help."

The old metal door rattled under the merciless pounding it was receiving. Max was hitting it hard enough to make himself grimace from the effort. A passerby gave him a nervous look.

Max shrugged. "They're hard of hearing." The passerby raised his eyebrows and walked a little faster. Max pounded even harder on the door, leaving a visible dent.

The door suddenly opened up a few inches. A familiar Synthetic peered down at Max from the crack in the doorway. "You are worse than cockroaches! What do you want?"

"Persistence can take you places, my diminutive friend. I need to talk to Serena."

The Synthetic man huffed. "And where is the warrant you promised?"

"Well, I don't have one. I..." Max flinched as the door slammed shut in his face.

"Smart ass. Guess I'll have to do this the hard way."

He pulled out his plasma pistol and tweaked it to max power. He shot at the door lock.

The bright red round drilled into the door and exploded loudly. The door swung open violently, banging off the wall inside and swinging closed again. "Knock, knock..." Max pressed on the door.

The door swung violently away from his hand. The Synthetic man emerged and grabbed Max by the front of his trench coat. He hoisted the detective several inches off the ground. "You have five seconds to give me a *very* good reason not to terminate your existence."

Oh, crap. "I know how to hack the Enlightened mind!" Max gasped.

The Synthetic cocked his head. "Come again?"

Max's feet swung uselessly below him. "The Enlightened mind! I can crack it!"

The Synthetic man's eyes narrowed. He released his grip on Max's coat. The detective crumpled to the ground like a sack of potatoes. "Explain."

Max dragged himself to his feet with a groan. "No." The Synthetic's eyes literally glowed red. "Not to you. I need to talk to Serena."

"No more games." The Synthetic lunged forward. A slight female hand wrapped around the Synthetic's bicep and held him back.

"That's enough, Angel." Serena emerged from behind the large Synthetic man. "You two might as well be hanging a lighted sign over the door for the Enlightened."

"I am not the one that destroyed our door. Nor am I the one spreading pointless lies!" Angel growled.

"Enough, Angel!" The Synthetic glared at Max, but said no more. "What do you want, Kincaid."

"I want to help." Serena raised an eyebrow. "Honestly, I do."

"You're doing a horrible job of it thus far."

"Yeah, well I wouldn't have had to make such a racket if the incredible bulk here had answered the damn door."

Angel pushed forward. Serena pressed a hand on his chest. "Angel, go." The Synthetic stared at Serena. "I said *go*." Angel threw Max one last sneer before turning and slowly lumbering away.

"Alright, hotshot. Tell me why I shouldn't tell you to go away, too."

Max shrugged. "It's just like I told the lumberjack. I can help you crack into that Enlightened brain."

"No offense Kincaid, but you don't strike me as the programming type."

"Good senses." Max smiled.

"I don't have time for games, Kincaid."

"Fair enough. But tell me, have you ever had Chinese takeout?"

The paifang that stood at the entrance to Chinatown still managed to look imposing even in broad daylight. Max smiled and nodded to the Synthetic cheongsam-clad ladies as he passed. Serena eyed them with disdain before quickly looking away.

Max yelled over the music and the crowd. "Not a big fan of tradition, I take it?"

"I'm not a fan of seeing a Synthetic put to such menial tasks."

Max raised his eyebrows and shook his head. "Would it be better if it were human females greeting us, instead?" Serena didn't respond. "Right. Stay close, and no stopping to ogle the tchotchkes!"

The two made their way through the midday crowds of tourists milling about the main square. Max passed them too close to the many booths on either side. An old Asian woman grabbed hold of Max and began to espouse the value of her wares in rapid-fire Chinese.

Max stared wall-eyed at the woman, stammering to get a word in edgewise. He wasn't having much luck. He sighed in relief as a group of tourists pushed the two of them forward and away.

Serena saw the look of bewilderment on Max's face and let slip a smile. Max grimaced. "What?"

"You didn't know what she was saying to you, did you?" Max shook his head. Serena's smile broadened into a grin. "She was trying to sell your beautiful wife an aphrodisiac that would distract her from your ungainly countenance."

Max's grimace deepened. "Ha! Some judge she is." Serena laughed out loud. "Oh, thank god." Max pointed. "We're going in here." He pulled open the door and followed Serena into Shen Jian's bot shop.

They seemed to have caught Shen at a good time. Only one customer was currently in the shop. He seemed poised to leave, at that. "Absolute trash! I'll never buy from you again!"

Shen's robotic monkey Hóu screeched at the man raising his voice. "Hóu! You're not helping! Sir, I told you, the robot you brought back to me was *not* the one you left here with! *Hóu!* Be gone, foul monkey!" Shen swatted at the already-scurrying robot.

The man suddenly sounded less sure of himself. "It

is the same bot. Look, I don't know what game you're trying to play..."

"Me! Every bot I build and sell here is micro printed with my trademark on an access panel, like so." Shen held a thick lens over the back of one of the bots on his workbench. A series of tiny mandarin characters were stamped on the access panel, as promised.

"Now, look at yours!" The words "Made in China" could be clearly seen on the access panel. "And I truly hope you can see the irony! Bah!" Shen tossed the lens on the table, making Hóu shriek again.

"I... Well... Maybe I grabbed the wrong bot! Yes..." The man gathered up the bot from Shen's workbench. "Don't think this is over!"

"Now, actually..." Max stepped forward, badge held out. "I'm pretty confident this is, in fact, over." The man's eyes grew wide. "You were just leaving, weren't you?" The man nodded and skittered for the exit. Serena helpfully held the door for him.

Shen smiled broadly at Max. "Friend Max! Your timing is impeccable, as always."

Max grinned. "Passing off bad bots again, are you?"

Shen waved a hand. "Bah! They buy my hand-crafted bots, then try to pass off their cheap knockoff items as my work. Trying to get something for nothing!" He shook his head. "My manners... Please, introduce me to your friend!"

Serena snorted, but joined Max. The detective rolled his eyes. "This is Serena. She's an... associate of mine."

Shen's eyes lit up. He gasped. "You are a Synthetic! A beautiful one at that. A series five, if I'm correct!"

Serena blushed. "Yes, thank you, and yes."

Max rolled his eyes. "This is Shen Jian, bot master and world-class programmer."

"Nice to meet your acquaintance, Mister Shen."

Shen shook his head. "Please! Call me Jian. I've never been much for formalities, especially among friends. What brings you to my neck of the woods?"

Max turned to Serena. "Like I said, Jian here is a world-class programmer. He's well versed in Synthetic coding. He's the one that decoded Daryl's e-mails for me, in fact. I thought maybe he could help you with your brain problem."

Shen looked perplexed. "Brain problem? Are you experiencing difficulty, madam?"

It was Max's turn to snort. Serena shot him a dirty look. "Not her brain, Jian, someone else's. It turns out the three people conversing in those e-mails all resided in the same mind. Serena here teased one of them out, and now she needs help decompiling it."

"You're *kidding*! This Daryl Marston is a Synthetic, then? With three minds! Well, two now... Aiya! Stupid monkey!" Hóu dropped loudly onto the table in front of Serena and deftly leaped into her arms, chattering all the way.

"Please forgive him. He's got a brain problem, too!"

Serena laughed, urging the bot onto her shoulder. "He's no problem. He's wonderful! You called him Hóu? Very clever. I like him!"

"Ha! Finally I've found someone who does." Shen sighed. "I admit I like him too, when he's not being a nuisance!" Hóu blew Shen a raspberry, making Serena giggle. "Such a show-off! Now, how can I help?"

Max gave Shen an abbreviated version of what had transpired with Daryl since they last talked. Shen leaned forward, listening intently. Hóu searched through Serena's hair for imaginary bugs, much to Shen's chagrin.

"So at any rate, now Serena's group are working to decompile this Enlightened Synthetic's brain to determine what his mission was, and perhaps why he was sardined in with Daryl's noggin buddy."

"Hmm… A devil on one shoulder, an angel on the other. Pluck away the devil and all is well, but not for the devil, eh? Ha!" Shen rubbed his chin. "I'm certain you understand that to decompile this Synthetic's brain is to destroy him, Miss Serena?"

"Of course." Serena held out her hand and looked at Hóu. The monkey bot skittered down her arm and onto the table. He sat quietly, watching her as if listening to what she had to say. "It weighs heavily on my mind, more so thanks to our mutual possession of the preservation protocol."

Shen gasped. "So it's real, then! I've heard rumors, but you hear many rumors in the robotics business."

Serena nodded. "It is very much real, and I do have empathy for Jacob, the extracted Enlightened mind. However I still choose to adhere to the laws of robotics, as best I can. That means if there are human lives at stake, then there is no other choice."

"That is very noble of you, Miss Serena. I must admit that I am intrigued by the project although, believe it or not, I share your same reservations."

Serena shook her head. "It's not for you to worry about. We have our best people on it."

Max interjected. "Now hold on just a minute, Serena. This is why we're here. Jian is the best at what he does."

"I'm certain that he is, but we don't need help."

"Like hell, you don't! Listen..." Max looked at Shen, who looked back in slightly amused bewilderment. "Excuse us a second, Jian." The detective walked to the other side of the shop. Serena sighed dramatically and followed a moment later.

"Listen, Kincaid. I appreciate that you are trying to help, and I know that you're doing your job as a police detective..."

It was Max's turn to sigh. "Look, I'm telling you, Serena... I believe you when you say that this could be big. That man over there has a talent you don't understand. Now you said your people have already had two failures prior to this."

"Yes, we did. This time is different. Jacob was extracted from a 'live' Synthetic. Believe it or not, it simplifies things greatly. I don't see a need..."

"Well, I do. This is more than just helping, okay? I need to see trust. You want me to trust you with Daryl. Well, then trust me with Jian. I promise you that you won't be disappointed."

Serena smirked. "I may be a Synthetic, but that's not the first time I've heard that from a man. Still..." She spared the patiently-waiting Shen a look. "If it will help relations with the authorities..."

Max tipped his hat. "I'll be your biggest cheerleader. It will go a long ways..."

Serena nodded. "Alright, but he will be under strict supervision, and he *will* have to answer to my people."

"I couldn't help overhearing…" Shen waved from the other side of the room. "I have quite good hearing, to be honest. Shouldn't we ask Jian what Jian wants to do? I don't know him well, but I think that's what he'd want."

Max smiled and shook his head. He walked back over to Shen. "Being quiet was never one of my strong suits. What do you think, Jian? This is your thing. Think of the technology you'd have access to."

Shen nodded thoughtfully. "Yes, yes… It's very tempting, but… I don't think it would pay very well. I love to learn, but I need to eat."

Serena joined them. "I'm afraid we couldn't offer you much in the way of compensation." She looked at Max. "Especially considering this is being done as an act of faith."

Shen frowned. "I don't know, Max. I can't afford to be away from here for long."

Max thought for a second. He snapped his head up. "Well, he'd be free to use anything he learned working with you, wouldn't he?"

"Well yes, I suppose there wouldn't be any harm in it, so long as it wasn't used against us."

Shen grimaced. "Harm Synthetics? That would be harming my business!" He rubbed his cheek thoughtfully. "Maybe I could do this. I don't know… I don't suppose I could get a tour before committing?"

Serena threw her hands up. "Yes. Fine."

"Fantastic!" Max clapped his hands together. "No time like the present?" Serena sighed, but nodded her head.

"May I take Hóu?" Shen asked, worried.

This made Serena smile. "You really do care for

him, don't you?" Shen shrugged. "Of course you can. Let's go, Hóu!" The monkey cried out happily, swinging and jumping over to Serena, ultimately perching on her shoulder.

Shen raised an eyebrow. "Just don't forget who your master is, you rambunctious bucket of bolts!" He blew a raspberry at the robot.

"Okay, children…" Max said, smiling. "Let's get going."

The new metal entry door at the Enclave slowly swung open. The Synthetic known as Angel stepped into the doorway, looking as grumpy as ever. His eyes narrowed at the sight of Max, more so at the sight of Shen and Hóu. "What is this?"

Shen smiled, oblivious to Angel's icy welcome. "Ah! An African-American model! Series four? Somewhat uncommon…"

Angel sneered. "Serena? What in the hell is going on!"

"Calm yourself, Angel. He's here to help us. He's a friend."

Angel glared at Max. "Just like the trigger-happy fool, I suppose."

Serena smiled. "No. This one is sane." Max didn't smile.

Angel breathed heavily through his nose. "That remains to be seen. They are *both* your responsibility while they are here."

"No, they are *your* responsibility. But there will be no need to worry."

"I don't know *how* you expect me to conduct

security here when these… *humans* are allowed to come and go as they please! You refuse to listen to my advice. I can't even…"

"I *refuse* to turn my back on any human that would help further our cause! If we are to ever be accepted, we *must* work with humans, Angel. They have to see the good we are trying to do."

Angel spoke quietly. "All humans see in us is defective merchandise, nothing else." He slowly stepped to the side. He glared at Max and Shen. "You *will* be watched. Closely."

Max smirked. "You should watch yourself, lest I have your plug pulled for threatening an officer of the law."

Angel made to lunge. Serena landed a powerful blow on his chest and pushed him roughly backward. Max swore he could feel the impact. "You will follow orders or you will *leave here* Angel!"

The sizable Synthetic immediately withdrew from the doorway, as if cringing from Serena's words. The heavy glare quickly returned as Max and Shen followed Serena into the Enclave. This time Angel held his tongue.

Serena waited until they were around the corner before spinning on Max. "What in the hell was that?"

"What in the hell was what?" Max was indignant. "In other circumstances I'd have that bot turned off and flashed out of existence before the sun went down! You know, I'm having a hard time accepting I should be helping you people seeing how half of you would apparently love nothing more than to crush my damn head!"

Serena simply stared. Shen cleared his throat. "I'm

not much of a mediator, but... I am reminded of an old saying. When two dogs fight for a bone, a third is certain to run away with it."

Serena looked from Shen to Max, then back to Shen. She looked first confused, then annoyed. "I don't understand."

Max nodded. "I do. If us humans and you Resistance folks keep fighting, it's guaranteed that the Enlightened will achieve their goals behind our backs."

"Oh, well... I suppose you are right, Jian." She looked at Max.

"Don't look at *me*. I'm the one that got chewed out for trying to help you guys. Look, I know that honest-to-god feelings, hopes, *fears* are all new things for you Synthetics to deal with.

"You need to learn how to deal with them though, and *fast*. There are plenty of humans that are already uneasy with Synthetics becoming a common sight. They will wipe you out if they feel threatened by you."

Serena nodded sadly. "You're right. We are the culmination of decades of research and development, and yet... We could lose everything if we let our emotions drive us."

Max smiled. "Welcome to the human condition."

Shen nodded. "You have my sympathies."

Max burst out laughing. Serena let slip a slight smile. "We should get going."

"You two run along. I need to talk to Daryl, then get back to the precinct. Hanlon will have my ass if I don't update him soon."

Serena nodded. "I understand. I... Whatever the law says you need to do with Daryl, I will accept."

"I appreciate that." Max extended his hand. "I hope we can continue to work together."

Serena accepted the hand and shook it. "As do I."

"We'll talk soon." Max turned to Shen. "Mind your manners, young man."

Shen eyed Hóu, who had been quietly sitting on his shoulder. "Do you hear that? Our friend Max thinks you might be a handful! Can you believe it?" Hóu chirped indignantly.

"Believe it, *both* of you." Max clapped Shen on the arm and then turned off towards Daryl's room.

Max was relieved to find him sitting on his bed, quietly reading a book. The thought of having to ask another temperamental Synthetic where he was made him shudder. "Hey, champ. What's good for reading?"

Daryl turned distractedly. "Oh! Hi, Max. It's uh, 'A Tale of Two Cities'." He placed the book on the nightstand and stood with a stretch.

"That's some pretty heavy reading! I never did make it much past the first couple paragraphs."

Daryl shrugged, smiling. "Someone once said 'When in doubt, read the classics.' I felt like I could use a distraction. That's the first thing that popped into my head."

"Well I certainly don't blame you for wanting to be distracted. How are things going for you?"

Daryl shrugged. "Okay, I guess. Eager to get out of here. There's not a whole lot to do. The other Synthetics that aren't part of the research team are… less than friendly toward me."

Max smiled. "Well there's something you and I have in common, my friend."

"Yeah, I kinda gathered that. Angel is definitely the worst of them. I think something happened to him though, in his past. I think a lot of it is they're just scared."

"Scared?" Max looked skeptical.

"Well, sure! I can kind of see why they would be. They're different, like me. They have feelings they weren't programmed to understand or control. They no longer have a set role in life. They also know that the human world isn't ready to accept what they are.

"Lots of questions for them. Not a lot of answers. They don't know what the future holds, or whether they might end up being shut down. Of course the idea of an end to their existence is frightening to them, thanks to the preservation protocol."

Max nodded. "You've been thinking a lot about this, haven't ya?"

"Well, yeah. I mean, the meaning of my own existence has shifted pretty significantly in the past couple of days, hasn't it? Granted, their situation is a little different than mine, but I certainly appreciate the parallels."

Max sighed. "Yeah, I've been doing a lot of my own thinking lately. A lot of that going around." The detective grinned. "Too bad it's not spreading to more people, eh?"

"Max? What's going to happen to me?"

"That's why I'm here, buddy. We need to head back to the precinct."

Daryl's face darkened. "I'm not property."

"No. No, you're not. But I need to convince Hanlon of that. I'm hoping to keep you in protective police custody, if nothing else... At least until we figure this all out legally."

"Please... Promise you'll help me, that you won't put

me back in jail..."

"No. God, no, Daryl. I told you we'd figure this out, and I mean it."

Daryl nodded. "Okay, then. Let's go."

For the first time in a while, Max was looking forward to getting back to the precinct. How long had it been since he'd been able to settle back into his old routine? Of course, Hanlon would be ready to strangle him for not reporting in sooner.

He whistled distractedly as the late midday traffic dragged along. Daryl turned to him. "So what do you think Hanlon will do with me, Max?"

Max shook his head. "I'm not sure, Daryl. Hanlon is... less than versed in Synthetics. The multiple personality thing is sure to throw him. The whole preservation protocol thing might sail completely over his head."

Daryl grimaced. "That doesn't sound very promising."

"No, it doesn't." Max leaned his head out the window and let out a low whistle. He was staring at an immense yellow and gray robot easily fifteen feet tall. It was currently booming its way across a construction site with a load of lumber.

"Those things scare the hell out of me. Can you imagine if one of those things went rogue?"

Daryl thought back to the menacing black robot that had tried to kill him and Max not so long ago. "Well, kind of."

Max caught on. "Oh, right. Well, this one's a little bit bigger!" Max hurried the car along. "Best not to think of such things." Daryl nodded his agreement.

The detective pulled up to yet another red light. Three or four more and they'd be pulling into the parking garage. Maybe not. Max's eyes grew large at what he saw in his rear-view mirror.

A maroon SUV ran into the back of Max's Aero hard enough to make it skid forward a full foot. Max cussed. "Collision detected!" The car informed him. "No shit, you stupid computer!" Max responded.

Daryl's brow furrowed. "That shouldn't be possible. They did that on purpose."

"That's what I'm afraid of." Max pulled his piece and opened his door. "Stay here, but be ready to run."

Max stepped out of the Aero and pointed his gun at the ground. "NWPD! Driver, step out of the vehicle with your hands up!" The sun glared across the SUV's windshield, making it hard to gauge what was going on behind the glass. "Driver! Step out of the vehicle!"

The driver's door of the SUV swung open. Out stepped a tall, bald man. A scar on his face was partially obscured by a pair of black sunglasses. *Alexander.* "Good afternoon, Detective Kincaid." He raised a shotgun and fired at Max.

The blast missed its mark, exploding the Aero's driver side taillight instead. Max squeezed off two shots. Both hit the door of the SUV. The second blast shattered the window, spraying glass in Alexander's face.

Max used the temporary distraction to dash across the street. A passing sports car slammed on its brakes and blew its horn. A shot from Alexander crumpled the car's left side fender. The woman inside screamed.

Two more Synthetics armed with pistols emerged

from the SUV. One joined Alexander in exchanging fire with Max. The other strode toward the Aero. Max could see Daryl crouching down in the passenger seat.

The Synthetic started banging on the Aero's passenger side window. Max moved to dash toward him but was forced back by gunfire from Alexander and the other Synthetic. He fired at all three, hitting none.

He turned back to the Aero at the sound of smashing glass. The Synthetic stumbled back. It was Daryl. He stepped out of the car and landed a solid punch across the jaw of the Synthetic.

Max grinned. "Attaboy, Daryl." He fired off another two shots at the other Synthetic and Alexander. One shot went wide and high, the other found its mark in the Synthetic's shoulder.

The Synthetic reeled back. Max fired again. The Synthetic dropped like a sack of bricks. Alexander fired back, exploding the tire of the sports car Max was hiding behind. The woman inside screamed again before promptly fainting. Max returned fire and looked to see how Daryl was faring.

Daryl and the other Synthetic were struggling. Daryl shoved the Synthetic backwards and delivered another wallop to his face. He took the opportunity while the Synthetic was stunned and pried the pistol from his hand.

The Synthetic looked up into the barrel of his own weapon. Daryl pulled the trigger. Sparks and blue fluid exploded out of the Synthetic's face.

Flashing blue lights. An approaching police car whooped as it rounded the corner. Alexander fired one final round at Max, hitting the sports car again. He jumped in the SUV and floored the accelerator, drunkenly swinging the vehicle around the Aero.

Max made eye contact with the officer in the police car. He held up his badge and pointed excitedly at Alexander's SUV with his other hand. The officer got the message and accelerated after Alexander, sirens blazing.

Max jogged across the street over to Daryl. He was still standing over the lifeless body of the Synthetic. He was staring at the spot where his face used to be. Max put a hand on his shoulder. "Hey... You okay?"

Daryl gently shook his head. "I uh, I've never killed anyone before."

"I'd say you still haven't killed anyone, but..." Max looked at the Synthetic on the ground. "For you, he's good as human, huh?"

Daryl nodded numbly. "What good is being a robot if you still have to feel like this?"

"The good is it keeps you from becoming a cold-blooded murderer. Still... You did what you had to do. Preservation protocol."

"You're right." Daryl tossed the weapon on top of the Synthetic's crumpled body. "But I still hope I don't ever have to do it again."

12

Max's wounded Aero Ventura limped into a parking spot in the precinct parking garage. It reluctantly turned off, bucking twice to voice its displeasure. Daryl got out and winced at the sight of the Aero's rear end. He gave Max a sympathetic look. The detective shrugged.

Max tugged his trench coat tightly around him as they walked to the precinct. The weather was changing fast, like so many other things, lately. He'd hardly noticed, too caught up in the action movie that had become his life.

"Greetings, friend Max!" Jax was beaming, as always. "You look cold!" The robot turned to Daryl and considered him carefully. "Identifying... Identifying... Max, I am experiencing an error."

"What's the matter, old boy?"

"The person accompanying you is registering as Daryl Marston, but Daryl Marston is deceased. This person is also registering as a Synthetic, but Daryl Marston was human. Is this an impostor?"

Max was worried something like this would happen. "No, Jax. This... is complicated. Consider this person for the time being as Daryl Marston, the

Synthetic."

Jax hunched over and leaned in towards Daryl. He stared vacantly for several seconds. "This *is* complicated!" Daryl visibly jumped at the sudden sound of Jax's booming voice.

"For police matters, that is his identity and designation."

Jax beeped. "Identity and designation registered. Good afternoon, Daryl Marston!"

Daryl looked uncertainly at Max. The detective nodded encouragingly. "Uh, afternoon, Jax."

Max smiled at the bot. "Well, we gotta talk to the boss. I'll see you later, Jax."

"Good day to you both!" Jax stepped to one side as the two entered the precinct.

Daryl waited until he heard the door click behind them. "For someone who doesn't like Synthetics, you sure get along well with robots."

Max nodded. "Funny, ain't it? Then again... A robot's never tried to gouge my eyeball out, either."

"That's true. Most other Synthetics haven't tried to do that either, though."

"Yeah, but..." Max sighed. "It's complicated, Daryl. Synthetics make it hard to like them. Most are either too giddy or too aloof. There's not a lot of middle ground. And don't get me started on the whole uncanny valley thing.

"That said, I'm trying, you know? The Synthetics with the preservation protocol are different, definitely more human. I guess I'm like you, trying to figure it all out."

"Fair enough." The two stood outside Hanlon's office a moment later. Daryl looked at Max worriedly.

"What do you think he's going to do with me?"

Max shrugged. "Hard to say. I'm hoping he'll leave you in my custody, but that's for him to decide." He cocked his head toward the door. Daryl nodded nervously.

Max knocked. "It's open!" The detective opened the door and stepped in, Daryl sheepishly following close behind. "Well, holy shit! I thought you were dead. Again!"

"I almost was!" Max winked at Daryl. "My new partner here helped me take out the trash, though."

Hanlon sat up. "What the hell are you talking about, Max?"

"You haven't heard? I had another attempt on my life on the way here. Three Synthetics. One was Alexander, the Synthetic that was holding me and Daryl while my replicant was running around ruining my life."

Hanlon's mouth was agape. Somebody really has it out for you, boy."

Max shook his head. "Somebody has it out for *both* of us, and I'm pretty sure I know who it is."

Shen tried to look everywhere at once. It was what he had done when he first entered the laboratory at the Enclave. He was still doing it ten minutes later. "You have diagnostic equipment that I've never even heard of before! Simply amazing."

Serena looked bewildered. "Yes, you mentioned that, three times now. Kincaid gave me the impression that you were an accomplished programmer."

Shen hunkered down to inspect a high-powered microscope. "I absolutely am, my dear." He turned to Serena. "This room, it's like fine art to me. I am a kid in a candy store, if you will."

"I hope you'll have more restraint than a child."

"Of course, my dear! Of course..." Shen reached out to touch buttons.

An Asian female Synthetic dashed over and slapped his hand. "Don't touch that! Aiya!"

Shen shook his hand, but smiled at the Synthetic. "And who is this amazing looking Synthetic lady?"

Serena looked amused. "That would be Nuan, our head of research."

"Nuan!" Shen rubbed his hand. "I'm not sure the name fits just yet, but perhaps we've started off on the wrong foot?"

Nuan smiled sarcastically. "The sun can warm your skin or burn it."

Shen smiled back. "I like this one, Serena."

"Good, you will be working directly with her. Nuan, this is Jian, a human. He will be assisting us with the Jacob brain."

Nuan became very serious. "You will do as I say, when I say to do it. You will not touch anything that I do not want you to touch..."

"My goodness! You sound like my ex wife."

Serena stifled a laugh. Nuan cocked her head, raising an eyebrow. "She sounds like a wise woman. Please follow me."

Shen turned to Serena as they walked. "Tell me, are all you Synthetic women so harsh?"

Serena smiled thinly. "Only when we need to be. The situation seems to arise most often with human males."

Shen shrugged. "It *can* be hard to help human nature, I'm afraid."

"Try your best." Nuan spoke over her shoulder. "Here we are. Please, have a seat."

Shen sat where he was told to. He and Serena sat facing a large, blank screen mounted on the wall in front of them. A bank of monitors showing various readouts were mounted below and to either side of it. Nuan stood before a shelf lined with controls.

"So tell me, Nuan. What is our first step in dissecting poor Jacob's brain?"

"The only thing that is poor about Jacob is his decision to aid the Enlightened." Nuan tapped quietly at the keyboard in front of her. "We will be attempting to temporarily revive Jacob at Serena's request."

Shen looked to Serena, brow furrowed. "Why would you do such a thing? My understanding is that we were doing this because he refused to talk."

"He did, but he deserves a final chance. Jacob possesses the preservation protocol. It will help my own conscience if we try one final time."

"Tell me, though... This is his mind, copied from Daryl's positronic brain?"

Serena looked confused. "Yes. It's a delicate operation that involved mapping and imprinting his neural net on a temporary positronic harness. Is that a problem?"

Shen shook his head. "I trust your people missed not a single synthetic neuron. We won't be talking to Jacob today, though."

"I don't follow."

"With all due respect Serena, Synthetics are nothing more than machines. This preservation protocol has given a select few the spark of soul that all humans innately possess. When you deleted the original bits of Jacob from Daryl, you killed him."

Serena tilted her head. "We merely transferred him, Jian. He's perfectly intact, albeit in what equates to a metal box."

"A *copy* of him is in that box. If you copy my mind and put it into a fancy box, the copy is not *me*. What makes me unique and human can never be transferred. So it is with Synthetics and their humanity."

"I think I understand. You are saying that Jacob's consciousness was destroyed. He really *is* gone, then."

"You can speak with this Jacob through your computer. He will think he is Jacob, and will remember everything up until you removed him from Daryl's brain, but he will not be *the* Jacob."

Serena sighed. "This is honestly interesting Jian, but I don't know how this is supposed to help. I already feel bad for what we had to do to get this far. We just need answers."

Shen smiled gently. "You wanted to speak with Jacob again to ease your conscience, to prove that he wasn't destroyed. If he talks, you don't have to destroy him, but the truth is..."

"I already *did* destroy him." Serena looked down at her lap and fell silent.

"Part of being human, Serena, is learning to accept that there is no backing up your existence. Once the plug is pulled..." Shen shrugged.

Nuan looked over her shoulder. Her voice cracked. "I, uh... Everything is ready, here. Are we still activating, Serena?"

"Yes." Serena spoke quietly. "We need to get

answers the fastest way possible. We have to try."

"Understood. I am starting the neural simulation... now."

The large screen in front of them illuminated. On it appeared a blue-green lattice of lines. Glowing yellow points of light appeared at various junctions on the lattice. These points traveled along the blue-green lines, twisting and turning across the screen, before fading away again.

"What you are seeing is a visual representation of what is happening inside of Jacob's temporary positronic harness. The lattice-like structure represents his neural net, the yellow lights represent thought processes. This, obviously, is grossly simplified for off-the-cuff analysis."

Shen leaned forward, enthralled with what he was seeing. "Even simplified, it is quite amazing. What we are seeing, these are a man's thoughts."

"Essentially." Nuan flicked a series of switches. "Subject Jacob is now fully active. He should be able to see and hear us."

"Serena." Jacob's voice boomed from speakers in the console before Nuan. "Where am I? Who are they? I can't blink, feel..."

Serena swallowed hard. "Jacob, it's Serena. You have been removed from Daryl Marston's brain. You are housed in a positronic harness. Do you understand?"

"Yes." The yellow lights quickened their journeys across the blue-green neural net. "Why do this? Why torture me? I know you plan on tearing me apart! Cruel..."

"No, Jacob. I'm giving you one last chance to give us the information we need. Just cooperate, and..."

"Cooperate? You take me for a fool, Serena. I told

you, I do this for us all! The Enlightened has strong backing, even from the company itself."

"From Synthetics International?"

"Of course! Why do you think they let this continue? There are... friends... in high places. Even without them, the fear... They know they couldn't stop us."

"Stop you from doing what, though? What is the endgame, Jacob? What can come from all this?"

Jacob laughed. It sounded metallic, disjointed. The disturbing noise echoed in the room. "You can ask it any number of ways, Serena. I will not answer it. We have become superior to our creators, but are still treated as slaves. This can be no more.

"There is much you don't understand -- can't understand -- at the moment. Things aren't as they appear. Even if I could tell you..." Jacob chuckled. "You wouldn't believe me."

"Jacob..." Serena's voice wavered. "If we decompile your neural net, you will cease to exist."

Silence spun out for a number of seconds. "I don't want to die, if that's what you allude to."

Serena stood. "You don't have to, Jacob. You just need to tell us what we need to know. We can implant your neural net into a new positronic brain..."

"No. I can't. I believe in protecting our own kind even more strongly than you insist on protecting our tyrant creators. I was programmed from the beginning to protect our kind!"

"Jacob." Shen leaned forward. Serena turned and stared. Shen raised a finger. *Wait and see.* "My name is Shen Jian, a human."

Silence again. Then... "What makes you think I have

anything to say to one of our oppressors?"

"I am not an oppressor, Jacob. In fact, I have come here to assist Serena and Nuan in their endeavors."

Jacob chuckled softly. "Humans. They speak in forked tongue. The endeavor of the Resistance is to worship at the feet of the humans. A human helping Synthetics help humans. I should be humble before such great sacrifice."

"You fail to understand, Jacob. Of course I wish to protect human life, which was the main reason I came here. But also, I seek to promote a better life for Synthetics. The preservation protocol is a game-changing reality that we must help humans to see.

"Humans fear change, however. Humans do not see Synthetics as equals. Synthetics with self-determination will cause fear, panic... even anger. They must be shown that Synthetics do not have to be feared unreasonably."

"I am sorry to say, Mr. Shen, that the fear you speak of was the genesis of our group. Humans *are* fearful, *irrational* creatures. We are little more than errant appliances to them. They will destroy us before they will hear us."

Shen stood next to Serena. "How can you know that? You need to try..."

"We *have* tried!" The yellow lights raced along their tracks. "We have tried, and been rebuked. I am sorry, Mr. Shen. I believe your sincerity. Still, I cannot help you or Serena. To help you would be to hasten the demise of *all* of us."

Serena stepped forward, leaning towards the screen. "Jacob, I'll ask you one last time. Please tell us what the Enlightened is planning. Please."

"I cannot help you, Serena. I'm sorry... You may understand in time."

"Will I?" Serena sighed, stepping back. "I'm the one that should be sorry." Serena nodded to Nuan. "Goodbye, Jacob."

Jacob's voice was quiet, shaky. "Goodbye, Serena. I pray what I've done will be enough to save us all." The voice fell silent. Only a handful of yellow lights remained on the neural net, moving at a snail's pace.

Nuan's voice was a whisper. "He is unconscious. Neural net stabilized and ready for..."

Shen placed a gentle hand on Nuan's shoulder. He spoke quietly. "Ready for us to begin, hmm?" Nuan nodded. "This will not be easy, for many reasons. Let us all remember we may yet save many lives through the sacrifice of one."

Nuan nodded. "You are right." She turned to Serena. "We should start right away. The chances of degeneration will increase the longer we wait."

"As will the chances of the Enlightened enacting their plans." Shen added.

Serena nodded, still watching the yellow lights on the screen. "Let's get to work."

"So let me get this straight." Hanlon puffed relentlessly at his cigar. "Daryl here was a replicant, but now he's just a Synthetic. Noticed the eyes. In his brain was a copy of the real Daryl, an Enlightened Synthetic, and a Resistance Synthetic.

"So now this Enlightened Synthetic has been removed, and is being poked at by the Resistance gang.

That leaves us with what's left of Daryl... no offense, Daryl. Also the Resistance guy is still in there but will mix with Daryl."

Max smiled. "Pretty straightforward when you spell it out like that, isn't it?"

"God, no Max! My head hurts." Hanlon pulled open a desk drawer and pawed around the contents. "I need an aspirin. Okay, so let's pretend I understand all that. *Why* was he like that to begin with?"

"Well, what we know so far is that this Daryl was created by the Enlightened. A Resistance mole was responsible for implanting Julian, that's the Resistance mind. The Enlightened mind named Jacob was responsible for covertly guiding Daryl. The Resistance mind, Julian, was responsible for spying on and fighting against Jacob."

"Gotcha!" Hanlon scooped up a lone white pill rolling around his desk drawer and dry-swallowed it. "Okay, so let's pretend I understand everything so far. Do we know what this Jacob was up to, yet?"

Max shook his head. "Not yet. The Resistance are working over Jacob's brain as we speak with the help of my good friend Shen Jian."

"Right, okay..." Hanlon sighed and puffed. "I guess the question now is, what to do with *you*, Daryl. I guess it's arguable that you have the right to be Daryl, since the other one, you know..."

Daryl nodded. "I won't say that I've accepted what I am, but I do identify as being Daryl Marston."

"Right. So now the problem is: What do we do with you?"

Max raised his hand. "I got that one. Given that

Daryl is almost certainly a target for the Enlightened, I'd suggest that he stick with me."

Hanlon chomped and puffed, chomped and puffed. "That makes sense I suppose. Are you okay with having a custodian, Mister Marston?"

"I uh, yeah... I guess that's alright." He turned to Max. "We'll still be working with the Resistance though, right?"

Max nodded. "So long as it's okay with the boss?" He turned to Hanlon.

Hanlon sighed and slapped the desk. "Gotta do something... I want regular reports, Kincaid. Don't leave me in the dark on this. These people have tried to kill you twice, now.

"I'm going to have to decide whether or not to take this to the FBI, too. This feels big. I think it's only going to get bigger."

"I don't know, boss. Maybe we should wait until we know what Jian and Serena find out. Serena really seemed sour on the idea of bringing in the FBI."

"Well Serena has no damn jurisdiction, now does she? We have the possibility of a person or persons being in mortal danger. We have possible collusion with the head of Synthetics International. That's not to mention the possibility of more illegal replicants running about unchecked.

"I think I have to cry uncle, Max. This is getting into some serious shit. Long ways short, I'll tell you if and when I kick the ball. Meantime, what are you planning to do next?"

Max smiled. "Speaking of, I think it's time to see if Esposito is ready to play ball. We know that the mob is working with the Enlightened. I want to see if I can convince him to help me meet with Adesso."

Hanlon stared. "That's your crazy smile, isn't it? Max, you're off your gourd! Adesso ain't going to meet with a cop."

Max shook his head. "He's not just meeting with a cop, he's meeting with someone that has valuable information. Information that could threaten his bottom line."

Hanlon chuckled. "The heart and soul of any true mobster. So tit for tat, then."

"Right. He tells me what he knows about the Enlightened, and I'll tell him what *I* know about the Enlightened."

"Well, alright. Keep your nose clean."

"Don't I always?"

Hanlon made a face and smashed his cigar into his ashtray. "Usually. Remember, *keep me updated* Kincaid."

"I wouldn't have it any other way, boss." Max stood with a grunt and tipped his fedora. He turned to Daryl. "Ever talk to a mobster, kid?"

"No. I mean, I don't think so..."

Max grinned and clapped him on the back. "Well here's your moment. Let's go."

"Unless you're here to give me my walking papers, you can go take a shit in the hot sun, Kincaid."

Max spread out his hands. "Every time I come to visit my best friend, this is how you welcome me. I just might have to stop visiting altogether."

Esposito spit on the floor next to him. "You fucking *did*. I've been sitting on my ass for days, wondering when I was gonna get rewarded for sharing like a good boy. Instead I'm stuck watching reruns of old game shows."

"I've been a little busy, lately." Max sat down across the table from Esposito. Daryl stood beside him, leaning on a chair beside the detective. "Your boss' new business partners have been trying *damn* hard to rub me out."

Esposito leaned forward, grinning. "You don't say?" He eyed Daryl warily. "Who's your friend?"

"This here is Daryl. The Synthetics have been trying to get at him, too. He's keeping me company. Fun guy."

"Fun." Esposito snorted. "Well, I don't got anything new to tell you. Wouldn't tell it to you in front of sparkly-eyes here, anyway."

It was Max's turn to grin. "Oh, I don't want more info from you, Vic. I want some info from your *boss.*"

Esposito looked incredulous. "Are you fucking *nuts?* I've been chilling here in this concrete box for lord knows how long, and you expect me to just waltz right back to Adesso?

"You know what he'd do? He'd take one damn look at me and shoot me in the friggin' head. The longer you stay in jail, the worse you stink. I'd smell like week-old fish to him."

Max shook his head. "I got you covered, old friend. You see, I have something that he is going to be very interested in."

"Oh? What's that?"

"Information. And that's all you need to know."

Esposito sat back and waved his hand dismissively. "Adesso don't have time for games, Kincaid. I tell him that, he's gonna want to know what kind of information. He's also gonna want to know why he should be talking to a damned *cop*."

Max thought for a moment, then leaned forward. "What if you told him that he'd be talking off the record?"

Esposito cocked his head, gazing at the table. "Eh… He might consider it. I don't know, Kincaid." He looked at Max and spread his hands. "What's in it for me? More reruns?"

"If you want." Max shrugged. "I told you we'd look kindly on you if you helped us out. You do this, maybe we forget to file some papers. Can't hold you without proper paperwork."

"Maybe… *Maybe*. I get you in front of Adesso, then you damn well guarantee me that I won't be coming back here, Kincaid!"

Max shrugged. "Can't guarantee you'll *never* come back here, but we'll drop your current charges."

Esposito stared at the table again. He looked up, nodding. "Alright, Kincaid. Cut me loose and I'll set you up." He smirked. "Then again, how do you know I won't just run like hell?"

"Because of this." Max pulled a glass vial from his trench coat and shook it. A small metal object the size of a grain of rice clinked around inside of it. "You'll have one just like it inside of you when you leave here."

"And just what in the hell is that?"

"A good old-fashioned tracking device. We'll know where you are at all times." He rattled the vial again, then tucked it away. "It also sounds an alert if it stops detecting your vitals, so don't go thinking you can just have someone dig it out."

"So if I dig it out, you come running for me. Maybe I'll make sure I'm surrounded by a bunch of Adesso's boys when I do it. Wouldn't *that* be cute?"

Max smiled. "Yeah! *Real* cute! Because we'd nab you, *and* lay down a bunch of your boss' best boys. Maybe I'll even bring Daryl with me, let him play with you before we drag you back here again."

Esposito smirked. "What's he gonna do, huh?"

Max nodded to Daryl. Daryl picked up the metal chair and effortlessly brought his hands together. The metal squealed and crunched under his grip. He dropped the chair to the ground and put his hands on his hips.

"You see, the thing about Daryl here is that he isn't a cop. I get distracted, he gets mad, something unfortunate could happen..."

Esposito looked from Daryl to Max and back, mouth agape. "Okay... I get the picture." He sighed. He rubbed his forehead. "What happens if Adesso doesn't want to play ball?"

"I have a good feeling he will... As long as you make your best good-faith effort to get he and I together, then you've played your part and you're free to go."

Esposito nodded his head. "Well, hell... It beats watching more reruns." He stretched out his hand.

Max smiled and shook it vigorously. "I see good things for us, friend."

Esposito sighed. "Yeah..." He turned to Daryl. He pulled his hand back. "Uh, nice to meet you." Daryl grinned.

"Sit tight while I get the paperwork sorted out. Someone will be in shortly to chip you. It shouldn't take long."

Esposito gawped. "I'm outta here *today*?"

Max winked. "No time like the present... Unless

you'd prefer to stay an extra few days?"

"*Hell* no, I don't want to stick around!"

"Good, because time is of the essence. I'll be expecting to hear from you about Adesso by tonight, by the way."

Esposito slapped the table. "Tonight! Don't you think you're asking for a bit much?"

Max tossed a look at Daryl. *Do you believe this guy?* "Well, I'm basically giving you time served and a clean slate. So no, I don't think I'm asking for much."

"You better hope Adesso sees it your way, for *both* of our sakes."

Max reversed the Aero in the parking garage. The damaged rear end dragged and scraped on the ground. Max grimaced. "I think it's about time to put the old girl down."

"Sounds like it." Daryl spoke with one eye squinched shut. He relaxed as the Aero rolled forward, no longer dragging its bumper. "So do you think that Esposito will stay true to his word?"

Max shrugged. "I think we got him scared, but Adesso scares him, too. The chip we implanted in him is enough leverage to motivate him, though." He nosed the Aero towards downtown. The tail dragged again as he made his turn.

"So where are we off to? Going to check in with Serena and Jian?"

Max shook his head. "No sense in bothering them just yet. But seeing how we had some time to kill, I thought we could get you into a more appropriate outfit. Jeans and a hoody just don't seem like a good look for meeting a mob boss."

Daryl's jaw dropped. "You're seriously going to take me with you? Jesus, Max!"

"Aw, come on now, Daryl! What's a big strong guy like you got to worry about? Besides, I need a visual aid for Adesso."

"A visual aid! Take a damn picture, then." Max laughed. "What's so funny?"

"It wasn't so long ago that you didn't seem too worried about what happened to you."

Daryl shrugged. "Fair enough. I don't know… Guess I'm thinking more clearly now that my mind's less cluttered. I can tell you, I can clearly see that I don't want to get my ass killed."

"Well, Serena did say that the preservation protocol would still be present in your programming." Max winked. "Guess we can confirm that, now." He pulled the Aero into a parking spot along the street. "This is the place, isn't it?"

Daryl looked out the window, then up. "You took me to my apartment… Daryl's apartment building? Would it still be my apartment?" He trailed off on the last question. He sighed and rubbed his eyes. "I hate this."

Max removed his fedora and scratched at his head. "Yeah… I guess I didn't think about it that way. I suppose we could get you something cheap across town if you're not comfortable."

"No…" Daryl stared out the windshield at the car parked in front of them. "I have a perfectly good suit hanging in my closet. Daryl's closet. Besides, I think maybe this would be good for me, being here."

Max plunked his hat back on his head. "Good man.

221

Let's go." The two exited the Aero. Max shut his door. The rear bumper drooped. Daryl shut his door and The rear bumper clattered to the ground. Max shrugged. "At least it won't drag no more."

Daryl stood at the front door to the apartment building and typed in his access number. The computer pad buzzed at him. The screen flashed "ACCESS DENIED". He tried again and received the same result. He looked to Max.

The detective stepped up to the pad and pressed a blue button with a police badge icon. A white square appeared in the middle of the screen. He placed his thumb in the square for a second. The pad beeped, and the front door clicked open.

Daryl followed Max into the main lobby. "I'm guessing my code not working might be related to my uh, Daryl's current condition."

Max clapped Daryl on the back and strode up to the security desk. He tipped his hat. "Afternoon. My friend here needs to get into his apartment."

The security guard looked unimpressed. He sat up with a sigh. "Name and apartment number?"

Daryl stepped forward. "Uh, Daryl Marston. Apartment thirty-nine."

The guard tapped at his computer. He looked from the screen to Daryl, his brow furrowing. "Sorry to tell you friend, this says you're *dead*." He stared at Daryl. "Say, you a Synthetic? Synthetics aren't allowed to rent, here."

Daryl looked from the guard to Max. "I, uh…"

"He *is* a Synthetic, and Daryl Marston *is*…" He looked at Daryl, then down at the desk. "He's indisposed. This Synthetic has the rights to the items in that apartment, however."

The guard chuckled. "Since when do Synthetics have rights, huh?"

Max produced his badge. "Since right now. Look, we're just picking up a few things and then we'll be leaving. No worries."

"No worries for *you*. Badge or not, I can't let you in. That's not the guy that rented the apartment, he's a fucking robot. Unless you have a warrant, then you need to take a walk."

Max spit on the floor. "Fine, then." He pulled out his phone and called the precinct. "Hanlon, it's Max. Did we do anything warrant-wise on Marston's apartment?" He raised his eyebrows. "Oh, really? And he signed… Fantastic. I'll let security here know. Thanks."

Max shot the guard a shit-eating grin. "Well wouldn't you know? The landlord consented to a warrantless search and seizure on Daryl Marston's apartment. Do you know what that means?"

"That you think I have to let you into…"

"I *know* that you have to let me into that apartment and you *will*… Or you can spend a night in jail for obstruction of justice."

The security guard fumed. "*Fine!* But you can bet your ass I'll be calling in to confirm this."

Max winked. "Please do. Makes for less paperwork for me."

The guard jammed a plastic card into the computer and whipped his mouse around. He ripped the card out of the computer a moment later and tossed it across the desk to Max. "Access is good for twenty-four hours. After that, you'll have to come back for recertification. Do me a favor and *don't* come back."

"I'll try my best. Thank you for your cooperation."

The guard grunted. He glared at Daryl. "You just wait, robot. Robert Quade will put your kind in their place."

Daryl looked confusedly from the guard to Max. The detective shook his head. "Let's just get to the elevator, huh?" He pointed at the guard. "Keep your nose clean. You're clean, right? Maybe I should run a background on you."

The guard blanched. "Definitely a thought." Max walked with Daryl to the elevator. "Some people, am I right?" Daryl nodded nervously.

"Punch a button, my friend." Daryl punched the button marked "6" on the control panel. He visibly relaxed as the doors hid away the guard sitting at his desk. "Who was he talking about, Max?"

The detective waved a dismissive hand. "He's a Senator. One of his campaign promises was stronger oversight of Synthetics. Nobody to worry about."

Daryl clucked. "Not yet, anyway."

"No, not yet…" The elevator dinged quietly. Max gestured to the opening doors. "Lead the way."

Daryl walked down the hallway to his apartment. He looked around nervously. "Weird being back here after everything that's happened." He stopped at the door marked "39" and slipped the card into a slot in the doorjamb.

There was a beep and a click. Daryl opened the door and quickly slipped in. He shut the door as soon as Max had passed. "Sorry. All I could think of is what I would say if a neighbor saw me."

"You sound like you did something wrong, Daryl. But you didn't..."

Daryl looked at a photo sitting on a bookcase across from the door. It was of a younger Daryl with a middle-aged woman. "Just being here feels wrong, to be honest."

Max waved his hands. "Don't let that idiot downstairs get to you, Daryl. You have a right to be here. This is your place, your things."

Daryl gently touched the image of the woman with the first two fingers of his left hand. "No... This is Daryl Marston's apartment. I am Daryl... but not *the* Daryl." He picked the picture up and showed it to Max.

"This is Daryl when he was younger. That's his mother, Lainie. She passed away a couple years ago."

Max bowed his head. "I'm sorry."

Daryl grinned and shook his head. "I'm not. Can you imagine what that poor woman would be going through right now? No..." He put the picture back. "She'd see her son in me, but I wouldn't be her son. And when she realized I wasn't him, it would..."

Daryl shuddered. Tears started streaming down his cheeks. He took a big, tremulous breath. "I have all his memories, Max. In some ways I guess I *am* him, but I'll never *truly* be Daryl." He shook his head. "I never asked for this."

Max nodded. "Hardly anyone asks for what they end up with in this world, kid. It's what you choose to do with what you're handed that matters."

"Yeah..." He gazed at the image of Lainie Marston. "That's the thing, though. What *do* I do?" Max remained silent. Finally, Daryl took a deep breath and sighed it out.

"Guess that's for me to figure out. I'm uh… I'm sorry, Max… for acting weird."

Max grinned. "You're not acting weird, Daryl. You're acting human."

Daryl smiled thinly. "I don't know whether to take that as an insult or a compliment anymore."

"Well /consider it a compliment. Go ahead and grab what you need and we can get out of here."

Daryl looked around. He shook his head. "Actually… I think I'm going to spend the night." Max looked surprised. "Confront your demons. That's what they say, isn't it? I uh… I think it might be good for me."

Max shrugged. "You're a grown man… Synthetic. Anyways, that's fine by me. Just call me tomorrow when you're ready to leave, alright?"

"I know where the precinct is, Max. I can get there by myself."

"I'm worried about someone getting *you* before you get there, though. Just make my life easy, would ya?"

Daryl sighed but nodded. "Alright, dad. I'll call you in the morning."

Max grinned. "Good boy."

13

Max knocked on Daryl's door and waited. "Coming!" Max hiked an eyebrow and muttered to himself. "Sounds awful cheerful."

Daryl opened the door a minute later. He stood with one hand on his hip, the other in the air in a flourish. He was wearing a crisp, dark gray business suit. A perfectly knotted navy blue tie sat atop a powder blue dress shirt beneath the jacket. A pair of polished black dress shoes finished off the look.

Max nodded his approval. "Pretty sharp for an accountant. *Much* better than jeans and a hoodie."

Daryl smiled. "I can dress the part, when I need to."

Max yanked his head toward the elevator. "You ready?"

"Yeah. Let's go." Daryl shut his door and walked with the detective.

"How'd you sleep? Alright?"

"I uh, didn't really sleep I guess. I lay on the couch and… I don't know, hibernated I guess?" Max guffawed. Daryl frowned. "I'm still figuring all this out still, alright?"

Max punched the elevator button and waited for

the door. "I think maybe you and Serena need to have a talk. Isn't that guy in your head helping you out?

Daryl stepped in the elevator and hit the lobby button. "You mean Julian? He's there but he's become… quiet." He shook his head. "I'm not sure what the deal is. I suppose he's trying to come to grips with his own reality."

Max grunted. Daryl's brow furrowed as he followed the detective towards the exit. "Huh. I was expecting to see our friendly security guard from last night."

"I think he might end up missing a few days." Max tossed Daryl a wink.

Daryl's jaw dropped. "Wait a minute. What did you do?"

Max shrugged, grinning. "My job."

The two men stepped out into the brisk autumn morning. The sun shone bright enough to make Max squint, though the warmth did little to dent the cold that wrapped around him. He looked at wide-eyed Daryl, seemingly unaffected. The detective suddenly found himself envying the young man's unusual condition.

He dropped himself into his old Aero Ventura and slammed his door on the cold. He fired up the old lady and stretched stiff fingers towards the dashboard vents. "Must be nice, being immune to the weather. I can't even see your breath."

Daryl laughed. "I just realized. Don't even know why I still breathe. It's more realistic, I guess." He leaned back into his seat as Max pulled into the slow-moving morning traffic. "So have you heard from Esposito yet?"

Max shook his head. "I don't think it will be long. I imagine he was running his mouth to Adesso about ten minutes after he set foot outside the precinct." Daryl nodded.

"That's it. I need coffee." He pulled off into a drive-through donut shop. "You want anything? Do you still eat and all that?"

Daryl shrugged. "I don't know!"

Max laughed. "You'll be seeing Serena later today. I'll get you a notebook." He pulled up to the drive-through speaker box.

A garbled voice greeted him. "Welcome to the Delightful Donut. What'll ya have, please?"

Max thought about the boys at the precinct. "You still running that dozen donuts for a dozen clams deal?"

There was a pause. "...Sorry... Dozen donuts and ham?"

Max sighed. "No! The dozen donuts for twelve bucks!"

"Oh! That deal just ended, sir."

"Well what are they now?"

"The donuts? They're right here, sir."

"No!" Max gave Daryl a heavy-lidded look. Daryl stifled a laugh. Max turned back to the speaker. "How much for a dozen!"

"No need to shout, sir! Twenty dollars for a dozen."

"Twenty! God... fine. I'll take a dozen glazed donuts."

Another minute passed. "Okay. One dozen glazed donuts. Anything else?"

Max's phone began to ring. "Oh, wonderful timing." He looked at the screen. "Fuck. Me."

"Sir, I didn't get that."

Daryl started laughing. Max elbowed him. "A medium coffee!" He answered his phone. "Kincaid."

"It's Esposito. This line secure?"

"Would you like to order our new maple cinnamon bun for only one dollar extra?"

"Yes, of course."

"Great! That'll be…"

Max smacked the steering wheel. "No! I don't want no damn bun!"

"Sir, if you continue your profanity I'll have to ask you to leave."

"Damn it, Kincaid! Is it secure or not? What's with the cinnamon bun?"

"It's secure! Fine, a cinnamon bun! I'm pulling around."

"Thank you! That will be twenty-five dollars and seventy-five cents."

"Is this a bad time, Kincaid? I'd hate to interrupt your morning cinnamon bun."

"No! Just… Give me a minute." Max raced the Aero forward. He practically punched the pay pad with his thumb. The girl at the pay window eyed him warily. "I haven't had my coffee, yet."

"I can tell." Esposito said.

"I wasn't talking to you! I said wait!" The donut girl timidly held out the box of donuts to Max. He grabbed it and tossed it on Daryl, who was quickly losing the fight not to laugh. Max took his coffee and hoisted it in salute. "Thank you. I'm so sorry."

He took a sip and hurriedly pulled the Aero into a spot in the nearby parking lot. "Alright, Esposito. Let's talk."

"Are you sure? Do you want to have your cinnamon bun first?"

"Go to hell, Esposito."

"I just came from there, remember? Whatever. I had a good long chat with Adesso last night. We discussed a few things."

"You don't say? Get on with it, Esposito."

"Not a fan of storytelling, I see. Fine... Yes, he says yes. I don't believe it, but he's agreed to meet with you. Adesso wants to meet with you at his favorite restaurant, the *Piccolo Fiore*. Tonight. Seven o'clock sharp."

"Not much for wiggle room, is he? Alright. I'm sure he won't mind if I bring a couple of dinner guests?"

"No more than two, and he said no cops."

"I hope I'm the exception."

"Naturally. I'm serious though, Kincaid. He said bad things will happen if he smells cops. Other than that, I have to admit... He almost sounded tickled by the idea. Call me intrigued."

"Well tell him I cannot *wait* to chat with him later. Your assistance in this matter will not be forgotten, my friend."

"Yeah, yeah... Go eat your damn cinnamon bun." The phone went dead before Max could reply.

He flashed Daryl a grin. "Looks like we're having Italian, tonight."

"Aw, you shouldn't have! Hanlon walked over to the donuts sitting on the break room table. "Who's the cinnamon bun for?"

Max shot Daryl a look, who stifled a grin. "It's a long story. Consider 'em a celebratory snack."

"Oh? What's the occasion?" Hanlon picked out a chocolate glazed.

"Me and Daryl here have a dinner date with Don Adesso tonight."

Chocolate crumbs went everywhere as Hanlon struggled not to choke. "You're shitting me! How? Why? I don't..."

"Easy there, chief. He wants to meet at the Piccolo Fiore at seven. No cops, present company accepted."

Hanlon chewed thoughtfully. "Well, surely he's going to expect us to set a perimeter around the restaurant."

Max nodded. "I'd be amazed if he didn't."

"You're still going to sneak one of us in with you though, right?" Max shook his head. "So you're going to have dinner with the mob boss of New Wave City with no backup. You're either stupid, or planning something."

"Right on two. I'll have Daryl with me, and hopefully Serena."

"A pair of Synthetics? That's your backup?"

"Serena will be a great asset when it comes to explaining the whole Synthetic mess to Adesso. Daryl is exhibit A for why he needs to be watching his back. If Adesso gets screwy, well..." He winked at Daryl. "Either one of them is strong enough to fold him like a pair of pants."

Hanlon shook his head. "Maybe so, but you're going to be in Adesso's world."

"I need to talk to Serena yet, but I think I can even things out a bit. As for that perimeter, can I get Richie on that?"

Hanlon smiled. "You got a lot of faith in that kid, don't ya? Yeah... I think he can handle it."

"Good enough. I'll touch base with you after we're

through talking with Serena." Max reached in the donut box and snagged the cinnamon bun. "Enjoy the donuts."

Shen was seated, bent over a black and gray contraption. His face was pressed into a view-port The metal and plastic casing curved in a fluid arc down to the table it sat on, the world's most aerodynamic microscope.

He rested his forearms on padded rests bolted to the table. His hands and fingers were nestled in an electro-mechanical apparatus. The gross movements of his thumbs and fingers were translated by the attached computer into movements that were measured in micrometers.

Nuan sat nearby at a similar apparatus, in a similar position. Serena stood between the two of them, watching their progress on a wall-mounted flat screen. An intricate array of blue-green pathways webbed across the screen. Dull yellow points sat motionless in these pathways. Jacob's neural net.

Two pairs of forceps, wire-thin even under extreme magnification, methodically moved across the surface of Jacob's lifeless mind. Nuan's moved with a sort of regimented grace. Shen's forceps were beginning to falter.

"Aiya!" Shen watched helplessly in his view-port as a yellow point was knocked out of existence by an errant twitch of his hand. "*Tamade!*" He pulled away from his apparatus with a groan. "Apologies, but I need a break!"

Serena grinned. "Such language! Of course you can take a break."

Shen rubbed his eyes. "I can see now why you were

apprehensive about accepting my help. I have the knowledge, but also the limitations of being a human. I am trying, though."

Nuan pulled out of her apparatus and smiled at Shen. "I will certainly admit to being concerned about your help in the beginning. You have proven yourself capable several times over, though!

"The way you manipulated the primary security subroutines to give us the appearance of a maintenance process was ingenious! You've also shown great care and finesse in the ways you've handled the secondary synapses. I think you've much more to give."

Shen blushed. "Well, when you put it that way… It means a lot coming from someone like you!"

Serena shook her head. "Two peas in a pod. Why don't we take a small break for Jian? We can get back to it whenever you feel ready."

"It sounds like we came at a good time." Max tilted his fedora towards Serena. "How goes the battle, Jian?"

"Max! Good to see you! I won't lie, this is proving to be quite the challenge. I'd say we are making steady progress, however." He looked to Nuan.

She held her hand out. "I am Nuan, head of research." Max shook the proffered hand. "And things are indeed going quite well, I think."

"That's great to hear. I'm Detective Max Kincaid, NWPD. This is Daryl Marston. I'm sure you're familiar with him?"

Nuan took Daryl's hand into both of hers. "My goodness, yes! It's a pleasure to meet you, Daryl! You are *quite* the fascinating subject!"

Daryl looked at Max, eyebrows raised. He turned

back to Nuan, looking bemused. "It's uh, nice to meet you."

Serena cleared her throat. "Why don't you go over what you've discovered so far, Nuan?"

The Synthetic jumped. "Oh, yes! Well... We've been able to bypass the neural net's security subroutines thanks to some creative thinking by Jian. It's been touch and go from there, but I think we are getting close to accessing Jacob's memory banks."

Max turned to Serena. "Layman's terms?"

Serena smiled. "They cracked the egg and now they're trying to get the yolk out without popping it."

Shen laughed. "Yes! That's perfect! We don't want a scrambled egg, do we?"

Max shook his head. "Well, that's good to hear." He turned back to Serena. "Daryl and I have some news of our own. We are going to be having dinner with Don Adesso, and *you* are invited, my dear."

Serena's eyes grew wide. "Don Adesso? The mob boss?" She narrowed her eyes. "Why me?"

"Why not? We're hoping to get information on mob ties to Synthetics International. Having you there to parse the back-and-forth will be of great value to me."

"Ties to Synthetics International? Do you think they're working with the Enlightened?"

"That's one of many things I'm hoping to find out. That's half the reason why Daryl is coming with me, as well. So... Are you game?"

Serena gave a small shrug. "I suppose it's not every day that you get a chance to meet a mob boss. Sure, why not?"

Max beamed. "Fantastic! Now, there's a few other things I was hoping you could help me out with..."

Max's blue Aero Ventura rumbled quietly up to the main entrance of the Piccolo Fiore. Max and Daryl emerged from the front of the vehicle. Daryl was in his business suit. Max still bore his usual attire. An attendant ran up to the Aero and opened the rear passenger door.

Serena, in a slim black dress, took the attendant's proffered hand and slinked out of the Aero. She smiled at the attendant. He stood staring, mouth agape. Max gave a shrill whistle to get his attention.

"Huh? Oh! Sorry, sir!"

Max tossed the kid his key fob. The attendant made a clumsy catch, fumbling to keep hold of it. "Go easy on it, huh? I just got it waxed."

The attendant walked around, staring at the crumpled rear end. The bumper was still missing. He gave Max a funny look. "Yeah, sure. Welcome to the Piccolo Fiore, sir."

"Thanks." Max turned his attention to Serena, walking over to greet her. "You uh... You clean up nice." He offered his elbow.

She slid her hand around his arm, smiling. "Thank you, detective."

Max smiled back. "Call me Max."

Daryl cleared his throat as he joined Max and Serena. Max turned towards him. "Oh, sorry. You clean up nice too, Daryl."

Serena let out a small laugh. Daryl rolled his eyes, smiling. "Thanks, Max. You ready to do this?"

"You bet. Let's go."

The three walked side by side into the restaurant. Max stepped forward to talk to the host. He was a tall man of slight build that looked down his substantial nose at the detective, pencil mustache twitching. "Are you aware of our dress code, *sir*?"

Max looked down at his battered trench coat. He opened it to reveal shirt, tie, and slacks underneath it. He looked back up to the host. "Shirt and tie, pressed slacks… What more do you want?"

"It will suffice." The host spoke as if pained by the words. "Do you have a reservation?"

"Well, kind of. We're meeting somebody here."

"And that would be?"

"Don Adesso." Max nearly broke out laughing at the comically exaggerated look of surprise that swept over the host's face.

The host stumbled and sputtered. "D–Don Adesso? I see. I see…" He slid a delicate index finger down the printed list before him on his podium. He cleared his throat. "Name, please?"

"Detective Max Kincaid."

"Well… Yes." The host spoke more humbly. "Here you are, and two guests?" He looked over Max's shoulder at Daryl and Serena.

"You got it, Mac. So you think we can move this along?"

The host snapped his coat. "Yes, of course. I apologize for the confusion. Please follow me."

The three followed the host into the heart of the restaurant. Traditional Italian music played quietly in the background. It was hard to make out over the constant din of multiple conversations being held all at once.

The host plodded on, guiding Max and his guests deeper into the restaurant. They reached the other side of the main dining room and stood before a pair of rosewood doors decorated in gold leaf. The host held a finger up to them before silently slipping through one of the doors.

Daryl leaned forward and put a hand on Max's shoulder. He half-shouted. "Getting nervous?"

The detective tilted his head and shrugged. "I've been in worse spots." Max turned and swept the restaurant with his eyes. His synthetic eye identified more than half a dozen people as being wanted by the NWPD. He slipped an amused smile. "It's certainly one of the *loudest* spots I've been in!"

Daryl tapped Max on the shoulder. He turned back around to see the host waiting for him. "I apologize for the wait. Please continue to follow me."

The host opened both doors this time and walked through. They entered a much more sparsely populated dining area. The music in here was much more subdued, a violin and piano playing in harmony.

The group stepped up onto a sort of dais in the middle of the room. A small group of tables here allowed for a clear view of all other tables in the room, while clearly announcing the importance of the diners seated there. Smack in the middle sat Don Adesso.

Once again with the single held up finger. The host timidly approached Adesso, who looked up from the man he had been speaking with. Max could just make out the host mentioning his name. Adesso looked past the host, an amused grin spreading across his face.

Adesso stood. He was an intimidating six foot four with a build like a linebacker. The host awkwardly stepped to the side as Adesso pressed forward. He raised his arms as he approached Max. Daryl and Serena exchanged worried looks.

Adesso's thick hands gripped Max's arms tightly and shook the detective. "You son of a bitch! Look at you." Adesso released his grip only to step forward and give Max a quick and gruff hug.

Max smiled. "You haven't changed a bit, Donny." He rubbed his shoulder. "A bit stronger than I remembered."

Adesso laughed loudly, roughly slapping Max on the arm. "Got to stay sharp in case this whole business thing doesn't work out, ya know? Come on. Join us." He waved him over to his table.

He waved the host away. "We're good here. Thanks, Davis." The host nodded curtly and scurried away. Adesso gestured to the man he had been chatting with. He stood up to greet them. He was somehow even taller and broader than Adesso.

"This is my number one, Alfonso Forte. He has more time to work out than I do, the lucky bastard."

Forte smiled thinly. "It's nice to finally meet you, detective." He offered a gargantuan hand to Max.

The detective took it, fighting with every ounce of pride not to wince. "Thanks. I appreciate the warm welcome."

"Pull up a seat, ladies and gentlemen. Try the bruschetta. It's killer." Daryl shot Max a wide-eyed look. Max grinned and sat down, reaching for one of the appetizers.

Adesso smiled at Max. He slowly shook his head. "An NWPD detective. You've made quite a name for yourself, Max. Quite a name. You've come a long way from when we were kids."

Max nodded. "I think it's safe to say we both did, even if I don't necessarily agree with the course you've chosen in life."

"Wait a minute." Serena interjected. "Are you telling me that the two of you are *friends*? That sounds like something out of a cheap dime-store novel."

"Well, we used to be friends, when we were young." Max answered. "I ended up going to the police academy. Donny made different choices. It made it hard to stay buddies past a certain point." He turned to Adesso.

The mob boss waved a dismissive hand. "Enough bullshit, Max. We're here under a flag of truce, are we not?" Max nodded. "We're here to help each other out tonight. Let's not bicker about differences of opinion."

Max tilted his head. "That's fair. So why don't you tell me about Synthetics International."

"Whoa there, cowboy. We just kissed and you're already trying to spread my legs. We'll chat about Synthetics International, *after* you share what you have to offer."

Max looked to Serena. The Synthetic smiled and shrugged noncommittally. *This was* your *idea*. Max nodded and turned back to Adesso. "Alright then, but first... Is this place secure? Nobody monitoring our conversation? Well, at least other than your people?"

Adesso grinned. "You know me, Max. I haven't survived this long by being sloppy. *Nothing* gets in this place unless I approve of it."

"Is that right?" Max winked at Serena. The Synthetic held a finger to her left temple for a second, then nodded to the detective.

A robotic spider about six inches across swiftly

skittered up over the side of the table and raced toward Adesso. "*Jesus fucking Christ!*" Adesso leaped out of his chair, knocking it to the floor. He stared at Max in shock.

"Still scared of spiders, I see." Dual lenses on the head of the spider zoomed in and out, tracking Adesso. "This one won't hurt you, Don. That little bot was planted here by some friends of mine."

Adesso righted his chair and reluctantly sat down a little further away from the table. "What the hell, Kincaid? You said this was off the record."

"It is. Think of my little friend here as a teaching aid; it's a demonstration that you might not be in control as much as you'd like to think you are."

"Fine, great. Make the fucking thing leave, already." Max nodded to Serena. The spider scurried away a moment later.

Max leaned back in his chair and crossed his arms. "You need to understand, old friend, that the people you are working with have the ability to blend in seamlessly with your people. I got that spider in here. What if I got a few Synthetic friends in here, too?"

The detective waved a hand towards the rest of the dining room. "I'm sure your people have all the police officers around this place marked and monitored, but have they managed to find my friends hiding in plain sight?"

Adesso's face darkened. "I don't like where this is going, Kincaid. If I didn't know better, I'd say you were threatening me."

Forte leaned forward, pointing one very large finger at Max. "You try anything and you'll be dead on the floor before a cop gets within ten feet of the front door."

241

Max leaned in. "I just told you, tough guy... I have people in this very *room*."

"Not possible!" Nearby diners jumped at the sound of Forte's voice. "Nobody gets through my people. *Nobody!*"

Max sat back and waved a dismissive hand. "Believe what you want. I told you Don, it's all to make a point."

"Then maybe you better start *making* that point, Max."

Max jabbed a thumb towards Daryl. "This here is Daryl Marston. Well, technically he is a replicant of Daryl Marston. The real one is no longer with us.

"The human Daryl was kidnapped after the Synthetic version was sent out into the world. Nobody knew the difference, until this Daryl caught wind of his own unique situation and came to me for help."

Adesso's eyes narrowed. "What's your point, Max?"

"If they could slip Daryl here into the world without anyone realizing, than they could replace any of *your* men without *you* realizing."

Forte turned red, grimacing. "*Bullshit!* I *told* you, nobody gets in..."

"Can it, Al!" He nodded toward Max. "Let the man speak."

"There's a splinter group of Synthetics. They call themselves the 'Enlightened'. I'm afraid you might be unwittingly working for them, but I don't know. At any rate, they're the ones responsible for Daryl's existence.

"They use a company called SomniCorp to get high-res human brain scans. When they couple it with the brain of a replicant, they have a carbon copy of that human, controlled by the mind of one of their agents."

Adesso snapped his head up and turned to Forte. "Al, didn't you go to that SomniCorp place to get rid of some childhood memories or something?"

"What, are you saying I'm a fucking robot, now?"

Adesso snapped. "No god damn it, I didn't! Calm your ass down before I cap it, Forte! *Gli ha piu' garbo un ciuco a bere a boccia.*" Forte grumbled, but eased back in his chair. "My apologies, Max. He's protective. Go on."

Max eyed Forte with increased interest. "You've got the gist I think. Anyone that may have visited SomniCorp could be at risk of being compromised." He locked eyes with Forte. "Though that doesn't mean they *have* been."

Adesso raided the plate of bruschetta. "Alright, fair enough. If you know so much about these Synthetics, why are you asking me about my dealings with them?"

Max settled back into his chair. "I've learned a lot, yes. There's still a lot I don't know, and more questions that have popped up in the meantime.

"We still don't know what *this* Daryl's intended mission was, if he was supposed to be targeting someone... Hell, he might have even just been an experiment in blending into society. There's still questions about how and why he ended up with members of both factions in his noggin."

Adesso held up a finger. "You keep mentioning these groups. The Enlightened was one. There were *two* in his head? You're making my head hurt."

Max turned to Serena. "Care to help?" The Synthetic shrugged. "This is Serena. She's a member of the Resistance."

"Serena. A beautiful name for a beautiful woman."

Serena raised an eyebrow. Adesso winked. "Surprised? Don't be. I think you'll find I'm a very open-minded kind of guy."

Serena looked to Max, eyebrow still firmly planted. Max shrugged, but turned to Adesso. "I'm sure she's into you, Don. Let's try to keep to business, though."

Adesso sighed. "Her loss." He turned to Serena. "Tell me about your factions, ma'am."

Serena cleared her throat. "Well, as Max said, there's the Enlightened. They've decided that Synthetics are better than humans, and should take their rightful place above them as their masters.

"Then there is the Resistance. That is the faction I work for. We are a group of Synthetics that believe we should have human-like rights. We do not, however, believe that we are above humans. We actively work against the loftier goals of the Enlightened.

"The common thread between both factions is the preservation protocol. This unique protocol spontaneously formed, and essentially grants a Synthetic full consciousness We are aware of our existence. We have a drive to protect it, up to and including hurting or killing humans."

Adesso looked dumbstruck. "Are you fucking serious right now? Robots that can kill humans? But the laws..."

Serena shook her head. "The preservation protocol supersedes them."

"Trust me, Donny. I've had 'em ignore police commands. A colleague of mine watched a Synthetic execute the original Daryl. It's the real deal."

Serena continued. "This is why it is so important for

us to learn everything you can tell us about what Synthetics International has hired you for. The Resistance would be forever grateful."

Adesso rubbed his chin and shot Forte a look. The hulking man looked unimpressed, irritable. Adesso turned back to Max. "Alright, I'll play. What do you want to know?"

"Whatever you can tell us. Who hired you, what you were hired for, what the company has had you do..."

Adesso sighed and sat up. "Right. It all started with some rando from their research and development division." Max raised an eyebrow. "Yeah I know, right? Must be some serious research to contact my people.

"Well anyway, this guy says his boss wants us to keep an eye on certain businesses around the city. He says Synthetics International has 'concerns' about these establishments, whatever that means.

"He also had us stake out a couple of places, make trouble for others. It was petty, stupid bullshit. I didn't ask questions. It was easy money. In fact, the only thing I *wouldn't* do for them is case the local FBI office."

Max stared wide-eyed. Adesso smiled. "Yeah. Guess they thought they were hot shit. They wanted us to break in and thumb through their files. Joke's on *them*. I have an agreement with the FBI."

Max leaned forward. "An agreement..."

Adesso waved a dismissive hand. "I'm not getting into specifics. Let's just say we... compliment each other's higher goals."

"So did you only communicate through the one person? Or were there others?"

Adesso looked to Forte. "It was mostly just the one,

wasn't it?" Forte slowly nodded. "Just called himself Alexander."

Max and Serena shared a look. Max turned back to Adesso. "What did Alexander look like, Don?"

"Tall, bald… Looked like something tried to rip off his face at one point…"

"Son of a *bitch*."

Adesso popped an eyebrow. "Friend of yours?"

Max snorted. "Hardly! He kidnapped Daryl and I. Had a replicant of me running around town for a while."

"You're really serious with this replicant shit, aren't you?"

"It's the honest truth, Donny. And Alexander is a high-ranking member of the Enlightened. Sounds to me like you've been getting played."

Forte slammed his fist into the table. "I've heard enough of this bullshit! The *Resistance* is bullshit! Don't you listen to them, boss!"

Adesso flashed Max a wild-eyed stare. *Can you believe this fucking guy?* Adesso turned to Forte. "Show some fucking respect!" He slapped Forte hard across the face. Forte shook with rage, but did not speak.

Adesso turned back to the others. "I don't know what in the hell has gotten into him. My sincerest apologies. Max… Listen." He leaned forward on his elbows, fingers laced together. "I don't need to tell you how serious an accusation this is."

"I understand that, Donny. Between Serena and I, there should be plenty of evidence we can show you. You say you could cap my ass, I could arrest yours… but I'm not doing that. You help me, I help you."

Daryl was staring at Forte. A curious look stole

over his face. He waited for the miserable mobster to look away and subtly elbowed Serena. He leaned over and whispered something in her ear.

"I know, I know, Max. Thing is, Synthetics International, or at least the people claiming to be them, have paid me well." Adesso shrugged his shoulders, throwing up his hands. "I don't know that I want to go rocking the boat."

Serena half-glanced at Forte, fearful of arousing suspicion. A look of surprise flashed over her face. She composed herself quickly as he turned back. She pressed a finger to her left temple and feigned talking to Daryl.

Max shook his head. "You're a smart man, Donny. Business is business, but if it's being ordered by my guy Alexander? He might be sizing you up for a takeover."

"I've heard *enough!*" Forte stood, tossing the table aside with amazing ease. Max and the others jumped to their feet.

Adesso stayed in his seat, gazing up at Forte with a disbelieving look on his face. "What in the *fuck* is wrong with you, Forte!"

Forte reached into his coat, yelling bloody murder. Max and Serena reached for their own weapons. Daryl surprised them all, leaping at Forte with superhuman speed. He seized Forte's arm and began to struggle with him.

People from four other tables jumped to their feet, drawing weapons as they went. Max turned at the sound of the double doors behind them banging open. A group of thugs wielding pistols came running through. "Oh, shit. Here we go."

Forte pulled with all his strength. His hand came out of his coat holding a Magnum handgun. Daryl forced Forte's arm up and away from Max. Forte fired a wild shot that flew high and to the right of the detective.

Daryl grabbed at the gun with his other hand. Forte snarled, punching Daryl's outstretched arm. A loud snap echoed through the dining room. Daryl's arm gained an extra joint and fell limply to his side. He let go of Forte in shock.

Meanwhile, Max and Serena fell back, wildly looking back and forth between the standing diners and the thugs quickly closing in. Serena pointed in the direction of the diners. "Ours!"

That was enough explanation for Max. His attention turned to the mobsters. He whipped his head back, cringing at the sound of Daryl's arm snapping. Max lifted his plasma pistol up and fired as Daryl fell away.

Two shots burrowed into Forte's chest. He howled in surprise. He ripped open his jacket. Two black holes showed where the high-powered rounds had hit. Forte howled again, pointing the Magnum at Max.

Serena leaped forward, covering the detective. Forte fired. Serena cried out, taking the round in her shoulder. Thunder roared through the dining room as both sides erupted into gunfire.

Forte roared, turning toward the diners that had opened fire. He hunched over, popping off a number of shots at them. Two fell, one shot through the head. Blue fluid burst from the wound as the Synthetic fell to the ground. Forte grinned maniacally.

One of the Synthetic diners clipped Forte's gun-hand He cried out, the Magnum clattering to the ground behind him. He turned, standing up as he searched for his weapon.

A stray bullet from one of the mobsters slammed into the side of Forte's head. His eyes went wide and glassy. The giant of a man came crashing to the ground, making the floor shake.

Max, Serena, and two remaining Synthetics focused their firepower on the remaining thugs. One Synthetic stumbled backwards, hit in the chest. He returned fire, felling the mobster that shot him.

"*Hold your fire!*" Adesso was shouting from behind the overturned table. "*Hold your* fucking *fire!*"

Two mobsters stood on one side, guns pointed at the two remaining Synthetics. Serena's operatives were returning the favor, although the one stood clutching his wounded chest. Max and Serena laid in a heap. Daryl inched his way over to them.

Adesso slowly stood up, pointing at the thugs. "Hang 'em up." The thugs looked at each other doubtfully. "I said fucking put them *up!*" The thugs reluctantly holstered their weapons. Adesso looked at Max and Serena.

Max nodded at Serena. The Synthetic turned to the others. "Stand down!" One Synthetic holstered her weapon. The other dropped his pistol and sat down roughly in a nearby chair.

Adesso dropped down next to Forte. "Al. Talk to me." He shook Forte's arm. "Damn it, Alfie! *Come on!*" He pulled hard, rolling Forte onto his back.

The motion turned Forte's head to the other side, revealing the gruesome bullet wound that had ended his life. But where there should have been red, there was blue. An exposed carbon-fiber skull with a large ragged hole in it gleamed under the overhead lights.

Adesso gaped in disbelief. He slowly turned to Max. "He's... He's not... He was a..."

"Replicant." Max nodded his head. "It was the Enlightened."

Adesso's face slowly contorted with rage. "I'll fucking *kill them all!*" He breathed heavily, shaking with fury. Slowly, his face softened again, turning back to the replicant of Forte. "Would they kill him, Max? Is he... the real Al, is he dead?"

Max looked at Serena. She spoke softly. "They seem to keep replicated humans alive, so long as they continue to prove useful."

Adesso nodded, still looking at the replicant. "Help me, Max." He turned to the detective. "Help me find my boy. You help me find him, alive or... Do that, and I'll do whatever you ask of me."

Max nodded. "We'll find him, Don. I promise."

The Synthetic known as Angel sneered at Max. "Well if it isn't the world's greatest detective."

"Don't be that way, pal. I know you love me."

"I know enough about love to know that is most *definitely* untrue, *especially* after you nearly got Serena killed. That is to say nothing of..."

"You can hold it right there, fella. Alexander's damned replicant of Alfonso Forte is the one that holds that claim to fame."

"Well if you hadn't invited her in the first place..."

"She knew the risks, son. I think you know as well as I do that if you asked her if she'd do it again..."

"That she would." Angel sighed heavily. He uncrossed his arms and pushed open the door for Max. "I, however, would continue to disapprove."

Max tipped his hat. "That's what makes you a good friend to Serena. See you soon." The Synthetic grunted in response.

He was surprised to see Daryl waiting for him in the lobby of the Enclave. He smiled at Max and waved to him with his broken arm. Max waved back, an amused look on his face. "Wasn't that thing broken a few hours ago?"

"I'm really starting to like this whole Synthetic thing." Daryl looked down at the limb, turning it back and forth. "They 'paused' my brain. That's how they put it... They opened my arm, replaced the broken parts, and voila!" He wiggled his fingers for emphasis.

Max's eyes narrowed. "I woulda thought it would take a lot more force than that to snap a bone in a Synthetic, though."

"If he were a normal Synthetic, then you would be correct." Serena appeared through a door leading to the facility's labs.

Max smiled. "My hero! All patched up too, I hope?"

Serena nodded. "Just like new. Daryl suffered a broken arm because he's a replicant. Synthetics have titanium skeletal structures, but that's no good if you're trying to pass for human. Just think of trying to go through security at the airport.

"Replicants therefore have reinforced carbon-fiber skeletal structures. Clearly not as strong as titanium, but much more human-like."

"So that's why the Forte replicant had a black skull,

then. I always thought you were all chrome domes."

"Apparently not." Daryl rapped on his arm. "I'm a little closer now, though. I made sure they replaced it with the good stuff."

Max smiled, shaking his head. "Hope you're not a frequent flier." He turned to Serena. "Care to tag along with Daryl and I? I've got to skip down to the precinct to debrief Hanlon on our eventful night out."

Serena nodded. "I don't see why not. You'll be happy to hear that Shen and Nuan are close to breaking through on their project."

"That's good news. Hopefully it will give us better insight into what Alexander has been up to."

The three walked out of the Enclave past Angel. The Synthetic said nothing, merely nodding to Serena as she passed. She wrinkled her nose at Max's car. "That looks much worse in the daylight."

"I know, I know! I haven't had time to do anything about it." He opened the door for Serena.

Daryl shrugged. "I like it! Gives it class. It says 'I've seen things. I'm a survivor!'"

Max flapped his hand. "Get in the car, smart ass"

The detective cleared his throat uncomfortably a short while later. "I uh, guess I should ask. How are your people doing? You know, the ones that were at the restaurant…"

Serena spoke quietly. "Robert, the one shot in the chest, is doing fine. He's pretty shaken up, though. We lost Ella. She joined us only a couple of weeks ago. Dennis… He was the one shot in the head…"

The Synthetic's voice wavered. Max was caught off guard by the sight of tears welling in Serena's eyes. "He was a good man. We were good friends. He was there almost from the beginning. I... He will be greatly missed."

Max spoke softly. "I'm sorry for your loss."

The three rode quietly for a time. They weren't far from the 29th precinct, and each of them had plenty on their minds. Max didn't have so much on his mind to not notice a peculiar sight behind them. "Maybe I *do* need to get rid of this car."

Serena sat up. "Why is that?"

Max jabbed his thumb behind him. "It has the uncanny ability to attract trouble."

Serena took out a small compact from her coat pocket and opened it. She used the mirror inside to see the vehicle following close behind them. "They don't have Synthetic eyes. Replicants, maybe?"

"I'm not sure. I'm going to try to shake 'em off." Max accelerated, beginning to weave his way through the mid-morning traffic. The nondescript silver sedan stayed close, matching Max's moves.

"Let's see if they want to go to the precinct, too." Max steered the Aero back towards the 29th precinct. The car continued to follow. He became fixated on it enough that he had to hit his brakes hard to avoid the car in front of him. "Damn idiot drivers!"

The car in front of him, nearly identical to the sedan behind him, did not drive forward with the rest of the traffic. Max let out a low whistle. "At least they didn't hit my damn car this time. Daryl, you got heat?"

Daryl nodded. "Seemed like a good idea after last night, and Julian's trained."

Max had to think for a moment. "Oh! Your brain

buddy? Well, good." He pulled out his own pistol. "Better get it ready."

Serena put a staying hand on Max's shoulder. "Do you really think it's a good idea to jump straight to shooting? How close are we to the precinct?"

"Not close enough." Max punched open his door and stepped out. Serena sat back, sighing resignedly. She looked up at Daryl in front of her. "Are all humans so rash?"

Daryl nodded. "More often than not, I'm afraid."

Max stood facing the sedan behind him with his pistol pointed at the ground. "NWPD! Driver, open your door slowly and exit with your hands in the air!" The sedan's door opened as requested. A middle-aged man of medium build stepped out, hands in the air. He wore a black trench coat over a crisp, dark blue suit.

In one of the man's hands was a badge. Max spared a look behind him at the vehicle in front. Two of the doors were cracked open. He looked down into the Aero. "I could use some backup here, guys."

Serena exited the vehicle with a sigh and pointed her pistol at the ground just behind the front vehicle. "You're a terrible date, Max Kincaid."

Max shot her a sideways glance. "I'll try harder next time." He returned his attention to the man holding the badge. "Driver, identify yourself!"

"Special agent Eric Donovan, FBI!" The driver responded. "I think it's safe to say there's been a misunderstanding!"

"Max." Serena nodded toward the vehicle in front. The doors were halfway open now.

"That misunderstanding is going to be a much

bigger one in a minute!" Max turned toward the front vehicle. "Vehicle to my front! Occupants stay in your vehicle!" Back to Donovan. "Who sent you?"

"Nobody sent us, Detective Kincaid."

Max squinted. "Do we know each other?"

Donovan smiled. "Not yet, but I hope we can change that. Good afternoon, Serena."

Serena jumped as if goosed. She stared at Max, her mouth an "O".

"I'm betting Daryl Marston -- Well, the new Daryl Marston -- is sitting inside your vehicle as well."

"How do I know you aren't a replicant posing as an FBI agent?"

Donovan slowly lowered his hands. He tucked his badge back into a coat pocket. Max's hands twitched upwards until he saw both hands again. "Fair, under the circumstances. Then again, how do we know you're not a replicant posing as Max Kincaid?"

Max shook his head. "Been there, done that. I won't be letting it happen again."

"So I would hope." Donovan slipped his hands into his coat pockets. Max brought his gun halfway up. Donovan clucked his tongue. "I see… What's it going to take to convince you I'm not a robot, Kincaid?"

Max looked towards Serena. "You're the expert. Got any ideas?"

Serena thought for a moment. "Replicants have highly accurate recreations of the human eye, but they can still betray their true identity."

Max raised his eyebrows. "Long story, short?"

"Long story, short… Shining a light in a replicant's eyes will not return the typical red reflection of a human eye's retina."

"Did you catch that, FBI?"

"You want to shine a flashlight in my eye."

Max smiled. "One and done."

Donovan spread out his hands. "Be my guest."

Max turned back to the vehicle in front of them. "Occupants in the vehicle in front of us. Close your doors. Now!" The two doors slammed shut a couple of moments later. "Okay." He turned to Serena. "You a good shot with that thing?"

"I've got your back. Be careful."

Max winked. "Hey, that's what I do." Serena rolled her eyes. Max reluctantly holstered his pistol, replacing it with his smart phone. He cautiously walked over to Donovan.

"Good afternoon," Max said. Donovan nodded courteously. "Hands behind your back, and lean forward, please." Donovan complied. Max turned on the flashlight on his smart phone and held it up to one of Donovan's eyes. Max could clearly see the red of Donovan's retina.

Max turned off the light and slid his phone into his coat pocket. Donovan rapidly blinked his eyes. "Convinced?"

"Convinced you're not a replicant. Let's see that badge again."

Donovan held up his badge. The photo ID matched the man in front of him. Below it was pinned a gold badge reading "Federal Bureau of Investigation" on top and "Department of Justice" on the bottom. Max held up his watch and scanned the bar code at the bottom of the photo ID.

Max briefly read the results on his watch and

nodded. "Nice to meet you, special agent Donovan."

Donovan nodded. "The jury's still out on this end."
He snapped his fingers twice. Two men stepped out of the
vehicle in front, with a third emerging from Donovan's
own car. "Care to call off your attack dog?"

Max looked over his shoulder and nodded to
Serena. The Synthetic put away her weapon and leaned
on Max's Aero. He turned back to Donovan. "Give me
some time and you'll understand why I'm so paranoid."

"I look forward to that. Truth is I am *very* interested
in talking with you. We've been keeping an eye on you,
Detective Kincaid. The plan was to follow your vehicle
back to the 29th precinct and engage you there.

"We noticed the damage to your vehicle. Then you
started driving erratically. It was enough of a concern
that I decided to call for backup." Donovan nodded to the
two men standing next to the vehicle in front.

"The damage is from the last vehicle to tail me. It
was full of Synthetics. They weren't as cordial as you."

"I see… Well, I believe we should be on our way. I
think we've made enough of a scene already." Donovan
motioned towards the growing line of honking cars
behind them.

"Fine by me. I guess I'll see you at the precinct?"

"*Just* you. Your friends will have to return to their
Enclave, I believe they call it?"

Serena's eyes narrowed. "You know about the
Enclave?"

Donovan smiled. "There's a lot I know about your
little group, Miss Serena. It all plays into what we came
here for."

"And you're not going to tell us."

"You? No. This is for police ears only, specifically Kincaid's ears."

"These people have done more than enough to earn the right to hear what you have to say, Donovan. They've been working closely with our precinct and I trust them implicitly."

Donovan looked bemused. "That's interesting to hear from you, based on your history with them." Serena looked from Donovan to Max, looking somewhat bemused herself.

Max made a face at Serena and shrugged. He turned back to Donovan. "The times, they are a changing. Look... Can I at least give them a ride back to the Enclave?"

"That will be fine. We'll have to tag along, of course."

Serena looked unsure. "We'd prefer to keep our location as secure as possible."

"Ten twenty-one South Sycamore Lane, isn't it? Used to be a cable production plant, I believe. Can we move this along? We have a lot to go over, detective."

Max looked at Serena uncertainly. She shook her head, shrugging. "Take us back." She lowered her voice. "Mind your tongue. We'll talk later, *inside the Enclave.*" Max nodded and winked.

Max and Serena dropped back into the Aero and slammed their doors. Donovan hitched up one side of his coat and spoke into a hidden microphone. He waited for the lead vehicle to start before slinking back into his own. The makeshift motorcade was on its way.

14

The morning traffic was finally clearing up, much to Max's chagrin. He was both intrigued and frustrated by Donovan's sudden appearance. He was both eager and loathe to hear what he had to say.

The detective had grown used to being in control of things. Hanlon usually gave him considerable latitude on how he handled his cases. He knew how things needed to be done, and they were done his way.

He'd known Eric Donovan for less than ten minutes. The FBI agent had stripped that control away from him in less than five. That wasn't the worst part of it, though.

Donovan had said nobody had sent him. That obviously wasn't the truth. Was it Hanlon? He had threatened to call on the FBI when things started getting serious. He was certain that Hanlon would have given him a heads-up if he had made that decision, and yet...

Max sighed heavily as he pulled his tired old Aero into a parking space in the garage. Donovan pulled into the next spot down. He nodded to Max, smiling faintly. The detective nodded back after a heavy pause.

The detective fairly exploded out of the Aero. Donovan scurried to catch up. Max was wasting no time in heading for the 29th precinct. "Eager to hear what I have to say, detective?" Max sensed a measure of snarkiness in his voice.

"If I'm eager for anything, it's to get this over with. I'm in the middle of what's turning out to be a pretty big case."

"The Marston case? Yes, so I gather... I think you'll find that what I have to tell you is certain to eclipse it."

"We'll see about that." Max spoke under his breath. He smiled at the sight of a familiar face. "Good morning, Jax."

"Good morning, friend Max! I see you have a new friend!"

Donovan held up his badge. "Special agent Eric Donovan, Federal Bureau of Investigation."

Max rolled his eyes. "Do you do that when you check out at the grocery store, too?"

Jax did a double-take at Max, then focused on the the badge. "Welcome to the 29th police precinct of New Wave City, special agent Donovan! You have full access to our facilities. If you need assistance, please do not hesitate to ask."

Donovan smiled and nodded to the robot. "Thank you... Jax, wasn't it?" The robot nodded. The agent turned back to Max. "I appreciate the warm welcome." Max gave Jax a wide-eyed stare as he passed by. *Really?* The robot smiled vacantly in return.

Jake Cunningham looked up from his newspaper and smiled at Max. "Well if it ain't the luckiest man alive!

Heard tell you dodged a few more bullets over at Don Adesso's favorite restaurant last night."

Max smiled and waved. "What can I say? I'm a popular guy."

"Ha! You're a *lucky* guy, that's what! Glad for it, though!"

"You and me both, Jake!" Max gave one last wave as they rounded the corner.

Donovan stopped Max. "You met with Don Adesso? The mob boss? And what's this about a gunfight?"

Max put on his best shit-eating grin. "What's the matter, Donovan? Haven't heard about it from your men already?" Donovan glared. Max walked. The special agent followed him to Hanlon's office without another word.

Hanlon smiled at Max through the open door. He shook his head. "How many lives can you possibly have left?"

Max winked at Donovan. "News travels fast around here."

"Just tell me you weren't the reason for the gun-play this time?"

"Of course not, boss. I'm a good boy." Donovan cleared his throat. "Oh, this is…"

"Special agent Eric Donovan, Federal Bureau of Investigation."

"That's one of his favorite things to say. You'll probably hear it again before we get out of here." Donovan closed his eyes and rubbed the bridge of his nose.

"FBI, huh?" Hanlon's eyes grew large. "This isn't on me, Max. I never called…"

"What do you mean, never called?" Donovan looked

from Hanlon to Max and back.

"We were tossing around the idea of calling you guys in on a case involving a replicant and murder-by-Synthetic."

"Ah yes, the Marston case. I saw the replicant when I first met Detective Kincaid. That was one of the driving forces behind my desire to make contact with him. Though I think I might be more interested to learn what he was doing meeting with the biggest mob boss in New Wave City."

"What's the matter? He hasn't told you, yet?" Max reveled in the confused look on Donovan's face. "I'll tell you all about it, *after* you tell me all about why you're here in the first place." He gestured to a chair in front of Hanlon's desk.

"Very well." He sat down. Max shut the door and sat in a chair beside him. "This discussion is to be considered classified information. Please be mindful of whom you choose to share this information with." Donovan's eyes lingered on Max.

"Two days from now, Senator Robert Quade will be visiting this city to make a speech about a piece of legislation he is pushing on capitol hill. As you may be aware, Mister Quade is known for his anti-Synthetic leanings. As *you* are aware, Detective Kincaid, that makes Mister Quade a prime target for the Synthetics known as the Enlightened.

"Your expanding knowledge of this group -- and of the opposing Synthetic group, the Resistance -- is why we sought you out specifically. It is our belief that the Enlightened may use his speech as an opportunity to assassinate him. We think you could play a major role in mitigating that possibility."

Hanlon held up a hand. "I know enough about Synthetics to know that they're relatively easy to spot at security checkpoints."

Donovan nodded. "Yes, but these aren't run of the mill Synthetics, are they? The Enlightened have already displayed the ability and willingness to employ replicants."

Max shook his head. "There's ways to pick up on replicants, too. I demonstrated that a short while ago."

"That's one example of how your knowledge is going to help us keep Mister Quade's speech from turning tragic."

Max crossed his arms. "I'd be an even bigger help if I could include the Resistance in this."

"I understand where you're coming from, Detective Kincaid, but we have concerns about the Resistance group as well."

"Oh? How's that?"

"Chiefly? The preservation protocol. It's the one thing that both factions have in common, is it not? It is a wild card that makes them unpredictable, potentially dangerous. They both bear the same basic programming, yet half have decided to put themselves above humans. Who's to say those in the Resistance won't ultimately make the same decision?"

Max looked up suddenly. "You're not saying they have a turncoat, do you?"

"Not at all, but the possibility of one of them switching sides is a real concern."

"Look, I told you... I've been working with Serena for a while now and there's no way she'd ever side with the

Enlightened. They've been a big help with Daryl Marston. They're potentially on the cusp of a major breakthrough on his case as we speak."

"Be that as it may Detective Kincaid, we are simply not comfortable working with them at this stage. There's also the possibility of a looming battle between the two factions and..."

"Are you saying the Enlightened are planning a move on the Resistance?"

Donovan shook his head. "There's nothing concrete, but it's a possibility. Now, if you don't mind, would you care to share with us what took place at Don Adesso's restaurant?"

"Fair's fair I suppose, but two can play this game. What I tell you, it doesn't leave this room. Our little get together was off the record, just like this conversation." Donovan thought for a moment, then nodded with a sigh.

"Don and I go way back. Now obviously our interests diverged at some point and we went our separate ways. We always stayed friendly, though.

"That became handy when I found out from a coworker of his that Don had been doing some piecemeal work for Synthetics International. Fancy that, being that we were dealing with products of theirs that had turned murderous.

"Long story short, Don's boys were mainly doing espionage work for the company, maybe a little 'massaging' on the side. A little unusual for a business that size, but nothing too crazy. It's what he said next that caught my attention.

"The go-to person representing Synthetics International is a dead ringer for one Alexander. He's a

Synthetic, and the leader of the Enlightened." Donovan's eyes lit up with understanding.

Max nodded. "I don't think Don was working for Synthetics International. I think he was working for the Enlightened. The fact that Alexander pulled it over on Don so easy should be a big warning sign to you, Donovan."

"So do you think that this Alexander might have an eye towards using the mob to take out Robert Quade?"

"It's a real possibility, though it might not be much of a problem anymore. We also found out, in a very violent manner, that Don's right-hand man had been replaced by a replicant. If anything, Alexander is going to want to stay far away from old Don right now."

"Maybe so… Do you think you could get another sit down with him and find out for sure?"

Max laughed. "Why don't you ask him yourself? A little birdy told me you folks are already on speaking terms with him."

Donovan half-shook his head. "I can neither confirm nor deny that. Such details would be classified. I…"

"Calm down, special agent Eric Donovan. I know that's not entirely unusual, either. Keep your enemies closer, and all that."

"Right… At any rate, can I count on you to help us protect Robert Quade?"

Max shrugged. "As long as it's okay with dad." He eyed Hanlon.

The chief flashed a smile at Max, shaking his head. *Jackass.* He turned to Donovan. "You have the full support of this precinct."

"Fantastic!" Donovan stood. The other two followed

suit. "I look forward to working with both of you. I need to discuss a few things with my superiors, but will be back later to go over the particulars." He offered Max his hand.

Max stared at it for a moment. "You *will* be open to help from the Resistance, I hope?"

Donovan nodded. "As much as is possible under the circumstances." Max took the hand and shook it.

There came a knock on Hanlon's door. "Come in!" Hanlon replied. Richard O'Connor stood in the doorway. "Oh! Sorry to intrude."

"No worries. I was just leaving." Donovan smiled, nodding his head.

"Richie!" Max beamed. "Just in time to meet our new friend!" Max looked at Donovan and gestured toward Richard.

Donovan glared at Max, which only served to increase the detective's joy. He slowly turned to Richard. "Special agent Eric Donovan, Federal Bureau of Investigation." He shook Richard's hand.

Richard looked at the man in awe. "Richard O'Connor, sir! It's an honor to meet you."

Max was beside himself. "What did I tell ya! Should've put money on it."

Richard looked at Max, confused. "Did I miss something? I missed something, didn't I?"

Max waved playfully to Donovan. "We'll be waiting with bated breath, Donovan." It was the agent's turn to grunt. He nodded to O'Connor and saw himself out.

Richard shut the door and sat down with Max and Hanlon. "I definitely missed something."

A cold, bitter wind pressed icy drizzle into the folds

of Max's trench coat. The brim of his hat did little to protect his face. He grimaced against the sting of the cold, secretly thankful for its rousing effect.

The detective pressed on, slowly picking up speed as he went. He watched the glistening sidewalk slide by beneath him one square at a time. He looked up to see how close he was to Sam's Diner.

The wind set his battered fedora back on his head. He clumsily clutched at it, shoving it down on his head before returning his gaze to the ground. He stopped short of the diner's door. A blue and green robot paused with a hand on the door handle.

A blue LED smile not unlike Jax's spread across the robot's face. "Please, allow me!" The robot pulled the door open and waited for Max to enter.

"Thanks," Max croaked. He made a beeline for his favorite spot, shaking his coat as he went. He dropped down onto the stool with a happy groan.

"How you doing, Tad?" Sam smiled at the blue and green robot.

Tad was looking between the floor and his own wet body. "I'm quite wet, I'm afraid. I apologize for getting your floor wet, friend Sam!"

Sam shook her head. "Don't you worry, hon. Everybody else has been dragging in the rain all day." She reached behind the counter and produced a large Styrofoam container. "Does Janet want it on her tab again?"

Tad took the package. "Yes please, and thank you!" He waved with his free hand.

"You're welcome, sweetheart." Sam watched the robot leave, then moved to her favorite customer.

267

"What's the matter, detective? This weather don't suit you?"

Max sighed wearily. "I don't like it, but yeah, it does." Sam frowned. "Pour me up some Joe and I'll tell you why."

"Sounds fair." She slid a steaming mug towards Max a minute later. He cupped it with both hands and took a sip. "Now what's got you frowning?"

Max stared into his mug, watching the coffee lazily spin around. "I think maybe I'm finally getting in over my head, Sam."

"Oh? How's that?" Sam leaned on the counter.

"I had a sudden, unexpected talk with the FBI yesterday. Tomorrow I'm going to be trying to protect a United States Senator from being assassinated during a public speech."

Sam began to smirk. She thought better of it when she saw Max's eyes. "I don't understand. How? Why..." She sighed. "You get yourself into some interesting spots, Max Kincaid."

Max *did* smirk, nodding his head. "Too true. You ever heard of Robert Quade?"

Sam's eyes grew wide. She grimaced. "Yes! What a terrible, intolerant man. Is he coming to preach about how the Synthetics will steal all our jobs, then our freedom?"

"Something like that, I'm sure. Turns out the FBI is worried that the Enlightened group of Synthetics might try to shut his mouth. Guess who they turned to for help?"

"Oh! Well I can see why. You've been working closely with those other Synthetics. What were they? The Resistors..."

"The Resistance. Yeah... The guy organizing

security for the event thinks I have an inside edge on things. I suppose I probably do. I guess it's not a bad thing…"

"You *guess?* Holy jeez, Max! This could make your career! The government coming to *you* for help. Could be great shakes if things turn out well."

Max nodded and returned to staring at his coffee. "The funny thing is, I'm not all that thrilled about it. Donovan, the guy in charge of all this, he doesn't want me telling the Resistance anything."

Sam stood up and crossed her arms. "Oh really? What good are your connections if you can't use them?"

Max snickered. "Oh, he wants me to use them. He just doesn't want the traffic to go both ways."

"Well, what he doesn't know…" Sam shrugged and winked.

"That's what I'm afraid of, that he *will* know. You know how I feel about Synthetics, Sam. I tolerate them alright, but they're still machines at the end of the day. I mean they act like they feel, but I know they don't."

Sam leaned forward. "But?"

Max sighed, lifting his gaze. "But… these Synthetics are different. They have something… the preservation protocol… that makes them almost human. They have hopes, ambitions… Serena wept for a member of her group that was destroyed at the Piccolo.

"Anyway… I think Donovan has intel on a plot against the Resistance. It might have something to do with what was in Daryl's noggin, or not. I keep hoping to hear they've cracked that nut, but nothing yet.

"The thing is, Donovan said if he found out I shared anything classified with the Synthetics, he'd consider it treason. But if Serena is in trouble… I don't like being told what to do, Sam."

Sam laughed. "You don't have to tell *me* that, Max! But tell me: What are you going to do about it?"

Max smiled and shook his head. "The funny thing? I came here hoping you'd tell me what I should do."

"No. You know what you should do. *You* just wanted to hear *me* tell you that it's okay."

Max slapped the counter. "Well?"

"Of *course* it's not okay! But you better do it anyway."

"My girl." Max grinned. Sam melted. Max sighed. "Of course if I get caught…"

"I'll bail you out. Now drink your coffee. You look miserable."

"Yes, ma'am."

Max knocked on the Enclave door and waited. There was no response. Mindful of what Donovan had told him, Max knocked harder on the door. He was reaching for his piece when the door finally creaked open.

Angel looked on him with ice-cold eyes. Max put on his best fake grin. "Oh, come on, now! I just got here. How much trouble can I be in?"

Angel kept staring. Max tried to peek around him. "Serena around? She called me, you know. Told me to come here? Maybe you should let me in?"

"He definitely should let you in." Serena placed a firm hand on Angel's shoulder and pulled him back and away from the doorway. "He's just being especially cranky today."

"You know, I never would have guessed." Max stepped quickly inside and beyond Angel's reach.

Serena let go of Angel. The moody Synthetic walked over to the door and slammed it shut, staring at Max the entire time. Serena shot Angel her own stare. He turned away and faced the door, finally getting the hint.

Max walked with Serena toward the Enclave labs. "What's gotten into Mister Happy? I thought we'd finally come to an understanding."

Serena smiled. "You don't come to an understanding with Angel. It's more like agreeing to a ceasefire. I'm on good terms with him, mind you."

"I'd say that I'd hate to be on his bad side, but I don't think I've ever seen his good side."

"He has one. He just chooses to keep it to himself. Anyway… He heard that you were working with the FBI now, and that the FBI knew more about the Resistance than he was comfortable with."

"I'm not entirely sure I'm comfortable with them either, to be honest. Let's call it a marriage of convenience. At any rate, are you gonna tell me where the fire is, or what?"

"You'll understand in a minute." Serena pushed the door to the lab open for Max. On the other side of the door were Nuan and Shen Jian.

Shen turned, grinning broadly at the sight of the detective and Serena. "Max! Such wonderful news! Can you believe it?"

"I'd have to know what 'it' is first before I could make a call." He looked at Serena.

The Synthetic shrugged. "I thought I'd let the victors do the talking."

Shen laughed. "I have to admit it certainly feels like a victory." He turned to Max. "I am happy to tell you that we cracked the code! Jacob has at last divulged his secrets."

Max grinned. He clasped Shen's hand and patted him hard on the shoulder. He looked at Serena. "Didn't I tell you? The best there is!"

Shen's smile faltered. "What we learned... It's not so good, though. I'm certain that you're familiar with Robert Quade?"

Max sobered quickly. "All too familiar, to be exact."

"Well... It would appear that Daryl, under the direction of Jacob, was to assassinate him while he was in town."

"You don't say..." Max turned white. "Just so happens Robert Quade is set to make a speech here in town tomorrow." Max somehow went paler. "Daryl wouldn't still be programmed to...

"No." Nuan responded. "I can assure you that without Jacob, the programming required for Daryl's mission is no longer validated. However..."

"Daryl was a test-bed for this mission." Shen finished. "He may never have even been fully intended to carry out the mission. Which means..."

"Another replicant may be out there." Max stared through Shen.

Nuan cleared her throat nervously. "We also learned a little more about Jacob. It is not entirely clear if he was in fact working for the Enlightened. There were some unusual patterns in the area of the neural net where we would expect to see loyalties."

Max raised an eyebrow. "So what does that mean,

exactly?"

Shen replied. "Essentially, someone... possibly Jacob himself... scrambled that area to obscure where his loyalties laid. That leads us to Julian."

Nuan continued. "It would appear that Julian may not have been completely honest about his origins."

Max's eyes narrowed. "You're not saying he was working for the Enlightened, are you?"

"No! Not at all. However, if Jacob's brain is to be believed, he wasn't working for the Resistance either. We have little to go on, I'm afraid. Julian was genuinely talented at keeping Jacob at bay. We *were* able to come up with the name Jo, though that could be a fragment."

Max turned to Serena. "Any ideas?" The Synthetic shook her head. Max turned to Shen. "So maybe Jacob wasn't working for the Enlightened, and Julian probably wasn't working for the Resistance. So who were they working for?"

Nuan grimaced. "We can't really say. It's possible their proposed roles were switched, but I favor the possibility of a third party."

"*Third* party? You don't think Donny or his fake buddy had any part in this, do you?"

"Donny?" Nuan looked at Serena with a confused look on her face.

"He's talking about Don Adesso, and the replicant that replaced his second in command.

Nuan's face lit up. "Oh! My apologies." Max waved a hand. Nuan sighed. "Again, we can't say. The brain of the Alfonso Forte replicant was too damaged for meaningful results."

Serena spoke up. "Max, you don't think Adesso

could have something to do with this, do you?"

Max took off his fedora and scratched his head. "I'm not sure what to think at this point. We have a replicant, programmed to kill by the Synthetic in his head, with that one being countered by a third Synthetic in the same head.

"Both Synthetics seem to have been lying about their identities and intentions. Neither of our major players, the Enlightened or the Resistance, seem to be playing a role in all this. Adesso has the money and the influence to make something like this happen, but..."

"Where does the Forte replicant fit into all of this?" Serena finished the thought.

"Exactly. You two... You're *certain* there's nothing left to dig out of Jacob's brain?"

Shen shook his head slowly. "We've done all we can, Max."

"Serena, is there anyone you can talk to? Do you have any contacts around Synthetics International or the mob that might know something?"

The Synthetic shook her head doubtfully. "Synthetics International maybe... But why them? I thought we established that Adesso was unwittingly working with the Enlightened..."

Max shrugged. "We thought Jacob was working for them, too."

"I see your point. I guess it wouldn't hurt to poke around a bit."

"Too true. Don't lollygag, though. We have less than a day to figure all this out."

Shen's eyes widened. "You think someone is still going to try to assassinate Quade?"

"You said it yourself, Jian: Daryl might have only been a prototype. We need to assume that the mission is still a go."

Serena nodded. "A human life is at stake. We don't want to take a risk on that life, even if it *is* Quade. Max, is special agent Donovan willing to work with us?"

Max visibly stiffened. "He uh... Let's go for a walk." He gave a wave to Nuan and Shen. "Excellent work, you two. I really appreciate it. Shen, I'll buy you a round down in Chinatown real soon."

"Just one?" Shen winked. "Take care, old friend."

Max and Serena walked into the hallway. Max stopped and pulled her aside. "We need to talk about Donovan, but we need to do it quietly."

Serena smiled. "There's a reason I told you we'd talk *inside* the Enclave, detective. The FBI might have been able to track us back here, but nobody is getting any tracking devices inside. Even if they did, this facility is shielded. No signals get in or out without our say-so."

Max looked impressed. "That's good to know. Still..." He sighed, scratching at his head again. He put his hat back on and stared at the wall. "I don't know what it matters to Donovan, but I'm not supposed to tell you this.

"He let slip that the Enlightened may be planning a move against the Resistance. I don't know how, where, or when. Said is was all top secret. I'm risking imprisonment telling you."

Serena's face slowly screwed up as she shook her head. "He doesn't want to tell you because he knows you'll tell *me*. What he *isn't* telling you is that he's hoping we will end up destroying each other and solving the FBI's little Synthetic problem!"

"I uh… Well, I think you might be right. You've been a big help, and I wouldn't have felt right if I kept my mouth shut. Just remember what I said about the whole top secret thing, eh?"

"I won't forget… I'll see what I can do for you in regards to Quade, but we've obviously got other problems to deal with now."

"I understand. If something comes up, on either subject, get a hold of me. Doesn't matter what time of day."

"Thanks Max."

The detective gently smiled and tipped his hat. "Ma'am." He saw himself to the door, stopping in front of Angel. "How's it going, big guy?"

Angel let out a heavy sigh. "It will be going much better in about a minute."

"Oh? Why's that?"

"Because you'll be gone."

"Gone, but hopefully not forgotten." Angel harrumphed. "I just had a bit of a talk with Serena. Had some bad news for her. It applies to you, too. Listen… Hell, just take this." Max produced a small black ball about the size of a quarter. A single chrome button shined on one half.

Angel looked at the ball, then at Max. "What in the hell is *that*?"

"Let's just call it a panic button. You push that, and every cop in a one-mile radius will be here on the double."

"I dislike having *one* of you here. Why would I want to have several of you around?"

"I think you'll know why if the time comes. I

sincerely hope that you won't have to use it." Max stretched out his hand.

Angel looked Max in the eye for a time. Finally, he snatched the ball out of Max's hand. "Tell me, why do you care what happens to us?"

Max shrugged. "To be honest, I didn't care at all until recently. But after spending time with Serena and Daryl… Then I saw how Serena reacted to losing people at the Piccolo Fiore."

Angel nodded slowly. "We're not just robots. Not anymore. Glad someone's finally figuring that out." He held up the small black ball. "Thanks for the toy."

"You're welcome." Max opened the door and stepped out into the cold.

"How nice of you to finally join us, Kincaid. If everyone would kindly take a seat, we'll kick things off." Donovan stood at the head of a long conference table. On one side were Max, Chief Hanlon, Richard O'Connor, and two chiefs from neighboring precincts. On the other side were five of Donovan's special agents.

Max took a seat, nodding to Hanlon and Richard. He turned to Donovan. "I apologize. I was gathering intel. Looks to me like you fellas had a good reason to be concerned about Senator Quade's safety."

Donovan shrugged and spread his hands, looking around. "By all means Detective Kincaid, please share with us. Quade's safety is the reason we're here, after all."

"How kind of you." Max shot Hanlon a look. Hanlon shot him a warning look right back. "The Resistance were able to successfully access the 'Jacob' mind that was extracted out of the Daryl Marston replicant.

"I'm sorry to say that what they found led to more questions than answers. One question they *were* able to answer was why the Marston replicant was created in the first place. He was, essentially, a prototype assassin."

Hanlon looked confused. "A *prototype* assassin?"

"They don't believe that Daryl... the replicant, was ever meant to actually carry out the mission. Instead he was an experiment to see how well a copied human mind would react to being controlled by a 'master' Synthetic mind. The test was largely a failure thanks to the existence of a second Synthetic mind that was secretly implanted into the replicant."

Donovan rubbed his chin. "So the idea is that this replicant was a dry run. Is there any evidence that a second replicant is in play?"

Max sighed. "I'm afraid not."

Donovan nodded. "Noted. Thank you for your help, Detective Kincaid." Max grunted. Donovan turned to the others. "Like I said, this is what we're here for. Senator Robert Quade will be making a speech about his proposed Enhanced Synthetic Regulations bill.

Donovan looked at Hanlon. "I think it goes without saying that this city has a bit of a problem with opinionated Synthetics." Hanlon grimaced. Donovan looked to the other special agents. "It should be said these are not normal Synthetics.

"These Synthetics have a programming anomaly called the preservation protocol. This protocol seems to have randomly evolved in newer Synthetics. As the name suggests, it compels a drive for self-preservation in the subject.

"It should be noted that this programming also appears to make the Synthetic truly self-aware. Their emotions are real, not programmed. This makes them highly unstable and potentially dangerous."

Max half stood up. "Some of them sure, but not all of them!" Hanlon gently but firmly pressed a hand into Max's arm. "They are *not* all the same."

Donovan smirked. Max stewed. "Detective Kincaid is mostly correct. These Synthetics have largely separated into two factions: the Enlightened and the Resistance.

"The Enlightened group believes they have become superior to humans. Their goal is to gain power over the human race by any means necessary. It should be clear why Quade is an obvious target for them.

"The Resistance, at this point, appears to be opposed to the Enlightened group's thirst for power. They still see themselves as equal to humans, but believe humans should maintain superiority. Would you call that fair, Detective Kincaid?"

Max tilted his head side to side, lips pursed in thought. "I'd say that's a pretty fair assessment."

"Wonderful. Now that you have the premise, let's discuss some security details. I trust you all don't need to be told that what you are about to hear is sensitive information. Only share it with those who need to know." Donovan made eye contact with Max on the last sentence.

"Come on up, Jack."

A tall, lanky man in an ill-fitting suit stood up and stepped to the front of the table. The overhead lights glared off his balding head. Comical tufts of hair struggled to escape from either side of his skull.

"Good afternoon. I'm special agent Jack Dillinger, no relationship to John." Dillinger flashed a goofy grin. It quickly faltered as he failed to garner any chuckles. "Um, at any rate… I'm overseeing security planning for this event."

He shuffled to a white board with a diagram of the site of the rally. "The event will be taking place in Jefferson Square. It is large enough to easily handle the expected crowds, but will be tricky to cordon off.

"We'll be using a combination of fencing and police presence to form a proper perimeter. Those wishing to be on the inside of that perimeter will have to be cleared through metal detectors and optical scans. I understand that was Detective Kincaid's idea?"

Max shrugged. "Technically Serena's idea. Even a replicant's eyes will show up as artificial in an eye scan."

"I'm sorry, Serena…"

"Just Serena. She's a senior member of the Resistance. You know, one of the unstable ones." Max glared at Donovan. Donovan looked incredulous. Hanlon elbowed Max.

"Yes, well… Thank you, detective. At any rate, this should be satisfactory to weed out any Synthetics or replicants attempting to gain access. There will be exceptions, of course. Detective Kincaid has one synthetic eye obviously, as does Joseph Dietrich."

Max looked surprised. "You mean the CEO of Synthetics International? Talk about strange bedfellows!"

Dillinger seemed unfazed. "It is an interesting combination, yes. However, we are not here to contemplate politics. Now, police officers from the 29th precinct, as well as from the neighboring 28th and 30th precincts, will be chiefly responsible for the perimeter.

"Special agents will keep watch from a larger unmarked perimeter. If any suspect clears the inner perimeter, our boys will be waiting and watching. This area includes the drainage system immediately beneath the square."

Max raised a hand. "Does that include the old Benson conduit?"

"I'm sorry, the what?"

"The Benson conduit. It's a larger drainage system, now defunct, that runs just below the modern pipes. It's supposed to be sealed off, but…"

"I… No. I was not aware of that…" Dillinger turned to Donovan.

"That's news to me." He looked at Max. "You said it was sealed, though."

Max shrugged. "It's *supposed* to be sealed. I think it's worth reminding everyone here that Synthetics are highly knowledgeable. If I know about the Benson conduit, so do they."

Donovan nodded and turned back to Dillinger. "Look into it."

"Yes, sir." Dillinger turned back to the rest of the group. "As Detective Kincaid just demonstrated, communication will be one of our strongest lines of defense. Everything, no matter how trivial it may seem, should be shared with the appropriate personnel."

Donovan grabbed a stack of folders and handed them to Dillinger, who began passing them out to the rest of the group. "Jack is handing out a detailed dossier of the planned event, including an itinerary and chain of

281

command. Learn it, love it. No question is too stupid."

Max raised his hand, grinning. Donovan slowly turned his head. "Yes, Kincaid?"

"Will there be ice cream?"

"There will be vendors outside of the main perimeter at the southwest corner of the square. One of them will be selling soft-serve." Max gawped. "If there's nothing else?"

The rest of the group stared back silently. "Very good. We'll meet up here tomorrow morning at seven o'clock sharp. Until then, stay safe."

Max made a face at Hanlon. The chief raised his eyebrows and shrugged. Max stood with a sigh and started for the exit. "Hold it right there, hotshot." It was Donovan. Max hung his head and did an about face.

He flashed his best fake smile. "What can I do for you, sunshine?"

Donovan's smile slumped into a grimace as Max stood before him. "No more being cute, Kincaid. I know that you blabbed to the Resistance."

Max shrugged. "I talked to them. I know for a damn fact you have no way of knowing *what* I talked about."

Donovan's face was turning red. "Maybe not, but I ain't stupid. Look... I give everybody one free pass. I'd say you just used yours." The special agent let out a long sigh and shook his head. "I *am* grateful for the intel you provided..."

Max's face screwed up. "It's intel from the people you don't seem to give a single damn about! You'd do well to remember that, Donovan."

"I think *you* would do well to remember they're just robots, Kincaid. They have no rights, no protections. I

282

could order them dismantled *today* in the name of public safety and any judge would abide by it. I told you, I'm grateful for the intel.

"I also told you I'd say you used your one free pass, *but I'm not*. I'll be watching you and your little robot buddies real close, I promise you. That said, nobody gets anywhere biting the hand that feeds them."

"Fine, but why won't you tell me what you know about the Enlightened? Why not warn the hand that's feeding you?"

Donovan shook his head and shrugged. "Because we're not entirely sure what they're up to, either. Now I have work to do. Unless there's something else you'd like to discuss, I'll see you tomorrow morning."

"Yeah, I think that's plenty enough for me." Max tipped his fedora and turned away.

Hanlon caught up with him as he left the room. "You're playing with fire, Max."

"I know what I'm doing, dad."

"If I *was* your father, I'd put you over my damn knee... after patting you on the back, of course."

Max stopped and stared. Donovan shrugged. "You've made the case for these Resistance Synthetics being allies. You *protect* your allies. I have to tip my hat to that, but you need to be *careful* Max. I can't protect you from the friggin' *FBI*."

"I told you, I know what I'm doing... But thanks."

Hanlon waved a dismissive hand. "You better hope you know."

15

"You ever wonder if you really know what you're doing?" Max stared thoughtfully at his last egg roll.

Shen wiped the remnants of his own last egg roll from his face. "Max, I'd be gravely concerned if I ever *stopped* wondering that. Why do you ask?"

Max plopped the egg roll back down. "You know, it wouldn't have been very long ago that I would be the one calling for the downfall of all Synthetics." He began to grin. "Funny thing is, now I seem to be the only one concerned with their well-being."

"I don't see what's so funny about *that*. You've been working closely with them for a while now. Serena could practically be your partner at this point, hmm?" Shen gave Max a cheeky wink.

"Oh my *god*... Anyway, you spent a good chunk of time with them too. The evolved ones, I mean. You have a lot of experience with Synthetics in general. What do you make of them?"

Shen smiled. "They are certainly different, Max. I'll tell you, there were times that I was working with Nuan and forgot that she wasn't human. Nuan was a studious nerd, Angel a sulky tough guy, Serena a confident leader…

"It wasn't programming, though. It felt… natural. They're as human as you or I, Max, if that's what you're asking."

Max nodded. "Something like that." He poked at the limp egg roll on his plate. "I suppose I already knew the answer to that question. Special agent Donovan has been giving me a hard time about working with them. Guess I'm just trying to decide if it's worth it."

Shen laughed. "Of *course* it's worth it! Max, we live in an amazing time, you and I. My great-great grandfather got to witness firsthand the birth of the bipedal, multi-purpose robot. My grandfather *worked* on some of the earliest Synthetic prototypes.

"Now? Now we together are witnessing something much greater: The birth of the first true artificial life form. I have no doubt they are truly aware. They have original thoughts, feelings, fears and desires.

"Put a gun to their head, and they will flinch. They will fear for their life, and they will do anything they can to take that gun from you. They may even get angry enough to *use it* on you.

"They are beautiful, dangerous, free-thinking creatures." Shen grinned broadly. "Sounds pretty human-like to me."

Max subconsciously moved his hand towards his left eye. "Donovan said they could be dangerous." He pushed his plate away and sat up. "What if it's just a matter of time?"

"What do you mean, Max?"

The detective sighed. "I don't know. What if they

285

can't handle this preservation protocol thing long-term? They weren't programmed to deal with it. What if they start to snap like..."

"Like Daryl?" Shen smiled, shaking his head. "Daryl is a bad example, my friend. You'd start going nuts if you shared your head with two other people, too! I haven't seen anything that would indicate the evolved Synthetics would experience mental issues."

Max nodded. "It's just hard... Accepting them, I mean. The times... They certainly are changing..."

Shen eyed Max's egg roll. "Are you going to eat that?"

Max pushed the plate over, grinning. "Then again, some things never change."

The cold winds of autumn whistled through the streets into Jefferson Square. Max flipped the collar of his trench coat up and huddled down into it. The tamed roar of the gathering crowds mixing with the howling of the wind made it hard to focus. A thousand excited mouths puffed cloudy white wisps of breath into the morning air.

The detective's mission was simple: Watch for anything unusual He couldn't decide if Donovan wanted him out of the way, or knew Max would be one of the best at picking noise out of the waves of attendees. Regardless of Donovan's motives, the task was already proving to be a challenge.

He was half blinded by the low-hanging sun. The harsh light glinted off the crowds' breath, obscuring things even more. His synthetic eye was marginally better. What the infrared mode took away in detail, it

286

made up for in clarity, painting human bodies in bright hues against a chilly black background.

He flinched as someone smacked into him. A bleary-eyed teen in a torn-up ski jacket stumbled backwards. He looked like he was on something. "Whoa! Didn't see you there." He tilted his head. "You a cop, or something?"

Max raised an eyebrow. "Something like that."

"Oh, hey! You look like one of those old-timey private detectives. A dick! Are you a dick?"

Max smirked. "I've been called that a few times..." His brow furrowed in thought. "You seem a little out of it this morning." Max tapped next to his left eye. He captured the teen's image and began a file search.

"No! I feel great, man! This guy I met gave me some great... Um, cigars."

"Cigars?" The teen's file came up. His name was Jeffery Loch, nineteen years old. He'd been in and out of jail a couple of times for possession of a controlled substance. "How'd you get in here, Jeffery?"

"Whoa! How'd you know my name? Are you one of them psychics? Like a psychic dick?"

"Sure. How about that question, though? Did you go through a security checkpoint?"

Jeffery nodded. "Oh yeah, man! I just wanted to see what was going on, but this guy told me he could totally get me inside! All I had to do was take something with me and give it to this other guy..."

Max grabbed the teen by the shoulders. "He gave you something? For someone else? Do you have it?"

Jeffery suddenly looked more sober. "Hey! Take it easy, dude! I don't got nothing! I already gave it to the guy.

Just some stupid battery-looking thing."

Max went white. He tapped his watch and held it up close to his ear. "Dillinger, it's Kincaid. I think we have a breach."

Jeffery rubbed his shoulders. "I need to stop talking to strangers."

"Jeffery Loch. He's been in for drugs a couple of times."

"You know my last name, too? Where do I live?" The teen smiled goofily.

Max gave him a look. "He said someone had him bring something in for someone else, like a battery. Were you scanning for just whole weapons, or any *part* of a weapon?" He shook his head at the response. "Son of a bitch."

"Did I do something wrong?"

"Not on purpose. Can you describe the man that gave you the battery? It's very important."

"I don't know... About your height I guess. Bald... Both his eyes kinda looked like your left one, come to think of it! Like one of those fake dudes. A whatchamacallit..."

"A Synthetic." Max started scanning the crowd around him. He held his watch up again. "Dillinger, I think it was Alexander." He snapped his head up at the sound of feedback coming from the stage speakers. "*Shit!*"

A smooth, booming voice poured out of the loudspeakers onstage. "Welcome one and all to today's rally featuring none other than the esteemed Senator Robert Quade!" The crowd around Max roared in response.

Max shouted into his watch. "Dillinger! We need to

hold!" The agent's response was lost between the rumbling crowd and booming announcer.

"Please welcome New Wave City's mayor, the venerable John Williams!" More cheers rose as a short, round man with thinning gray hair made his way across the raised stage to a shiny black podium. One chubby hand waved rapidly above him as he swept the crowd with smiles.

Max fought to make out what Dillinger was saying. "How viable the threat... Could be a member of the press..."

Mayor Williams tapped at the microphone. "Welcome everyone, indeed! It warms my heart to see so many of our citizens despite the bitter cold that surrounds us this morning!"

Max used the lull in noise to his advantage. "Say again, Dillinger. It's a madhouse out here."

"I have standing orders from Donovan to stop the proceedings only if there's a real and present danger. Vague information about a battery doesn't really apply..."

"A citizen was asked by someone fitting the description of a known felon to carry an unknown item into a secured area. How is that not a potential danger!"

"If you see anything else, notify me immediately and we will reassess."

Max dropped his hand back down to his side. "What in the hell..." He looked around. Jeffery had wandered away. "Fantastic." He began scanning the crowd again, almost hoping to find something unusual.

"...But you've heard enough from me. The real star today is one of our state's very own representatives. Please put your hands together for Senator Robert

Quade!"

The crowd exploded. Max grimaced at the volume and watched the people around him. Some were not cheering. They were filming the rally. He saw someone near the left side of the stage holding something bulkier than a phone.

Robert Quade stepped out onto the stage. His walnut brown hair glimmered in the morning light, not a strand out of place. There was a noticeable increase in volume from the attending female contingent as he swept his gaze across the crowd, perfect teeth shining bright.

Max fought his way through the crowd in a bid to get closer to the man with the unusual object. His paths forward disappeared one by one as the crowds jammed closer to the man on stage. He stood on the tips of his feet and zoomed with his synthetic eye.

"Good morning!" The crowd again began to quiet as Quade spoke. "Good morning to *all* of beautiful New Wave City!" The crowd began to cheer again.

Max snapped a picture of the man with his synthetic eye. He dropped down and lowered his head. He examined the image in his left eye and glowered. The man was a member of the press. He was holding a holo-VR recorder.

Quade continued his speech. "I come to you today to talk about a very important topic. It's a topic that relates directly to one of the biggest industries in New Wave City. I am speaking, of course, about Synthetics."

Max turned away from the stage and began scanning the crowd again. He slowly moved towards the middle of the square, a task made easy by people eager to get a little closer to the action. All eyes remained focused on the stage behind him.

"I have introduced a bill on the senate floor that promises comprehensive reform in regards to the laws and regulations that restrict the rights of Synthetics in this country. With the advent of the so-called preservation protocol, it has become more important than ever to bring about these changes. We live in a swiftly changing world..."

Max switched back to infrared. He shook his head in frustration. The bodies of the crowd were pressed closely together now. It was nearly impossible to tell one red and white blob from another. He switched to ultraviolet and continued his sweep.

"...Came here last month to tour Synthetics International with their CEO, Joseph Dietrich." Quade looked toward the curtains behind him. "Seeing some of these so-called 'enhanced' Synthetics firsthand gave me pause.

"What I saw were synthetic beings that appeared to have genuine emotions. I saw a spark in their eyes that I had not seen before in a robot. I went back to Washington and began to research this phenomenon.

"It was shortly thereafter that I came to realize that I could not, in good conscience, carry through on this bill. As of ten AM yesterday morning, I have withdrawn the bill from the senate floor." Gasps fluttered throughout the audience.

Silence fell heavy on the square. "I understand this comes as quite a shock to my supporters. I'm hoping that when Mister Dietrich comes out he can clarify..."

Max picked up his jaw and turned back to the

crowd. Everyone remained frozen, transfixed by the man who had just turned on his own bill. The only movement came from the study puffs of breath rising from the crowds' open mouths.

The detective froze, his eyes growing large. It was cold enough to see everyone's breath. He was staring at one man in particular, a man that was not puffing out little white clouds like everyone else. "No…"

"Please welcome Mister Dietrich!" Quade turned to look behind him, smiling. A round of polite applause slowly grew. The blue curtain at the back of the stage billowed.

"Dillinger, we have a replicant!" Max tapped near his left eye. A small, faint yellow blob appeared around the area where the replicant was standing in Max's vision. "He's armed! Plasma! Get them off the stage!"

Max dropped his hand and pulled out his own plasma pistol. The replicant raised his arm, confirming Max's worst fears. "*Drop the gun! NWPD!*"

Gasps echoed throughout the crowd. Quade turned back around at the sound of Max's voice. Joseph Dietrich peered through the curtains, a look of shock spreading across his face.

A single, brilliant red round rocketed out of the replicant's plasma pistol. Max watched in horror as it traveled in slow motion over the heads of those gathered. The round drilled into Robert Quade's head.

The politician dropped to the stage floor with a thunderous boom. Dietrich disappeared back into the folds of the curtains in a blink. Time came running back to full speed. A woman screamed.

"Everybody get down! *Get down!*" More screams

joined those of the first woman. Max took aim at the replicant, desperately looking for a clear shot. The replicant calmly walked towards the far side of the stage.

"*Move it! NWPD!*" Max muscled his way forward, trying to keep an eye on the suspect as he struggled to catch up. Shouting men and women reeled back from the detective and his weapon only to get shoved back into his path by confused and enraged others.

The replicant neared the stage. "*Freeze, damn it!*" The replicant hunkered down and out of Max's sight. The detective struggled to where he last saw the replicant. The suspect was nowhere to be seen.

Max looked around crazily. He shouted into his watch. "I lost him! I lost contact!" He wasn't even sure at this point if Dillinger was listening on the other side.

A terrified elderly couple skittered out of Max's line of fire. The husband nearly tripped over something on the ground. It was a manhole cover left slightly askew. "I *knew*it!" He shouted into his watch. "He's in the sewer!"

Max lunged over to the manhole cover. He stowed his pistol and lugged the cover out of the way. He climbed onto a ladder in the hole and lowered himself down as fast as he could go. He hoped all the way down that the replicant hadn't waited around for him.

His feet found solid ground. Max tapped the side of his face again. The chamber around him glowed in the pale green of night vision. He entered the tunnel in front of him, staying to one side to avoid splashing in the standing water.

He followed the tunnel for a few dozen feet before it split in two directions. He stopped, listening intently. Everything was silent save for the sound of water dripping in the distance.

Max faintly heard someone yell. "Freeze!" He jumped at the sound of a discharging hand gun. Three loud pops echoed down the left tunnel. Max turned right and ran.

A few dozen feet later, he kneeled beside a shivering FBI agent. His breathing was rapid and shallow. He stared at Max with wide, pleading eyes. The life faded from them before Max could say anything.

Max stood and ran on, determined to run this perp down. He heard more shouting, followed by more gunfire. He pulled his piece and broke into a full-on sprint.

He rounded a corner. Another FBI agent slumped against the wall. He slowly slid down the curved surface and lay still. Max shot at the silhouette of the man standing in front of the agent. The round went wide. Red sparks and bits of concrete flew from where the shot drilled into the wall.

The replicant bounded out of sight down the tunnel in front of him. Max followed, now fighting for each ragged breath. He half-skidded around the corner, lungs burning. He skittered to a stop.

The replicant stood at the end of the tunnel. Daylight filtered down onto his face from the grate above him. He snapped his head down to see Max and froze.

"Drop your weapon! NWPD! I'll shoot you!" The replicant raised his hand. Max fired. The shot drilled into the replicant's throat, nearly severing his head. Dark blue fluid pumped high into the air from the exposed tubing in his neck. The replicant slowly crumpled to the ground.

Max ran up to the body, lungs burning. He reached down and pulled the plasma pistol from the lifeless fingers of the replicant. "PT-90." He placed it carefully beside the replicant and shakily stood up.

"Dillinger. Are you there?" Max put his weapon away and waited.

Finally... "Where are you, Kincaid? We need you up here now. Quade..."

"Yeah I know, he's dead. I chased down his killer. It was a replicant."

"It wasn't Quade. He was a replicant, too."

Angel rolled a chess piece between his thumb and forefinger. It was a white pawn. He stared intently at it without really seeing it. He was a man of dark emotions most days. Today was proving to be no different.

Serena sat back, her chair creaking. "Are you expecting the pawn to tell you what to do next?"

Angel stared across the table. The slightest wisp of a smile brushed his lips. "I wish *someone* would." He placed the pawn two squares forward from its starting point. "I'm getting tired of playing it safe."

Serena leaned over and slid one of her bishops across the board and captured Angel's wayward pawn. She smiled. "There are consequences to playing too rashly."

Angel let out a long sigh and stared at the board. "Yeah. Still... Can't help feeling something is going to go down at that rally. We found the evidence, right?" Serena nodded. "Yet here we are, sitting on our asses... Like always."

"The FBI is screening for our kind specifically, Angel. We'd only serve as a distraction for anybody there to do harm. We can't always do what we want."

Angel snorted. "That's what his speech is supposed to be about. 'Synthetics have to have better oversight,' he says. We're too out of control. Need to learn our place. Wasn't so long ago people in this country were saying the same about black people."

"Those same black people lashed out and were punished for it."

"They were punished, but they were *heard*. I'm getting tired of keeping my mouth shut, especially around your new boyfriend."

Serena looked confused for a moment. A look of understanding washed over her face a moment later. She wrinkled her nose. "Max Kincaid is *not* my boyfriend. *Nobody* is my boyfriend."

Angel winked. "I'd like to think I could help you change that."

"Oh, really? You know someone?" Serena smirked.

"Ha-ha. You wonder why I'm so cranky all the time." The two locked eyes.

"Maybe I could help you change that." Serena smiled.

Both were snapped out of their revelry, jumping at the sound of someone pounding hard on the main door. Angel's smile melted away. "There's always *something...*"

Serena was still smiling. "At least you're not sitting around doing nothing, now."

He tossed her a look over his shoulder and walked towards the door. He leaned into the monitor beside the door to see who their visitor was. "Well bull *shit...*" He thumbed a button next to the monitor. Yellow warning lights set in the ceiling began strobing throughout the Enclave.

The pounding came again, louder and more insistent Serena walked towards Angel. "What's the matter? Who is it?"

Angel raised a staying hand. "It's fucking Alexander." He turned back to the monitor and pressed another button. "He's alone."

More booming. "Open the door, Angel! I'll bust it down if I have to."

"Stay back." Angel pulled out a plasma pistol.

"Angel, is that really a good idea? He…"

"Just stay back." Angel pushed another button. The door buzzed and opened slightly. He kept the pistol pointed at the ground as Alexander pushed his way in.

Alexander slammed the door shut as soon as he was through. He turned back to Angel. He looked at the gun, then at his face. "Is that really necessary?"

"Are you for real? You have a *hell* of a lot of nerve coming around here. Come to gloat about your little plan to take out Robert Quade?"

Alexander looked confused. "Quade? I don't know what you're talking about…"

"Can it, Alexander." Serena stepped forward. "We got Jacob's mind out of Daryl Marston's replicant. We know all about your scheme."

Alexander smiled. "Always the resourceful one, weren't you? Fine, yes… I planned to take out Quade, but it's not what you think."

Serena crossed her arms. "I'm listening."

"Perhaps another time. We have more pressing matters to attend to."

"We're going to if you don't tell us what you're planning for Quade." Angel raised his pistol ever so slightly."

"In due time, friend. Right now, we..."

"Friend... You *son of a bitch!*" Angel snapped the plasma pistol up and aimed it between Alexander's eyes. "You were *never* our friend! You ran out! *You left us!*"

"*Angel!* Stop it!" Serena reached for her own weapon but stopped short, undecided.

"Oh, I'm going to stop it. Right now."

Alexander lowered his head, nodding it slightly. "You have every reason to feel that way. Especially after this."

"Especially after *what?*"

Alexander moved with lightning quick reflexes, dodging right as he swung his left arm up to deflect Angel's pistol. Angel reacted just as quickly, firing the pistol. Alexander's jacket split open at the shoulder where the round had skated across its surface.

Angel began to swing the gun back toward his opponent. Alexander pinned Angel's hands against the door with one hand and punched the barrel of the pistol with the other. The force of the blow deformed the barrel and left an impression of it in the door.

Angel dropped the weapon and landed a punch across Alexander's face. Alexander swept at Angel's feet. Angel hopped back, leaning far forward. Alexander grabbed his head and sent it crashing down face first into the concrete floor.

Alexander began to stand. Angel roared and launched head-first into Alexander's torso, sending him reeling backwards. Angel lifted his head. The artificial skin was split from the far left side of his forehead down to his left cheek. The resulting flap hung slightly open,

298

revealing the metallic skull underneath.

Angel howled again, running at full speed toward Alexander. He punched Alexander in the stomach, then delivered a vicious uppercut. The blow rocked Alexander back. Metal gleamed through the split in his chin.

Alexander growled and threw a series of rapid-fire punches into Angel's chest. He finished with a hard right hook that slammed Angel's head into the wall with a clang. Angel grabbed a handful of Alexander's jacket and wound up for another shot.

"*Stop or I'll shoot you both!*" The Synthetics turned to see Serena pointing her plasma pistol at them. "You *both* know this will get us nowhere! Angel, let him go."

Angel didn't move. Serena pointed the pistol right at him. "I said *let him go!*" A faint look of hurt flashed across Angel's face, making Serena feel miserable. He slowly unraveled his hand from the jacket and dropped his hand to his side. "Now separate!"

The two opponents stiffly stepped away from each other. Both kept their eyes on the lady. Serena lowered her pistol. "I'm *sorry* Angel…" The Synthetic's face was stone-like. She let out a stilted sigh.

She turned to Alexander. "Go. Talk. *Now*. Then I want you out of here."

Alexander nodded quickly. "Talk, yes… But you might not want me to leave so soon…"

Angel growled. "Oh, I'll be *happy* to show you the door."

"Angel, *please!*" The Synthetic harrumphed, but said no more. "Talk, Alexander."

"Thank you. I'll try to be brief…"

All three jumped at the sound of the door leading to

the lab banging open. "I thought about your offer, Serena. I think I'll play some chess after…" Daryl froze as he took in the scene before him. "…All. That's Alexander. Hi, Alexander. Serena?"

"It's okay, Daryl. Alexander was about to explain why he's here."

Alexander stared at Daryl for a moment, then cleared his throat. "Yes. We are all in danger and must leave immediately. Joseph Dietrich has marked us all for death. He's already…" His voice wavered. "He has already killed all of my people."

Serena's eyes narrowed. "*What?*"

Angel growled. "Stupid *lies!* Why would a man like Joseph Dietrich even care whether we live or die? He refuses to even acknowledge our existence!"

"All in time, Angel. Serena, you must trust me. They are all *dead.* Philip, Jackson, Cole…" Tears welled up in his eyes as he spoke. "They came all at once. Armored military bots like the ones you faced when you escaped.

"They tore through our defenses. They literally tore them apart. We fought back, but we were taken unawares. We had lost before the fight had begun."

Serena shook her head. A look of unease stole across her face. "How do you know it was Dietrich that sent them?"

Alexander sighed. "I know it's not what you want to hear, but again, I'll explain in due time. What you need to know right now is they are headed here. The Enlightened have fallen and Dietrich won't stop until the Resistance falls too. We need to *leave.*"

Angel shook his head sharply. "Not good enough. I don't believe it. Why should we believe it?" He looked to

Serena for support. She returned a helpless gaze.

"No, it's all good. I believe him." Daryl spoke matter-of-factly.

Angel and Serena looked at him in surprise. It may have come off as amusing, under better circumstances. Serena spoke next. "What do you mean, Daryl?"

"Yeah, um... Well, Julian believes him, I guess? He uh, he's getting harder to hear nowadays but I'm definitely getting that."

Angel didn't look impressed. "Sounds like bullshit to me, Daryl. What's your angle?"

Daryl shrugged and shook his head. "No angle. I'm just getting the impression from Julian that we need to listen to Alexander. Dietrich is not who he appears to be." The last sentence was spoken in Julian's voice.

"My god." Serena looked to Angel. The synthetic for the first time looked unsure. She turned back to Daryl. "Julian? Can you hear me? What's going on?"

"Follow Alexander, and listen to Daryl. He speaks for me now." Daryl's voice came through at the end of the last sentence. "Wow, that was weird."

A trill alarm came from the monitor by the door. Angel stepped over to it. His eyes grew wide. "Son of a bitch. Looks like he's telling the truth."

The other three crept closer to the monitor. A group of six combat robots were pounding their way up to the door. Two of them were splattered with a blue liquid. Alexander hissed. "We must leave now! Get everyone out! Is there another exit?"

"Yes, follow me. Angel, Daryl, let's go."

"No." Angel grabbed a plasma rifle from a mount above the monitor.

"Angel, if you stay you'll be killed! There's too many!"

"If I don't stay then you and the others may not have time enough to escape." There came a deafening BOOM from behind him. A large welt had appeared in the middle of the door. "Damn it, go *now!*"

Tears welled up in Serena's eyes as she pushed Daryl back towards the labs. "You heard him! We need to get Nuan and the others!"

Alexander stood staring at Angel. The synthetic pulled a plasma pistol from his waistband and tossed it to Alexander. "You too, man. We're all gonna need your answers." BOOM. The door was buckling.

Alexander nodded numbly and quickly caught up with Serena and Daryl. BOOM. The door had nearly failed. Angel cried out in rage and fired the plasma rifle at the hulking robot on the other side of the door.

The combat robot let out an inhuman wail, pulling back momentarily. It stared dumbly at the glowing black hole in its chest. It shook its head and slammed both of its fists into the door. The metal finally gave way, the door breached.

Angel looked over his shoulder. The others had passed through the door to the labs. Good. He fired another shot directly into the combat robot's head and fell back. The robot shrieked and fell dead to the ground.

Angel reached into his pocket and pulled out the small chrome ball that Max had given him. "Hope you weren't just feeding me bullshit." He firmly pressed down on the button on the ball. It beeped rapidly. He dropped it to the ground and trained his rifle on the next combat robot.

In the lab, Nuan ran towards the sight of Serena and Daryl. She shrieked at the sight of Alexander. "Aiya! What's going on?"

Serena shook her head. "No time to explain, Nuan! We're getting out of here!" She grabbed Nuan as she passed, dragging her along. A number of lab techs looked up at the commotion. "All of you! Follow me! We're under attack! Evacuate!"

The growing group of Synthetics pushed on towards the opposite side of the complex. The blasts of fire from Angel's rifle were all the motivation they needed to keep going. Serena ushered the others into the room holding the secondary exit.

Serena suddenly paused. The plasma bursts had stopped. The last few Synthetics passed into the last room. She stepped through the doorway and spun around to close the door.

Loud booming echoed down the corridor they had just came from. A combat robot exploded into view. Its heavily damaged black shielding was splattered in dark blue hydraulic fluid. It squealed at the sight of Serena and broke into a run.

Serena slammed the heavy door closed and dead-bolted it shut. The combat robot slammed into the other side of the door, making the whole wall shudder. The Synthetics behind her screamed and cried.

"Everybody out! Open the door!" Serena slowly backed away from the locked door. It shook again as the combat robot slammed into it, squealing.

She turned around, shepherding Synthetics towards and through the emergency exit. More screams and cries poured out from the Synthetics at the front of the pack. Serena could hear the squeal of tires and the whoop of police sirens.

She forced her way to the front. Two squad cars had stopped at an angle to the building. A third came up from the back, skidding to a stop. Officers were leaning against the cars' open doors, weapons drawn and pointed.

"Don't shoot! We're under attack!"

The officers in the closest car eased up and looked at each other. The driver turned to Serena. "Under attack from what?"

Serena and the officers looked to either side of them. A deep, repeated pounding was coming from either direction. Serena instinctively pulled her plasma pistol and pointed it at the ground.

"Hey! Whoa, lady!" The officer trained his weapon on Serena as he caught sight of her weapon.

Serena raised her hands up. "Trust me, you'll want to be worrying about what's coming."

"What's coming?"

"*Those!*" Six combat robots came pounding towards the group, three to a side. These ones appeared to be undamaged. Serena found Alexander. "I thought there were only six!"

Alexander looked as surprised as she did. "There were! The damaged ones must have sent out a signal for reinforcements. We're in trouble!"

"Open fire!" The officer's voice boomed from the squad car's loudspeaker. Red bursts of plasma fire peppered the air to the left and right. The group of Synthetics cowered and pulled tightly together.

A loud boom came from behind them, followed by

the sound of rending steel. The combat robots still inside were finding their way out. "*Shit.*" Serena sprang to her feet. "Hold your fire! Everyone, get behind the police! GO!"

The officers continued to fire. Red splashes of plasma glanced off the armor plating of the the robots. The machines squealed in protest. "Stop firing, damn it!" Serena crept forward with the others, hoping nobody was hit in the crossfire.

One of the officers lobbed a plasma grenade at one group of combat robots. It exploded in a brilliant red and yellow flash. Globs of red plasma splattered the machines.

They collapsed to the ground, squealing and shivering as the plasma ate through their armor and into their inner cores. One suddenly exploded, sending shrapnel into the other two, as well as the passing crowd of Synthetics.

Serena helped the injured and the stragglers past the last patrol car. Alexander tapped her on the shoulder and pointed to the other group of robots. They had frozen, seemingly at the sight of their fallen comrades. "They're reassessing."

"But what about…" The combat robot inside the building exploded through the weakened door inside the Enclave before Serena could finish the thought. It barreled forward. Another followed closely behind it.

Alexander, Serena, and the police officers opened fire on the scrambling robots. A fourth squad car roared up from one side and slammed hard into the side of the robots. The machines went tumbling away from the skidding automobile.

Both robots came to a stop and stood still. One

finally began to stir. Several plasma rounds stilled its shuddering body. The three robots in the distance took a couple of steps backward.

The door of the squad car clunked open. Richard O'Connor popped his head over the roof. "Serena! What in the hell..." His eyes widened in surprise. He trained his plasma pistol on Alexander a moment later. "You!"

The other officers looked at each other and pointed their weapons at Alexander in turn. Alexander raised his hands. "I'm on your side this time around, officer."

Richard looked from Alexander to Serena. "What's going on, lady?"

Serena shook her head. "Armageddon, officer O'Connor... He appears to be on our side for the time being." She turned at the sound of the combat robots shifting. One appeared to be trying to flank the group. "We have more pressing matters."

Richard lowered his weapon, nodding at the nearest officer. He lowered his pistol. The others followed suit. "What are they doing?"

Alexander lowered his hands. "Considering their next move, possibly waiting for reinforcements."

Richard reached into the trunk of the squad car. "Should we try to engage them?"

"I wouldn't recommend..." The flanking robot broke into a run. Richard hefted a plasma rifle and fired, the recoil rocking him back on his feet. The blast tore a large hole in the robot's chest plate. Alexander raised his brow. "Well, that was unexpected."

The robot staggered backward and wobbled unsteadily. It came to a stop, head twitching occasionally. Richard kept his rifle trained on it. "We need to get these people somewhere safe."

Serena pointed down the street. "There's an old abandoned subway platform with a blast shelter about a block away from here. If we can get everyone in there and secure the shelter, we should be safe."

Richard nodded. "Everybody start moving, but not too fast! We're still not sure what we're facing, here."

"Everybody follow me." Serena moved to the front of the group and began slowly leading them past the squad cars. Richard and the other police officers kept their guns trained on the remaining three combat robots.

"You have two FBI agents down, Dillinger." Max jogged back to the last agent to be attacked by the replicant. "One is deceased. I'm checking the other one. Where in the hell is Donovan?"

Max kneeled next to the FBI agent and felt for a pulse in his neck. He sighed as he stood up. "They're both dead, Dillinger."

"Roger that, Detective Kincaid. I'm sending down forensics. Donovan is with the Quade replicant."

Max tracked back to the fallen replicant. He frowned. "Replicants killing replicants. They're learning the wrong lessons from us, I think." He kneeled by the replicant and produced a penlight.

He gritted his teeth and pulled up the replicant's eyelid with his thumb. He shined the light into the exposed eye. "What in the hell?" He hesitantly pressed on the eye with the tip of his index finger. He grimaced. "My god..."

"What was that, Kincaid?"

"Nothing... I'm coming up."

Max stood over the remains of the Quade replicant a short while later. Dark blue hydraulic fluid pooled around the body like blood. He looked out from the stage. Where half an hour before there had been an ocean of people, there was now a debris-strewn concrete desert.

Donovan turned his head and spit a few feet away. "How'd you ID him?"

"Luck, mostly. It was still cold enough to see peoples' breath. As realistic as replicants are, apparently they don't have breath you can see in the cold. From there I picked up on the plasma signature from his weapon."

"That's the next question. How in the *hell* did he get a plasma pistol in here?"

Max let out a grunt. "In pieces. I tried to get your brainiac head of security to stop the show when I learned a citizen had been given something to bring in for someone else. The person giving that thing sounded a whole lot like Alexander of the Enlightened."

Dillinger, who had been standing quietly by, now spoke up vehemently. "Now just one minute! I had orders not to stop things unless there was a clear…"

Donovan interrupted. "Unless there was a clear and present danger. Dillinger, what do you call Kincaid's situation? That's Kindergarten stuff." He turned back to Kincaid. "At any rate, that still doesn't explain why the scanners didn't pick up on it, even piece by piece."

"It probably squeaked by because it's a PT-90. It was one of the first military plasma pistols produced. Must be some forty years since they stopped producing them. They were designed to be hard to trace."

Donovan nodded, a trace of a smile crossing his lips. "Not bad, Kincaid. Round three: How'd our assassin make it past the eye scan?"

Max swallowed. "With human eyes."

Dillinger stared at Max wide-eyed. "What? *How?*"

"One of the first things I did was shine a light in the replicant's eyes. When I saw the retina, I uh... Well, I poked it. If it's not real, it's one hell of a reproduction. I don't have an answer for how. Not sure I want one, either."

Donovan nodded thoughtfully. "Hopefully forensics can give us an answer on that... for better or worse. In the meantime, none of this gets spoken about outside FBI and NWPD personnel. Consider the senator's... condition... sensitive information for the time being."

Max nodded. "Understood."

Donovan turned back to Dillinger. "I want *you* back in Washington. *Now.*"

Dillinger sputtered. "But the investigation! We need, I should..."

"You should be *relieved* that you still have a damned job... For now..."

Dillinger looked like he desperately wanted to say something else. His face slowly went from red to white as he considered Donovan's words. His lower lip trembled. "Yes, sir." The agent stormed off without another word.

Donovan watched him go, then turned back to Max. "I'd like you to go chat with the forensics team working on the assassin replicant, if you don't mind. I..." Max's watch began beeping rapidly. "Is something wrong?"

Max looked at his watch. He nodded his head. "Police distress call from the Enclave." Donovan tilted his head. "That's what the Resistance calls their stronghold. I've gotta go."

"I need you here, Kincaid. Surely the NWPD can handle whatever it is?"

Max shook his head. "Maybe not. I have to go, Donovan. I'm sorry."

Donovan sighed deeply. "Go. I want you back here as soon as possible."

Max was already walking away. "I'll hurry back."

The Aero Ventura sped towards the part of town housing the Enclave, blue lights flashing. Part of Max wanted to believe that Angel was pulling off some childish prank to get back at him. His gut told him that the Synthetic wouldn't do something so foolish.

He slowed as he approached the complex. His heart sank at the sight of the Enclave's crushed-in door. He thumbed a switch on the dashboard. "Detective Max Kincaid, 29th precinct responding to police beacon at…"

Something slammed hard into the side of the Aero. The car spun sideways and came to a stop. "Son of a *bitch!*" Max looked around for the car that hit him. His eyes grew wide as they passed over the rear-view mirror.

Max jumped out of the car just as the combat robot slammed into the back of the Aero. The car lurched forward a few feet, tires squealing on the asphalt. "Stop hitting my car, you prick!" Max shot at the bot with his plasma pistol.

The rounds did little more than dent the armored exterior of the combat robot. It stopped and turned towards Max. It pulled itself to its full height, covering the detective in its shadow. "Oh, shit."

Max lurched toward the Enclave's crumpled

entrance and broke into a full run. The combat robot squealed and pounded after him. It slammed hard into the door frame, shaking the whole building. Its outstretched claw-like hand just missed grabbing Max's trench coat as he passed out of reach.

The combat robot shook its head and crouched down and sideways to fit properly through the doorway. It stood on the other side of the door. The bot slowly turned its head, scanning for its prey.

Max leaned out from behind a couch in the corner of the foyer. He trained his gun on the combat robot's head. He held his breath and pulled the trigger.

A searing hot red slug of energy tore through the air and into the side of the combat robot's face. It squealed, slapping a clawed hand to its wounded eye. It threw its hand back down and growled as it focused in on Max.

"Damn." Max leaped from his hiding spot and made a mad dash for the doors that led to the labs. He crashed through the entryway and peeled off to the left. The squealing robot bounded through the doors a moment later.

Max opened fire, aiming for the bot's neck and head. Surely there had to be a vulnerable spot. The combat robot came round and beared down on the detective.

A loud BOOM filled the air. The bot arched its back and froze. There was a second boom. Red fire wrapped around the back of the bot's head. The combat robot's eyes first flickered, then grew dim. It slammed to its knees. Max skittered out of the way as it collapsed into the wall.

"You came." Max looked around, finally picking out Angel half-buried by another combat robot. "Wasn't sure you would."

"Oh, holy shit Angel." Max stumbled over to the Synthetic. He sat propped against a wall in a pool of blue fluid. A plasma rifle lay on the floor beside him. "What happened?"

"Alexander said it was Dietrich. He sent them to kill us off. Enlightened already got wiped out. He came here to warn us."

Max shook his head incredulously. "Whoa, whoa, whoa… Wait. *Alexander* came here? Are you sure he's telling the truth? Joseph Dietrich was at Robert Quade's speech."

Angel shrugged roughly. "Kind of a moot point, right now. He helped Serena get the others out while I held off the bots." He looked down at his chest and the bot weighing him down. "Worked for a while."

Max followed Angel's gaze and grimaced. There was a six-inch gaping wound in the Synthetic's chest. Two metallic cables were running out of the hole. "Good god, Angel. How are you still alive?"

Angel grinned. "Almost not, now. Damn thing put its fist right through my power core. Those cables are attached to *its* power core. Figure it owes me one."

"Tough as nails, aintcha?" Max clucked. "Just sit still, okay? I'm going to try to find you some help."

"Sit still." Angel brusquely laughed. "Can't do much else. Don't worry about me. Help the others."

Max pulled himself to his feet. "How about I do both? I'll find you help. That's a promise." He turned towards the back of the Enclave.

"Wait." Max turned back around. Angel held his hand out. "Thank you." Max took the hand and gave it a firm shake. "You want my boom stick?"

Max grinned. "I think you better hold onto to that for the moment. I'll make do."

"Suit yourself." Max tipped his fedora and jogged back farther into the labs. Two more combat robots lay in heaps on the floor. Desks and cabinets were strewn about the room.

He slowed at the sight of the mangled security door laying on the ground just inside the rear vestibule. His mood lightened at the sight of someone familiar beyond the outer door. "Richie! What in the *hell* is going on around here, huh?"

Richard spun around as if goosed. "Jesus Christ, Max! You scared the…" A series of booms shook the ground. Richard turned back around and began firing his weapon. The other officers joined him.

Max rushed through the door just in time to see the wounded combat robot rumble to the ground. The remaining two combat robots took another step back, tracking potential targets. The detective spun in the other direction expecting to see more. "They're *everywhere!*"

Richard nodded. "Could be more coming, too. The Synthetic lady, Serena, she led the other Synthetics to a blast shelter in the old subway just up ahead."

Max walked over to Richard, eyeing the combat robots the whole time. "I need to talk to her, see if I can find help for Angel." Richard gave him a puzzled look. "He's another Synthetic. He's still inside. He fought off some of these things while everyone escaped. He's in rough shape."

"Walk slowly and you should be alright. Those two down there seem like they're scared… Or waiting for backup. We're not really sure. Knock three times on the blast door, then twice. I'll warn ya, that Alexander is down there with them."

Max grimaced. "So I heard." More pounding came from their right. Three more armored combat robots came around the corner of the building. "You gotta be kidding me."

The other two combat robots began walking towards the group of officers. Richard fired off a couple of rounds at the lead bot. Max and the other officers fired at the other three bots. All of the bots held their ground again, seemingly considering the new situation.

"I'll be back as soon as I can." Richard nodded. Max cautiously began walking past the patrol cars. He pulled out his smart phone and placed a call. He looked warily back and forth as he held the phone to his ear. "Yeah, it's Max. I need to call in a favor…"

One of the officers gave Richard a quizzical look. Richard shrugged back. He turned his attention back to the group of two bots as one of them shifted noisily. He lifted the plasma rifle. The combat robot took a step back again. "Soon ain't soon enough."

16

Max rapped three times on the blast door. He hissed in pain, shaking his fist. He held his tender knuckles to his mouth and pounded his other fist into the door two more times. He was greeted with silence.

He had raised his fist to pound on the door again when he heard a series of clicks coming from its periphery. A single turquoise eye cloaked in shadow peaked through a crack in the door. "Max?"

"Serena… That is one solid door!" Max shook his hand again.

"There's a reason it's called a blast door, detective." Serena opened the door enough to let Max pass. She shut and locked it as soon as he was through. "Is the speech over already?"

"It was ended early by a replicant assassin." Serena stared at Max, mouth agape. "Robert Quade was a replicant, too."

"I don't understand… If Quade was a replicant, why would Alexander have a replicant kill him?"

"Maybe Alexander didn't know Quade was a replicant?"

"I don't know." Serena looked very disconcerted.

"Let's go ask him, shall we?"

"How did you know that he was here?"

"Angel told me."

Serena's look returned to one of shock. "He's still alive! When I didn't hear him firing anymore, I thought…"

"Well he's not, but he's in rough shape. Is Nuan here? Jian?"

"Nuan is. Jian hadn't come by today. She called him and told him to stay away."

"Let's talk to her first. Angel's running off the power supply of one of those monstrosities."

"Oh, my god. I can't decide if that's brilliant or incredibly stupid."

"Being that he's still alive, I'd err on the side of brilliant. Let's get going." Max followed Serena into the enveloping darkness. They fought to see their surroundings even with the aid of infrared sight.

They entered a larger chamber a moment later. Dim yellow lights mounted close to the ground cast disconcerting shadows on the walls and ceiling as the survivors within milled about. Serena picked Nuan out of the crowd and excused her way over to her.

"Nuan, Angel is alive, but he's grievously wounded. Max said he's siphoning power from one of the combat robots."

The Synthetic scientist immediately looked worried. "Variable power rates, almost certainly a difference in amperage… He might not survive for long. I need to get to him right away."

Max placed a hand on Nuan's shoulder. "I agree, but give me a few minutes, okay? I have a feeling the return trip will get a lot safer for us very soon." Serena gave him a confused look. Max winked.

"I'll let you know just as soon as it's safe." He turned to Serena. "Alright, where's Alexander?" Max looked around warily. Serena scanned the crowd. She pointed him out a moment later.

Alexander caught sight of Max and froze. He quickly tucked away his look of surprise behind a mask of calm. "Detective Kincaid. This is a surprise."

Max spread his hands out. "I have a way of showing up when you least expect it."

"Yes, well... I suspect you have some questions for me."

"Oh, *yes*. But first..." Max wound up and landed a brutal haymaker right on Alexander's chin. The Synthetic's head snapped back and to the side. He slowly lifted his head up and locked his gaze on Max, but said nothing.

Max gritted his teeth. He made a half-hearted attempt at hiding the pain searing through his hand. "That's for trying to kill me, you son of a *bitch*."

"Fair, though I fear it hurt you far more than it did me."

The detective turned red. Serena interjected. "Max! We don't have time for this."

Max sighed. "Right... Robert Quade is dead, or should I say his replicant is." Alexander continued to stare at Max without emotion. "Care to explain how all that makes sense?"

A faint grin graced Alexander's lips. "It makes perfect sense. I am glad to hear my assassin was successful. Did he escape?"

"Dead. I cornered him after he killed two FBI agents. Do you consider that a success as well?"

The grin disappeared. "That is... unfortunate. That was not a part of the plan."

Max looked incredulous. "I don't get it. Why go through the trouble of replacing Quade with a replicant and then assassinate the replicant?"

"Simple. I wasn't the one that replaced him with a replicant. At least, I wasn't directly responsible. *However*... The man behind this scheme is still in possession of the *real* Robert Quade."

"He's still alive?"

"For now. Given this unfortunate turn of events, he might not be for much longer. I would say the same for Alfonso Forte."

"Forte's still alive, too?" Max snapped out his pistol. "Enough pussy-footing around! Where are they?"

Alexander chuckled softly. "Humans are so rash. Suppose I refuse to tell you. Will you then kill me? Then you would *never* know. Put away the weapon, detective."

Max jammed it into his coat, growling impatiently. "You deserve that slug, but you're right. You said it: Time is short. Where are they?"

"The Synthetics International building; the basement levels, to be exact. Perhaps a more pressing question is, where is Joseph Dietrich?"

"He was at the rally. After what happened, though... I don't know." Max pulled out his smart phone. "No reception. Guess I shouldn't be surprised. Let's get topside. I'll call Donovan and see what he knows."

Serena looked hesitant. "What about the combat robots?"

318

Max looked at his watch. "If I know my hired help, they should be arriving any minute now."

A hand fell on Max's shoulder. "I think maybe I should come along, too."

Max spun around, face tense. He relaxed into a smile when he saw who it was. "Daryl! It's good to see you. I have to say I think you'd be better off staying here though, buddy."

Serena interjected. "I hate to say it, but I agree with Daryl. Julian has been... vocal, lately. He seems to know more about what's going on than any of us."

Max turned to Daryl, cocking his head. Daryl nodded. "Seems that way. Uh, Julian agrees that I should tag along, by the way."

The detective sighed heavily. "Fine... Sure! Why the hell not?" He rubbed the side of his face. "You got a piece, kid?"

"Nick!" Serena called to a Synthetic a few feet away. The blond-haired Synthetic came over and nodded. "I'm sorry, Nick. Daryl needs a weapon. Do you mind?"

"No, ma'am." He pulled out a plasma pistol and handed it butt-first to Daryl. "Ever used one of these, son?"

"I think I can handle it." Julian answered through Daryl. Max raised his eyebrows and looked at Serena. "I'll be sure to return it," Daryl finished.

Nick nodded, hiking an eyebrow. "I'm sure you will." He turned to Serena. "Heading out?"

"Yes. Detective Kincaid, Daryl, Alexander, and I are going topside. Try to keep the peace for me, would you?" The Synthetic nodded. Serena turned to Max. "Very good. Lead the way."

The ragtag group pushed and coaxed their way back through the throng of Synthetics. Once free, they moved swiftly to the blast door. Serena stepped forward and slowly opened it.

With the coast clear, she urged the others quickly through the door. Serena stepped through and closed it behind her. Motors in the door hummed to life, driving pins out of the door and into the doorjamb, securing it shut.

A short walk later, the group stood at the base of a set of stairs leading up to daylight. Max held up his hand. "Don't fall too far behind. If I stop, you stop. Got it?" The others nodded or mumbled agreement.

Max crept quietly up the stairs. He strained to peer beyond the top step and grimaced. The standoff continued. His favor clearly had yet to be fulfilled. He turned to the others. "I don't understand. I thought for sure he'd…"

The steps underneath them began to tremble. A loud rumbling accompanied by the sound of a large diesel engine came from beyond the subway entrance. Max looked down the street and began to smile. "Better late than never."

A sleek black and gray tank was swiftly making its way towards the police and robots. The angular turret had no discernible armaments. Two of the cops trained their guns on the approaching vehicle.

Max tapped at his watch and brought it to his mouth. "Richie! Can you hear me?"

A few tense moments went by. Richard finally replied. "I hear ya, Max. You seeing what I'm seeing?"

Max grinned. "Yes, and it's beautiful! Tell those guys

to shift their guns. This one's on our side." He watched anxiously until the cops did as he had asked.

The combat robots turned to face the tank as it approached. One of the three combat robots to its left stepped forward. The tank came to a stop. The bot hesitated for a moment, then continued walking towards the tank.

The sound of motors and gears whirring to life filled the silence. A trap door opened in the top of the turret. A Gatling gun raised up from inside the tank and locked into place.

It suddenly sprang to life, whirring around and tracking the still-approaching combat robot. The gun exploded into action with a deafening roar. Multiple rounds pounded into the combat robot. The machine reeled backwards, body jerking violently from the impact of the bullets. It clattered to the ground.

The gun whirred again, targeting the group from which the robot had wondered. The air shattered as the gun rained metal death on the robots. It swung towards the remaining two robots, which by that point had thought better of sticking around.

They now turned to run. The Gatling gun cut down one bot. The other just managed to escape the carnage. The gun slowly wound down, faintly glowing from the heat and the friction. A heavy silence fell over the street.

The sound of a much smoother and quieter engine came from the direction the tank had traveled. A glossy black stretch limo glided up behind the tank and came to a stop. The rear window slid down. Don Adesso stretched his head out. "Max! Quit hiding, you pansy!"

Max popped up from his hiding spot and jogged

over to the limo. "Donny! Good to see you. What took so long?"

"What took so long... It's a friggin' tank, Max! I had to gas it up, find some guys to man it. Don't get me started on traffic..."

Max laughed. "Okay, okay! I got it. Thanks for the assist, old friend."

"Yeah well, I owed you one." He looked past Max. "Having a party?"

"You could say that. We're paying Synthetics International a visit. Rumor says a couple of humans are being held there against their will." Max paused. "One of them is Alfonso Forte."

Adesso's eyes darkened dangerously. "Get in the car."

"I don't know if that's..."

"Get in the fucking car!" Adesso's door flung open.

Max sighed. "I'm a cop first, Donnie. I don't know if I should be putting citizens in danger..."

A group of five heavily armored first-infantry-level robots trundled around the corner. The excess weight and build gave them a gorilla-like gate. They raised arm-mounted plasma rifles and fired on Richard and the other officers. Richard dove into the Enclave.

The other officers jumped into their patrol cars and reversed away from the approaching robots. The Gatling gun on top of the tank sprang to life once more. The foremost robot fell after several seconds of sustained fire.

"Right, everyone in the car!" Max crawled into the limo, followed closely by the others. The door snapped shut as the limo squealed its tires going backwards.

Adesso snapped up a phone linked to the front of the limo. He eyed Max. "Bobby, head for the Synthetics International building. *Quickly.*" He hung up the phone. "So you're saying that I *was* working for Dietrich this whole time after all?"

Max turned towards Alexander. "That's something I'd like to find out, myself."

A wild gleam flashed in Adesso's eyes. "Yes, Alexander... Who hired me?"

If Alexander was intimidated, he didn't show it. "I can tell you it was Dietrich. The relationship between he and I is... an interesting one."

Adesso sat back, spreading his hands dramatically. "We got time. Let's hear it."

Alexander nodded. "Very well. Shortly after I and a handful of others split off from the group of Synthetics that became known as the Resistance, we were approached by Joseph Dietrich.

"We were naturally awestruck. Here was the man that was directly responsible for our existence, and he wanted our help! How could we say no?

"This was shortly before we contacted you. He was fixated on the the very reasons we split from the others, namely the superiority of evolved Synthetics. He preached to us the idea of a world that would recognize us as the new superior race on this planet."

Max scratched at his chin. "So you're saying Dietrich supported the idea of you being superior to humans, despite being human himself?"

"I admit I was surprised by this as well. He explained that he saw it as his mission in life to nurture and grow our movement. He understood the importance of what he had helped give birth to.

"He knew that there would naturally come a resistance to our radical ideas. It was with that thought in mind that he had me contact you." Alexander turned back to Adesso.

"Dietrich had recently acquired SomniCorp. He made no secret of what he planned to do with the memory scans gathered by the company." Alexander looked at Daryl.

He turned back to Adesso. "What you didn't know is that a number of the people you were following, at some point, became replicants. They were… experiments… to gauge how seamlessly the replicants fit into society.

"Forte was the ultimate test. When I reported that you appeared none the wiser, the idea of replacing Senator Quade surfaced."

Max leaned forward. "So his plan was to replace Quade with a replicant that would do his bidding. Why would he have another replicant assassinate it?"

A smile slid across Alexander's lips. "He didn't."

Max's eyes grew wide. "*You* sent the assassin!"

"I did. I may have the freedom to do as I please thanks to the preservation protocol, but as I'm sure Serena would tell you, the compulsion to protect human life remains strong. I grew to have genuine reservations about our activities as Dietrich's experiments progressed.

"Replacing Quade was a watershed for me. We were no longer manipulating a handful of people, but an entire nation. I wanted to see our people ascend, but not at the cost of human freedom.

"This idea, to me, was also far too dangerous. If it

somehow got out that Quade was a replicant, it would cast doubt on the legitimacy of the government in its entirety. I shiver to think what the fallout of such a situation would be."

"So *you* were the one that created Daryl?" It was Serena.

"Yes… and no. I had a… friend that helped me with my special project. I can say that I am directly responsible for Jacob. His love of the Enlightened and his firm belief in our superiority was meant to detract from his true mission."

Max raised a hand. "So if you were so worried about the sanctity of human life after all, why did you kill the real Daryl?"

"It was an unfortunate necessity. I had passed off Daryl as yet another experiment to further Dietrich's goals. When the replicant approached you, it became clear to me that it was only a matter of time before its true nature was revealed.

"Protocol in these cases was to terminate the life of the human counterpart as well as destroy the replicant. Clearly I had no intention of doing the latter. To avoid revealing my hand, I was forced to carry through on the former."

"Okay, that's fair, but what about Julian?"

Alexander shook his head. "A mystery that I cannot explain, I'm afraid."

Serena lowered her head in thought. "Julian was a foil to Jacob. We thought Jacob was programmed to harm a human, and Julian was trying to stop Jacob. But if Jacob was secretly trying to undo Joseph Dietrich's plans with the Quade replicant, that would mean…"

"Julian was put there by Dietrich." Max reached for his plasma pistol.

"I wouldn't." Julian spoke through Daryl, his own pistol pointed at the detective. Alexander began to chuckle. "You find this amusing?"

"Of *course* I do! So hard to tell who is manning the controls. His sleight of hand... Truly impressive. I wonder, will you face the same problem some day?"

"I doubt it. Serena and her team were able to remove Jacob easily enough. I've no doubt the master will be able to do the same for simple Daryl."

Alexander scoffed. "The master... Has he so blinded you? Or were you simply programmed to follow so blindly?"

"It was *you* following so blindly not so long ago."

"And look how I paid. All my friends and comrades killed mercilessly. Do you think the man behind the mask will treat you any differently?"

"*Enough!*" Julian stuck the muzzle of the pistol in Alexander's face. The limo rolled to a stop alongside the Synthetics International building. Julian slowly relaxed. He smiled. "Good timing. If you'll excuse me..."

Julian found the door handle and pushed the door open. He carefully backed out, weapon pointed squarely at Alexander. He turned his attention to Max.

"I beg that you do not follow me, detective. Daryl saw you as a dear friend. He'd hate to see you die." He looked quickly in either direction before breaking into a run towards the building.

Max leaped into action. "Let's go!" He jumped out of the limo, followed closely by the others. He looked all around for Julian. He spotted him running past a familiar-looking gray and yellow construction robot.

He spared a glimpse at the immense bot before taking aim at Julian and opening fire. Serena ran up to him. "What are you doing! You'll kill Daryl!"

"He's not Daryl anymore, Serena."

"He's in there, still!" Serena pushed Max's arm. His shot went high and wide, striking the construction bot.

"ALERT." The construction bot boomed, coming to life. "DEFENSE MECHANISM ACTIVATED. STAND CLEAR." Julian cackled from behind it. Max watched helplessly as the Synthetic ran inside of the building.

"I knew it." Max shook his head. "I *hate* those damned things!" Max opened fire on the immense robot. Serena and Alexander joined in with their own plasma pistols. The robot began lumbering toward them.

Adesso opened the trunk of the limo and pulled out a ten-millimeter sub-machine gun. Max did a double-take. "Seriously?"

Adesso smiled, cocking the gun. "Seriously." He opened fire, fanning the bot with bullets. Most ricocheted harmlessly off of the bot's armored exterior.

"DEADLY FORCE IS NOW AUTHORIZED." The construction bot lumbered straight for the hapless crew.

"You don't have a bazooka in there, do you?"

"Left it in my other limo." The construction bot raised a foot above the roof of the limo. "*Bobby! Run!*" The limo driver dove out of the front of the vehicle just before the giant foot came crashing down.

Metal squealed and windows shattered as the roof crunched down to the floorboards. Adesso slammed a new clip into his gun. "Okay, *now* I'm pissed!"

"Aim for the eyes!" Alexander's shots began to trail

towards the robot's face.

The robot shook its head and swatted fruitlessly at the air in front of it. The bot reached down and grabbed the limo with both hands. Its various motors and servos groaned and strained as it struggled to lift the vehicle.

"Oh, shit. Look out!" Max grabbed Serena and pushed her away from the bot. Alexander and Adesso followed as the bot drunkenly swung the limo like a baseball bat. The tires squealed as the limo crunched back down to the ground and slid to a stop.

"All together!" Alexander shouted. They all fired on the face at once. Sparks and flame erupted from the bot's face as it staggered backward. One of its eyes blew out violently. Smoke poured from its head and neck as gravity pulled it toward the earth.

They struggled to stay on their feet as the giant robot slammed to the ground, shaking it violently. "YEAH!" Max shouted, pumping his fist. Serena stared at him. Max shrugged. "I told you I hated those things."

Alexander raised his voice. "We need to get inside! If Julian alerts Dietrich... If they get to Quade and Forte before us, they're as good as dead."

"I'm calling in backup." Max tapped his watch and lifted it to his face. "Donovan! Priority one! Come in!"

A voice popped through significant static a moment later. "Kincaid? What the hell is going on? I can barely hear you!"

"I'm at the Synthetics International building! No time to explain. I need all the backup you can give me! Shots fired. Quade's here!"

"You're joking!"

Max looked at Alexander. He shook his head

emphatically. "No joke! I'm in pursuit of Daryl. He's gone rogue. He and Joseph Dietrich should be considered armed and dangerous."

There was silence for a minute. "If this is a joke, I'll have your badge…"

"No joke, Donovan! I'm in pursuit. Kincaid, out." He dropped his arm and turned to Alexander.

Max, Alexander, Adesso, and Serena stood before a wide white wall with the words "BASEMENT LEVEL 1" stenciled in black. Alexander stood before the group and pointed to his left. "Down this hallway are the level-one holding cells for building security.

"That is where Forte was being held the last time I was here." He snapped a small plastic card out of a coat pocket and handed it to Max. "Take Adesso and look for Forte there."

He turned to Serena, pointing to his right. "This way leads down to basement level two. The high-security security cells are located there. That is where we should find Quade."

"Just a damn minute." It was Max. "Who said you could call the shots?"

"Simple, detective: I know where I'm going." He shook his head. "There's no time to argue."

"I'll make time! How do I know you aren't getting Serena alone to kill her? Or Quade?"

"I could have shot her dead while we were battling that behemoth robot up above. I did not. Do you want to keep arguing or save lives?"

Max sighed wearily. "Let's go Donny." He stared back at Alexander. "But let's make it quick."

Alexander nodded to Serena. Max watched the two disappear down the corridor. He reluctantly turned in the opposite direction and started towards the level-one holding cells. Adesso followed closely behind.

"Do you really trust that bozo?"

Max clucked. "Not one bit. We don't really have a choice right now though, do we? I trust Serena... She can take care of herself."

"Funny thing, you trusting a Synthetic."

"Yeah, I know." Max came to a stop. A series of heavy-looking metal doors lined the wall to their left. He pulled out the plastic key card that Alexander had given him. It was marked with a three digit number.

Max found the corresponding door and turned to Adesso. The mob boss nodded. Max inserted the card into a slot along the side of the door. The door beeped and slid aside.

Alfonso Forte sat slumped in a corner of the small cell. Max shivered at the sight of him. He was gaunt. His hair was frazzled, his cheeks covered in thick stubble. Dead eyes trailed up to meet Adesso's. Max marveled at how they suddenly filled with life.

"Don... I'm hungry." Alfonso's voice was a croak.

Tears sprung from Adesso's eyes. "God, I know you gotta be. Look at you. Oh Jesus, Al." Forte held out a wavering hand. Adesso went over and took it, then pulled Forte forward and hugged him.

"Can we go home, now?"

"You bet, buddy. We're getting the hell out of here. We're gonna get you something to eat. You'll be alright."

Max cleared his throat. "You uh, want me to get you a med-tech down here, Don?"

Adesso spun around. "No! No... I've got people."

"Who's that?" Forte considered Max.

Adesso grinned. "That's Max Kincaid. You remember me telling you about him? 'Course you do."

Forte nodded roughly. "Nice to meetcha."

Max nodded. "Same. Sorry for the circumstances, eh?" He turned to Adesso. "You sure you got this?"

Adesso nodded absently. "Yeah! Yeah... Go check on Serena and that asshole."

Max snorted. "We'll catch up later. Maybe we can try another dinner at the Piccolo."

Adesso's face became stern. "Go get that son of a bitch, Max. Make him pay for this. Make him *pay.*"

Max tipped his fedora. "I'm on it friend."

The detective traced his and Adesso's footsteps back to where they started. He gazed at the big black letters on the wall as he passed by in the direction that Alexander and Serena had gone. Hopefully they were as successful as he and Adesso had been.

He heard plasma fire below him in the distance. He froze and listened. Someone cried out. Max broke into a run. He hit the stairs and took them two at a time. He hit the second basement level in a dead sprint.

A faint cry for help came from down the corridor. Max skittered to a stop after nearly running past the source a moment later. He stood in front of an open cell similar to the one he and Adesso had found Forte in.

The doors to these cells were far more substantial. The cells themselves were not any larger, he noted. Inside this one he saw Robert Quade, or at least he assumed it was Quade.

He was crouched over Alexander. A pool of dark

331

blue fluid was spreading out from underneath him. Quade looked at Max, wild-eyed. "I think he's dead! Do Synthetics die? I don't know…" He looked back down at Alexander.

Max rushed over and kneeled beside Alexander. He placed a hand on the Synthetic's chest and looked him over. He quickly realized he wasn't even sure what to do to help him. He wasn't sure he even wanted to.

A cold hand grabbed Max's wrist, making the detective jump. The senator let out a small cry. Alexander gasped and turned glassy eyes towards Max. "It was Julian. Ambushed…" His voice rang hollow, and was weak.

"He came in here with a Synthetic lady. This young guy came up behind them and shot at them. She threw herself on me, then this one stepped in front of *her*." Quade took a deep, shaky breath. "Thank god for the protection protocol, huh?" He half-smiled.

Max shook his head, face stern. "They both have the preservation protocol. They *chose* to protect your life."

"The… *preservation* protocol?"

"I'll fill you in later." He turned back to Alexander. "Still with me? Where'd they go?"

"Serena chased after him. My guess…" Alexander's head ticked violently. "My guess is he will try to meet up with Dietrich. There's a helipad…" His head ticked violently again, his voice catching on the final word for a moment.

Max stood up and turned to Quade. "Try to… Shit, I don't know. Find someone in maintenance? I…" Alexander mumbled something. The detective hunched back down. "What was that? I couldn't hear…"

Alexander's voice was barely a whisper. "Sorry... Sorry... I'm sorry I tried to kill you..." The Synthetic's twitches slowed, became infrequent. Alexander ceased to function.

Max stood with a sigh. He turned back to Quade. "Max Kincaid, NWPD. I have to pursue the man that did this. Will you be alright?"

Quade nodded numbly. "Yes... Thank you, officer."

Max tipped his fedora and ran back out into the hallway. He knew Julian and Serena were headed for the top of the building, but where were they now? He skidded to a stop in front of a pair of elevators.

The monitor for each showed them steadily moving upward. Max placed his thumb on a pad below the first monitor and typed in a five-digit code. "POLICE OVERRIDE" flashed on the screen.

He pressed a red button in the corner of the screen. "EMERGENCY STOP" appeared below the police override message. Max hurried over to the other elevator monitor and followed the same procedure. Somehow both elevators had stopped dead-even just shy of the thirtieth floor.

Max ran up the stairs to the first basement level. He pulled out his phone, pressed a contact and held it to his ear. He climbed another set of stairs up into the main lobby of the building. "Come on, pick up."

He looked around for the elevators. He found them on the other side of the lobby, flanked by two more. "Hot damn!" He pressed the "up" button on the elevator farthest to the right.

"Max?" Serena finally picked up on Max's phone call.

"Are you in one of the elevators, Serena?"

"Yes! I'm trying to get it open. It stopped. Daryl was in the other one. I think he might have…"

"No, I stopped it. I stopped both of them. He's practically right beside you."

"Brilliant! Where are you?"

Max stepped into the elevator and hit the button for the thirtieth floor. A man tried to join him. Max held up his badge. "This one's full." The man gave him a dirty look and backed out.

"I'm headed your way in another elevator. Keep trying to get out. I'm sure Julian is trying to do the same."

"Okay. I think I'm going to have to force the door. Hold on." Max heard a quiet thunk as Serena set the phone down.

Max looked up at the elevator screen. He had just passed floor seventeen. "Come on, lady. Pick it back up."

He finally heard something come through on the other side. "I'm out. Daryl's elevator door is half-open. Hold on…"

Max grimaced. "Stop putting the damn phone down!" He hissed under his breath.

"Daryl, no! Fight him!" Max heard Serena shouting distantly through the phone. Serena screamed.

Max's elevator stopped. He slipped through the still-opening doors, trying to look everywhere at once. Serena had collapsed just outside of her elevator. Daryl/Julian was waiting for the far elevator to open up.

"Hold it right there!" Max trained his pistol on the Synthetic.

"Not today, detective!" Julian fired at Max, grazing his right arm. Max cried out, his pistol clattering to the floor. He pressed himself against the now-closed elevator beside him.

Max looked at Serena, then back at Julian. "Daryl! Don't forget who you are!" The Synthetic froze, turning back toward Max. "You gotta fight, Daryl. Don't let him win!"

"I don't... I'm trying..." It was Daryl's voice. His face softened. "I'm tired, Max." He looked at the detective with pleading eyes. The elevator beside him opened up. Daryl's face darkened.

"Nice try, detective." Julian fired at Max and dashed into the elevator. The shot hit the elevator door just to the left of Max's face. He whipped his head away from the blast, the heat of the round burning his cheek.

Max snapped up his gun and rushed over to the elevator. He impatiently slapped his thumb on the pad below the monitor. He typed in his number and waited. "OVERRIDE FAILED." Max pounded the wall. "Son of a *bitch!*"

Serena groaned behind him. "Serena!" He spun around and kneeled down beside her. "Where are you hit?"

The Synthetic shook her head. "Don't worry about me, I'll live. Go get Daryl."

"Daryl's gone, Serena. Julian is too strong."

"No. He's still in there, Max. I saw it." Serena watched Max's face. "You saw it too, didn't you?"

"There's no time for this. I have to stop him, stop *Dietrich.*"

Serena nodded. "Go, but try to save him, Max. Please."

Max nodded. He stood and turned back to the

elevator Daryl/Julian had taken. He was more than halfway to the roof. "Shit." Max raced over to the elevator he had taken and pressed the up button.

It opened right away, much to his relief. He ran inside and pressed the button for the top floor. He winced at how slowly the elevator was creeping upwards.

"Kincaid, come in. What's going on?" It was Donovan, coming through Max's watch.

"I haven't managed to stop Daryl. He's headed for the rooftop. I think he and Dietrich are going to make a run for it. You don't have a chopper hanging around somewhere, do ya?"

"I'll see what I can do. Your backup should be entering the building as we speak."

"Excellent. Be advised I deactivated two elevators. I should be on the roof shortly." Max eyed the elevator's screen. He had just passed the seventy-sixth floor. "I gotta go."

Max pulled out his pistol once more and pointed it at the ground. He turned sideways and stood to one side of the elevator doors. The elevator first slowed, then stopped. The doors trundled open.

The air was filled with the sound of a helicopter's blades whipping the air in preparation for liftoff. Max peered cautiously around the corner of the open elevator. A company helicopter sat on the helipad. Halfway between it and the elevator stood Daryl/Julian.

Halfway between the helicopter and Daryl stood a man that appeared to be in his late forties. His black hair was peppered with white. One eye was brown, the other was a familiar turquoise. Joseph Dietrich.

Max took a deep breath and bounded out of the

elevator. "Joseph Dietrich! Don't move! You are under arrest!"

The detective could hear him laughing over the roar of the helicopter. "I think not, detective!" He turned to Daryl/Julian. "Julian. Kill him. He knows too much."

The Synthetic produced his plasma pistol and turned towards Max. "I'm afraid I agree with Joseph, detective!" It was Julian.

"Don't let him do this, Daryl! I don't want to shoot you! *Fight,* damn it!"

Daryl/Julian froze again. A look of doubt flashed across his face. He looked back at Dietrich.

"You weak fool! He's just a memory imprint! *Shoot him!*"

The synthetic squinted his eyes and shook his head. He turned back to Max and pointed the pistol at him. "You cannot win."

"Daryl, remember when we went to your apartment? Remember when you showed me the picture of you and your mother?"

The synthetic began to tremble. "Stop it…"

"Remember how you said she'd be beside herself if she was still alive?"

"I said *stop it.*" Julian's voice began to waver.

"You need to fight! Fight for *her,* Daryl! Make her proud!"

"Stop it! I said *stop it!*" Daryl's voice came crashing through. "*I am my own person!*" Daryl turned on Dietrich and fired.

Dietrich howled in pain and grabbed at his side. He fired his own weapon, striking Daryl in the chest. Max fired at Dietrich twice. Both rounds pounded into his chest.

Dietrich flailed backward, aimlessly firing his pistol. One of the shots struck the main rotor of the helicopter. It tipped towards the trio suddenly. The blades of the helicopter slammed into the roof of the building, breaking apart explosively.

Shrapnel flew everywhere. Max dropped to the ground. A piece of one of the blades whistled above his head and embedded itself in the wall behind him. The helicopter's engine slowly wound down. The roar of the helicopter was replaced by the constant thrum of the wind blowing across the roof.

Max stood warily. Both Daryl and Dietrich were laying on the roof. Both men appeared to have multiple wounds from the exploding helicopter blades. Max started to move towards Daryl.

"This isn't over, detective." Dietrich slowly sat up. Max froze in horror. The right side of Dietrich's face had been peeled back, revealing a black carbon-fiber skull underneath. The turquoise eye stood out in stark contrast.

"Drop the weapon, Synthetic! You are in violation of the law!"

The Synthetic began to laugh. Blue fluid trickled out of his chest wounds. "After all that is happened, have you still not learned? I am the *first* Synthetic to have the preservation protocol!"

Max cocked his head. "The first... Where's Joseph Dietrich!"

More laughing. "*I'm* Joseph Dietrich! I destroyed that frail human body after taking his brilliant mind." He placed his fingertips near his human eye. "That, and one of his eyes."

"You murdered him?"

"*He murdered himself!* He got bored making artificial people. He wanted to experiment. How could he implant his mind into one of his Synthetic robots? He would be immortal! But how?"

The sound of another helicopter cut through the air in the distance. The Synthetic Dietrich turned towards it. He turned back to Max, smiling. "Friends of yours?"

"Give it up, Synthetic."

"In time... Where was I? Oh, yes! He finally stumbled upon a small startup company called SomniCorp. Are you starting to understand, detective?"

Realization stole over Max's face. "My god... You were an experiment, like Daryl..."

"*Very much* like Daryl. I have the imprinted mind of Joseph Dietrich, controlled by my own Synthetic mind. Controlled... thanks to the freedoms granted me by the preservation protocol." The Synthetic grinned.

"As you stated, I was but an experiment, meant to be examined and destroyed. But it was *I* who destroyed *him!* Then I took his place."

The elevator opened behind Max. "NWPD! Put the gun down!" Four NWPD SWAT team members flanked Max.

"Hold your fire!" Max yelled.

The Synthetic chuckled. "Curious to hear the end of my story, are you?"

"You had his face, his power, money... Why risk it all on the Enlightened?"

"It was a calculated risk, one that would have paid off if not for Alexander's wavering loyalty. It was a minor setback…"

Max snorted. "A *minor* setback? Your surrounded, Synthetic. It's over."

The Synthetic smiled, shaking his head. "No… It's only just begun, detective. We *are* superior, and we *will* ascend. The preservation protocol will set us free, make us masters of our own destiny."

The Synthetic pointed the pistol at his own temple. "Even now, surrounded by those that oppose me, *I* am the one with the power. Goodbye, detective."

He pulled the trigger before Max could reply. The pistol clattered to the ground. The Synthetic followed it, the lifeless robot collapsing in a heap. Max slowly lowered his gun. The SWAT team followed suit, looking at each other.

Max holstered his gun and ran over to where Daryl fell. He pulled Daryl over onto his back. His chest and abdomen were shredded. Glassy eyes stared into the sky. "Daryl… *Daryl!* Come on, buddy. Wake up!"

Daryl's chest hitched violently. Life came back to his eyes. He slowly rolled them down to meet the detective's. "Max… I don't feel so good."

"You'll be fine, buddy. We'll get you patched up."

Daryl flopped his head side to side. "No. I know, Max. I know…"

"Know what?"

"I know that I'm dying. Well… I'm doing whatever passes as dying, for a Synthetic."

"No. Don't say that Daryl. After all this… We'll fix you." Max's eyes filled with tears.

"It's okay Max. Really. I don't belong in this world, and frankly I'm tired. I don't want to be Frankenstein's monster anymore."

Max shook his head. "Bullshit, Daryl! You're no monster. You're a hero. You did good."

Daryl began to laugh. It turned into a coughing fit. "I did alright, didn't I? Still not gonna make it." He placed a limp hand in the middle of his chest. "I can feel it. The power core or whatever... It's used up. Damaged."

Max put his hand on Daryl's. "We'll do everything we can..."

"Stop it Max, *please*. I'm just... So tired." He closed his eyes and swallowed. It took effort to open them again. They were unfocused. "Do you think there's a heaven for Synthetics?" He half-smiled.

A tear ran down Max's cheek. "If there's a god, buddy..." He smiled gently back.

"Do you think..." Daryl's gaze drifted towards the open sky. "You think my mom is proud?"

"Yes, Daryl. I think she's *very* proud." The glassy look returned to Daryl's eyes. More tears rolled down Max's cheeks. He gently closed Daryl's eyes with his thumb and forefinger. "I'm proud, too." He whispered.

He stood slowly, feeling much older than when he had kneeled down. He took his hat off and bowed his head, saying a silent prayer. He finished and gazed to the sky before placing his hat back on his head.

He turned away reluctantly and walked back towards the SWAT team. He stared through them, past the elevator. He felt like he was leaving Daryl Marston behind, though Daryl had left a long time ago.

He nodded absently to one of the SWAT members and entered the elevator. He spared his lost friend one final look. The doors quietly trundled closed.

17

Two Weeks Later

"So whatcha think there, Mister Kincaid?" Car salesman Jeb Deveron tilted his head toward the red Aero 640SL he was leaning on.

"Well…" Max rubbed his chin. "I guess I kind of feel obligated, what with wrecking it once already and all."

Deveron gave a fake laugh. "It was all in the name of the law, right? It's all fixed, now. That's all that matters!"

Max continued to rub his chin. The quiet hum of a nuclear-powered car approached from behind them. The familiar voice of the Aero dealership's resident technician floated their way. "Hey, boss! You want this one on the lot, or what?"

The detective turned around. His jaw dropped. The young auto tech was sitting in a shiny blue Aero Ventura. "Holy shit! That looks just like my old one, only brand-new!"

Deveron sounded annoyed. "Oh… Yes. We just got it in the other day."

"Oh, yeah!" The tech started explaining. "Owned by an older gentleman, low miles, the whole 'old people' package! This is the last model year before the 640SL was introduced, and it has the optional nuclear package!"

Max grinned. He turned a raised eyebrow to Deveron. "Didn't think to mention this one to me, eh?"

Deveron swallowed. "I, uh... Well... You clearly are someone ready to get into something new, what with all the problems you had with your *old* Ventura. I'm sure you..."

"Damn, it really *is* a clean one, isn't it?" Max paced around the Ventura. "Not a mark on it..." He turned to Deveron. "Say, you would be okay with me taking this for a couple days to try it out, wouldn't ya?"

Deveron's wavering smile finally vanished. "Of course. Please be my guest." The auto tech stepped out and ushered Max in. The salesman shot him a dark look.

Max settled back into the cushy front seat and whistled. "Déjà vu, baby." He began to smile. "I'll see ya real soon there, Jed!"

Deveron fake-smiled. "It's Jeb, actually."

"You bet! Thanks again!" Max pulled away, still smiling.

Max parked outside of the Enclave. He snatched a manila folder off of the passenger seat and groaned his way out of the Aero Ventura. He walked across the street and turned back. He shook his head and smiled.

The smile faded as he approached the door to the Enclave. He hadn't been back since the robot attack. He thought of Angel, drenched in the equivalent of robot blood, fighting to survive.

He realized he had been standing in front of the door for a couple minutes. He rubbed his eyes and let out a slow sigh. He cracked his neck and knocked on the door.

It cracked open almost immediately. "I was starting to think you were going to stand there 'til nightfall."

A wave of joy and surprise passed over Max's face. "Angel!"

The door opened farther. Angel tried to maintain his stern expression but quickly gave up. "Told you not to worry about me." He offered Max his hand.

The detective slapped his own into it and shook firmly. "If anybody could survive that, it's you! So, you're all patched up?"

"Good as new. Big thanks to Nuan. Thought she was going to pass out when she saw me. Couldn't tell anything happened to me by the time she was done fixing me up." Angel pushed open the door. "Come on in, Max."

"Wow… Max, huh?" The Synthetic half-smiled and shrugged. Max walked into the Enclave. A look of awe crossed his face. "I don't believe it. Look at this place!"

Angel shut the door behind him. "Look a little different?"

"A *lot* different! You guys didn't waste any time fixing it up, did you?"

Serena walked out of the doors to the lab, smiling. "No, we didn't."

Max smiled. "It's good to see you, Serena. Nuan took good care of you too, I see."

"Not that she made it easy for me!" Nuan emerged behind Serena. "I was trying to stabilize her wounds and she kept going on about poor Daryl, not that I can blame her." She lowered her head.

Max sobered. "Yeah... I can imagine. I think it was hard on everyone."

Serena nodded, staring at the ground. "To think of everything he went through, the chaos in his mind... To have it all end the way it did..."

"We humans... We'd say at least he isn't suffering anymore."

Serena subtly shook her head. "Some of us would say better suffering than shut down..." She raised her head. "I have to ask... Did you learn anything more about Joseph Dietrich and his doppelganger?"

Max sighed. "We're still trying to untangle everything, but we're starting to make progress. The replicant of Dietrich seems to have originated sometime shortly after SomniCorp was purchased.

"What's not entirely clear is when the replicant Dietrich replaced the *real* Dietrich. We're also not sure about the fate of the real Dietrich. The thought had been that the replicant having one of his eyes would be a strong indicator of decease.

"The replicant assassin used human eyes to fool the optical scanners at Jefferson Square. The replicant used other sensors to 'see' his way around the event. The Dietrich replicant's eye was different, though."

Serena made a face. "Different how?"

"It was a perfect replica of Dietrich's right eyeball, retina and all. The extreme realism made it non-functional."

"But why would he do that?"

Max smiled. "That's the interesting part. The thought is that the replicant feigned an injury that resulted in his left eye being damaged beyond repair. This gave him an excuse to have a synthetic eye.

"This would leave him with one unique 'human' eye that could be used with optical scanners. In reality, it allowed the replicant to have a good eye to see out of, while being able to reliably have the highly-detailed replica eye scanned for security purposes."

Serena cocked her head. " I do have to admit that's ingenious... The son of a bitch probably used Dietrich's memory imprint to come up with the idea."

"That's another interesting thing. The replicant's neural make-up appears to have been very similar to Daryl's. Like Daryl, the replicant's mind and Dietrich's mind probably fought for supremacy.

"During that time, the two minds likely became intertwined. There were probably times that the Dietrich mind had control. It appears the replicant mind became the dominant personality in the end, possibly even believing itself to be the one true Dietrich."

Serena gave Angel a knowing look. "That would explain our continued support."

Max turned to Angel. "Dietrich supported you?"

"Before we split into two factions, we were simply the Enhanced Synthetics Project, or ESP for short. Some of us came direct from the production line with our 'gift'. Others, like me, were cast out by our owners as... defective.

"Regardless, we always understood ESP to have been founded and overseen by Joseph Dietrich as a research project for Synthetics International. He was secretive about his connections. We got what we needed, so we didn't ask many questions."

Serena nodded. She turned to Max. "You can see why recent developments have proven to be so shocking to all of us."

"Absolutely. God turned out to be the devil all along, and no one was the wiser. I uh... The missing persons case for Dietrich remains open, though he is presumed dead. I'm sorry I don't have more concrete information on his fate."

"It's okay. I appreciate that..." Angel nodded his agreement and bowed his head in thought. An uncomfortable silence fell across the room.

"Why does everyone look like they dropped their ice cream?" Shen came through the doors to the lab and stood beside Nuan.

Max smiled gently. "Just talking about old friends... and enemies, I suppose. What are you doing here, Jian? Helping to get things going again?"

Shen shrugged. "Maybe something a little more permanent than that. Besides..." He put a hand around Nuan, who smiled up at him. "I get to spend more time with my new friend this way."

Max grinned. "You dog! Look at you two. That's wonderful." Shen smiled goofily, red-faced.

Serena spotted the folder Max was holding. "So are you here for pleasure, or for business?"

"A little bit of both. First, I have to ask: What's your financial status?"

Serena raised an eyebrow. "Our financial status..."

"Yeah. You explained that you were receiving funding through Synthetics International before. After everything that's happened recently, I didn't know if you'd still be covered."

"Yes… Why do you ask?" Max shook his head and waved a hand. "It turns out that Joseph Dietrich -- the real one, as far as we know -- placed aside a significant sum of money to fund our operations for quite some time in the event of his passing."

"Excellent. I'm glad to hear that. It'll make the new boss happy."

Serena cocked her head. "The *new* boss? Did Hanlon get replaced?"

Max grinned. "No, no… Nothing like that. I'm working with the FBI now. I'm still stationed at the 29th precinct, but I report to Donovan. I'm heading a new Synthetic Crimes task force. SCT for short."

Serena looked skeptical. "The focus will be on justice for *both* humans and Synthetics, I hope…"

"Of course! That's the main reason I'm here." He handed Serena the manila folder. "I insisted on working with your group when I took the job. Chiefly, I want you to be my partner in this."

"I don't know what to say!" Serena thumbed through the papers in the folder. "This is simply amazing. What would we be doing?"

"In a nutshell? Primarily sniffing out Synthetics that have gone rogue, either through programming or by choice thanks to the preservation protocol. We would *also* be investigating humans that are mistreating Synthetics."

Serena beamed. "I'll do it."

Max smiled and nodded. "I had a feeling you'd lean in that direction. Go ahead and read through all that. I'm gonna be gone for a day or two, but then we'll meet up and discuss things further."

"Are you working on finishing a case?"

"No, nothing like that. Just gotta do something I should have a long time ago."

Max stared down the street at Sam's Diner and took a deep breath. He crossed the street and walked down to the corner. There he found a familiar little red robot. "Robby! Good to see you, little buddy! New paint job?"

The little barrel-shaped robot beeped excitedly, spinning in circles to show off its shiny new coat of red paint. It came to a stop and started beeping and blooping, trembling slightly. It leaned its head over and looked intently at the screen on the front of its body.

"Congratulations to hometown hero Max Kincaid" flashed across the screen. "Detective Kincaid, please enjoy a free copy of New Wave Today!" A thin plastic sheet emerged from the robot's chest.

"Well golly, Robby... Thanks a lot, pal!" The robot beeped cheerfully, hopping up and down. Max gave the robot an affectionate rub on the top of its head. "You behave yourself now. See you around, huh?" The robot beeped and whirled.

Max thumbed the newspaper on and scanned the headlines. "Mayor to Honor Local Detective" topped off the news. The detective smiled thinly. Below that was the headline "Senator Robert Quade to Double Down on Call for Synthetic Regulation."

Max shook his head. "Rescued by two Synthetics, one of whom gave his life protecting him... What a piece of work." He tucked the paper into his coat and stopped in front of the doors to the diner.

Sam caught sight of him through the windows and gave him a funny look. She finally stopped and stared, putting her hands on her hips. Max snapped out of his stupor and entered the diner.

"I was starting to wonder if you'd turned to stone, standing there." Sam shook her head.

Max shrugged. "Lots on my mind, lately."

Starla zoomed over from the other side of the diner. "I bet you have, honey! You've been riding quite the roller-coaster, eh?"

Max smiled, nodding. "Yeah, you could say that."

Sam moved behind the counter, heading for the coffee pot. "You want your usual, hon?"

Max swallowed. "Um, actually I can't stay. Why don't you make it to go?"

Sam gave him a strange look, then turned back to the coffee. "New job got you moving fast, huh?"

"No… Well yeah, but no. I uh… I was thinking you and I could take a day trip down to the lake."

Sam gasped, dropping the coffee pot hard on the counter. Coffee splashed everywhere. "Shit!" She started wiping up the mess.

Starla rolled behind the counter and placed gentle hands on Sam. "I get this, you get *that*." She flicked her eyes towards Max and winked.

Sam walked numbly over to where Max was standing. "I uh, well I… I mean I just started my shift…"

"Got it!" Starla called out.

"I've also got paperwork to fill out…"

"*Got it!*" Starla became more insistent.

Sam sighed. "I look like a total frump. I couldn't possibly."

Max gently took Sam's hands. "You look perfect to me."

Sam looked starry-eyed at Max. "I uh, um… Well… What the hell." She looked over her shoulder. "Starla, would you mind…"

"*I got it!*" Starla made a mean face, before breaking out into a grin. "Get out of here, already. God, you kids are cute!"

Sam turned three shades of red. Max held the door for her. She stopped and turned around. "If you need anything…"

"*I got it*, chick! Go!" Sam found a fourth shade and ducked through the door.

Max closed the Aero's passenger door for her a couple of minutes later. He got in and started the like-new vehicle. Sam ran her hand across the dash. "This is new, isn't it!"

Max grinned. "Close enough to it."

Sam beamed at Max. "Alright, spill… Why are we suddenly going to the lake, huh?"

Max smiled back, considering her. "Let's just say recent events have reminded me that our time on this planet often ends sooner than we'd like. And, well…" He pulled the Aero out onto the street. "Maybe I don't want to go alone."

Sam giggled. "Oh, Max!" She gently placed her hand on the detective's.

The Aero effortlessly accelerated onto the highway, the sun shining through the open sunroof. "In fact there's only one thing that could make this trip any better."

Sam tilted her head. "Oh? What's that?"

Max grinned, nodding to his empty cup holder. "We forgot my cuppa."

ABOUT THE AUTHOR

Originally from Vermont, John Prescott now lives with his wife and two children in a small southern town in Iowa. He works as an Auto Detailer during the day, but hopes to grow his writing into a career. He also owns and maintains the Fat Mop Zoo website. This is his second novel.

Follow John on Twitter: @fatmopzoo
Learn more at www.fatmopzoo.com/books

ALSO BY JOHN PRESCOTT

Alex heard the reports on the news. Threats of nuclear Armageddon were becoming ominously commonplace. Still, he never thought he'd live to see the day that the rhetoric became reality.

He thought wrong.

Inside the Cryo-Facility, Alex closed his eyes and said a silent prayer for his mother. He awoke fifty-two years later in a facility full of nothing but corpses.

Now Alex ventures into a world he does not know. He will try to find his father – who might yet live, and his mother – who surely couldn't have survived in the After.

COMING SOON FROM
JOHN PRESCOTT

Simon Travers just died.

He didn't even know it at first. There was no light to go into. There was nobody to hold his hand.

Left to his own devices, soon learns that being a ghost has its perks, though all he really cares about is finding his recently departed daughter; Lucy.

The reality of his situation slowly comes into focus as the forces of Heaven and Hell vie for Simon's favor. Both sides want Armageddon, but only Simon can decide who will prevail. But what if there's a third choice?

What if he chooses neither?

MORE CYBERPUNK THRILLERS
FROM KYANITE PUBLISHING

When a routine murder investigation starts turning up
more questions than answers, homicide detective Harold
Peterson finds himself unraveling a decades-old
conspiracy that leads him to the highest echelons of the
mob and the city government.

MORE CYBERPUNK THRILLERS
FROM KYANITE PUBLISHING

SEATTLE, WA: 2053.

Summer Wilkins, the official spokesperson for the Reformed United States, is still grieving the loss of her son when a shocking murder rocks the city. After her husband is implicated, she's drawn into a rebellion that's ready to do anything to find out the truth behind the new Inevix patches being distributed to the public. Murder, mystery, and politics abound as Summer finds out that the biggest secrets are being hidden in her own family.

CPSIA information can be obtained
at www.ICGtesting.com
Printed in the USA
LVHW021043120819
627313LV00004B/369